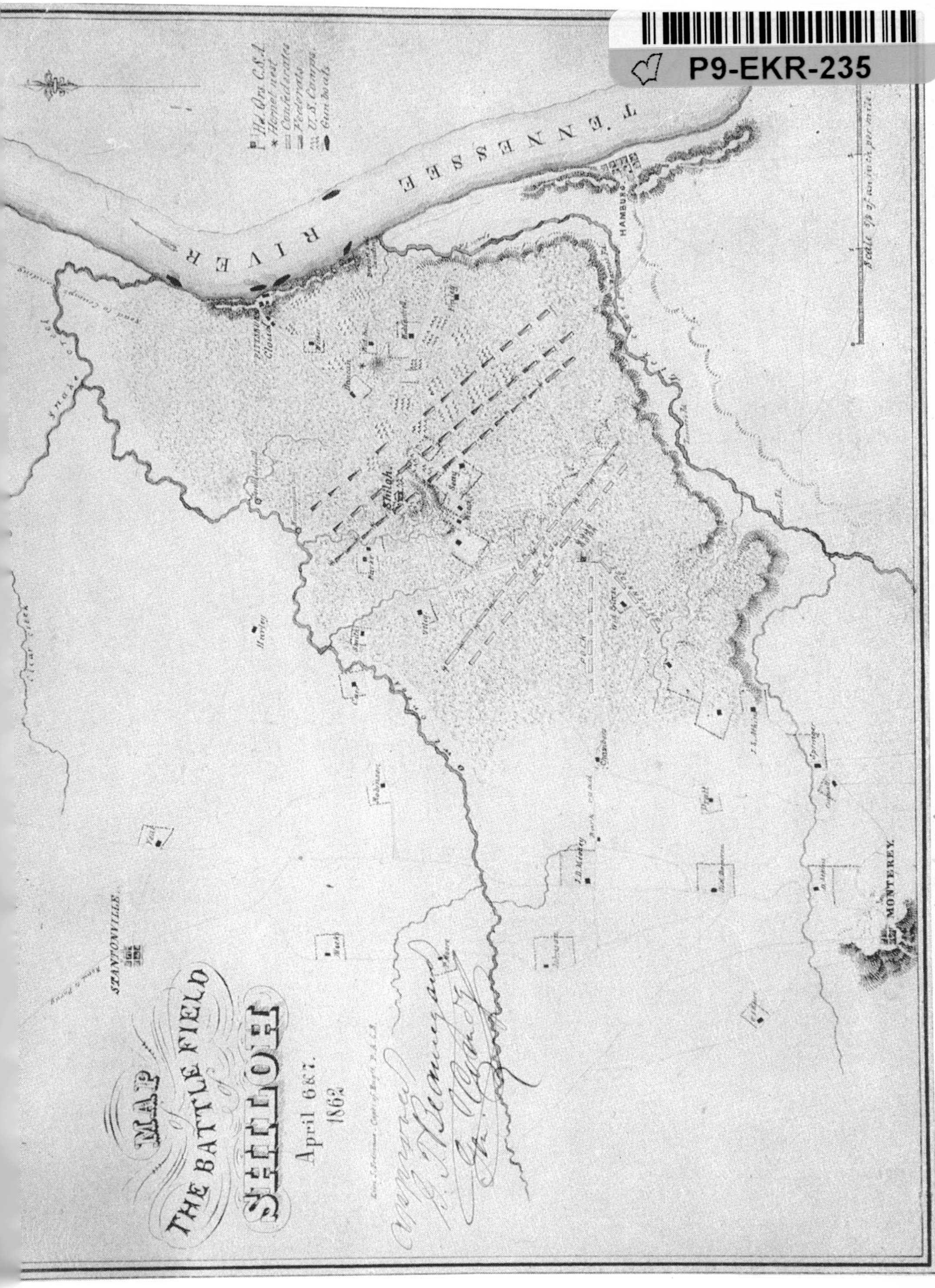

LÉON J. FRÉMAUX'S SKETCH
MAP OF THE BATTLEFIELD OF SHILOH, TENNESSEE, APRIL 6–7, 1862

Geography and Map Division, Library of Congress, Washington, D. C.

FAITH *of our* FATHERS

TO MAKE MEN FREE

Volume 2

OTHER BOOKS AND BOOKS ON CASSETTE
N.C. ALLEN

Faith of Our Fathers, Volume 1: A House Divided

FAITH *of our* FATHERS

TO MAKE MEN FREE

Volume 2

a novel by

N.C. ALLEN

Covenant Communications, Inc.

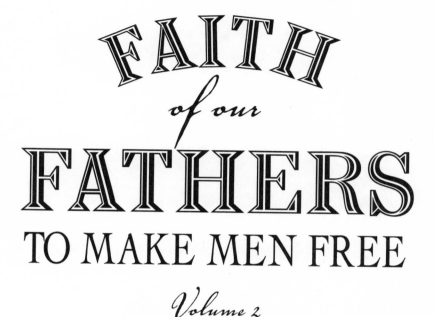

Cover and interior photographs © Al Thelin
Cover flag illustration by Joe Flores

Published by Covenant Communications, Inc.
American Fork, Utah

Printed in Canada
First Printing: September 2002

09 08 07 06 05 04 03 02 10 9 8 7 6 5 4 3 2 1

ISBN 1-59156-121-3

For Mark

LIST OF CHARACTERS

The Boston, Massachusetts, Birmingham Family

James Birmingham, the father. A wealthy iron magnate.

Elizabeth Stein Birmingham, the mother. Abolitionist descendant of Rhode Island Quakers.

Luke, oldest son. Ardent abolitionist.

Anne, daughter.

Camille, daughter.

Robert, son.

Jimmy, son.

The Charleston, South Carolina, Birmingham Family

Jeffrey, the father. Also James's twin brother, married to plantation heiress.

Sarah Matthews Birmingham, the mother. Plantation owner.

Ben, oldest son. Left home after joining the Mormon Church.

Charlotte Birmingham Ellis. Married to William Ellis.

Richard, son.

Emily, daughter.

Clara, daughter.

The Birmingham Slaves

Ruth, head house servant. The "matriarch" of the majority of the slaves.

Joshua, raised as Ben's companion.

Mary, Ruth's granddaughter. Joshua's biological sister; close friend to Emily.

Rose, Mary's little sister. Companion to Clara.

The O'Shea family, New York

Gavin, the father.
Brenna, the mother.
Daniel, son.

The Brissot family, New Orleans

Jean-Pierre, the father.
Genevieve (Jenny) Stein Brissot. The mother; sister to Elizabeth Stein Birmingham.
Marie, daughter

The Gundersen family, Cleveland, Ohio

Per, the father.
Amanda, the mother.
Ivar, son.
Inger, Ivar's daughter.

Other Fictional Characters

Isabelle Webb
Dolly and Abigail Van Dyke
Jacob Taylor, Boston newspaper editor
Lucy Lockhart, associate of Isabelle Webb
Eli and Ellen Dobranski and their children
Earl Dobranski, Utah resident and temporary enlistee

Nonfictional characters to whom reference is made or who play a minor role, interacting with the fictional characters:

President Abraham Lincoln.
William Lloyd Garrison, abolitionist and editor of *The Liberator.*
Jefferson Davis, President of the Confederacy.
Allan Pinkerton, private investigator.
James Chestnut, former U.S. senator.
Mary Chestnut, his wife and famed diarist.
P. G. T. Beauregard, Confederate General.
Robert E. Lee, Confederate General.

Thomas "Stonewall" Jackson, Confederate General.
Irving McDowell, Union Army General.
George McClellan, Union General.
Winfield Scott, Union General.
William Seward, Union Secretary of State.
"Fighting Joe" Hooker, Union army general

"In the beauty of the lilies, Christ was born across the sea,
With a glory in his bosom that transfigures you and me.
As he died to make men holy, let us die to make men free,
While God is marching on."

—Julia Ward Howe

CHAPTER 1

"Come on you volunteers, come on! This is your chance. You volunteered to be killed for love of your country and now you can be. You are only damned volunteers. I am only a soldier and don't want to be killed, but you came to be killed and now you can be."
—Charles F. Smith, General Grant's former West Point commandant, speaking to the 2nd Iowa

* * *

7 January 1862
Near Romney, Virginia

Anne Birmingham glanced over her shoulder in the blinding snow at the faces of her fellow soldiers, illuminated pale and drawn in the bright, moonlit night. They had been out in the weather for over twenty-four hours and were now marching back to the main camp in Romney. Anne's feet protested the blistering cold, and judging by the expressions on the faces of the men she marched beside, she was not the only one in pain.

The snow collected on the front of her wool overcoat in layers, but she couldn't summon the desire to brush it away. Everything hurt, from the tip of her head to the soles of her feet, and she wondered numbly at her ability to plod along, placing one foot interminably in front of the other in the deep drifts.

"You're managing, then?"

The voice beside Anne was deep and quiet, meant for her ears alone. She glanced aside at Ivar Gundersen, and pulled her face out of its frozen mask long enough to reply, "And why wouldn't I be?"

His answering reply was a quick smile that was gone almost before it appeared. That smile was given grudgingly, she knew, for Ivar didn't approve of her presence with the Ohio 7th. He didn't approve of her appearance in the Union army altogether. Most men wouldn't.

Her mind drifted back to the day over two weeks before when he had discovered proof of her gender via a letter from home she had unwittingly left open atop her satchel for all and sundry to view. "You'll be reporting me," she had said, knowing full well that any man in his right mind would. It wasn't every day that a woman encountered freethinkers like her brother Luke or her newspaper editor, Jacob Taylor.

"No, I won't," had been Ivar's reply, and it had caught her off guard. "What you do is your own business." He had turned to leave the tent they shared with two other men, and seemingly as an afterthought, turned back to her and murmured as he passed, "I should tell you though, I knew you for a woman the moment I first laid eyes on you. If I know the truth, surely others will deduce the same."

He paused, and she said nothing.

"It's a risky game you play," he said, his hands still resting in his pockets, his spectacles upon his rugged features. The eyes behind the round glass lenses were a piercing blue.

Anne nodded once in reply, her hand still clutching the throat of her overcoat.

"Would it be an imposition to ask why?"

She cleared her throat. "It's my job."

He shook his head and turned again to leave. "Seems to me that a person with any sense at all would consider a change in vocation."

Anne's mind returned to the present, and she glanced at Ivar again, his head bent against the snow that collected atop his Union army cap. "I daresay I'm not any more cold than you are," she gritted out of a throat that was scratchy and dry.

From somewhere behind them, a rough cough sounded against the shuffling of feet and occasional murmur of low voices. Anne grimaced. The cough belonged to Jed Dietrich, a tent mate and Ivar's good friend from home. It was worsening, from the sound of it, and Anne worried for the man.

"Not much longer now." Major Casement walked back through the ranks and offered the words of encouragement. "We're nearly home."

Home . . . The word echoed through Anne's head. Boston seemed an eternity away, and she wondered how her family fared. Luke had enlisted with her cousin Ben and was serving in a cavalry regiment currently training in Annapolis, Maryland. Camille was reportedly attending Society meetings (would wonders never cease?), and Robert and Jimmy were doing who knew what. At times she wished she did. She missed them all much more than she ever would have believed possible.

It was with a measure of relief that Anne finally viewed their camp from a distance. The sight was a welcome one, and she found herself grateful for the shelter of the tent she shared with Ivar, Jed, and Mark Stephenson, although she knew it wouldn't be warm, only relatively dry.

Upon reaching the makeshift shelter, she stamped her feet on the ground, wincing in pain, and brushed the snow from her coat and hat. Beside her, Ivar, Mark, and Jed all did the same, and they shuffled their way into the tent wordlessly, exhausted.

Anne situated her bedroll between Mark's and Ivar's; Jed slept next to Mark on the other side. The close proximity provided not only body heat, but comfort that none of them ever openly acknowledged. She mused that if her father knew she was sleeping at night between two men, he would perish of an apoplectic fit. It was hardly intimate, though, except under the bonds of deep friendship forged from extremely unpleasant conditions. *Besides,* she told herself as she straightened her blankets, *only Ivar knows I'm a woman, and it doesn't seem to affect him.*

With those exhausted thoughts, she climbed into her bedroll fully clothed and grateful for the closeness of the other men. Maybe, with their added body heat, she wouldn't freeze to death by morning.

* * *

Ivar lay close to the woman, listening to her even breathing. She was insane, that was all there was to it. What he wouldn't give to be in his warm little home in Ohio, sitting before the fire in his rocking chair with his sweet, two-year-old daughter snuggled in his lap. And Anne could leave at will! She could, at any moment, reveal her gender to their commanding officers, and within a matter of days she would find herself in her own warm Boston bed.

He knew little about her home—she shared a few details, but never much. He imagined she came from wealth. Her bearing was regal and confident; she was ever poised and possessed a certain social polish his late wife had always tried to imitate but had never actually accomplished.

Anne looked so young! He often found himself thinking that the other men in the regiment must be either extremely unobservant or blind. *Do you not think this boy is a mite too pretty?* he imagined himself saying to them. But no one batted a suspecting eye at her, and "Aaron Johnson," or so she called herself, lived in all the male splendor the Union army could provide.

He turned on his side and viewed her profile, barely visible in the dark night. She was completely spent, and he had known it from the moment they left camp the night before. His mind rolled over the events of the Blue's Gap Affair, as the men were already calling it. They had marched, all told, thirty-two miles through the wintry mountains, found and routed a rebel encampment, engaged in a skirmish, and taken prisoners. Here they were, back again, trying to rest and wondering what the next twenty-four hours would bring.

The even cadence of Anne's breathing was interrupted by the harsh, barklike cough emanating from the far side of the small tent. Jed was doing his best to smother the noise, but it sounded painful and was apparently worsening. The dry cough was punctuated with short, choking sounds that had Ivar wincing.

Waving a hand at Jed's mumbled apology, he rose and quietly exited the tent after locating his tin cup in his personal belongings. The weather accosted him in a steady, unrelenting stream, and he knelt quickly beside the thin walls of the tent, filling the cup with wet snow. He reentered the tent, fastened the flaps securely behind him, and, reaching over the two sleeping forms, handed Jed the cup.

"Put some of this in your mouth. It will help your dry throat," he whispered to the sick man.

"Thank you," came the croaked response, and amidst subdued coughing, Jed sucked on the snow.

It was ironic, Ivar mused as he settled back in for the night, that he had assumed their worst enemy would be, well, the enemy. They might lose one another to illness, and it was a prospect he hadn't anticipated. Jed and Mark had been his friends from boyhood. He knew their wives, their children, their various relatives back home in Ohio, and he didn't relish the thought of those good folk living the rest of their lives without their husbands, fathers, and loved ones.

He couldn't stop a bullet, but he could well care for his friends when they were sick. Ivar again registered Anne's breathing and her face in the dark. *And as for you,* he thought, *how can I, in good conscience, keep your secret?* But it really wasn't his business, and he would do well to remember that. Her life was her own, and had little, if anything, to do with his.

* * *

7 January 1862
Boston, Massachusetts

Elizabeth Birmingham sat upright in her bed, her breathing shallow and rapid. The dream had seemed so real! Anne was in the snow, and she was cold, hungry, and in pain! As Elizabeth gazed about her bedroom, her eyes falling upon familiar objects in the dim light of dawn, her breathing gradually returned to its normal pace and her heart calmed.

Of course it was foolish. Anne was working in Chicago for Allan Pinkerton. It might not be the most conventional employment, but she was safe to be sure. In the snow, indeed! Elizabeth shook her head and swung her feet over the side of her large bed, glancing at the door connecting her bedroom with James's. She entertained the notion of sharing her silly dream with her husband, but decided against it. James was worried enough about Anne as it was; he might think her dream was some kind of premonition, and then there would be no living with the man.

She rose from the bed and readied herself for the day, eventually emerging from her bedroom with face scrubbed, hair neatly in place, and clothing pressed to perfection. Her skirts rustled about her as she traversed the length of the hallway and made her way down the back stairs and into the kitchen. As she went about the activities of the morning, seeing to it that breakfast was on its way and the household maids had their proper instructions, she wondered at the reason she should imagine Anne in such an odd place.

More likely than not, she was taking her fears for Luke's safety and placing them upon her daughter. It was only natural, after all. Anne had been gone for over six months, and her odd pronouncement that she would be staying in Chicago for the holidays had been a painful surprise. Elizabeth wanted to see Anne; she had never been so far away from home for so long, even when she had been attending school, and Elizabeth thought of her often. It was no wonder, really, that a mother might have strange dreams about a child who was far from the nest.

Anne, however, was independent and always had been. Of one thing Elizabeth was certain; Anne could care for herself.

* * *

Elizabeth's younger daughter, Camille Birmingham, sat at the breakfast table, her pretty, nineteen-year-old brow wrinkled in a frown.

"What is it?" her brother Robert asked her as he took a sip of hot tea.

"A note from Olivia."

"An invitation to a party?"

Camille shook her head. "Quite the contrary. Olivia informs me that as I have been seen at 'those atrocious Society meetings on more than one occasion,' she'll be unable to continue our acquaintance."

Robert looked at Camille for a moment, his expression unreadable. "I can't say I'm sorry, Cammy, except for your feelings."

Camille tried to shake the sense of sadness that had descended upon her when she read the note. "I know. It's only that she's been my dearest friend for years . . ."

"She's a complete cake and you know it. You've been avoiding her for weeks now—months even. She doesn't deserve your company. She never has." He paused. "I don't see Nathaniel much anymore, either."

Camille shrugged and placed the note to the side of her plate, trying to turn her attention toward the breakfast she no longer wanted to eat. "Does he still talk of enlisting?"

Robert nodded and broke apart a breakfast roll that was soft and warm. "I think he wants to prove he can fight."

Camille wrinkled her nose in distaste. "Does he not remember his reaction to the last battle he witnessed?"

"He never did admit to his father that he threw up."

"He's only sixteen. His father will allow him to enlist?"

Robert shrugged. "I don't know."

Camille turned her gaze toward the large wall of windows that overlooked the back gardens. The beautiful flowers and plants slept beneath the winter snow, and the somber gray morning matched her spirits. "It's of no account, I suppose," she murmured, more to herself than to Robert. "I spend most of my social time with Abigail, anymore."

Robert placed his roll to one side and gave his sister the benefit of his full regard. "Camille, Olivia is a brainless twit. You're much better off having Abigail as a friend."

"It wasn't so very long ago that I was a brainless twit, Robert. Abigail has been an intelligent person her entire life. I don't belong with either friend."

"Camille, a person doesn't suddenly become intelligent. You always have been—you were just . . . uninformed."

Camille laughed. "Suddenly you're my champion. You used to think I was an idiot." She slowly sobered. "I liked it better when we annoyed each other, Robert. Life was predictable then."

She rose and left the table, her breakfast untouched. Making her way to her bedroom, she retrieved a warm woolen cloak with a matching bonnet and gloves. She walked back down the front stairs to the entryway and informed Griffen, the family butler, that she would be out for a few hours, should anyone inquire after her whereabouts.

Once ensconced in the family's smallest carriage, a young groom atop to manage the horses and guide the vehicle, she chewed on her bottom lip, her focus turned inward. "To the Van Dykes' home," she had told the lad when asked of her intended destination. It was the only logical place, really. Whenever there was a matter to stew over, Abigail was the best confidant. Ironic that Abby herself was part of the object of Camille's stewing.

Upon admittance to the Van Dyke parlor, Camille paced the length of the room completely unaware that she was the very image of her older brother, Luke, who had paced that very room in much the same fashion a few months earlier. Abigail remarked on the similarities as she entered to greet her friend.

"You are your brother's sister," Abigail said, her hands outstretched.

Camille took the woman's hands and pressed her cheek against her friend's with a quick kiss.

"And to what do I owe the honor of this visit?"

Camille sighed and tugged on Abigail's hands as she made her way toward a settee by the hearth wherein glowed a cozy fire. The women sat upon it together, and Camille released Abigail's hands, pulling on the fingers of her own gloves. "I am two people, Abby. I find myself most vexed."

"Do you suppose you might consider sharing a few more specific details?"

"I'm a well-informed idiot."

"Hmm. And here I found you bright. I'm so very rarely wrong, too. Now *I'm* vexed."

Camille's mouth turned up in a smile that was quick to fade. "Olivia has informed me that we are no longer friends."

"I see. And you mourn the loss?"

"No, not exactly. I find her extremely annoying."

"Well, then?"

"I had once considered her my dearest friend." Camille rose and moved closer to the fire, extending her fingers toward the warmth. "We were inseparable, and not only that, we were so very much alike."

She turned her back to the flames and folded her hands together, studying Abigail's strong, beautiful features.

"You are not like Olivia Sylvester anymore, Camille. Is that your concern?"

Camille shrugged. "I don't belong anywhere. I float between Society meetings and society itself. I am not as intelligent as you, nor as stupid as Olivia."

Abigail laughed. "Even in your most innocent youth, you were never as stupid as Olivia. And you're every bit as intelligent as I, or your mother, or anyone else in the Society. Speaking of your mother," she added, "you need look no further for a perfect example of how to float between the two worlds. She's done it for years, and with great style, might I add."

"My mother doesn't care one whit for what people think, and yet she still manages to never offend anyone. I don't believe I can do that. I care too much for the good opinion of others, yet I lack my mother's diplomacy."

"You discredit yourself, Camille," Abigail murmured. "You are bright and witty and charming. And beautiful. The world is yours to grasp, if you so choose."

"I don't know how."

"You will."

Camille glanced at her friend's earnest face and was suddenly chagrined. "I apologize for taking your time with such silliness, Abby. You must think me the veriest goose."

"Nonsense. Come sit beside me and tell me what you hear from Luke."

Camille resumed her vacated position on the settee, her expression brightening. "We probably hear less than you do. We receive one letter for your every two!"

Abigail blushed, and Camille was amazed by it. "What is it?"

"Your brother and I continue to grow . . . close . . ."

"Abby! Has he proposed marriage?"

"No, no. Not yet."

"Not yet?" Camille's voice raised a notch. "Abby, I'm delighted! That is, I'm delighted that you say 'yet'! I would so dearly love to have you as a sister. Please, when he proposes, you must say yes."

Abigail laughed. "So that we can be sisters?"

"Yes!"

"I suppose people have married for reasons stranger than that. I would love it too, Camille. I just hope he comes home in one piece."

"Oh, yes. There is that."
"Yes. There is that."

* * *

14 January 1862
Annapolis, Maryland

"The second and third battalions left New York yesterday for Hilton Head." Luke Birmingham joined his cousin Ben in their barracks.

Ben glanced up at him from his position on his cot, where he sat writing letters to his friends in the Utah Territory. He studied Luke's face with an inscrutable expression, and in the end, Luke was left wondering what he was thinking, because Ben remained silent.

Luke sat on his own cot and quietly watched as Ben returned to his letter. "Rumor has it that we won't be far behind," Luke said.

"Just my luck," Ben finally said. He shook his head, still looking down at his paper. "I can't complain. This is what I wanted."

When he didn't seem inclined to say more, Luke left his cousin to his own thoughts and reached for his haversack, pulling from it Abigail's most recent letter. His heart skipped each time he viewed the neat script; her pragmatic personality and cynical sense of humor showed through each phrase, each sentence. He had definite hopes for when he returned home, and while it was his intention to be with her in person before proposing, he wasn't sure he could wait so long to ask her to be his. He was trying to be fair, to allow her room for socialization in case she met someone who could make her happy. But with each letter, indeed with each passing day, he grew more enamored of her and experienced an ugly surge of jealousy when thinking of her in the company of other men.

Luke pulled a pen and paper from his small leather writing kit and began his second letter to Abigail in three days. He glanced up, feeling a twinge of guilt for being relatively happy, as Ben stood and announced he was going for a walk outside. "Would you care for company?" Luke asked, trying to assuage his conscience.

"No, thank you. I need some time to think."

* * *

Be careful what you wish for . . . It was a trite little phrase that Ben had often heard before, yet never had it applied so accurately to his life. When he had traveled east to enlist with his cousin, he never imagined he would eventually find himself in his former backyard. Hilton Head was easily within traveling distance from Charleston and Bentley Plantation, his family home.

Well, it was done, that's all there was to it. He couldn't very well have enlisted and said, "I want to help the North overthrow my homeland; I just don't want to have to do it up close. Keep me away from South Carolina." If there was a bright side, a proverbial silver lining to the cloud, it was that being stationed so close to his home might afford him an opportunity to see people he had missed for years. His sisters, Emily and Clara. Ruth, Mary, Rose, and Joshua—slaves he was closer to than his own parents. Yet how would they receive him? He had abandoned them, really—had left them to their fates in an effort to preserve his own life. He knew they probably didn't fault him for it, yet how could they not resent him, even just a little bit? He knew Emily did—she had told him as much on more than one occasion in the few letters she had managed to get to him over the last five or so years.

His heart ached to see them, and he knew that if he hadn't already become a man of religion, that he would have soon. Either that, or become a firm believer in fate. It was too fantastic, really, to discount. He was destined to again see the people who, for good or ill, had influenced his life in so many ways.

"And what wouldst Thou have me do, once there?" he whispered toward the heavens. The white sky offered no answer, and so he was left to continue his own train of thought.

CHAPTER 2

"Were [this position] offered to me now, and I at home on no account would I accept of it—knowing from experience what it is. I am in it now and will do the best I can, trusting, hoping, praying that very soon the time will come when I can leave it."

—Josiah Parker Higgins, new recruit aboard the Kennebec

* * *

9 February 1862
Atlantic Ocean

Daniel O'Shea stood aboard the deck of the *Kennebec* and looked out over the blue expanse. The newly commissioned gunboat had pulled away from shore the day before, and was on course for an eventual union with Rear Admiral David Farragut's West Gulf Blockading Squadron, a fleet of warships and mortar vessels of impressive magnitude, situated near the coast of Louisiana.

It was the eventual destination that had initially engaged Daniel's interest and held it fast. He was in drastic need of a change in circumstances, and hoped to find it in his enlistment. In his heart was a glimmer of hope that he might have a chance to meet in person one Marie Brissot, and thank her for her role in helping him maintain the one shred of sanity he felt he still possessed. Her letters in the preceding months had given him something on which to focus other than his own sorry state of affairs. He was an angry Irish-American man with a chip on his shoulder so large he was beginning to stagger under the weight of it.

The seas were rough, and Daniel fought a wave of nausea for what must have been the millionth time. His only consolation was that many of his fellow sailors were suffering worse than he was. At least he hadn't been up half the night hurling the contents of his stomach into a pail—instead he'd been forced to listen to those who did.

The quarters were close aboard the *Kennebec*. The hammocks were hung in tight rows, and Daniel missed the comfort of his own bed at home. *So why, then, did you leave?* he asked himself. Sea life was proving not only to be uncomfortable, but his shipmates were rowdy and often looked for trouble-causing diversions. He kept his past as a fighter to himself, and hoped he would never have cause to use his skills. His goal, he mused as he answered his own question, was to get away from his old life, not continue its unpleasantness.

Daniel's mind reviewed the past two days, which had sped by with alarming swiftness. One minute he had been working in his workshop at home, jaw grimly set and mind thirsting for escape, and the next his father, Gavin, had flown through his door, announcing that the *Kennebec* had just been commissioned and he had but a few hours to sign himself aboard. When Gavin told him breathlessly where the ship was headed, Daniel dropped his lathe and didn't look back.

"We'll care for your home, Danny boy," Gavin had said two hours later while Daniel was feverishly packing a bag with the barest of necessities inside.

His mother, Brenna, stood near Gavin's side, sniffling. "You go now. This will all be here when you return."

The wind caught Daniel's short hair and ruffled it across the top of his head. He wished he could say he'd enlisted for patriotic reasons; his father certainly would have, but Daniel's reasons were entirely self-serving. Daniel needed to leave New York and all that he knew. He needed to try to establish what kind of life he wanted to live, and he hoped to find some sort of peace. It was ironic, he supposed, to be looking for peace while going to war, but the peace he sought was internal. He was quite sure that the ravages of the current war were nothing compared to the turmoil that erupted daily in his heart. It wasn't even anything he could quite put a finger on, and perhaps that was the most puzzling and disconcerting thing of all.

Daniel made his way below deck to his quarters and decided to make use of what little free time he had by writing a few quick letters. The first was to Marie Brissot. Writing her name at the top of the paper felt as natural to him as breathing. He cherished his correspondence with her, and as he sat in the corner of the sailors' quarters, the ship pitching and rolling, he forgot for a moment his queasy stomach and instead tried to fight off a surge of panic. Suppose Marie found him foolish? She said in her letters to him that she enjoyed hearing from him, but perhaps she was merely polite. Her parents, after all, were very polished people—her father French, her mother a Rhode Island native, the descendant of a long line of proper Quaker folk.

Daniel was never confident in his skills at writing or academics, and Marie was a teacher, of all things! What if she went over his letters to her with a correcting pencil? He imagined a stack of papers sitting on her desk, a sea of unforgiving marks. His hand faltered for a bit after he scrawled her name, and for a moment he doubted himself. She was so beautiful—he knew it to be fact as he had viewed with his own eyes a daguerreotype of her likeness—and she was also very intelligent. What would she think of him, a bad-tempered Irishman with no formal education?

He shook his head. It may be that they would never meet. Perhaps once near New Orleans he would never get the chance to find her, or it may be that she wouldn't want to meet him. Most likely he was stewing over an association that would be limited to letters.

He unconsciously clenched his teeth and considered his options. He detested the thought that he might find himself, in the end, looking the part of a fool. He had fought for respect ever since he could remember, and he never willingly placed himself in situations where he might emerge embarrassed or ashamed. He was a proud man of twenty-eight, and his pride, Gavin often told him, would be his downfall.

If a man didn't have his pride, though, he argued to himself as he looked at the blank page before him that moved up and down with the roll of the ship, *then he might as well have nothing at all.* He steadied himself against the constant movement of the craft upon the depths of the tumultuous sea and gripped his pen. He would keep writing to Marie, and if she didn't find him good enough, should they ever meet, then the devil take her, because it really didn't matter to him one way or the other.

* * *

15 February 1862
New Orleans, Louisiana

Marie Brissot took a sip of her tea and, with pleasure, sighed as she leaned back into her chair. Her "houseguests" were settled for the night, and she smiled as she thought of the family that rested in the beds upstairs. The Fromeres were free blacks, and had been for a number of years, but their very lives were at stake because of the meddling trouble of some local white boys. The Fromeres' reaction to Marie's generous offer to hide them in her home had at first been shock and utter disbelief, and Marie smiled at the way they now repaid her hospitality. When Marie returned home each day from her small schoolhouse, she found the house in absolute order and a warm meal waiting.

She now sat in the parlor near her father's study, where she slept. She looked at the unopened letter she held in her hand and smiled in anticipation. Her heart gave a small leap as she set her cup in its saucer on the small table at her left and opened the letter, her eyes glancing over the scrawled, masculine script. There were no frills or elegant touches to the handwriting, and Marie imagined that it matched its creator to perfection.

Her heart began to beat a bit harder as her eyes perused the contents, falling to midpage where he stated:

You may find this as strange as do I, but as I sit writing this letter to you, I am traveling ever closer to New Orleans. By the time you receive this, I expect to find myself at the Florida Keys, if not at the Louisiana coast. As you might have guessed with this information, I have enlisted in the Union navy. The reasons are complex, and I do not wish to outline them here. I—

Marie squinted to read the scrawled words that had been crossed out repeatedly. What had he started to say, only to change his mind? The letter continued:

There is every possibility that we may meet, if you would be interested. I fully understand if you wish otherwise. We have never been formally introduced, and I would hate to cause undue harm to your reputation, especially given that we are currently on opposing sides of a war . . .

Marie let her hands fall heavily into her lap, and brought her gaze slowly from the parchment to the window, where the drapes were closed firmly against the dark night. *Her reputation*. It was laughable that he would think an association with him would bring it further harm. To the contrary; it was nothing less than the locals would expect of her. Daniel didn't know, however, that most people considered her to be of loose moral fiber because of a moment's indiscretion in a society matron's garden over seven years before.

Her warm association with Daniel through letters written over the last few months had brought her more joy than she had realized. He was kind and interesting, and there wasn't even one time when she hadn't laughed right out loud at something or other he wrote to her. She detected a bent to his personality that was slightly irreverent, and her lonely soul was drawn to it.

He did, however, have two extremely honorable parents who had worked very hard to give their son a good life. She had read it both in the things he did and didn't say about Gavin and Brenna O'Shea. What would they think of their son's association with a Southern girl whom the locals viewed with a certain amount of superior distaste? Especially if he developed feelings for her? Men often did; she frequently heard remarks about her physical beauty, but she had learned to find such comments abhorrent because they were always followed by a commentary on her lack of upstanding character.

She couldn't bear to lose his companionship, limited though it was, and she surely would if he knew the truth about her—about how other people viewed her. She rose from the settee with a sigh and walked slowly to the window, parting the heavy drapes with one hand. The sky was black, filled with the brilliance of a million white stars. Perhaps Daniel was, at that very moment, looking at those very same stars.

Marie let the drapes fall back into place, and she wandered toward the small desk in the corner of the room. She lit a lamp that sat on the desk and withdrew a piece of paper from the center drawer. With resignation, she began her letter.

Dear Daniel,

You can imagine my surprise at learning you will soon be stationed so close to my home! I hope all goes well with your career at sea, and I pray you will be kept safe. I do not, however, think it a good idea that we meet. My days are so busy, you see, and . . .

* * *

20 February 1862
Florida Keys

Daniel stared at the letter in his hand with a blank expression. His initial delight that Marie's letter had reached his docked location at the islands was quickly squelched as he internalized her response to his tentative request that they meet. It was well that he had braced himself for this eventuality, because he told himself he hardly felt the sting.

Marie didn't want to meet him. It was just as he had suspected; he wasn't nearly refined enough for someone of her standing and upbringing. He felt a flash of anger followed by a stab of dull pain that caught him by surprise. He barely knew the woman. Why should it matter to him one way or another if she did or didn't want to meet him? She meant little to him, if that, and he would be better off focusing on his duties as a yeoman as opposed to obsessing about Marie Brissot.

He didn't need her in his life, and come to think of it, he had been wasting his time writing to her. The problem was that he had written so many things to her over the past months that he had come to view the writing itself as a comfort, in an odd way. He had learned many things about himself as he had penned those letters. Well, if he wanted to keep writing to someone, there was always his mother. Brenna loved him without reservation, as only a mother could, and she didn't judge him by his lack of social polish or education.

Yes, letters to Brenna would do just fine. Who needed Marie Brissot, after all?

* * *

9 February 1862
Utah Territory

Earl Dobranski strolled down Main Street, whistling a merry tune. He was generally of a good-natured disposition, prone to optimism and very few bursts of melancholy. He blended well with nearly every assembled crowd, and found himself in very few circumstances to which he was not able to quickly adapt. As the oldest of eight strapping boys, he indubitably owed his patience and flexibility to his role as the elder brother.

In his hand Earl held a letter written to one Ben Birmingham, who had left his home with the Saints in Utah and was fighting a war of which the latter felt very much a part. In each letter the Dobranskis received from Ben, he told them that he loved them, he missed them and counted the days until they would again meet, but that he knew he was where he needed to be.

Earl, of all the Dobranski boys, missed Ben the most. When Ben had arrived in the Utah Territory as a freshly baptized Saint, he was lost and alone and needing a family. The Dobranskis, among others, filled that void, and in turn, Ben became the older-brother figure Earl so desperately needed, as his own father was a missionary for the Church.

Earl supposed the day would soon come when he would be a missionary himself, but he didn't feel ready somehow. It was as though he were in limbo—not really a child anymore, but certainly not feeling yet like a man. He wished Ben were there to talk with him about it. Earl's father had returned, but somehow things were still a bit different.

In the letter to Ben, Earl had told him all about recent political happenings in the desert valley—about how at the end of last year, Governor Dawson had left his post after a mere three weeks because he improperly propositioned one of the city's good ladies. He cited his health as reasons for his immediate return east, but upon leaving, he was set upon by a band of rowdy young men and beaten rather badly.

He also told Ben of the Saints' pity for the states involved in the current conflict, and of President Young's condemnation of those states and cities that had offered the Church nothing but trouble in the past. President Young was nearly like a parent speaking to a recalcitrant child at times when speaking in reference to the states the Church members had left behind. He maintained that the war, in part, was a direct result of the murder of a prophet.

Earl mentioned the frustrations the Saints had encountered when dealing with the United States government. They applied for statehood and were continually rebuffed because of the polygamy still practiced by some of the members of the Church. Brigham Young had repeatedly asked that they be permitted to be governed by one of their own rather than a political appointee who knew nothing of the culture or lifestyle. Sometimes Washington listened—often it did not.

Earl continued to whistle as he made his way to the post office and tapped the letter in time against his thigh as he walked. He passed familiar faces, offering a quick smile and nod of the head in response to their greetings. Finally, at the door to the post office, he was stopped by Acting Governor Fuller.

"Young Dobranski! How nice to see you today."

"And you as well, sir."

"Sending a letter to your friend again?"

"I am."

Fuller cleared his throat. "I wonder if I might have a word with you," he said, and drew Earl a bit away from the door. "I have it on good authority that before long, the word will come from Washington that we need to raise a militia to protect the mail and telegraph lines from Indian attack. I was hoping I might come to you for support."

Earl nodded. "I'll certainly consider it."

The governor patted Earl's arm, his eyes widening slightly at its solidity and size. "I'm glad to hear it. Give my best to your parents."

Earl nodded and made his way into the mail office. He knew Ben would enjoy hearing from his old friend, and hoped desperately that he hadn't forgotten him. Ben was a good man, and Earl missed him greatly.

CHAPTER 3

"No terms except an unconditional and immediate surrender can be accepted. I propose to move immediately upon your works."
—Missive from General Grant to Simon B. Buckner in response to the Confederate request for terms of the surrender of Fort Donelson

* * *

20 February 1862
Charleston, South Carolina

"You don't say!" Emily Birmingham waved her fan gently across her neck and was grateful that she had something to do with her hands. Being a young Southern socialite was still not a role in which she felt completely at ease, despite the fact that she had given over two months of study to it.

The ample woman Emily stood with on the fringes of the ballroom was much more at ease in the setting. "Yes! And I told her repeatedly that yellow was not a becoming color for her, but she simply wouldn't hear me. I suppose that once a girl has married and left home, a mother's good opinion no longer matters," the woman sniffed, her massive chest lifting in response.

"Now, Mrs. Appleby, I'm certain Eliza still values your opinion greatly," Emily said, trying to ignore the twinges of irritating pain gathering behind her eyes and threatening to become a full-blown headache by the time the evening was through. Emily had been trying, in vain, to gather Confederate information that might be of use to the Union, and for her cause had subjected herself to an endless round of socializing and mundane events that, night after night, had her metaphorically rolling her eyes in disgust. The social scene was not one in which Emily took a natural interest, and her efforts were beginning to try her nerves. It might have been different altogether if she had been able to unearth some interesting tidbits of information, but to come home empty-handed each night was disheartening.

The discussion with Mrs. Appleby was gaining her nothing. Emily determined with an internal sigh of relief that it was time to move on. After murmuring a polite good-bye with an excuse that she needed to speak with her father, Emily strolled away from the woman and, spying Jeffrey Birmingham across the room, made her way in his direction.

He smiled as she approached. "Are you enjoying yourself, Emily?"

She returned his smile with slightly less enthusiasm, and tried for a suitable response. "Yes, I am indeed, although I was wondering if you would accompany me to the card room."

Jeffrey's eyebrows shot up in mild surprise, and Emily scrutinized her father with an objective eye. He was extraordinarily handsome, with dark hair that was only just beginning to turn to gray, and vibrant green eyes. He was fit for a man in his midfifties, and he blended well into the Southern society he had adopted for his own with his marriage to Emily's mother, Sarah Matthews, nearly thirty years before.

"The card room, dear? Whatever for?"

Emily sighed. "I'm bored."

"Bored? I suggest you keep that from your mother. You're supposed to be looking for a husband, and I'm supposed to be helping you find one."

Emily wondered if the slight grimace that passed across her father's features was real or if she only imagined it.

"Well what better place for me to find one than in the card room?"

"That all depends on what kind of husband you're looking for. Would you fancy one who likes to gamble? I should think you'd have better luck finding someone suitable out here."

"Father, look closely at this ensemble. No, truly, look closely. There," Emily said behind her fan as she lightly pointed to her left. "That is Mr. Bodean. He vows that regardless of the state of affairs in his future, he will never live a day without his mother under the same roof. He also has malodorous breath and complicated sinuses."

Jeffrey chuckled softly as Emily continued. "And over here. Mr. Price. He maintains that the good Lord put him here on this earth to continue the legacy of Adam, and saints preserve us all, he intends that his wife bear him as many children as did our first father. Do you realize how many children Adam and Eve produced?"

Jeffrey's lips twitched, and he nodded his head toward the center of the floor where a dandy and his young, blushing dance partner moved to the rhythm of the live band. "How about Alexander Croxton?"

"There are too many *x*'s in his name."

"Emily, be reasonable."

"Father, he whines! I have danced with him on no less than three different occasions during the past month, and all I've heard him do is complain about the fact that if the war doesn't go the way all good Southerners hope it will, then the price of cravats and snuff boxes will be absolutely exorbitant. Something tells me he hasn't considered the fact that if the war doesn't go the way 'all good Southerners hope it will,' he won't be able to find a cravat or snuff box within several hundred miles."

"One might think Mr. Croxton is lacking faith in the Confederate cause."

Emily did as well, but she wasn't about to admit as much to her father. Jeffrey Birmingham moved in some very powerful political circles. It was the one thing at which he completely excelled. "Father," she said, "if you were in my shoes, would you honestly choose any man in this room?"

"Well, not necessarily," he finally admitted after some thought. "But I'm not altogether certain you'll find anything better in the card room."

"It can't be any worse." Emily was growing desperate. She didn't want to watch the men play cards so that she might look over potential husband material; she wanted to be privy to their conversations.

Jeffrey must have agreed with her statement because he gave her his arm and led her from the ballroom into the adjoining billiard and card room, where people sat at tables playing a wide variety of games. The majority of the room's occupants were men, but there were a few women sprinkled here and there, trying their hands at the less innocuous and more socially acceptable games like faro and hearts. Emily scanned the room, eyeing the tables and trying to decide which one would yield the most fruit.

As luck would have it, Jeffrey guided her to a table around which sat men of a wide combination of ages; some were fathers and sons, others just friends. A total of eight men circled the table, and they greeted Jeffrey warmly when he asked if they might sit and observe their play.

Some of the younger men knew Emily from prior parties and balls; some of the older ones greeted her with glints in their eyes that Emily found particularly nauseating. She knew she was turning out quite nicely; her young body was beginning to take the shape that would define her womanhood, and her rich, auburn hair was pulled to the crown and cascading down in ringlets about her head and lightly touching her shoulders. She was not impressed, however, that several of the men who were eyeing her with such interest had wives that strolled about in the ballroom not twenty feet away.

Emily bestowed smiles upon the group and sat in a chair a small space apart from the table, arranging her skirts to their best advantage. "Do continue," she said with a wave of her hand when the men seemed reluctant to continue their play. "I apologize for interrupting, but I told Father I simply *had* to escape the busyness of the ballroom for a moment. It's quite the crush tonight."

Mr. Reid, the husband of the hostess, glanced in Emily's direction with a slight grunt. Emily was unable to discern whether or not the reaction was a favorable one. "Mrs. Reid will be thrilled to hear that you think so, Miss Birmingham. She was quite pleased to be able to draw in the most influential folk from around the county."

"Yes," drawled a young man seated just to Emily's left. "Important folk such as ourselves are a must-have at any successful function." He glanced at Emily with a wink. "Wouldn't you agree, Miss Birmingham?"

Emily glanced at the young man. "I don't believe we've been introduced, Mr. . . ."

Jeffrey Birmingham cleared his throat. "Emily, dear, this is Mr. Austin Stanhope, of the Savannah Stanhopes."

"Of course, the Savannah Stanhopes," Emily said, with no prior knowledge of any Stanhopes, Savannah or otherwise, and offered her gloved hand to the man. He stood and took her fingers between his, placing a ghost of a kiss on her hand.

Austin Stanhope resumed his seat, and the card game continued, the conversation mostly as dull as that she'd left behind in the ballroom. Emily was nearly ready to admit despair and whisper to her father that she wasn't feeling well when the talk finally turned toward recent military campaigns. Her ears perked up, and she made an effort to keep the motion of the fan in her hand as casual as it had been before.

"That cur Grant took not only Fort Henry, but Donelson as well," Mr. Reid said.

"Yes," said a man to his immediate left, "and did you hear that Floyd and Pillow ran like cowards? Were I there, I should like to have followed and thrashed them both!"

"True enough," Reid grunted, "but Grant's comment about Pillow to Simon Buckner was beyond the pale."

"And what comment was that?" Austin Stanhope asked.

"He said, 'If I had got him, I'd let him go again. He will do us more good commanding you fellows.'"

Emily was startled to hear what sounded suspiciously like a snicker come from Stanhope's general direction, but he covered it with a cough.

"Perhaps you need your glass refilled," Jeffrey commented to Stanhope, his tone dry.

Emily's lips twitched. Her father, no doubt, had already heard all about the entire scenario that had just been outlined, but he rarely offered comment in general conversation unless specifically asked, and even then he was often evasive and noncommittal. He was the very essence of diplomacy, but nothing political ever escaped his notice. It was because of these qualities and Jeffrey's social habits that Emily had decided to embark upon her scheme in the first place.

"Yes," Stanhope said between coughs, "I think that would be wise."

Reid signaled to an aging black man standing at his post with a tray full of drinks. The man moved forward, his back straight, and as Reid pointed to Stanhope's empty glass, replaced it with one already filled with two fingers of brandy. Emily tried not to cringe as the man slowly made his way to his corner by the windows and resumed his former position. The hour was late, and the man should have been resting his old bones in a comfortable bed. *More to the point*, Emily mused, *he shouldn't have to be here in the first place.*

Emily felt the familiar fire in her veins and stiffened her resolve to do something, *anything*, for the Union cause. She was sure that if the Union prevailed, they would eventually free the slaves, if for no other reason than to economically cripple the South. It was the best way she could think of to win a sure advantage, and although the Union government had not yet stated freedom for slaves as an official objective of the war, she hoped and prayed daily that it would happen.

"Perhaps you gentlemen have heard that Simon Buckner and Ulysses Grant were classmates at West Point and then fought in the Mexican war together?" Austin Stanhope asked as he took a sip of his brandy.

There were several murmurs of surprise around the table as the men continued to look over their cards. One voice dissented, however. "It so happens I did know that, Stanhope, and furthermore, I have it on good authority that Buckner loaned Grant money to pay a hotel bill when he first resigned from the army. One might suppose that Grant would behave in a gentlemanly fashion and return the favor!"

"One might," Stanhope conceded, "but then again, this is war."

Reid grunted again, and this time Emily was left with no question as to whether or not it was a positive response. "Grant is obviously a Yank. A Southerner is a gentleman at all times, even in war."

Stanhope raised a brow but refrained from further comment. He took another sip of his brandy and studied his cards instead. He surprised Emily by turning his hand to her and saying, "What say you, Miss Birmingham? Do I have a chance of winning this hand?"

Emily looked at his cards, which revealed three aces and two kings. She glanced into the man's face, and found it pleasant, almost handsome. "I wouldn't know, sir," she lied. "You had best not lean heavily on my advice."

"Well, perhaps I'll not turn to you for help, in that case, but I will claim you as my good luck charm." He turned back to the table at the grumbling of the other men, who were anxious to see his cards. Of course, he won the hand easily. "Did you know," he said to Emily as he accepted a pile of bills from the middle of the table, "that red is my favorite color?"

* * *

Emily wandered into her bedroom in the family mansion an hour later with much on her mind. She was supremely irritated, for one thing. Austin Stanhope had asked her father if he might have permission to call formally upon Emily in the future. She had received a fair amount of gentlemen callers in recent weeks, but she always found their company tedious at best, and inevitably they left with disappointment at her sharp tongue. She often found herself unable to control it, and when seated opposite a person who was of no value to her politically and could serve absolutely no purpose to help her seek out Confederate information, she said things better left unspoken.

Austin Stanhope was one in a long line of Southern dandies who had enough money to avoid enlistment and could spend their time in idle pursuits, even with a war on. She would undoubtedly send him on his way soon enough. He would come to wish he'd never set foot inside the Bentley mansion.

Emily studied her reflection in the mirror as she sat at her vanity and let her hair down. She could almost feel pity for the poor man. He had no idea Emily wasn't the docile Southern belle she appeared. She was startled and nearly let out a shriek as the shadow of a person appeared beyond her shoulder in the mirror. Spinning around, she gave a huge sigh of relief when she recognized the person emerging from Emily's sitting room.

"Mary! You nearly scared me senseless!" Emily rose with a smile and walked toward the girl, her arms extended.

The young slave met Emily halfway across the room and the two embraced. "What are you doing here so late? It's nearly three o'clock in the morning!" Emily asked, taking in her friend's eyes, tired and at odds with her crisp, formal maid's uniform.

"Your mother gave me permission to dust your sitting room before retiring for the night, and I only sat down for just the briefest of moments, but I must have fallen asleep."

"Oh, Mary, we've got to get you out of here." Emily's mother had been limiting contact between the two girls of late. "She thinks I'm going to try to get you a one-way ticket on the Underground Railroad. Of course, I am, but that's neither here nor there."

Mary slapped at Emily's hands with a smirk. "You're not."

"One way or another, Mary, we will find you freedom. But for now, come sit with me for a minute." Emily dragged Mary over to the enormous bed, raised on a dais, and climbed upon it, flopping down on her stomach like a young girl. She braced herself up on her elbows and patted the spot next to her across the exquisitely crafted quilt.

Mary hesitated but eventually joined Emily on the bed, lying on her side, her head propped in her hand. "If your mother finds me in here, she'll have me whipped," Mary whispered. "I was just waking up when I heard you come in."

"Mary, it's not like you to put yourself in a situation like this. I'm beginning to believe our association has finally had a negative effect on you. You're always the practical one."

"I've been tired, lately."

"Why? Is mother working you too hard? Oh, good heavens," Emily whispered, her hand covering her mouth. "Are you with child?"

"Mercy, no! Why would you think that?"

"My stupid brother took you once against your will—I figure if he can do it, just about anybody could."

"I'm much more careful now, Emily. I learned too many lessons the last time."

Emily patted Mary's free hand as it traced the tiny stitches along the differing patterns of blue fabric arranged in a log-cabin configuration. The blue quilt matched the décor of the bedroom, which was easily three times as big as the small shack Mary lived in with her grandmother. "I met another obnoxious man tonight," Emily said, changing the subject. "He's coming to call 'sometime soon,' he says."

"What's his name?"

"Austin Stanhope."

Mary's brow wrinkled slightly in contemplation. "Why does that name sound familiar to me?"

Emily shrugged. "I don't know. I'd never met him before. He's from Atlanta."

"There's something . . . something . . ."

"Something bad?"

"I don't know. I can't remember. I don't think it was bad, necessarily . . ."

"Hmm. Well, at any rate, when he comes to the house, I'll make sure you can get into the parlor. He's sure to be a bore like all the rest. Something tells me he likes to think he's charming."

"I'll ask Mama Ruth. Maybe she knows who he is."

"You do that. Mary," Emily said, clasping the hand that still traced the stitching on the quilt, "I've missed you so much. I haven't seen you for days."

Mary squeezed Emily's hand in return. "I've missed you too, Em. I've missed you, too."

Emily looked at her friend's tired face; the large, beautiful, golden-colored eyes, the gentle, light brown shade of her skin, and her thick hair pulled back into a bun at her nape. "You are so beautiful. Someday you're going to have the most wonderful life ever. Let's see if we can't make it happen."

"Oh, Em." Mary's eyes filmed over and she abruptly sat up, sliding down from the bed and making her way toward the door. When Emily caught her and gave her an affectionate squeeze, she returned the embrace and placed a kiss on her cheek. "You're good for me, white girl, but the kind of life you'd like to see me have will never happen."

"Nonsense." Emily rubbed her hands up and down Mary's arms and fought the burn of tears in her own eyes. "I'll make it happen if it kills me."

"That's what worries me."

CHAPTER 4

"Late in February a Negro woman who resided in Norfolk came to the Navy Department and desired a private interview with me. She and others had closely watched the work upon the Merrimac, *and she . . . had come to report that the ship was nearly finished. . . . The woman had passed through the lines, at great risk to herself, to bring me the information; and in confirmation of her statement, she took from the bosom of her dress a letter from a Union man, a mechanic in the Navy Yard, giving briefly the facts as stated by her."*

—Gideon Welles, Lincoln's Secretary of the Navy

* * *

6 March 1862
Brooklyn, New York

"Father was right," eleven-year-old Jimmy Birmingham stated. "It *does* look like a tin can on a shingle."

His brother Robert chuckled. "That it does. But I'd wager it'll do some damage. Do you see that turret? The guns spin in any direction and can fire from any position."

"But it'll sit barely a foot above the water line! It looks like nothing more than a glorified raft. That thing won't do well in heavy seas."

Robert glanced at his brother in some surprise. Jimmy hadn't shown much of an interest in volunteering his opinion in his young life. Questions usually comprised the bulk of his vocalization. He asked many, many questions, or quietly observed conversations and happenings around him. It was rare that the family heard him offer a definitive opinion. "Thankfully it won't have to spend much time in heavy seas," Robert commented. "All we need the *Monitor* to do is arrive safely at Chesapeake Bay, and then into Hampton Roads. Word has it that the rebs have completed their work on the *Merrimac* and that she's ready to start attacking our ships."

Robert thrust his hands into the pockets of his overcoat. The weather was a bit brisk at the Brooklyn shipyard where the boys' father, James, was conducting business. They had jumped at the chance to accompany James to New York and thereby avoid schoolwork for a while.

Jimmy was looking dubiously at the Union's newest creation, and Robert smiled to himself. "You'll see, Jim. The Union navy'll make you right proud."

Jimmy opened his mouth to respond but censored himself as he spied James walking toward them in deep conversation with another man. When the men reached the boys, James interrupted their talk for a brief introduction.

"Williams, I don't believe you've met my boys. This is Robert, my sixteen-year-old, and Jimmy, my eleven-year-old."

Robert and Jimmy took turns exchanging greetings and a quick hand clasp with the man whom James then introduced as one of the managers of the shipyard. He smiled as he shook hands with Jimmy. "Helping your father do some business, are you?"

"Yes, sir." The boy's expression was solemn.

The man laughed. "Well, it's a lucky man who has two healthy sons."

"Indeed it is," James agreed. Robert noticed his father didn't bother to tell the man that he had another son as well. He thought of Luke, off with his cavalry regiment, and wondered if it would be thusly for the rest of their lives: James introducing Robert and Jimmy with no mention of the other son. He was relieved when his father interrupted his thoughts.

"Now that we have Mr. Williams all to ourselves for a moment, is there anything you'd like to ask him about the Union's newest star?"

"Yes, sir," Jimmy said, imitating Robert's stance by thrusting his hands into his pockets. "There are two guns on the surface of the craft?"

"Yes, indeed."

"And they rotate on that revolving turret?"

"They do. They're eleven inches long, each. The pipe you see aft of the turret is a smoke pipe, and forward is the small iron pilothouse."

"And when she's in the water, my guess is there will be a foot, maybe two, of craft above the waterline?"

Williams grunted in some surprise. "That's right. You're a very perceptive young lad."

James placed a hand on the boy's shoulder. "That he is. Robert, any questions before we leave?"

"Just one, sir. Mr. Williams, how did the Union discover that the Confederacy was so close to finishing their own ironclad?"

Williams rubbed a chin that contained a good two days' worth of stubble and blinked eyes that were red and bloodshot, evidence of the long hours he'd spend in recent days working hard at getting the *Monitor* ready for battle. According to formal deadlines, she was to have been completed weeks before. "Well, I hear tell that there's a free black woman in Norfolk who carried a message from a Union sympathizer working in the Confederate navy yard. The Negress delivered the message to our Navy Department; the message said we had best make haste, that the *Merrimac,* or as the Confederacy now calls it, the *Virginia*, was nearly finished."

Robert nodded, his brow furrowed in thought. As the boys seemed content to ponder in silence for a moment, James took the opportunity to clasp Williams's hand and thank him for his time. "You'll be hearing from me shortly," he said.

"You'll be a wealthy man ten times over before this conflict is resolved, Mr. Birmingham," Williams said with a wink as he turned and left.

"Why did he say that?" Jimmy asked as the man retreated from view.

James sighed and, placing a hand on the shoulders of each boy, propelled them toward their waiting carriage outside the shipyard. "Because they're using large quantities of Birmingham iron to outfit the Union navy's ships."

Jimmy was quiet for a moment as he absorbed the information, and the trio listened to the sounds of the bustling shipyard; the shouts of the workers, the clang of tools hitting iron, and then beyond to other noises as horses and carriages traversed the length of the street beyond the shipyard.

"Why does the Confederate ironclad have two names?" Jimmy asked.

As the boys piled into the carriage, James brought up the rear and pulled the door closed behind him, tapping once on the roof to signal the driver. The vehicle gently jerked into motion as the well-trained horses pulled it forward on their journey back to the hotel.

James settled back into the cushioned seat opposite his sons and attempted to answer Jimmy's question. "When the war started a year ago, the Union was forced to abandon the Norfolk navy yard. There was a steam frigate in the yard with engines that were in very bad shape. Rather than leave the ship for the Confederates to fix and use, the navy set fire to it and then sunk it." James rested one ankle across his other knee and braced himself against the familiar rocking of the well-sprung carriage.

"The Confederates took possession of the navy yard," James continued, "and raised the hulk of the *Merrimac*. She was in good enough shape to be repaired; only just the upper works had burned. They must have been able to repair the engines as well, because by all accounts, she is in working order. They covered her hull in two feet of oak and an additional four inches of iron, renamed her the *Virginia,* and soon, I'm sure, we'll see exactly how well she performs in battle."

Robert noticed the grim expression that settled over his father's features and was almost willing to squelch his curiosity and change the nature of the conversation but for one burning question that had seized him after his father had started talking about the Confederates' new war toy.

"Father," he said, "how in heaven's name to do you know all this?"

"All what, son?"

"The details about the construction of the *Virginia?*"

The ghost of a smile played across James's face and quickly disappeared. "I have people who keep me informed."

"Who?" Robert was incredulous. Who on earth was so close to the enemy and yet so loyal to James Birmingham?

"Employees."

"Spies? Working for the rebs?"

"Son, I cannot offer details. To do so would be to jeopardize their safety." He paused for a moment. "Robert, this country is rife with intrigue. There are spies around every corner, on both sides of the conflict. This country is so enmeshed with itself that sometimes I'm amazed we're actually at war."

Robert was quiet for a moment, pensive, before posing his next question. "What do you hear from Uncle Jeffrey?"

"Very little. He wrote to me a few months back, but I don't believe he necessarily favors continuing close contact."

Robert frowned. "And Richard is somewhere in Virginia still?"

"I believe so."

"And Ben is fighting for the North."

James nodded absently, staring out the window at the passing buildings and trees only just beginning to show signs of pending spring.

"Odd. Two brothers, fighting on opposite sides of a war."

James nodded again, and only then did Robert realize the complexity of his statement. Not only were Ben and Richard brothers fighting against each other, but James and Jeffrey were brothers as well, each finding himself on the opposite side of a herculean conflict that baffled Robert the more he considered it. His life had been so much simpler when he had been content to obsess over military details and past wars. Being a student of the history of warfare was entirely different than actually living through a war itself.

* * *

9 March 1862
Hampton Roads Channel

Isabelle Webb stood on the banks of Hampton Roads, the channel that carried three of Virginia's rivers—the Nansemond, Elizabeth, and James—to the Chesapeake Bay. She was wearing a dress that was supported by inordinately large hoops and an inordinately tight corset. Her hair was coifed and curled to perfection, her Southern accent pronounced, definitive, aggressive, and entirely false.

Had the women surrounding her known she was a Pinkerton secret agent who actually hailed from Chicago, they would have dropped their delicate lace parasols into the mud.

"I still cannot grasp the fact that you spend the bulk of your time in Washington City, Miss Greene!" one of Isabelle's companions exclaimed.

"I do, indeed," Isabelle drawled, answering effortlessly to her assumed name. "You must admit there is an element of challenge and excitement wandering about the enemy capital," she said, casting the woman a glance meant to convey, without words, that she, Emma Greene, was a woman of adventure. An original. She was effective, as usual. The woman was suitably impressed. Isabelle saw it in the nearly imperceptible widening of the large blue eyes.

The young woman quickly hid her admiration, however, behind a delicate sniff. "Reginald would never allow me to do such a thing," she said. "I imagine that must be why you still find yourself lacking a husband, Miss Greene? You know any decent man would never approve of a woman who travels unaccompanied and places herself in danger."

"Bah," said an older woman who also stood in the circle. "Don't listen to such drivel, Miss Greene. Millicent only says those things because she can't draw a breath without Reginald telling her if she may."

The affronted Millicent gasped in outrage. "Well," she stammered, a pale flush mounting high in her cheeks, "If I might say so, it's statements like those that have kept you a spinster yourself all these years, Miss Lockhart!"

Isabelle raised an amused brow at Lucy Lockhart. The woman was probably only a couple of years older than Isabelle was—Lucy was twenty-five if she was a day. Still, Isabelle mused, if one reached her early to midtwenties and was still in the wretched and unfortunate state of being unmarried, she was without a doubt considered to be on the shelf.

Instead of taking offense, Lucy looked the poor Millicent straight in the face and laughed at her. "I'd rather die an old maid than be married to the likes of Reginald Baker," she said, and then laughed again as the outraged young woman marched off toward another group of ladies gathered with their husbands to observe the continued proceedings on the channel.

"It's true, you know," Lucy said to Isabelle as she watched Millicent recount the conversation with other society matrons, who glanced their way with disapproving glares. "Reginald Baker is a beast of a man. I would rather live the life of a woman of the streets than find myself shackled to him."

Isabelle fought but couldn't contain her surprise at the other woman's candid conversation.

"I see I've shocked you, Miss Greene."

"You have, Miss Lockhart. But not for the reasons you might suppose. I'm merely surprised to find someone whose lines of thinking run parallel to my own."

"Ah, so we are kindred spirits, then?"

"It appears so." Isabelle shared a grin with the woman and felt a stirring of kinship she hadn't experienced since helping Anne Birmingham enlist as a boy several months before. It was a pity she could never fully form any lasting friendship with Lucy Lockhart.

Lucy turned her eyes toward the water and the ships that sat upon it looking bruised and battered. "Were you witness to the battles yesterday, Miss Greene?"

"Regrettably, no. I was caring for my aunt, who is ill. Obviously the *Virginia* has crippled this little Union fleet." Isabelle's gaze followed Lucy's, and the women watched in silence for a moment as the sun rose more fully to shine upon the tired Union vessels.

"I should say so! The *Cumberland* was sunk entirely. She went down right about there." Lucy pointed off to their left with an elegantly gloved finger. "I watched it happen with my own eyes. Quite eerie, it was," she murmured, her brow creased in thought.

Isabelle cast a sidelong glance at her companion. "But a stunning victory, nonetheless."

Lucy dragged her gaze to Isabelle's. "Of course."

Isabelle turned her eyes back toward the water and considered the ships still making their homes upon the surface of the water. Supposedly, the *Virginia* was planning to come back and finish the job she had begun the day before. Pinkerton had dispatched Isabelle as soon as the rumors began circulating that the former *Merrimac* was on her way to becoming a Confederate wonder. Isabelle had been able to unearth precious little new information, however. For the first time since joining up with Allan Pinkerton's private detectives, she found herself on the sidelines, watching events unfold just as every other average citizen did. It was most frustrating.

"Do you believe in coincidence, Miss Greene?"

"I suppose so. Why do you ask?"

Lucy pursed her lips for a moment, her gaze upon the smoky remains of the Union vessel the *Congress,* which was grounded in shallow water and had been since the battle the day before. She pointed at it and said, "There was a young man on that ship yesterday by the name of Buchanan. When she was in flames and then surrendered, the commander of the *Virginia* ordered that his men board her and rescue the wounded. Buchanan was among those wounded, and I wonder if he knew at the time that the man who had just given the order to remove him from the burning ship was his own brother."

Isabelle stared. "The commander of the *Virginia* was that wounded man's brother?"

Lucy nodded. "So again I am forced to wonder—is there such a thing as coincidence?"

"You suppose everything in this life is divinely ordered? Orchestrated by a higher power? Those two brothers were meant to meet at sea?"

Lucy shrugged. "Who's to say? Do you not find it odd?"

"I suppose so; however, it isn't as though we are at war with a foreign power. We are at war with ourselves. It stands to reason that families living in different regions will eventually meet on the field of battle."

Lucy nodded, seeming almost reluctant. She added as an afterthought, "Would you believe that the Union batteries on the shore continued firing at the *Virginia,* even when it was perfectly clear that her men were aiding the wounded Union soldiers? Commodore Buchanan was so angry he armed himself and returned fire. He was wounded badly in the leg, they say."

Isabelle opened her mouth to reply, but it hung slack when she spied something in the distance. Lucy's gaze followed, and she looked out to the horizon, finally laughing in shock. "It looks like a giant beached whale!"

Isabelle's heart sank a fraction. It did indeed look like something ridiculously unprepared to fight, and she knew in her heart that she was looking at the Union's answer to the Confederate's new ironclad. The craft sat perhaps two feet above the waterline; it moved into Hampton Roads and drew the attention of the *Merrimac,* which was preparing to finish the job it had already begun.

And so it began. Shot followed shot as the two ironbound ships fired upon each other. Isabelle watched in fascination as the *Monitor* sent volley after volley into the side of the *Merrimac* from guns that swiveled about with ease. The shots, however, merely glanced off the side of the larger ship. As Isabelle watched, she witnessed the transformation of an age. The old manner of shipbuilding and naval combat was going to change forever, she knew. From now on, ships would not only be built to be steam propelled, but encased in protective iron as well.

Lucy and Isabelle eventually parted ways with a light promise to meet again under more socially favorable circumstances, and Isabelle made her way back to her hotel room. She removed her gloves and bonnet, tossing them onto her bed as she crossed the room to her window. From the third story, she had a perfect view of the water and the ensuing battle. She wasn't close enough to see minute details, but if one of the crafts sank, she would be aware.

She sighed a bit and stretched, rotating her neck from one side to the other, and wondered when she would ever lead a normal life. If she had things her way, and there was no reason on earth why she shouldn't, she would be a Pinkerton operative forever. True, the hotel rooms often felt empty and cold, and there were snatches of moments when, seeing that one happy couple in the midst of millions who weren't, she wished for a fairy-tale marriage of her own, but Isabelle was a woman of sound common sense and was extremely well rooted in reality. She had never been one to wallow in foolish daydreams or hope for the impossible. Her life suited her just fine, and furthermore, she wouldn't change a thing if given the opportunity.

Hours passed, and Isabelle caught up on neglected correspondence as the battle continued outside her window. She rose periodically to see if anything new had developed, but as far as battles went, this one seemed relatively benign. As the shadows of the afternoon lengthened, she rose one last time, took her spyglass from her satchel, and tried to get a closer view of the two warring vessels.

As she looked, a shot hit the pilothouse of the *Monitor*, and it appeared that the commander was blinded, because the craft sat in the water, unmoving and apparently trying to get its bearings. She shifted her focus to the *Merrimac* and watched as it changed course in the water and headed off as though returning to Norfolk. She wasn't surprised, really—the ironclad had sustained two days of continuous, furious battle, and she was beginning to show signs of wear. Her crew had to be exhausted and the ship herself weary of bombardment.

"Just like that?" Isabelle murmured aloud. "It's over, you're just leaving?"

And so it was. When Isabelle returned to Washington, D.C., her report to Pinkerton was blissfully uncomplicated. "They left," she told her employer, "and that was that."

CHAPTER 5

"The blue and the gray were mingled together. . . . It was no unusual thing to see the bodies of Federal and Confederate lying side by side as though they had bled to death while trying to aid each other."
—John A. Cockerill, Union regimental musician at Shiloh

* * *

6 April 1862
Corinth, Mississippi

Ma chère Marie,

The dawn hour approaches, and I find myself at the fringe of battle. That Union scoundrel, General Grant, has been sitting with his troops over the border at Pittsburg Landing for nearly a month. He is smug; he believes we will not attack, but will wait for him to find us here, some eleven miles south. We are strong, however; our number is forty thousand. We will send the Yankee dogs to their graves or crying home to their mamas.

I find this hard to write, Marie, but should I never make it home again, it would be my wish that you find it in your heart to remember me fondly. I proposed marriage to you more times than I can remember, and each time you refused. You always said to me, "But, Gustav, I am not the sort one marries." In this, sweet woman, you cannot be more mistaken. I am well aware of the reasons you feel you are unsuitable marriage material. The past is in the past, chère *Marie, and furthermore, you were never at fault.*

You always thought me silly, perhaps a bit frivolous, and in truth it was a perception I was content to portray, but in my heart of hearts I ached for you each time a society mama cast a slur upon your name. I wanted so badly to destroy the cur that hurt you all those years ago. I never permitted myself to delve beneath my happy surface because I suppose I hoped that if I was jovial and carefree enough, some of that might transfer to you, and I could take away your heavy burdens with my levity.

To my endless regret, I was unable to soothe your hurts. I do not know if I will live to again see your beautiful face, but this much I do know: you must not let the actions of one night, years ago when you were but a child, rob you of the happiness you so richly deserve. You were a trusting innocent, and he was an utter cad. You were in love and thought it was a sentiment returned; he sought to satisfy a juvenile wager. And you must remember, chèrie, *you know in your heart of hearts that your innocence remains. Mussed hair and a disheveled appearance do not equate to loss of virtue, regardless of what New Orleans's "finest" would have you believe.*

You are worthy of the best this world has to offer, and I pray with all my heart to that God who dwells above that you will find it. If I return home, I hope it will be me, because, of course, I am among the best ever. If I should die, however, find that someone who will love you and make you smile. Do not spend your life defined by the dictates of a society who condemns the most innocent of acts and yet perpetrates far worse behind closed doors. They are not worthy to trod in the dust dislodged from the soles of your boots, dear woman.

I hear now the bugle call, and so I must close. I will fold this missive and keep it in my jacket, close to my heart, addressed to you in hopes that, should I fall, some kind soul will see it through to its destination.

Ever yours,

Gustav

* * *

How was it possible for a mass of people, forty thousand strong, to so completely and silently catch an opposing foe by surprise? *They had not even heard us coming*, Gustav mused as he caught a Union blue uniform in his sights and pulled the trigger. Down the boy went, and Gustav gritted his teeth in satisfaction. The battle had begun, and by now, surely the rest of the Union troops gathered near the banks of the Tennessee were alerted and poised to strike back.

Finally, they would see some results! Gustav had only yet seen some minor picket action in his months as a Confederate enlistee, and he was yearning for the chance to make a difference. It wasn't fair, the way the Northerners thought they could just take over the Southern way of life. If the Yankees had their way, the entire Southern region would be industrialized, and the easy, slow pace that so hallmarked the charm of the Southern states would become a dead, rotting thing of the past.

Not if he could help it. Gustav ran to his left at the command of his company leader and steeled his nerves for conflict. He tore past a small, white church—Shiloh, it was called. The irony of the situation was not lost on him. *Shiloh*, translated, was a Hebrew word for "place of peace." To do battle so near a house of worship seemed the worst form of blasphemy, but there was no help for it. After all, God was on the side of right, and surely He would forgive.

The Confederate advance pressed forward, leveling lines of blue as they moved. The guns fired continually until Gustav felt he would surely hear the popping of his own rifle and the roar of the cannon in his sleep. He slipped and stepped on bodies of fallen blue, taking cover occasionally behind trees and reloading and firing his weapon with deadly accuracy.

A lead ball splintered the tree he currently sought refuge behind as he tore the cap from his cartridge, lining his lips with blue powder. He squeezed his eyes shut as the bark shattered and small pieces embedded themselves in the side of his face. Cringing, Gustav quickly plucked the largest pieces from his skin, ignoring the burning sensation and the trickle of liquid he felt flowing down the side of his cheek.

Minutes became hours as he fought alongside the members of his and other combined regiments, following orders, running first one way, then another, pressing the enemy ever closer to the banks of the river. He stepped on and tripped over more gore than he had ever seen in his entire life. He was a peaceful fisherman by trade, working up and down the gentle Louisiana bayous and enjoying the solitude. The sights and smells of battle pressed in upon his senses until his mind went numb with the horror. He was grateful for the mechanics of loading and firing his weapon because it gave him something on which to focus his tumultuous thoughts.

When night fell, Gustav sank to the ground as the sounds of the battle gradually faded away. His last impressions before he was overtaken by an exhausted slumber were of his commanding officer, who muttered to his second in command, "This thing will be decided tomorrow, one way or the other . . ."

* * *

Gustav heard the shouting before he opened his eyes. His face throbbed where the tree bark had shattered into it the day before, and he dared not raise his hand to it. As the world gradually came into focus through tired eyes, the one swollen and almost completely closed, he marveled at the beauty of the blue sky evident through the leafy, green trees. Surely, he was in heaven. It was only as he lowered his gaze that he realized his true location at the gaping jaws of purgatory.

Some of his comrades were wounded, moaning in pain, and others lay motionless and he knew them to be dead. There were medics attending the wounded, carrying them to the makeshift "hospitals" every soldier so dreaded to see, and he watched in numb shock as lifeless bodies were lifted gently and carried away. A great majority of his fellow soldiers, however, were already up and moving about, preparing for the day ahead. "What's the news?" he mumbled to a passing corporal.

"Buell's men have just arrived by boat as reinforcements for Grant. We're going again into battle."

Well, that's hardly a fair fight, Gustav found himself thinking, and yet knowing the thought to be irrational even as he believed it to be true. *They should wait for our reinforcements to arrive!* It wasn't to be, however, and he knew it.

The day blurred forward with a repeat of the first, only the impossible was occurring, and Gustav was loath to believe it even though his eyes bore evidence of its verity. The gore and mayhem was worse than before. He pushed onward, automatically following orders and commands until he at last felt the hot, searing pain in his midsection that he had known would eventually send him reeling to the ground. He fell upon a wounded Union soldier, his head cracking upon the hard ground and adding to the nausea he already felt rising into his throat.

He struggled to roll off the Yankee, who grunted in pain with Gustav's every movement, and eventually fell to one side, his face inches from that of the dying man. His first instinct was to clutch his weapon, and he was dismayed to realize it was out of reach. What if the blue belly shot him? He had no defense!

Gustav reached toward his abdomen and pulled his hand away, recoiling in horror at the red smear visible across his fingers and beginning to roll down into his sleeve. The young man next to him lifted his head, grunting with the effort, and looked quickly at Gustav's stomach. His pale face blanched further, and his freckles stood out in stark relief against the sick, white pallor of his skin.

"Don't look at it," the boy mumbled.

Gustav felt his heart race at the young soldier's statement even as he felt the blood surge from his exhausted body through the tear across his midsection.

"My leg," the Yankee said. "Is it gone?"

With extreme effort, Gustav lifted his head and looked down the young boy's body to the spot where the leg should have been. He again felt the bile rise in his throat as he finally found the limb in question, lying a good five yards away from its owner. The Yankee was losing blood from the open wound at an alarming rate; Gustav guessed that it would probably be a race to see which of the two of them would expire first.

"It's still there," Gustav told the boy. "I shouldn't worry overmuch if I were you." He coughed then, the metallic taste in his mouth a sure sign of his own mortality. He was so thirsty. If only he had his canteen.

The Yankee read his thoughts and unsnapped his own canteen, handing it weakly to Gustav.

Gustav gratefully accepted it and, grimacing in pain, twisted the cap and carefully tipped a few sips of the cool liquid into his mouth.

He handed it back to the man with a murmur of thanks and watched in shock as the boy's eyes took on a glazed expression.

"What's your name?" he rasped at the soldier in blue.

"Samuel," was the whispered reply. Samuel dropped the canteen of water to the side and grasped Gustav's hand instead. "I'm from Maine."

Samuel from Maine tightened his grip just slightly before his hand went slack altogether and his eyes froze on Gustav's face. Gustav felt the burning sensation behind his eyes and cursed it. He didn't want to die crying. His eyes blurred and dimmed as he felt his breathing grow shallow, the pain so intense he wished for death.

And then, peace. Suddenly it didn't hurt anymore. *Wait for me, Samuel from Maine,* he thought. *I'm coming with you.*

* * *

9 April 1862
Hilton Head, South Carolina

"I suppose, technically, it's a draw," Luke said to Ben, reading phrases from James's letter. "The Union calls it a victory, but the losses were horrifying."

The muscles along Ben's jaw worked as he glanced out over the water of the Atlantic. Hilton Head was a stunningly beautiful island, as well as a militarily sound hold for the Union. The current beauty, however, was eclipsed by the news Luke was sharing from his father's letter. "I worry that public sentiment will falter," Ben said. "We can ill afford a reversal of support at this point."

Luke's eyes continued to scan the letter, and he nodded absently at Ben's comment. He mumbled along with the words as he read, occasionally wincing.

"Grant wasn't worried at all that Johnston and Beauregard would attack. He didn't dig trenches or place the pickets far enough from the camp."

Ben shook his head. "And what was their position?"

"Pittsburg Landing, on the west banks of the Tennessee. Two days of fighting, all told, and the Union suffered thirteen thousand, dead or wounded."

Ben whistled softly under his breath. "And the Confederates?"

"Eleven thousand. A bright spot, though," Luke said, still reading the letter. "The Union took Island Number Ten."

Ben glanced at his cousin in surprise. "The fort on the Mississippi?"

Luke nodded. "Taken by General Foote. I suppose we must take the good news where we find it."

Ben nodded, his imagination still occupied with thoughts of the battle of Shiloh. "So many thousands gone," he murmured.

Luke grimaced, again reading from the letter. "Apparently General Grant has been quoted as saying that after the battle, he looked over an open field where there lay so many bodies it would have been possible to cross it in any direction without touching the ground."

Ben's face paled slightly under his increasingly tanned skin. "Do you wonder if we'll see battle the likes of that?"

Luke glanced up from his letter. "Well, I do now."

Ben looked out again over the water at the mainland. Who would mourn him if he died? He was filled with a momentary stab of longing for his family. He knew, though, that even under the best of circumstances, his mother would shove her grief so far below the surface that she would barely register its presence. It simply wasn't appropriate for women of stature in society to loudly proclaim their sadness. A few discreet tears were respected, but any outward show of emotion beyond that was frowned upon.

For Sarah Matthews Birmingham, it was doubly so. She had not only society to contend with—she had her own sense of self. In her estimation, a person of admirable strength didn't cower in the face of life's challenges, and Ben knew that even if he had remained behind to become the golden child they wished him to be, he would never feel an overabundance of warmth from his mother. Nor his father, for that matter, he mused with a frown. Jeffrey simply chose to absent himself, even if he was in the same room.

"What is it?" Luke asked him.

Nobody will miss me if I die. "Nothing."

Luke cleared his throat and folded the letter, placing it carefully in his haversack with the others he had received from his family and loved ones. "You know, there's talk of going into Charleston soon."

Ben nodded and picked up a smooth rock that lay at his feet. He rubbed its surface and examined the marbling blend of colors that swirled through it. "I've heard."

"Will you try to go to Bentley?"

Ben winced. "I don't know."

"I'll be glad to accompany you."

Ben looked over at his cousin. "Why are you so anxious for me to go there?"

"I think it would be a travesty to be this close and not at least see your family."

"They don't want to see me, Luke. My mother forbids the entire household from any contact with me whatsoever."

"I'm not speaking of your mother. I'm thinking of Emily and Clara. Not to mention Ruth, Mary, Rose, and Joshua." He ticked off his fingers as he talked. "Six people who loved you so much they probably haven't yet recovered from your absence."

Ben snorted. "I doubt that. Life keeps moving forward, even in the face of drastic change."

"That may be, but it doesn't mean they don't still love you. Well," Luke said as he stood and prepared to leave the small clearing they had retired to in order to read their mail in peace, "I won't pressure you anymore, but I urge you to consider it. If it were me, I should hate to live with regret."

Ben watched his cousin's retreating form for a moment before again casting his gaze over the water. The sun glinted and reflected off the waves in bright splendor. It seemed impossible that death and destruction occurred amidst such fantastic beauty. Ben thought of his childhood home and finally admitted the reason for his reluctance to visit it. *I'm scared,* he thought. *I'm scared they will all hate me for leaving and will have nothing to say to me.*

With a noise of disgust, he stood and hurled the rock through the air and watched its angry arc as it plummeted toward the waves and then disappeared. It was much easier to face the familiar anger than the fear. That was it. He was angry, he wasn't afraid. Fear was an alien emotion, and he wasn't comfortable with it, so he would abolish it, just as he had the sadness that had often overwhelmed him when he had first left home. Anger was much better because it was mobilizing.

Fear held him rooted to the spot, and that did him absolutely no good at all.

He turned and retraced his path, making his way back to camp, his hands shoved deep in his pockets and a scowl etched into his brow.

CHAPTER 6

"I have seen enough of the U.S. Navy to know that it is not a fitting place for a young man: I have learned enough in reference to that to last me a lifetime. Such screaming; such vulgarity, such wickedness I have never heard or seen."

—Josiah Parker Higgins, enlisted man aboard the Kennebec

* * *

17 April 1862

New Orleans Harbor, aboard the Kennebec

"Yep, he's the one."

Daniel looked up from his papers at the intruding voice. Standing opposite the small desk was an officer who had been a thorn in his side for the past two weeks, accompanied by another sailor he recognized only by sight.

Daniel cleared his throat. "Do you have issue with me?"

"Naw." The sailor from below deck jerked a thumb toward the officer. "He just wanted to know if you were the fighter the others're talking about."

Officer Nundry colored slightly but otherwise gave no outward sign that he was uncomfortable. "That will be all, Parker."

The enlisted man offered a salute that might have been interpreted as insolent, and then turned on his heel and sauntered from the officer's mess quarters.

"Is there a reason you're going to others about me, Nundry? You can ask me anything you like to my face," Daniel said.

"You're to address me as *Captain*, Yeoman."

When Daniel remained silent, Nundry's expression hardened. "You may have the commodore impressed with your bank experience, but I wonder how he'll feel at having a drunken brawler doing his documentation."

"I was never drunk," Daniel said, and turned his attention to the papers before him. It had come to the attention of the commodore that Daniel had worked at First Federal in New York just before his enlistment, and the man had wasted no time in beseeching Daniel for help with the ship's logs. His regular assistant was down with scarlet fever, and he considered Daniel a godsend.

Nundry, however, did not.

"I don't believe I've given you permission to turn your attention from me," Nundry snapped.

With a small sigh, Daniel again turned his gaze upward to the man who still stood stiffly across the desk. "I wasn't aware we were still having a discussion."

"Whether we are or not is beside the point, O'Shea!"

With that, Nundry spun on his heel and marched from the room. Daniel watched his angry strides with a sense of impatience. Nundry was a political appointee, a breed that was proving to be not quite so rare in the Union forces. It seemed that everyone who was even remotely connected to a Washington politician stood a good chance of gaining himself a fairly impressive military position. Nundry was the fiancé of a certain congressman's niece.

Daniel shook his head and envisioned the forthcoming scene. The commodore would request his presence, and when Daniel stood before the man, he would be told that he must watch himself with Nundry because the man was, after all, a senior officer. It wouldn't even be as harsh as a slap on the back of his hand, but it placated Nundry. It had happened before, and would undoubtedly happen many times before Daniel found himself home again in New York.

He glanced down at his ink-stained fingers. There was a time in the recent past when his fingers would find themselves thusly marked because he had been spending time writing to a particular New Orleans beauty. He hadn't written, however, since his receipt of her last letter. Marie didn't want to meet him, and it still stung. He had missed corresponding with her more than he ever dreamed possible. Perhaps what he missed most was her wit. Her sense of humor was evident, even though it was only through the printed word that he had become accustomed to it.

He glanced around himself and wondered how he had come to be in this place. Had someone told him a year earlier that he would one day soon find himself enlisted in the United States Navy, and that not only would he be a sailor, but a bookkeeping one at that, he would have laughed himself silly. Daniel's talents lay in his fingertips and his muscle, literally. He was a carpenter, a craftsman of fine, sturdy wooden furniture, not a banker.

His mind flew over the past six months, and he marveled at his current status. Sitting at a desk shifting through papers may not have been his ideal situation, but it was better than dealing all day with those who tried continually to goad him into fighting. Once the word got out that he was Daniel O'Shea, *the* Daniel O'Shea, New York's finest underground pugilist, he had had no rest. It was a mirror of the situation he had attempted to leave behind: men offering to go around placing bets, offering to pair him up with others guaranteed to lose, always suggesting that if he would only put his fate in their hands, they would make him a wealthy man. And through the efforts of his own muscle!

Therein lay the irony, he supposed. They all thought he was stupid enough not to realize that when everything was said and done, it was up to him to produce results. It was brawling that had brought him to his figurative knees, although the fighting itself wasn't at the root of his complex problems. It was merely a mask for pain that lay much deeper than he was even still willing to address. His solution had been to enlist, to escape his life for just a little while, but all it had taken was one sailor recognizing him from an obscure fight in New York, and his past had jumped neatly aboard with him, threatening to pick itself up where he had left it.

Marie must have known that he was a fighter, that his parents were humble Irish immigrants, *something!* Why else would she refuse to meet him after sharing such a warm and seemingly sincere correspondence with him for literally months? He had felt closer to her through her letters than he had any woman, even his late fiancée. It shamed him to admit it, but it was true. He thought of the small daguerreotype of Marie, nestled in with his other belongings below deck. Should he keep it? Throw it overboard? If he thought he could throw his lingering feelings of affection for her overboard, he might just do it.

It wasn't so easy, however. He had tried repeatedly to convince himself that she was selfish, that she was of the same caliber as those he despised in New York. Her mother had been dressed in rich clothing and had manners befitting a queen—he had seen that for himself when he had met the woman! But somehow, he couldn't quite make himself believe Marie was a shallow creature concerned only for her own comforts.

There was obviously a reason she didn't want to meet him, though. Another man, perhaps? That thought stung more than any that had crossed his mind thus far, and he found his heart giving a hard *thump.* Surely she wasn't involved with someone else; her mother would have said something, and she had made no mention of suitors when she spoke of her daughter who had stayed behind in New Orleans to teach a small, ragtag group of students.

That didn't necessarily have to mean anything, however. Marie was nearly twenty-five years old; she could easily be conducting an affair of the heart behind her parents' backs. It was unseemly, true, but not unheard of. And how much easier to do so with her parents far away in Boston!

Daniel shook his head. Marie's father lay in a coma, and her mother was nearly beside herself with worry. Jenny Brissot had told him of Marie's anxiety as well, and of her difficult decision to stay behind in New Orleans when her parents had left. If Marie was seeing someone of whom her parents didn't approve, however, what better excuse to stay behind and be with him than a desire to continue teaching?

It didn't paint Marie in a kind light, and he narrowed his eyes at his papers in thought. Could she be so duplicitous—so warm in her letters to him and yet in reality be so self-serving? And why write to him at all? One angry, solitary man in New York had nothing to offer her, and when they began exchanging letters, he had never told her of his intentions to enlist in the Navy and somehow end up in her locale. Indeed, at the time, he hadn't even known it to be in his future at all.

So why, then? What was she hiding? He rubbed the back of his neck and rotated it slightly from side to side. The long hours sorting through the ship's logs and attempting to make clear the smudges and messes left by his predecessor had taken their toll on his patience. He was not a man accustomed to sitting for long periods of time, and he found his fingers itching for the comfort of his tools and his workshop.

Well, he mused, his voluntary enlistment was serving its purpose, then. He sat back in his chair and stretched. It was his intention to stay away from home until he absolutely couldn't stand to be gone a moment longer. Then and only then might he be able to face the things he didn't want to think about. The ghost of his brother hung too heavily in the air around the small street where his house and his parents' house stood. Had they all stayed in Ireland, Colin would still be alive, and they would most likely both be married and raising their children together.

Daniel cleared his throat and rose abruptly, intending to go topside and catch a breath of fresh air. He determined to banish thoughts of his brother from the corners of his mind, where they were wont to linger. He didn't have to think about anything related to home until he was home again.

Perhaps, if he were wise, he would never go home.

* * *

17 April 1862
New Orleans, Louisiana

"The boys are learning so much more than I ever dared imagine they would," Pauline Fromere said as she dried a dish and placed it in the cupboard.

Marie smiled and glanced at the woman's face. "They're bright boys, Pauline. You've every right to be proud."

Pauline's eyes glassed over a bit, and Marie looked the other way, busying herself with the silver. "I am proud," the woman said, a catch in her voice that she tried to disguise by clearing her throat. "My mama would be so proud. I hope she knows that her grandsons ain't slaves."

"I'm sure she does. She probably watches over you each day." Marie finished with the silver and turned to Pauline with a smile. "Now you relax and put your feet up for a bit. I'm going into town."

Pauline frowned. "It'll be dark soon. Can't it wait until tomorrow?"

Marie moved forward and embraced the woman in a quick hug. "I'm glad you're here. You make me miss my mother less. And no, unfortunately, it can't wait. I need to leave for the schoolhouse early tomorrow to give a student some extra tutoring. Tonight I need to go see Michael at the paper."

"Is something wrong?"

"No. I just want to check on him."

Pauline looked at Marie for a moment as though she wished to question her further, but in the end, refrained. "You'll be cautious?"

"I will. You do the same. Will you please remind the boys to take care with the lights upstairs? People will be suspicious if the lamps are lit after I leave the house."

Pauline nodded, and after another embrace, Marie left her and exited the house at the back. She alone made ready her horse and carriage. The family groom had passed away only two short days after Marie had taken in the Fromeres. It was fortuitous, really; Marie couldn't have hoped to keep the knowledge of their presence from Winston indefinitely, and the thought of letting him go after so many years of service and companionship had pained her to no end.

She made her way into the heart of New Orleans, for a brief moment closing her eyes and enjoying the feel of the air on her face. The sun had nearly set, and the trees and flowers were lush in their growth. Not only was it her favorite time of year, it was her favorite time of the day as well. She loved the orange glow cast by the departing sun, which lit the vegetation and stately city buildings and homes with warm hues.

If only things were right—if only there was no war or hostile citizens, if only her father and mother were home, if only her father were healthy and whole again . . . Marie felt she could probably go on forever with her "if only's." Reality was harsh, and as much as she would have liked to avoid it, it was impossible to ignore. Her father lay thousands of miles away in Boston, his body still sleeping and his brain most likely dead. Her mother sat faithfully by his side, hoping every day would see an improvement.

Conditions in the city were impossible to ignore as well. The Union navy sat knocking at New Orleans's door, poised at any moment to strike. Marie shook her head as she absently registered the *clop* of her horse's hooves on the street. Jefferson Davis was convinced that the two forts at the mouth of the river would effectively keep the invading fleet at bay. Ships had been sent upriver to defend the Mississippi from invaders from the North, and Confederate troops and guns had been sent to join other armies, leaving New Orleans virtually unprotected.

Davis had total confidence in the two forts, but the citizens of New Orleans largely did not. Marie unconsciously shrugged a shoulder as she reached her father's newspaper office. It was as though she found herself detached. She did not believe in the Confederate cause, and she had personal reasons for viewing many in her family's close social circle with disdain and disgust, not the least of which was the fact that some of those people were responsible for putting her father in a coma.

The air around the city was tinged with tension, and she felt it as she secured her horse and carriage and entered the newspaper office. Detached she might be, but she couldn't deny the quick and nervous *thump* her heart made when she considered the possibility that Union troops may indeed succeed in taking over the city. Would they care that she wasn't sympathetic to the Southern cause? Would it matter that she wasn't a plantation owner, that her financial condition wasn't based upon the growth of cotton or sale of slaves? Would they care that she had influential Union relatives, and that her parents even now were safely within their residence?

She could only hope she might be viewed favorably and left in peace to assist Michael in running her father's newspaper. And therein lay the cause for her visit. Michael was a good family friend and had taken over the running of the paper after her father's misfortune. She spied the older man standing at one of the presses, pulling a freshly printed page from the machine.

His face wrinkled into a smile when he spied her, and he kissed both of her cheeks fondly in greeting. "And what brings you this way, *chérie?*"

"I'm coming to see how you're faring, Michael. Are people leaving you in peace?"

"Oui, Marie. I come and go unmolested. And you?"

"I'm fine."

Michael worked in silence for a moment, Marie watching thoughtfully. "I am thinking there is another purpose that brings you here?" Michael said after a moment.

Marie sighed and pulled a wooden chair from the corner of the shop. She sat near the press and continued to watch the older man's fluid movements as he worked the contraption. "I believe we're about to be invaded, Michael."

Michael said nothing for a long while, but eventually nodded. "I believe you're right."

"What will that mean for us?"

Again, the response was long in coming. "I do not know, *chérie*."

"Do you hear people talk? What do they say?"

He shrugged. "They say many things; some are wise, and some are not. Most people seem to think that Davis was wrong in his decision to leave the city so unprotected. We are very vulnerable, sitting here."

Marie nodded. "I can't imagine what he was thinking," she murmured, more to herself than Michael.

He heard her, however, and smiled. "He is thinking New Orleans is well enough protected at the mouth of the river."

"But if this city falls, surely the Confederacy stands no chance at all of gaining official recognition from foreign powers—from Britain and France."

"I would think not."

"So what *is* he thinking?"

"He isn't."

Marie's mouth lifted into a playful grin, one that Michael had not seen for a good long while. "I dare you to print that."

"If I thought I could without getting dragged out into the street and beaten, *chérie*, I might."

Marie's smile faded, and she thought of her father, bloodied and bruised because of the things he'd dared say that painted the Confederacy in a weak or foolish light. The paper had run no pieces of an editorial nature since.

Michael cursed lightly under his breath as he witnessed her reaction. He stopped working and turned to her, stooping to take her hands into his own and look into her face. His brilliant blue eyes were wise and apologetic.

"I am sorry, Marie. You finally show some signs of your old self, and I squash them flat like a bug."

A reluctant smile tugged at her mouth. "It's fine, Michael. I'm fine. I don't really know why I came tonight—I'm wondering what will become of the paper, I suppose . . ."

"The paper will run as long as the Union army allows it."

"So you do believe they're coming, then?"

"Oh yes, *chérie*. I do believe it. They are already here. The only thing left for them to do is walk through the open door."

CHAPTER 7

"The whole region seems literally filled with soldiery. One of the finest armies ever marshaled on the globe now wakes up these long stagnant fields and woods."

—The Reverend A. M. Stewart, 102nd Pennsylvania

* * *

20 April 1862
New Market, Virginia

"It's healing fine," Anne muttered under her breath as she left the camp medical tent. Ivar walked at her side, his hands thrust deeply into his pockets.

"It doesn't look fine."

Her head snapped around, and she glared at her companion. "And how would you know?"

Ivar exchanged polite smiles with a passing soldier before again subtly turning his attention toward her. "I saw it this morning before your visit to the doctor here," he said, gesturing with his shoulder to the tent she had only just vacated.

"When?"

"This morning in the tent when you examined it."

"I didn't know I wasn't alone," she mumbled, and shoved her own hands into her pockets, a mirror of Ivar. She winced slightly at the pain in her arm and turned her face away from him to hide it.

The skirmish at Stoney Creek while in the pursuit of retreating Confederate forces had been brief, but Anne had felt the first sting of an enemy bullet in her left arm. Thankfully it only grazed the surface, leaving a nasty, burnlike welt in its wake. Had the bullet penetrated her arm, she might well have found herself without a limb. Nearly every soldier who suffered bullet wounds to the extremities was then a victim of the physicians' amputation saws. It was just as well, she supposed as she walked along in silence. Better to be armless than lifeless. Still, she counted her lucky stars that she was still in possession of all of her limbs. It was her own bad luck that it hurt like the very devil.

"If I were home right now, my mother would have fits that I haven't washed it well."

"What did the doctor tell you?"

"To keep the bandage on."

"Is it still bleeding?"

Anne nodded. "A bit." The admission was followed by a grimace. "It's just that the bandage is so filthy it makes me gag."

"Can you get a clean one?"

She shook her head. "The doctor said I don't need a clean one, and that supplies often run short, at any rate. I need to keep this one."

Ivar glanced at her with an unreadable expression.

"What is it?" she finally asked out of exasperation when he didn't seem inclined to share his thoughts.

"My mother would be affected as well at the sight of a dirty bandage. It must be a mother's concern."

Anne shook her head. "I'm not a mother, and it concerns me."

"Perhaps, then, it is a gender issue." The statement was soft, meant for her ears alone.

She shivered at his tone, which was at once intimate and yet ambiguous. Clenching her teeth together, she cursed for the millionth time the day Ivar had discovered her true identity. The fact that someone else knew of her disguise made her restless. She could handle herself; she didn't like the unpredictable variable of another's interference.

Anne cast another glance in his direction, determined to put him in his place; exactly where or what that place was, she wasn't entirely sure. "I've seen you clean up as best as conditions allow in these past months, Ivar Gundersen. I don't imagine you would care for a dirty bandage, either."

He pursed his lips as though in serious thought. It was almost laughable, the attention they gave to such an innocuous subject. "No, I don't suppose I would."

"Well, then." She nodded once, feeling absurdly pleased, as though she had won a minor battle. They continued on in companionable silence, and Anne took in the view from her vantage point approaching their tent. The camp had all the appearances of a small city. There were tents stretched in neat rows over acres of land, thousands of men and horses could be seen, and numerous wagons dotted the landscape as well.

Anne had taken every opportunity to speak with as many men as possible, and where location permitted, she often found stations from which to transmit her articles to Jacob Taylor, her editor in Boston. According to the newspapers her mother sent via Isabelle Webb's sister in Chicago, Jacob printed every word she gave him. In turn, it gave her satisfaction to see that her experiences were being shared by a wide readership, even though it was under an assumed male name.

"Do you play chess?" Ivar asked her suddenly.

"I do, a bit. My father taught me when I was young."

"A bit unconventional, no?"

"A bit." She smiled. "It was at my mother's insistence. If he hadn't taught me, *she* would have. She wasn't content with trivial card games."

They had reached the tent they occupied with two friends from Ivar's hometown. Because the four of them shared sleeping quarters, they were possessors of one of a few Indian-style tepees, as opposed to the smaller affairs that provided shelter for one or two people at most. Ivar held the opening flap to one side and allowed Anne to enter before him.

"You shouldn't do that," she muttered, but entered anyway. "If you keep treating me with such chivalry, people will become suspicious."

He raised his eyebrows in surprise. "I can't open the tent for a friend? One of us had to enter first."

They were interrupted by a harsh cough, and Anne started in alarm. Glancing to the side, she relaxed slightly when she realized it was their friend Jed Dietrich, who had been sick for weeks. Her heart rate increased again, however, as she wondered how much he had overheard and what he would deduce from the conversation, if anything.

"How are you, Jed?" she asked, the concern in her voice real. His health had been failing steadily since the beginning of the year when they had all been exposed to marching in extremely cold conditions.

"I'm well enough," the man answered, unintentionally interrupting himself with another coughing fit. "And you?" he finally finished, gesturing to her arm.

"I'm fine," she said. "Just a few scratches."

Ivar glanced at her but said nothing. He alone, apparently, had seen the extent of the damage done to her arm, and she was grateful for his silence. In truth, the severity of the appearance of her wound caused her some concern.

"Are you well enough for a game of chess, then?" Ivar asked her.

"I am. Where did you find a chess set?"

"I bought it from a man in Company D," he said, gesturing toward the other end of the encampment. "It's small, but functional."

"Fine, then. Jed can play the winner."

"I don't know that we'll have so much time," Jed said, shoving himself into a sitting position on his bedding.

"Oh, I believe we will," Ivar answered as he reached into his bags for a small, wooden box that he extracted and placed upon his own bed area. "I spoke with the major a few minutes ago; he seems to think we'll be here for at least a few weeks."

In truth, his words came as a relief to Anne, who was weary of the never-ending marching. Every day they marched either in pursuit of an enemy or following orders to move to more strategic locations. A few weeks respite would do them all some good.

She glanced at Jed again as he was overcome by another fit of coughing. At least, she *hoped* it would do them all some good. The doctors had little to offer the sick man by way of help or medicine, and she worried for his health.

It was something on which she hadn't planned; nobody told her she would become so attached to the men she fought beside. It wasn't fair.

* * *

Ivar stood outside the tent later that night and watched the stars twinkle their way to life. Were he home right now, he would be eating dinner with his mother and father and his daughter, Inger. It pained him each time he received letters from home to realize how much of his young child's life he was missing. When a little one was so young, each passing month marked moments of achievement and growth. His eyes burned as he thought of the new photograph his mother had sent. It was Inger on her third birthday, which had come and gone while he was out marching in strange places.

His noble intentions to serve his country and fight for the Union cause hadn't diminished, and, truthfully, he hadn't carried any visions of glory in his breast when he left home. He supposed he hadn't realized, though, how empty it would feel to be gone from those he loved. He missed the feel of Inger's curly blonde hair after a bath and the sweet smell of his father's pipe after dinner each night.

The thought of dinner made his stomach rumble, and he was reminded of yet another thing he missed more than he could have imagined—his mother's good cooking. What he wouldn't give at that very moment for her fresh fish and new potatoes covered in a light, creamy sauce. With a nice glass of wine to complement the meal, he would gladly have died a happy man at that moment.

He studied the stars for a long time as the sky transformed itself through varying shades of blue until finally settling on black. *God,* he felt himself thinking without having decided to, *I don't suppose I have a right above any other man here to ask that I be allowed to live and resume my life with my family when this is over, but I will ask it anyway.* He paused, thinking of his father, Per, at home with a crippled leg and trying to manage two farms on his own. He was too proud to ask for help. *My father needs me. Inger needs me, and I need her. Please give me strength and luck enough to return home.*

He nodded once, decisively. It was a good prayer—to the point and direct, yet humble. He had never felt the need to bother God excessively with his troubles, and to his fortune, they had been few. He had thanked God for his blessings and prayed for the safety of his family. What more did a man need, really?

He heard, from within the thin walls of the tent, a light moan, and he felt himself unintentionally wincing. Ever since her injury, Anne often slept in pain, although she never admitted it. Each time she bumped or rolled over on her wounded arm, he heard a slight intake of breath or a noise that gave away the true nature of her condition. She was unaware of her discomfort—she usually slept through it, but Ivar found himself awakening each time she groaned, no matter how softly. It reminded him of when Inger had been an infant; his sleep had become very light and attuned to the slightest noise.

He wondered briefly at the paternal feelings he was experiencing for Anne. Was it because he was the only one who knew of her true identity? Did he feel some odd compulsion to care for her? She was a grown woman, obviously, and had made her own decisions long before she enlisted as a man. Her life was hers to conduct, and it was none of his affair.

Why, then, did he find himself walking toward the medical tent, bent on retrieving a clean, fresh bandage for her arm? Probably because he knew she wouldn't take the opportunity to do it for herself. She was so consumed in convincing the men of the regiment that she was the boy she claimed to be, that she was neglecting herself. What did he know, though? He was no doctor. If the physicians in camp had told her she'd be fine with a dirty bandage, what difference did it make to him?

He thought of the wound he'd seen only that morning and hardened his resolve to find her a clean piece of cloth. He might not be able to make her go home, but he could at least try to keep her in one piece until she got there. Ivar shook his head as he approached the medical tent. First his concern for Jed, and now the woman. He was becoming entirely too involved for his comfort. It was much easier to keep a safe distance.

CHAPTER 8

"How many pleasing recollections crowd upon the mind of each soldier as he walks over these grounds. The patriots of the Revolution were struggling for Liberty, and so are we."
—Texas chaplain

* * *

21 April 1862
Charleston, South Carolina

"And so I told Stanley, 'Don't you consider selling off anymore of the staff!' I tell you, Sarah, we can barely make do as it is." Mrs. Charlesworth sucked in as much air as her corset would allow and blew it out again in a puff of outrage. "I scarcely anticipated a change in our circumstances when the Confederacy formed, and truthfully we have yet to feel the sting some of our neighbors are experiencing, but Stanley is insisting we be prepared."

Sarah nodded but said nothing in reply, and her neighbor colored slightly when realizing she had committed the faux pas of speaking of financial difficulty. It was one thing to discuss the misfortune of others. A body simply did not admit to troubles in one's own realm, however.

"I'm certain all will be well," Mrs. Charlesworth said, and turned her head toward the picture hanging over the mantle. In an obvious attempt at subject change, she said, "It seems just yesterday you commissioned that portrait of Richard. How is he?"

Sarah glanced at the painting of her younger son. While it might have seemed that the fair hair and skin, the handsome face and frame had been painted with the generous hand artists sometimes employed to flatter the paying customer, those who knew him personally would realize the painting depicted his image as it truly was. He was as handsome in the flesh as he was in the portrait. There was a coldness about his eyes, however, that Sarah had often noticed but ignored.

"He is doing well," she answered, still gazing at her son's likeness. She was content to have her neighbor believe her gaze was one of longing. In truth, it was more objective speculation than anything. With Richard gone, she was more able to reflect upon his flaws without his affected charm to influence her conclusions. The boy was unscrupulous at best. She dared not consider the worst. When he came home, as he continued his life into adulthood, how would Bentley fare under his care? When she was dead and gone, what would become of the family legacy? Would he have the wherewithal to hold it together? How would he direct the lives of the servants?

The questions were endless and lacked the answers she was willing to dwell upon for more than a moment or two. She moved her eyes from the portrait and listened with half an ear to Mrs. Charlesworth's polite but inconsequential comments about Richard's nobility in fighting for the cause. A slight movement at the corner of her eye drew her gaze toward Emily, who sat demurely beside Charlotte on the divan.

Emily was turning out beautifully, having decided to take her rightful place in society and leave her childish braids behind. Her wardrobe was impeccable, the dresses showing off her becoming figure to its best advantage, her auburn hair a stunning contrast to her fair skin. All was right on the outside, it was true, but underneath, Sarah sensed a quiver of something that was probably a true reflection of the girl's inner core, and that something made her nervous.

As Emily listened with a polite smile to Mrs. Charlesworth's droning comments, Sarah watched as a slight movement at the hem of Emily's voluminous skirts puffed the lace outward—a gesture that would have been lost to a casual observer. What it told Sarah was that Emily's foot, which was undoubtedly crossed serenely over the other ankle, was bobbing in irritation. Sarah knew there was no love lost between Emily and Richard, and she would have bet her last Confederate dollar that Emily was figuratively, if not literally, biting her tongue at the neighbor's extolling of Richard's virtues.

Sarah didn't know whether to smile or frown, so she did neither. She finally took pity on her young redhead and said, "Emily, I know you have correspondence to answer. You may be excused if you wish."

Emily glanced at her, but she barely missed a beat at the falsehood. "Thank you, Mother. You know I should hate for it to stack up unanswered." She rose quickly from her seat in spite of the ruffles, petticoats, and hoops beneath her skirt, and after bobbing a quick curtsy to Mrs. Charlesworth, moved toward the door with a speed that was very nearly amusing.

* * *

Emily put her fingers to her temples as she dashed down the hallway, slowing to a more sedate pace as her breath quickened and was hampered by her whalebone stays. Her favorite time of day anymore was nighttime, when she changed out of the infernal thing and into her nightclothes. She had never imagined what a treat it would be to draw a decent breath.

Mrs. Charlesworth would surely be the death of her. Noble Richard, indeed. The thought made her nauseous. Richard was as noble as a weasel. It astounded her that she was apparently the only white person on earth who realized he was not all that he seemed. The Bentley slaves knew it well enough, especially Mary.

She massaged her temples gently with her fingertips and glanced at the waning light that filtered through the windows as she traversed the length of the hallway past the dining room, where the Birminghams and Charlesworths had just dined. The men were still at the table, enjoying a glass of port, and would soon join the women in the drawing room. She paused as she heard Stanley Charlesworth's voice booming at her father.

"I tell you, it's an outrage! Davis is mad, that's all there is to it."

"It was necessary." Emily heard Jeffrey's mild voice in reply.

"Necessary? A conscription act? It flies in the face of everything the seceded states hold dear!"

Emily peeked into the open doorway and saw her father's form, relaxed as always as he leaned back in his chair, his feet crossed at the ankles. He drew his glass to his lips and took a sip while Stanley leaned forward, his face a mottled red.

"You should speak to him, I say! You see Jeff Davis as often as does his own cabinet! Tell him that the Confederate States do not willingly support a draft!"

Jeffrey's sigh was quiet; Emily saw more than heard his tired reaction to his outspoken neighbor. "Stanley, we are running short on men. The initial term of enlistment is over for many of the original enlistees, and furthermore, we have lost thousands so far to battles and illness. Davis had little choice."

"He had plenty of choice, and I'm certainly not the only one who thinks so! He is trampling on the individual rights of the Confederate citizen, and I am astounded to think he believes he is justified. Why did we leave the Union in the first place? To establish our rights against a central government, that's why!"

Jeffrey rubbed his temple in much the same way Emily had, and he looked as though he'd rather abandon the subject altogether. Emily had to admire his resilience as he plunged back into the fore. "There are those who are exempt from the draft, Stanley . . ."

"Yes, railroad workers? Teachers? Miners and druggists? It is blatantly unfair to exempt such professions but yet expect society's finest to pick up a gun and sleep on the ground. You or I could be called up, Jeffrey, while some telegraph operator is allowed to remain in the comfort of home and hearth."

Stanley sat back in his chair and took a gulp of his port. Emily rolled her eyes and instantly regretted the movement as it aggravated her headache.

"I suspect there may come a point when plantation owners will be exempted as well."

Stanley leapt forward in his chair again. "Have you heard something?"

Jeffrey shrugged a bit. "There's talk of exempting from the draft those who own twenty or more slaves."

"Ah!" The light in Stanley's eyes made Emily want to scratch them out with her fingernails. "Finally, some sanity!"

Emily wondered if Stanley saw the look of derisive amusement on Jeffrey's face. "What of the individual rights for those still eligible?" he asked his neighbor. "Are you not still incensed?"

"Of course. But as you said, someone must fight the war. It makes ever so much more sense to protect the lives of those who wield influence, however. I hope to see this prophecy of yours come to pass."

"I wonder, Stanley, if you've heard of the latest congressional resolution signed by Lincoln?"

Charlesworth sniffed. "What is it?"

"The gradual, compensated emancipation of slaves. And slavery has been completely abolished in Washington."

Stanley slowly placed his glass of port on the table with a hand that trembled, and Emily watched in morbid fascination as the man's face blanched whiter than the tablecloth. Was he going to expire before her very eyes? "You jest," he finally whispered.

"No, I do not." Jeffrey took a sip of his port and studied the man. "Lincoln signed it on the tenth of this month."

Stanley's voice was choked and harsh. "How can you sit there so calmly, man? Are you batty?"

"What is there to fear, Stanley? It isn't as though Lincoln and the U.S. Congress have any say over the state of affairs in the Confederacy."

Emily slowly smiled at her father. They had never been close, true, but she had to inwardly laugh at the cat-and-mouse game he played with their officious neighbor. Her smile broadened at his next comment. "Why would you be concerned over the Union's activities?" He might as well have said, "What, Stanley, you don't believe the Confederacy will win the war?"

"Well, I . . . well—the very nature of it is outrageous! A country granting full citizenship to Negroes!"

"It's already happened in England and France. We seem to be the ones lagging behind."

"We're the ones who see the truth for what it is! Do you not remember the vice president's inaugural speech? The Confederacy is founded on the very truth that the white man is superior to the Negro!"

"I remember it well."

Emily squinted at her father. What was it he wasn't saying? Was he playing at annoying Stanley because he enjoyed it, or did he not hold to Southern beliefs as firmly as did their neighbor? She cocked her head to one side and regarded Jeffrey. Perhaps she didn't know her father as well as she thought she did. She firmly doubted he would ever abandon his comfortable home for the sake of principle, but perhaps, when the Confederacy fell, he would go down with it knowing all along that Alexander Stephens's "great philosophical and moral truth" was nothing but a perversity.

She walked slowly away from the door, her brow puckered in thought. She had learned something new about her father, and it might take awhile to digest. Her movement at the open door must have alerted Jeffrey to her presence because he called out to her from inside the room. She turned and met him as he approached the doorway.

"Yes?'

"Austin Stanhope has asked if he might formally be allowed to call on you. I wanted to mention it to you before I say yea or nay."

Emily narrowed her eyes. Since when was a daughter consulted on who was allowed to call? If the suitor was eligible, and Stanhope certainly was in the eyes of the society mamas, so much the better. "I suppose I wouldn't mind," Emily finally said, studying her father's face for signs that might give away his thoughts. She read nothing but innocence in his expression.

"Good enough, then. I'll tell him he may call at his earliest convenience." Jeffrey gave her the ghost of a smile, and she turned and made her way to her bedroom, brows drawn deep in thought.

* * *

Joshua lifted the front foot of the chestnut mare and examined the hoof by the light of his lantern. She had thrown a shoe earlier in the day; he would need to replace it in the morning. The young horse was Emily's favorite—Freedom, she had named her, and he wanted Emily to have her mount ready at a moment's notice.

As though his thoughts of her had made her materialize in the flesh, Joshua glanced up at the movement in the doorway. There she stood, looking like a vision in her grown-up finery, her hair piled in beautiful curls high on her head. The green print on her dress was a match for her emerald eyes, and Joshua found himself staring into her unflinching gaze for a few moments before he realized the lateness of the hour.

"Emily," he murmured, lifting his lantern from the overturned barrel where he had placed it. "You shouldn't be here."

"Posh," she said softly, and advanced toward him, her skirts rustling against the hay that lay strewn across the stable floor. "I've been coming into these stables to see you for years."

"You're not so young anymore," he said, averting his gaze and looking out a small window and into the night. "Your mother wouldn't approve."

"My mother is so pleased with me these days she doesn't know what to do with herself."

"I doubt that. Your mother always knows what to do with herself."

"Joshua."

He looked at her unwillingly. Her face was maturing in subtle ways he didn't want to acknowledge. Her cheeks were taking on lean lines, the arch of her brow accentuated by the new style of her hair.

"I've missed you. I've been out so much lately that I feel like I haven't seen you in weeks."

It had been weeks, but he didn't want to admit to her he'd been keeping track. He shrugged instead. "It's probably for the best anyway, Emily. You're too old now to be visiting the stables."

"I can visit the stables anytime I wish! My horse is in here!"

"I'm not speaking of your horse. I think you know that."

She closed her mouth and regarded him quietly for a moment. "My father is going to give Austin Stanhope permission to call on me," she said.

Joshua knew of Austin Stanhope. Mary had mentioned in passing that Emily repeatedly encountered the Savannah plantation owner on her outings with her parents. Stanhope was sweet on Emily, according to Mary, and Sarah had high expectations. "Congratulations," he said.

"Thank you." Emily cast him a sour look. "You know how very much I'm looking forward to being courted."

"Aren't you?"

This time, her expression was one of genuine surprise. "No! You know very well I've taken on this, this . . ." she gestured to her appearance in frustration ". . . this attire in order to learn Confederate secrets."

"And have you learned any?"

Her face fell, and he hated himself for being jealous. It was making him hurtful. "No, I haven't," she said. "But I have to keep trying, Joshua—it's the only thing keeping me sane!"

"I know that, Emily. I'm not trying to—" He cut himself off and rubbed his hand across the back of his neck. He walked away from her a bit, to the corner of the stable and collected his thoughts. What was it he was trying to do? He had no claim on Emily Birmingham. The very idea was laughable at best. At worst, he could get himself hanged. He had known her nearly all his life, though, and she was his breath of fresh air. Her newfound beauty only made it harder for him to deny his feelings.

"So, since your aim is not to find suitors, then, what will you do with them when they come calling?" He made an effort to keep his voice light, but wasn't sure if he was successful.

"I'd like to shove them out the parlor window," she said, and he heard her rustling skirts as she approached him. She was at his side in a moment, and he closed his eyes against her sweet scent. "But since I can't very well do that, I suppose I'll bat my eyes, say all the right things, and send them on their way."

He glanced over his shoulder and turned slightly to look at her. "I'm sure you'll do it very well," he murmured, hearing the husky tone in his voice. She must have heard it too, because her eyes widened almost imperceptibly, and her soft intake of breath was visible.

"As much as I wish you were free to live your life, sometimes I wish we could just stay here forever," she whispered, and lifted her hand.

He took it in his own and glanced down, noting the contrast between her skin and his. Hers was milky white. His was the color of lightly tanned leather. It wasn't the contrast it might have been had his father not been white, but it was enough. He pulled her hand softly to his lips and pressed them upon her knuckles, closing his eyes at the softness and the knowledge that he would never touch her again.

"Go," he said against her hand, his eyes still closed. "Go and don't come back here to see me alone again."

When he managed to finally open his eyes, he did so to find hers liquid and greener than he had ever seen them. She knew—he could see in her expression that she now knew without a doubt of the intensity of his feelings for her. What he hadn't expected to see was a return of those same feelings.

Heaven help her. Loving a slave wasn't a safe place for a white girl to be. He shook his head slightly at her, even as her eyes continued to fill and spill over, large tears falling down her cheeks. "It's not fair," she choked out. She pulled her hand from his and, reaching upward, entwined her arms around his neck and pressed the length of her slight body against his.

He took a shuddering breath and, for one brief moment, allowed his arms to close around her waist and hold her close, feeling her hot tears against his neck. "No, it isn't fair," he murmured. "But it's life. And if you don't want to see me swinging from the end of a rope, you need to leave."

She shook with a sob before tightening her arms around his neck and placing a kiss against his cheek. "I will always love you," she whispered through her tears. Then she tore herself from his arms and ran from the stable, leaving the hay to rustle and settle back into place in her wake.

CHAPTER 9

"I have put you in motion to offer battle to the invaders of your country. . . . You can but march to a decisive victory over . . . mercenaries sent to subjugate and despoil you of your liberties, property, and honor."
—Confederate General Albert Sidney Johnston

* * *

25 April 1862
Boston, Massachusetts

Camille clutched the small card in her gloved hand and watched out the window of the carriage as the houses passed in and out of her vision. She was nearly to Abigail's, and her heart gave a lurch. Glancing down again at the card, she read the words that had been hastily scrawled by her friend: *My mother has been in an accident. Please come.*

Camille did not consider herself to be of much use in times of turmoil. If anything, Abigail was the levelheaded one who knew what to say and how to soothe. She wished her mother had been home when the note had been delivered. She would have bullied her into coming along.

When she reached the stately, brick, colonial-style home that housed the Van Dykes, Camille took a deep breath, accepted the helping hand of the driver, and made her way toward the front door. It was flung open as she raised her fist to knock.

"Camille." Abigail grasped Camille's hands in her own and drew her into the house, nudging the door closed behind them. "I'm so glad you came. I was worried you wouldn't."

Camille was alarmed and unsettled at the sheen of tears in Abigail's eyes. "What has happened, Abby?"

Abigail drew a shaky breath. "My mother was out walking this morning when she was struck from behind by a horse and carriage. I wouldn't even know that much if it hadn't been for our parlor maid, who happened to be looking out the window at the time. The street was deserted otherwise."

Camille drew her brows together. "It happened right here?"

Abigail nodded. "Just right out front. I don't understand it," she said, her breath catching. "Glynis said Mother was on the side of the street, nearing our front gate. There was nobody else about, no other carriages in the street. It wasn't as though she was walking down the middle of the road in harm's way."

Camille stared, saying nothing. Who would run down Dolly Van Dyke? It was as though Abigail read her thoughts, however, because her eyes again filled with tears. Camille reached forward and clasped Abigail in a tight embrace. "I will help you," she said. "We will find those responsible. My family is wealthy, and my father is a powerful man." She pulled back a bit and moved her hands to Abigail's shoulders, squeezing gently. "Abby," she said when her friend ducked her head as a tear trickled down her cheek, "we will see this resolved. Your mother will be fine."

Abigail shook her head and looked down the hallway, drawing her finger across her cheek where the tear had fallen. "I don't think she will be," she said, sniffing. "You haven't seen her, Cammy . . ."

Abigail reached for Camille's hand and, securing it within her own, led her down the hallway, Camille still wearing her cloak and bonnet. Camille followed her friend into the parlor, where Dolly Van Dyke was lying on the sofa. She didn't see the woman at first because her view was blocked by a physician who bent over Dolly, his hand gently lifting a cloth that was against her head, the cloth soaked through with blood.

Upon hearing their entry, he stepped aside and turned to Abigail, his features tight. "Her pulse remains very weak," he murmured in an undertone to Abigail. "She is continuously losing blood from the wound in her head, and I suspect that some discoloring on her, ah, her abdomen," the man said, his face reddening, "might indicate internal bleeding as well." He cleared his throat and continued, "Is there not a male family member who might better handle these details, Miss Van Dyke?"

Abigail straightened her back. "There is only my mother and I, and I am capable of handling these details, sir."

"Of course. I hate to wound your sensibilities, however. I only wish to avoid causing you pain."

"I am here to help Miss Van Dyke," Camille said, and the doctor turned his attention to her. Had the circumstances been less serious, she might have laughed at his dubious expression. He offered a nearly imperceptible shrug, however, and apparently resigned himself to the reality of the situation. There were no men about to handle the ugliness, and so it fell to the young women.

"Who is he?" Camille asked as the doctor left after instructing them on how to change the bandage on Dolly's head.

Abigail sighed and sank down onto the floor next to her mother's inert side. "I sent Glynis out to find a doctor, and that's who she brought back."

"I wish we had known earlier; I'd have contacted our family physician. He's very competent. In fact," Camille said as she pulled her gloves from her hands and untied her bonnet, "I'll send a message home to have him sent for. He may be of more help."

* * *

Elizabeth read Camille's message with a frown of concern. She gestured to Robert, who was standing near the bed of his ailing uncle. He followed her out into the hallway.

"What is it?"

"It seems that Dolly Van Dyke was run down by a horse and carriage this morning. Camille is with Abigail and is requesting we send for Dr. Child."

"Well, it's fortuitous then that he's already on his way here."

Elizabeth shook her head and glanced into the bedroom where her sister, Jenny, sat at the side of her husband, Jean-Pierre. "Will you watch for the doctor at the front door and see if he will go to the Van Dykes when he's finished here? I don't want to burden Jenny with any more grief."

Robert nodded and glanced back through the open door at his uncle. Elizabeth watched with a wince as Robert's jaw tightened. The young man had been reading to his uncle almost daily in hopes that he would hear some of it—that he would eventually awaken. Since that morning, however, Jean-Pierre's breathing had become very shallow, and his body was bathed in sweat. It was the first time since arriving in Boston months ago that Jean-Pierre's body had exhibited signs of physical distress. Up until that very morning, it was as though he had been in a deep sleep, with nothing more ailing him.

Without saying another word, Robert turned and left the hallway, making his way down the front stairs to the foyer. Elizabeth reluctantly reentered the bedroom and walked to her sister's side, laying a hand upon her shoulder. She felt the hot sting of tears in her own eyes as Jenny reached up for Elizabeth's hand, pressing her wet cheek against it.

"He's leaving me," Jenny whispered.

"Don't talk so. You don't know that yet."

"Yes, I do." Jenny looked up at Elizabeth, her eyes glistening. "I can feel him leaving."

* * *

It was well past the dinner hour when Dr. Child finally arrived at the Van Dyke residence. Camille greeted him in the front hall with a breath of relief. "Oh, thank goodness," she said. "Mrs. Van Dyke is bleeding uncontrollably—Abby and I were starting to feel a bit desperate!" On an ordinary day, Camille might have worried over her appearance; she knew that the blood smears on her skirt and cuffs, combined with flushed cheeks and hair falling from its pins, cast her in a ghastly light. Her thoughts were consumed, however, with the welfare of the woman down the hall.

Dr. Child ran a hand through his windblown hair and cast an unreadable glance in Camille's direction. It sent a shiver of warning down her spine and she chose, for the moment, to ignore it. "Have you seen many injuries of this sort? Do you suppose anything can be done for Mrs. Van Dyke? Because I know you will do everything in your power to—"

Dr. Child placed a gentle touch on Camille's fluttering hands and said, "I shall surely do my best, Miss Birmingham."

Miss Birmingham? Camille couldn't remember a time when Dr. Child had ever addressed her so formally. He had delivered her and all of her siblings into this life and had seen personally to each individual illness. She could remember the days when he called her "little Cammy."

"What is it?" she finally said, giving voice to her fears. "Do you not think there is any hope for Abby's mother? You're behaving in a most worried fashion—I can't recall ever seeing you worried!"

"Camille, show me where Mrs. Van Dyke is, will you?"

Camille swallowed and nodded, gesturing down the hall toward the back sitting room.

* * *

It was nearing the midnight hour when, with a deep sigh of regret, the good doctor closed the eyes of one of the most vibrant women Boston society had ever seen. He might not approve of her unconventional personality, but without a doubt, the woman had been beautiful. And also without a doubt, Dr. Child knew the woman had loved her daughter with her whole heart and soul.

He turned to the two young women who sat opposite the dead woman, holding hands together on a richly upholstered divan, one eyeing him in shock and disbelief, the other with unspeakable grief. He wiped his hands clean on a cloth and moved to stoop next to Abigail Van Dyke.

"Do you have family who can help you attend to matters, Miss Van Dyke?"

The young woman looked at him through eyes bright with unshed tears. His concern for her raised a notch when her gaze continued upon his face uncomprehendingly.

"What are you saying, sir?" Camille asked, her voice cracking and approaching hysteria. "What matters would those be?"

He opened his mouth to speak, but was interrupted by Abigail. "She's gone, Cammy. My mother's gone."

Camille looked at her friend, and the doctor watched in sympathy as tears formed in Camille's eyes as well. "She was just here," was her whispered reply.

"Well, now she isn't." Abigail sniffed and looked into the empty hearth. "I need to tell Glynis to build a fire in here," she murmured.

Dr. Child looked upon the scene knowing full well he wouldn't be comfortable leaving the women alone for the night. His relief at the knock upon the front door was nearly palpable. Some moments later, James Birmingham appeared in the room, taking in the scene with one sweeping glance.

He walked to the front of the divan, where the two young women still sat motionless, and placed a hand upon their clasped hands. "I am deeply, deeply sorry, Abigail."

She nodded through her tears, which had now started to fall in earnest. "Thank you."

"Will you come and stay the night with our family?"

Abigail shook her head without hesitation. "I need to be here."

"I'll stay with you," Camille said, looking at her father as though daring him to disagree with her.

He finally nodded.

"Where's Mother? I would have thought she'd come with you," Camille said.

James hesitated a bit before responding. "She's home with your Aunt Jenny. We lost Uncle Jean-Pierre tonight, as well."

Camille stared at her father, and Dr. Child chose that moment to excuse himself from the small gathering. He made his way to the front door and gathered his coat and hat, feeling weary to his bones. He didn't envy Jenny the task of informing her young daughter of her father's death. Far away in New Orleans, there was nothing she could do to console her mother, and furthermore, according to the newspapers, Farragut had taken New Orleans that very day. Things were bound to be in chaos—compounded with the loss of a parent—no, he didn't wish to be in Brissot or Birmingham shoes anytime in the near future.

He hailed his driver, who had been waiting patiently in the kitchen, and made his way to the waiting carriage. He was looking forward to the comfort of his own home and bed. It was a hard thing to lose two patients in one night.

* * *

26 April 1862
New Orleans, Louisiana

Marie walked down the street from her father's newspaper shop and observed the citizens of New Orleans as they wandered to and fro in a state of shock. The Union navy had stormed its way past the two forts that guarded the city, and New Orleans was now in Union hands. People were outraged, of course, and angry that Jefferson Davis hadn't done more to protect the city.

She couldn't say she was upset; with New Orleans under Union control, perhaps the conflicts would soon end and the country would reunite. If only! Then her parents could return home and all would be as it had been.

Marie shook her head at her own folly. Things would never again be as they had been, and truthfully, that was probably a good thing. She would never again trust her neighbors, for she knew that many of them were responsible for her father's current state of incapacity. And the Fromeres—she would never wish that life return as it had been for them. They had yet to know more than a day or two of peace unmolested by society in general. She would keep them in her home for as long as was necessary—there might even be a chance that should a Union ship return to New England, they could book passage aboard. Her mother would help them once in Boston, she knew it.

As for now, she would keep to her routine as best she could. She had dismissed school for a few days in hopes that things would settle a bit. Once the citizens of New Orleans knew and understood their standings under Union control, she would have a better idea of what to expect.

With every passing sailor, Marie wondered if he were Daniel. He was undoubtedly among those who had taken control of the city—he could be that man right there! Or this one! She made herself feel batty with such thoughts. She had no idea what he looked like, and furthermore, she had been the one to insist they not meet. It was for his own good, she constantly reminded herself. He didn't need a woman like her in his life.

Still, if she only knew, just a bit, what he looked like, she might be able to put her active imagination to rest. She had missed him desperately. His letters in the past months had often been the bright point in her days, and knowing that she had been the one to cause their cessation was little comfort.

* * *

Daniel O'Shea watched the young woman maneuver her way down the crowded city street and marveled at her beauty. The image of her he carried in his knapsack didn't do her justice in the least. He knew she was Marie Brissot as surely as he knew his own name, and he was amazed that he had been able to pick her out of a crowd.

He had come ashore with several of the crew as a reward for his hard work with the ship's records. He was allowed but a few hours before his presence was expected again aboard the *Kennebec*, and he relished every moment on solid ground. The city itself was teeming with uncertainty and anger, literally smoldering in places.

When it had become evident that the Union advance was certain, the city's citizens burned cotton, corn, rice, sugar, and tobacco—tons of it—rather than see it fall into enemy hands as an asset. The acrid smell of smoke lay thick in the air, and Daniel wondered what the city had been like in its splendor, before the war.

He had chanced to see Marie as she purchased a few things and placed them in a basket that hung from her arm. He had known her upon sight, and felt his heart stop and then resume again with an incredible *thud*. He forced himself to observe her from a distance rather than rush to her and embrace her, as was his true desire. He must remind himself that she didn't want to meet him—that she must think him unworthy of her company. The truth of it caused him a flash of pain, and it angered him. He didn't have any room in his life for pain—he had left home to escape it.

Marie Brissot could go her way and the devil take her, for all he cared. He had enough on his mind, that much was certain. He caught another glimpse of her face as she turned and rounded a corner. She looked strained. He shrugged aside the momentary stab of concern. They were all strained; there was a war, and people were dying. Her troubles weren't any more unique than anybody else's.

He told himself that fact repeatedly as he followed her at a discreet distance to her home. He recognized the address from the letters he had sent—so many letters!—and watched as she rounded the house and apparently entered from the back entrance. It was a beautiful house with a large front porch and stately pillars, but it wasn't so big as to seem pretentious. It was just the sort of house he had imagined her in, and he found himself pleased that her dwelling wasn't an ostentatious affair.

He turned and left the street, making his way back into the heart of the city and toward the docks. He would do well to leave her be. He had satisfied his curiosity by following her home, and that would be the end of it. As long as he kept telling himself that, he might start to believe it.

* * *

29 April 1862
Utah Territory

Earl kissed his mother, Ellen, who patted his arm in an efficient manner and nodded her head. "You go and work hard, my boy. Remember all you've been taught."

His father, Eli, shook his hand and also nodded in agreement with Ellen. "You'll be fine," he said. "We'll pray for you each morning and night."

"Thank you, sir." Earl stood before his parents, outfitted in his new militia finery. Only last night the request for a militia had come over the wires from Washington. It was *extremely* telling that the U.S. Army Adjutant General Lorenzo Thomas had made the request of Brigham Young and not Acting Governor Fuller. It was plain proof that the folks back east knew exactly who was in control in Utah.

In typical competent Mormon fashion, immediately following the message he received from Thomas, Brigham Young had contacted Lieutenant General Daniel H. Wells of the militia, formally known as the Nauvoo Legion, and requested that he begin raising a militia that employed thirty officers and between fifty-six and seventy-two privates. The following day, a militia was formed, outfitted, and ready for camp.

So, there he was. Private Earl Dobranski. He was to meet with the rest of the militia at a camp just outside of Salt Lake City and remain there for a day, at which point they would begin marching east.

When he reached the camp, he was gratified to see many of his friends milling about as well. They eventually gathered together to listen to the words of Major Lot Smith, the man directly responsible for enlisting the company of men for their terms of ninety-day service.

"Our primary function," he told the men, "will be to examine the mail route, checking stations that have been victims of depredation, and to secure the mail and telegraph lines from any attack, Indian or otherwise. I have received explicit instructions from President Brigham Young," he continued, "that we are to conduct ourselves in a manner befitting Latter-day Saints. We are to observe strict sobriety in camp and avoid the use of all profane language or disorderly conduct of any kind."

Earl looked about himself at the springtime landscape of the valley. What had once been a barren, desolate piece of earth was beginning to blossom in aesthetic beauty. Trees, flowers, and beautiful gardens dotted the land, and the trees and shrubs along the mountains were green because of the recent moisture in spring snowmelt and rain.

It was a beautiful place, this desert, and he felt very much at home in it. He would miss it while gone and looked forward with anticipation to his return. If only he knew for certain what he would like to do when he returned, his mind might be at peace. It wasn't as though he were constantly troubled; his thoughts were nothing in comparison to Ben Birmingham's. That poor boy had always been thinking, thinking, thinking, and was angry. No, Earl's thoughts were simpler and calmer. He just felt a stirring, some kind of push that he couldn't define. He wanted something, wanted to do something, but couldn't put a finger on what it might be.

He shrugged slightly and smiled at a comment made by the man standing next to him, deciding that this was as good a place as any to think about his future. He would complete his ninety-day service and then maybe speak to his father. Eli was a wise man. Although Earl had found it difficult to talk with him since his return, he never doubted his father's wisdom or testimony of Christ. He simply didn't know his father anymore. He had been gone for years, and it would take some time to become reacquainted.

With one final glance at the mountaintops, which were beginning to see shadows of dusk, he made his way to his belongings so that he might settle in for the night.

CHAPTER 10

"He was too good for this earth. It is hard to have him die."
—Abraham Lincoln in reference to the death of his son Willie early in '62

* * *

10 May 1862
Charleston, South Carolina

Mary stood beneath the ancient tree, gazing up into the branches at the few planks that stubbornly held their positions as parts of a former tree house. It was Ben and Luke's creation, and had served them well until they climbed upon it with Joshua, a year after its initial completion, and one of the supporting branches had given way under their weight.

Taking advantage of the few moments she had to herself, Mary settled comfortably near the dilapidated tree house, still examining its remains as she leaned against the trunk of a neighboring tree. It wasn't often she found time for leisure; it was a treat she meant to savor. The heavy foliage in the small forest that connected Bentley to the Charlesworth's plantation blocked the afternoon sun and made for a restful thinking spot.

Mary wondered what Ben's life was like now. It had been nearly seven long years since she had last seen him, and she had been but a child when he'd left. He'd taken her heart with him, though, and she wished for a moment to see him so she could demand its return. How she had loved him! She realized those feelings were more likely than not an inevitable part of childhood, and that perhaps now she wouldn't feel so enamored of him, but she couldn't seem to make herself forget his face. Emily often said that if it weren't for the painting of Ben she herself had stashed under her bed, she might have forgotten his appearance altogether, but Mary saw him every time she closed her eyes. She didn't need a portrait to bring his face to view, but she never admitted as much to Emily. She and Emily were the best of friends, it was true, but Mary had never admitted her feelings for Ben to his sister. It was too personal—too private. Perhaps it was because she knew she'd never have the opportunity to be with Ben in this life. Whatever the reason, she kept it to herself.

He was probably married by now. Some lucky Mormon girl in the West had no doubt claimed him for her own—a white girl—a girl who was allowed to share his life. She wondered if he had any children. She wondered what his days entailed. He hadn't written to Emily in nearly nine months, so perhaps the separation that had thus far been one of only distance was now one in spirit as well. All these years he had managed to maintain contact with Emily, and now suddenly, nothing.

None of it did Mary any good anyway. Even if he were still here, awaiting the day when he would become lord of the plantation, he was well beyond Mary's reach. It was laughable, really; a slave girl pining away for the master and mistress's son. It was a scenario that undoubtedly repeated itself time after time in the South; she was not naive enough to believe it might ever be a reality for some fortunate couple. They would be ostracized at the very least, and the worst was unthinkable.

Mary's thoughts turned to Emily, and she smiled, if a bit wistfully. She knew the day would soon come when Emily would leave, too, and because her relationship with the girl was so much more concrete and real than her fantasies about Ben, she knew it would hurt even more than when Ben had left. Emily was a star that fairly burst with energy and fire. She would make something grand of her life once she could discern the direction in which she wished to head.

It wouldn't be long, in Mary's opinion, before Emily finally took a liking to one of the many suitors who called each day. Austin

Stanhope was calling with more frequency than any of his predecessors, in fact, and Mary wondered if Emily was encouraging his attention, even if she was unaware of it herself. Emily had been distant the past few weeks, as if she had something monumental and perhaps even painful on her mind, and Mary wasn't used to seeing her friend in such quiet turmoil. Emily's turmoil was typically much more vocal.

So where would Mary be, then, when Emily left? Mary felt her eyes sting and shook her head. A gentle breeze wafted through the trees, and she turned her face into it, relishing the cool sweep across her face. Closing her eyes against the unwanted tears, Mary stiffened her resolve to be strong. If Emily left, *when* Emily left, Mary wouldn't allow herself the luxury of crumbling, because there was no time for it in her life. Miz Sarah wouldn't take kindly to one of her primary house servants wailing and carrying on in her grief.

Mary felt a momentary stab of envy for Emily, and it surprised her. She had never been jealous of her friend before, and it was probably because Mary knew Emily loved her and wished things were different for her. Still, as Mary thought of Emily with her whole life before her—the freedom to marry whom she chose (provided Mr. Jeffrey and Miz Sarah didn't choose for her), the freedom to move about, to come and go—Mary was indeed envious. Emily possessed a freedom that even if she had been born to a family of limited means, she could find herself a respectable occupation and earn money that was hers to spend as she pleased.

These things, small things, really, were not a possibility for Mary, and to dream of them for herself was dangerous, yet still she did it. She dreamed of her own life even though she knew it wasn't possible. It was amazing, really, she mused as the breeze continued to waft cool upon her skin, that because *both* of Emily's parents were white, she was entitled to her own life. Only one of Mary's parents had been white, and therefore someone else owned her life.

She opened her eyes and turned her gaze toward heaven. *Someday,* she thought, *someday I'll see my sweet Jesus, and I'll ask Him why it had to be this way. He could make it right with the touch of His holy hand, and yet He doesn't.*

Or maybe He does. Emily had told her just that morning that the day before, a Union general, David Hunter, issued a proclamation freeing all slaves in Georgia, Florida, and South Carolina, but that Lincoln revoked the order. Emily and Mary both knew that the general had issued his proclamation as a strategic tactic against the Confederacy, but in the end, Mary wouldn't have cared overmuch about the reasons. Her freedom was what she wanted, and war tactic or no, if it was accomplished, she wouldn't complain.

Emily had expressed frustration over Lincoln's response, but it was murmured that he was well on his way to issuing a proclamation similar to General Hunter's, only the hope was that it would be even more sweeping in its effects. And besides, Mary had argued with Emily, if Lincoln gave the right to his generals to make such sweeping proclamations, he gave up his own power and rights as commander in chief. As he had said once before, generals do not make policy. The president and Congress make policy.

Emily was convinced that change was on the wind, and Mary could only hope that she was right. What would she do with her freedom? The very thought made her heart race, and she felt flushed. She would breathe differently! The very air in her lungs would be her own. She would be a seamstress, perhaps, or even work as a ladies' maid, and she would earn money that she would use to buy her own food and pay for a room in a boarding house, possibly. She would save her money and buy some bright yellow material, or maybe even purple, and she would make herself a beautiful dress to wear whenever she chose. She would throw away her serviceable brown slave dress and boots and buy some pretty shoes—maybe she would even make some matching ribbons for her hair!

She would do likewise for her little sister, Rose. She would make her look beautiful, and they would be happy. And Mama Ruth! She would be happy, too. They would be the family they always had been, but it would be according to their own terms and desires, not someone else's.

A rustle in the bushes to her left attracted her attention, and for a moment she thought she was losing her mind. She saw Ben's face, as clear as day, and in the next moment, it vanished. She stared at the spot, blinking, and truly questioned her sanity. Was she wishing to see him so much that she was conjuring up images of him and imagining they were real?

She shook her head and stood, brushing the twigs and dirt from her dress. *I must be mad,* she thought. *My poor brain needs a rest. That just goes to show what happens when I let my thoughts run wild with nonsense. Serves me right, really.*

Her time alone was spent, so she made her way back toward the mansion on the hill, walking slowly and thinking.

* * *

Ben caught his breath as Mary retreated from the forest, and cursed himself the most foolish of men. She had seen him! She probably thought she was seeing a ghost or some strange apparition from the past because she had shaken her head, as though questioning herself, and left.

She was beautiful. He turned away from her retreating form and felt his eyes burn at the years he had missed while those he loved grew closer to adulthood. She was probably nearly eighteen years old now, and although she had matured and grown since he had seen her last, her face was still undeniably hers. Her features were still the same: the large, brown-green eyes, the high cheekbones, the light brown skin, the beautiful hands and long fingers. Her fingers had been long as a child, too, and he remembered Sarah saying that they made for excellent handicrafting.

Mary had always had an exotic look about her, and as a young woman it was absolutely breathtaking. He envisioned her holding court as a queen in a lush, tropical island, and saw dozens of suitors sitting at her feet. The image made him smile, and he glanced back at her; she was opening the back door to the servants' entrance, and in an instant, she was inside the house.

His smile faded and the cold, harsh reality settled back into place. She wasn't a queen—she wasn't allowed to go to the front door and enter as would one of importance and stature. She was part of the supporting network that held the system in place—the part that was expected to enter and exit quietly, do the work, mind their manners, and retreat in peace.

The familiar anger settled like a lump in his heart, and he was reminded all over again why he had been forced to leave. It had been six years since he left home, and while his heart ached as he looked at the house and grounds that made the plantation what it was, the frustration that had never really gone away came rushing in with a vengeance.

* * *

10 May 1862
Hilton Head, South Carolina

"I wondered where you'd gone. Your note wasn't very specific." Luke brushed his horse and responded with a smile when the creature nudged his pocket, looking for a treat. He pulled forth a sugar lump and rubbed the horse's head as the enormous tongue shot forth and licked the sugar from the palm of his hand.

"I had to see the house," Ben said. He settled down with a sigh on a camp stool he'd purchased from a fellow soldier. "It hasn't changed."

"Did you see anybody?"

"Yes."

Luke paused, brush midair. "Who?"

"Mary."

Luke smiled and resumed brushing. "I'll bet she's all grown up now."

"That she is." Something in his tone must have given away the depth of his feelings because Luke glanced back at him with a speculative expression, but let it pass.

"Did she see you?"

"Yes, but I don't think she believed her eyes. She just left. I saw her at the old tree house. Do you remember it?"

Luke tipped his head slightly and laughed out loud. "Do I remember it? I still have the scars!" He pulled his sleeve up and pointed to his forearm, where a piece of shattered wood had pierced it when they had fallen from the tree house years ago. "Are any of the pieces still intact?"

Ben nodded, and the corner of his mouth twitched into a smile. "Most of the floorboards. The ones that didn't give way under us, that is."

"Mercy. That was a long time ago." Luke shook his head and smoothed his hand over the glossy coat of his horse. "Seems like another lifetime."

"It was."

Luke glanced at Ben again. "Are you all right?"

Ben shrugged slightly and looked over the regimental encampment. "I miss home, and I hate home."

Luke continued brushing his horse, leaving Ben to his thoughts. As though attempting to divert Ben's musings after a few moments, Luke asked, "So when are you going to tell me about your church?"

Ben saw the subject change for what it was, especially since he knew Luke was content with his mother's Quaker beliefs, but he smiled at his cousin's efforts. "Would you like to know the history behind it?"

"I would." Luke finished his task and secured his horse for the night, returning to sit on a fallen log next to Ben's camp stool.

Ben looked at his cousin with a fair amount of surprise and anticipation. He had wanted to share the story with someone, *anyone,* since he had learned of it himself. He took a deep breath and, with a prayer in his heart, began speaking. "A young boy named Joseph Smith was curious about which of the varied sects in his region of upstate New York the Lord would have him join. Following the admonition in James, chapter one, he went into a grove of trees near his home to pray . . ."

* * *

13 May 1862
Bentley Plantation

Sarah folded the newspaper slowly and with unnecessary care, a frown etched across her brow.

Ruth cast a glance at her over the butcher block table in the cookhouse. "Ma'am, are you well?"

Sarah looked at the woman and tilted her head to one side, regarding her fully, honestly. If Ruth had been one of a dozen other slaves, she might have said, "Missus, is you sick?" Or perhaps, "Somethin' got you ill, Miz?" But Ruth was different. Joshua had taught her everything he had learned from Ben, and Ben had taught Joshua everything he knew. Therefore, Joshua, Ruth, Mary, and even young Rose spoke as though they were white folk. Sarah hadn't minded so much at the time—in fact, she hadn't even been *exactly* sure that Joshua was actually teaching Ruth to read and write—but she had turned a blind eye nonetheless, and it had been to her own detriment. They had tried to leave.

For a moment as Sarah watched Ruth's intelligent eyes regarding her with concern, she felt a wild stab of fear that took her breath away. Natchez, Mississippi, had just surrendered to Farragut, and it didn't bode well for the Confederacy. They were literally losing ground. The loss of New Orleans had come as a huge blow, and Sarah tightened her jaw in frustration as she thought of Jefferson Davis. He was underestimating his adversaries, and it was putting them all in peril.

If there was a bright star on the horizon, it was that McClellan, the little poppycock, was still in a position of power, which was a boon to the Confederacy. In March, Lincoln had reduced him in rank from general-in-chief to commander of the Army of the Potomac only. Sarah shook her head slightly in derision. If Jeffrey's reports from Senator Chestnut were to be believed, McClellan had built a well-trained fighting machine, but he was afraid to use it. Despite the fact that he had taken both Yorktown and Williamsburg only a week before, he was constantly overestimating the size of the Confederate troops in Virginia, and although his numbers were vastly superior, his attacks were careful, if they materialized at all.

It was small comfort, however, what with Union troops situating themselves up and down the Mississippi and coming in through New Orleans. Now Natchez—what next? Memphis? Atlanta?

Sarah drew a sharp breath and tried to calm her racing heart. Her panic must have shown in her face because Ruth had quietly left her stool on the opposite side of the butcher block and was now at her side. The woman placed a gentle hand upon Sarah's own, which had tightly clenched the corner of the newspaper she had so carefully folded.

"Sarah."

Ruth's warm voice washed over her like a blanket. It had been absolutely years since she had addressed her mistress so informally. They had been but children then. She looked at Ruth's eyes and felt her breathing slow.

"What is it?"

"The Union," Sarah murmured, hoping her pounding heart would stay put in her chest. "They are working their way here."

Ruth nodded but said nothing. She still held Sarah's hand within her own.

"I don't suppose you'd mind that terribly, would you, Ruth?"

Ruth still remained silent, her intensely focused eyes still on Sarah's face.

Sarah took a deep, shuddering breath and let it out, sharply demanding that her mind pull itself together. It was beyond the pale that she should crumble so while a slave woman displayed all the strength. "Well," she said, shaking her hand free and smoothing the crumpled paper. "We have much to do. I've been informed by merchants in town that with the embargo, materials are now much more difficult to come by. We may find ourselves making do with what we have here on the plantation, so we'll need to take stock of what we have on hand and what we still should try to acquire."

Ruth nodded slowly, the intimate moment past, and made her way back around the table to her stool. She absently picked up the pen Sarah had been using earlier and pulled out a sheet of parchment. She suddenly looked up, her eyes startled, and shoved both the pen and paper to Sarah.

Sarah regarded Ruth silently for a moment, considering punishing Ruth for the outright proof that the woman was ready to make a list with a pen and paper. The fear in Ruth's eyes was enough to soothe Sarah's offended pride and sense of outrage; for now, it would do.

* * *

Ruth's hands shook as she walked from the cookhouse to the mansion. She went in through the servant's entrance on legs that trembled, and walked to the pantry, which was down the hall. She entered it on the pretense of obeying Sarah's orders to inventory it, but instead closed the door behind herself and sank to the floor.

Sarah didn't like being weak, didn't like to find herself in a position worthy of consolation, and she most assuredly didn't like the notion that she might not be superior, but merely an equal. When Ruth had reached for the pen and paper, she hadn't been thinking beyond Sarah's obvious reaction to something she had read in the paper. As Ruth had taken the opportunity to read it before presenting it to her mistress, she knew that the "something" was probably the news of Natchez falling to Farragut.

The fact that Sarah was so obviously frightened had shot through Ruth's frame like a ray of hope. Her concern for Sarah's welfare had been real enough; Ruth had wondered for a moment if Sarah was on the verge of physical collapse. Her face had been sickly pale, her skin clammy to the touch, and her eyes huge with fear.

Ruth knew she had blundered, however, when she had begun taking matters into her own hands with the pen and parchment. Never, *ever* had she made such a mistake. She often felt that Sarah was in considerable doubt as to whether or not Ruth was actually literate. Well, she had fixed that. Sarah now knew for a certainty, and with her fear very real, Ruth must watch herself.

There was a knock upon the pantry door, and Ruth rose, dusting herself off, and opened it. Angel, a young slave woman, stood on the other side with a puzzled expression. "Ruth, why's you there in the dark?"

"Oh, I . . ." Ruth cast about for a logical explanation. "I'm feeling a bit of a headache—I just wanted a few moments in the dark to soothe it . . ."

Angel accepted the excuse and said, "Oh. Well, Nellie needs a jar of molasses and she done sent me to fetch it."

Ruth moved back into the room, retrieved the jar with the benefit of the light spilling in from the hallway, and handed it to Angel. "Please tell Nellie that I'll be needing to know, from now on, exactly what she'll be using for meals. We must start exercising a certain amount of economy with our resources."

Angel looked at her in puzzlement, and Ruth didn't fault her confusion. Sarah was frugal, that much was true, but affairs at Bentley from the smallest breakfast to the grandest ball were handled with abundance. Economy was not a concept heretofore practiced.

Ruth watched the young girl move back down the hallway and out of her sight. Things were changing, and heaven only knew where they'd all be by the end.

CHAPTER 11

"Although you are United States soldiers, you are still members of The Church of Jesus Christ of Latter-day Saints, and while you have sworn allegiance to the constitution and government . . . and we have vowed to preserve the Union, the best way to accomplish this high purpose is to shun all evil associations and remember your prayers, and try to establish peace with the Indians, and always give ready obedience to the orders of your commanding officers. If you do this I promise you, as a servant of the Lord, that not one of you shall fall by the hand of an enemy."

—Brigham Young, speaking to departing troops at the mouth of Emigration Canyon

* * *

16 May 1862
Deer Creek, Wyoming

Dear Mother and Father,

You may well not receive this letter for a few weeks yet—we are still in the process of securing the mail and telegraph lines, and the mail, as you know, is still momentarily halted. I want you to know that I am well and healthy.

Thus far, our biggest problem has been the weather! The melting snow and rains have made for muddy passage; the horses seem to like it as little as do we, and just imagine the trial of moving ten supply wagons through such muck and mire! Yet we persevere, and are proud to aid the United States.

We have found deserted mail stations from Green River to our current location of Deer Creek, with stock and other property missing—Colonel Burton believes it to have been stolen. The mail stations are spaced at ten-mile intervals, and at each one we passed, we saw smoldering remains of what once were operating stations. Many of the mail stations had obviously only just been set fire to—they were smoking as we reached them. At Ice Creek Station we found locked mail of twenty-six sacks, many of which had been ripped open and tossed all over the prairie. The colonel wonders if there are some renegade white men causing all this ruckus as well as certain Indians—he has heard that some of the Snakes and Bannocks up north speak English, and one even supposedly speaks German.

We understand that we are to remain on the mail line until troops from the East are sent to relieve us. At that point we will return home. Please rest assured, however, that this journey has been one of surprisingly little event, and that I am safe and well. It may interest you to know that on the first of May, as we were departing the valley, President Young met us himself at the mouth of Emigration Canyon with General Wells. President Young admonished us to conduct ourselves as gentlemen, and to befriend the Indians wherever possible. He was most inspiring and yet firm in his speaking, and the lot of us are doing our very best to follow his counsel.

I endeavor daily to conduct myself in a manner befitting your approval, and look forward with great anticipation to seeing you all again.

Much love,
Earl

* * *

16 May 1862
Boston, Massachusetts

"The good news, I suppose, is that the fool did manage to take Yorktown and Williamsburg." Senator Crompton sat back in the chair James Birmingham offered him and cast an eye about the simple yet richly appointed office.

"It doesn't help much that he was driven back out of Virginia by a mere seventy-five thousand men when he was in command of one hundred fifty thousand himself," James answered, taking a seat beside his associate.

"You've heard, then? Johnston practically marched his men around in circles, confusing little Napoleon and fueling his paranoia."

James nodded and offered the man a cigar. Crompton took it, examined it with an appreciative sniff, and accepted the offered light. After blowing a few rings into the air, he turned to James with a smile.

"Have you thought about my offer?"

"I have. I've considered it long and hard."

"Well, I hate to withdraw it, but I hope you've decided to decline."

James looked at the man in surprise. "I had, but why do you say so?"

"In discussing the matter with my colleagues, we've come to the conclusion that while as valuable an asset you would be as a commander in the field, we need you more here at home, managing your business so that the Union can be assured further iron resources."

James nodded in response. "I had come to that conclusion myself. Truly, the only person I would trust with my business in my absence would be my wife, and your offer wouldn't have given me sufficient time to teach her all she would need to know."

"Your wife?"

"My wife. I trust her intellect above my own."

"What an odd thing to say, but then I hear you and Mrs. Birmingham have been frequenting abolition meetings of late."

"We've been frequenting abolition meetings for years."

Crompton shook his head. "Is it true that they also espouse the rights of women to work and to vote?"

"It is, indeed."

"I would no sooner turn my vocation over to my wife than fly to the moon. She is much too delicate of nature."

"How unfortunate."

Crompton stared at him over his smoke rings and James bit back a smile. He was undoubtedly one of the few men living who would express regret to a contemporary over the delicate nature of any man's wife. It was expected for women to be delicate, and it was the responsibility of the man in a woman's life to protect her from the glare of the harsh world.

Again, Crompton shook his head, tapping the ash from the end of his cigar into a glass-blown ashtray at his elbow. "I've heard stories about you, Birmingham—never believed 'em until now," he mumbled. Clearing his throat, he asked, "You have sons; surely they are of an age to take an interest in the family business."

"My oldest son, Luke, chose his own profession in the banking industry years ago, but that is a moot point, anyway. He's currently serving in a cavalry regiment in South Carolina. My other son Robert is but sixteen years of age. I feel him a bit young yet.

Crompton raised a brow but said nothing. It was obvious from his expression that he would have found a sixteen-year-old boy more capable of running a business than a man's wife, but he wisely kept those thoughts to himself. He blushed slightly and cleared his throat again. "I had forgotten your son enlisted. I hope he is well."

James nodded once. "He is. We pray daily for his health and welfare. He is serving alongside my nephew, and they seem in good spirits."

"Have they seen battle?"

"Nothing severe yet."

Crompton took another pull on his cigar and fell silent. He was a corpulent fellow—short of stature and wide of girth—and James had known him formally for years. The man thought highly of him and was in a position to grant a favor or two, should the occasion arise.

"My son Robert—he is a bright young man, and my instincts tell me that unless the war ends soon, we shall find him enlisted before long, as well. He has at least one more year before the enlistment offices will take him."

"They would take him this very day, and I think you and I both know this. The age of eligibility has been lowered once already—only God Himself knows how far it will drop before this conflict sees an end."

Crompton showed his assent with a slight incline of his balding head.

"I wonder, if the occasion does arise, if I might call upon your good graces for a favor."

"You want me to put him in a regiment guaranteed to see little action? Or assign him to an innocuous office position?"

"No. I don't mind him going into the field. I would like him to be placed with a commander who would be able to best use my son's talents."

"And what are those?"

"He's an excellent student of military history, and he thinks with a sound mind. I believe he would be an asset not only to a commander, but to fellow soldiers as well."

Crompton chuckled. "You almost sound as though you'd like to be rid of the boy."

James felt an uncustomary flush rise to his face, and he leaned forward in his chair. "I may well lose my oldest son, and I do not relish the thought of losing Robert, also. If I hold him back from these experiences, however, he may not develop the talents God has blessed him with."

Crompton raised a hand and said, "I mean no offense, James. I will do my best to see Robert placed in a good regiment, should the time arise."

James settled back into his chair and relaxed a bit, wondering how quickly he could end the visit without seeming rude. "Thank you. It is much appreciated."

* * *

"But graduating your studies early, what good will that do you?" Nathaniel Sylvester walked alongside Robert Birmingham as the boys made their way out of the barbershop.

"Are you daft?" Robert answered. "I'll be finished with schooling!"

"But that leaves me with a year by myself," Nathaniel said. "My mother's talking of Austria again, though, so maybe it's just as well."

"She is? That's wonderful!" Robert knew Nathaniel had been hoping to go to Austria for the past two years.

"I don't know."

Robert cast a glance at his friend as they strolled down the street toward their homes. Nathaniel had been uncharacteristically quiet the entire afternoon. "What troubles you today?"

"Nothing of consequence."

Robert frowned. He and Nathaniel had been friends since boyhood, and he couldn't remember a time when Nathaniel had felt uncomfortable about telling him anything.

"Do you ever think about Bull Run?" he asked Nathaniel.

Nathaniel nodded. "Often."

"Hard to believe it's been nearly a year."

"My aunt Helena is coming this way for a visit."

"The aunt we visited in Washington?"

Nathaniel nodded again. "She says she's long overdue for a visit with Mother."

Robert laughed. "You don't seem to be anticipating it very much."

"No, not with any happiness, anyway." Nathaniel paused, his expression uncomfortable. "Robert, you've been going to Abolition Society meetings lately, haven't you?"

Robert took a deep breath. "Yes, I have."

"It's not exactly the thing for those in our circles, you know. I mean, there are wealthy and influential people who are abolitionists, but it's not really the standard."

He glanced at Nathaniel, trying for levity he didn't feel. "You're starting to sound like your sister," he said with a chuckle.

Nathaniel flushed. "That's unfair."

"Are you worried about my social status?"

"No. I . . . no."

Robert stopped walking and thrust his hands into his pockets. He faced his friend squarely and said, "Nathaniel, what is it?"

Nathaniel sighed. "You need to tread carefully. There are those in our midst who would maintain the status quo."

Robert laughed. "Maintaining the status quo with the country torn apart? I'd say the status quo has been tossed into the trash heap."

"I mean the social status quo!" Nathaniel flushed again slightly as two free black women and a man dressed in finery that matched Robert's own passed. Robert tipped his hat to them with a quick smile, and then turned to his friend in impatience.

"What are you saying?"

"My mother is very dissatisfied with the current rise in abolition activity and all the literature that is circulating. It seems that supporters of abolition and influential Republican congressmen are pressuring Lincoln to state total abolition of all slaves as the war objective."

Robert stared at Nathaniel, his mouth going slack. "I'm of the opinion that such would be a good end, my friend."

"I'm not saying it wouldn't be," Nathaniel hissed and moved closer to Robert as more people passed them on the street. "But my parents don't think so, and they have some influential friends who are adamantly opposed to the Society."

Robert studied his friend's uncertain face with new interest. "What have you heard?"

"Nothing." Nathaniel resumed walking, this time at a brisk pace.

"You're lying," Robert said, jogging to catch up.

"I haven't heard anything specific. Just vague comments . . ."

"What kind of 'vague comments'?"

"Just something about some who may wish to find a way to end Society gatherings."

Robert drew his brows together in thought. "That could mean anything."

"Yes, it could. But the tone—I don't know anything specific, Robert, or I would tell you. Just watch out for yourself and your family. My mother is happy that Camille and Olivia don't spend time together anymore, and she's not anxious that we do, knowing you attend those meetings. I almost wonder if that's not why she's considering sending me to finish my last year in Austria."

"You jest! Your mother feels the need to protect you from *me?*"

Nathaniel shrugged. "She's a bit strange at times." They passed a storefront with a plate-glass window in which Nathaniel caught his reflection. "She'll want my valet to cut my hair again, just you wait and see. She won't like that I've gone to a common barber—she'll have it recut."

Robert shook his head slightly and walked along, grateful Nathaniel had slowed his pace. They looked a mirror of each other, both walking along with hands thrust deeply into pockets and eyes trained upon the ground, deep in thought. They had been similar for so many years, and now things were entirely different. Before Bull Run, the boys had desperately wanted to enlist in the Union army. Now, however, Nathaniel wanted nothing to do with war or military, and although Robert was reluctant, his interest had been rekindled in recent months. He was considering taking some part in the conflict if things were still actively moving when he became of age.

"I will write you from Austria, and you must promise me that you will take care."

"I will. And you as well."

Nathaniel nodded, and the boys continued on in silence, speaking again only at parting. Each continued on his way, still thoughtfully studying the ground until reaching his respective destination.

Robert reached his front steps only to change his course at the last minute and head for the stables instead. He requested that George, the family groom, saddle his mount. When the horse was ready, he swung his leg over its back and settled into the saddle, riding at a brisk pace to the Van Dyke home.

Upon reaching the dwelling, he took his horse to the stable, left him there with the groom, and went to the front door, pounding on it with more energy than he intended. Once shown to the parlor, his sister eventually appeared.

"Robert?" Camille didn't bother trying to hide her surprise. She had visited home only the night before, and they had talked at length over dinner. "I didn't expect to see you again so soon."

"I hadn't planned on coming—it's only that Nathaniel made some vague references today about people trying to put a stop to Society meetings or some such nonsense. Have you heard anything?"

"No, not a word. Come, sit down with me." She settled onto the settee and patted the spot next to her. "What do you think he meant?"

"I don't know. His mother is distraught that we are still friends—she would prefer he associate only with non-Society members—and her sister is on her way for a visit from Washington."

Camille looked horrified. "Aunt Helena? Oh, I did not like that woman."

"And do you remember? Almost a year ago Olivia said something to you about the Society—something negative. We came here, in fact!"

"Yes, to tell Dolly and Abigail." Camille winced.

Robert patted her hand awkwardly. He really was no good at comforting women. "How is Abigail?"

"She is doing remarkably well, actually. I think she feels her mother would expect her to hold herself together and not mourn her death excessively. It's just so strange."

"Have the police come by with any news?"

"Yes, but they were of little help. Upon investigation, they still don't know who was driving the carriage or why someone would want to hurt Dolly."

Robert nodded and looked around the room, wishing for some sort of distraction. Life had been so much easier before the war. And to think there was a time when he had gloried in it! Now it was a nuisance for some at best, and an unimaginable horror for others. He had witnessed some of the gore firsthand. And behind the terror of the battlefield, underneath the schematics of battle, there were opinions. Lifestyles. Heated debates and differing philosophies that had led to bloodshed. Philosophies that had led to Dolly's death. Robert knew as surely as the sun rose each day that Dolly's death had not been an accident. Someone had intentionally run her down because she was an ardent supporter of abolition.

Nathaniel's warnings echoed in his head, and he looked back at Camille. He felt the sting of fear as he thought of his sister hurt or molested by the Society's enemies.

She must have noticed the change in expression that he had surely felt upon his own face. "What is it, Robert?"

"I believe," he began slowly, "that we must take care. We must take special care wherever we go, whatever we do."

"Why do you say these things suddenly?"

"I should hate to see any one of us meet the same fate as Dolly."

Camille nodded and then looked into the hearth, where a small fire burned.

Robert thought of their aunt, whose husband was also dead because of fear and hatred. "How is Jenny?"

Camille shook her head, but her gaze remained on the gentle flames that licked the last pieces of a small log. "She is surviving. She merely goes through the motions, as does Abby. In an odd way, I believe they are a comfort for each other, though they converse little."

"Do you want to come home?"

Camille shook her head and finally turned her attention back to Robert. "No. I want to stay here. What would I do at home anyway? Receive callers I have no intention of marrying? At least I have a purpose here." She shrugged. "I'm helping two women grieve."

He felt himself flush slightly at the thought of Abigail Van Dyke, wishing he could offer a sympathetic shoulder himself. Cursing himself for thinking of his own desires during a time when she was hurting, he shook his head and rose. Thoughts of her were best left alone. Not only was she four years his senior, she was nearly engaged to his brother.

"I must go," he said, giving Camille an awkward pat on the arm. "I'll see you at the next meeting, if not sooner?"

She nodded. "Take care of yourself," she said.

"I will. And you."

CHAPTER 12

"It is called the Army of the Potomac but it is only McClellan's bodyguard. . . . If McClellan is not using the army, I should like to borrow it for a while."
—Abraham Lincoln

* * *

10 June 1862
Charleston, South Carolina

It was her second waltz with Austin Stanhope, and Emily realized that to dance a third with him in the same night would have the tongues wagging for certain. It was simply scandalous to favor any man with three waltzes at one event.

"I do hope the orchestra will favor me with a long piece. This will undoubtedly be my last chance to dance with you this evening," Mr. Stanhope commented as he swung her gently about the room, one large hand placed at the small of her back.

So, he was accustomed to convention. Emily was doing her best to get to know the man, as there was a particular spark in her mother's eyes these days whenever his name turned up in conversation. "I'm flattered you would wish to," she lied. Stanhope was handsome enough, she supposed, but her heart was broken, she was sure of it. The man she loved could never be hers, and ever since her one stolen moment in a warm embrace with Joshua, she had thought of little else. She hadn't even shared the experience with Mary.

"Your father tells me you enjoy horseback riding," he said as the music droned on.

"Yes, I do."

"And do you also enjoy traditional pursuits?"

"I'm absolutely dreadful at the pianoforte, I cannot carry a tune, and my stitching is horrid."

Instead of the shocked reaction Emily had expected, she was rewarded instead with laughter—long and hard. When he finally quieted a bit, his smile still remained. "I would hope for nothing less."

"You jest."

"Not at all. I've heard your opinions slip on occasion, and I've listened with avid interest. You attempt docility, but I fear you fail horribly."

Emily couldn't decide if she should be offended or flattered. She eyed him with suspicion as they swung to the continuing strains of the waltz.

"Please believe me, I intend to compliment, not insult. I find you refreshing." He sobered, and Emily fidgeted under his perceptive regard. "I have invited your father and mother to visit my home in Savannah. Please say you'll accompany them."

"I . . . I . . ." What was the matter with her tongue? "I'm not altogether certain they'd wish to have me along. As you've noticed, I lack convention entirely."

"Well, then I shall insist. I'll simply explain to them that the invitation is withdrawn unless they are willing to take you with them."

"Oh, no, I wouldn't want—"

"Miss Birmingham, I am teasing you."

Emily tried for a smile and wondered if it appeared as weak as it felt. Why on earth was her pulse pounding? Was she afraid of him? She cast a surreptitious glance upward through her lashes and looked at his face. No, no. It wasn't fear. She flushed when she realized she was staring at him. The corner of his mouth was lifted in a slight smile, and she wondered what he was thinking.

She didn't have long to wait. "I daresay it's not often that you're flustered, Miss Birmingham."

"Flustered? I'm not flustered."

"Flummoxed, then."

"I am not in the least flummoxed."

"Not even the least bit confused?"

Emily sniffed. "Why would I be, I wonder?"

His voice dropped to a whisper as the final strains of the waltz drifted to a close. "Because I am vastly interested in pursuing you, Miss Emily. I believe you know that."

Emily stopped moving, as had he. She stood, unable to form a response, and belatedly noticed that she had yet to remove her left hand from his shoulder and release his soft grip from her right hand. She snatched her arms down and cursed the fates that had given her a fair complexion. Her face felt afire, and she didn't enjoy not holding the upper hand in the exchange.

"You do what you will, Mr. Stanhope. I don't believe I care one way or the other." She turned her back and lifted her nose into the air, gritting her teeth at the soft laughter that followed her as she made her way to the side of the ballroom. It was with intense relief a few moments later that Emily watched as Stanhope made his polite good-byes to the party's hostess and exited the room with one final, steady glance in her direction.

Her mother noticed the brief exchange as well. "What do you think of Mr. Stanhope, Emily?" Sarah asked in a mild tone as she accepted a glass of punch from a passing footman.

Emily shrugged. "A bit conceited, I believe."

Sarah laughed. "Birds of a feather."

"Pardon me, Mother?" Emily turned to Sarah with an arched brow. "Surely you don't find me guilty of conceit?"

Sarah met Emily's gaze without comment. "Did he mention to you," she finally said, "that he's invited us to Willow Lane?"

"That would be his home, I assume?"

"Yes."

Emily nodded. "He did mention it."

"It so happens that he told me he'd be delighted if you were to come along."

"Are you certain you should be leaving Bentley at a time like this, Mother?"

"A time like what?"

"War? We are at war. It won't be long before we begin to feel the sting here in the Deep South," Emily murmured in an exaggerated drawl.

Sarah's nostrils flared slightly at Emily's impertinence, but she apparently chose to ignore the tone. "Bentley is flourishing and will continue to do so. We are well placed, Emily. It would behoove you to remember it."

"Indeed. I could never forget it."

Sarah looked at Emily's face for a long time before finally averting her gaze and looking out over the crowd of dancing neighbors, friends, and climbing social acquaintances. "What is it about you, I wonder, that makes you so hateful?" The question came out as little more than a murmur, and Emily knew Sarah probably addressed herself more than anyone.

"I am not hateful, Mother. I am dissatisfied."

"Dissatisfied with what?"

"Injustice."

"Oh, posh." Sarah firmly thumped her empty glass onto a small table at her back and looked at Emily with barely disguised contempt. "I should like to see how your world would fare with the rug pulled from beneath it."

"I would relish that prospect, madam. I would make my living by the sweat of my brow if I needed to. I would survive, and I would build a life for myself." Emily took a deep breath against the confines of her tight corset and released it, wondering why she felt no pleasure at Sarah's mottled expression.

"Emily Elizabeth Birmingham!" Sarah hissed, glancing quickly about. She took a deep breath herself and gazed at Emily with a steely expression. "Your father has taken an assignment from Jefferson Davis to serve abroad. He will leave soon, and after he does, we will travel to Savannah for a stay with Mr. Stanhope. You," she said, pointing at Emily with a finger that shook, "will come along, and you will *behave* yourself. Am I clear?"

Emily held Sarah's gaze for a long moment before she finally nodded once. As Sarah moved off to find Jeffrey, Emily watched her with a sense of despair. Why was she always so compelled to goad her mother and say such unimaginable things? Why couldn't things have been different? Why couldn't Sarah have been born in Boston, or California, even? Why did fate decree that she be born a plantation mistress and become queen over everything Emily so despised?

As she watched her mother with eyes that were suspiciously moist, she felt a light touch upon her elbow. Emily turned and looked into the face of Calista Charlesworth. The blonde beauty was a nuisance and had been since they were children. Her first words, however, caught Emily's attention.

"I see you've become quite taken with that Mr. Stanhope from Atlanta. You've obviously not heard all the rumors, Emily."

"What rumors, Calista?" Emily asked, striving for patience she didn't feel. She blinked back the tears that had been threatening and attempted to focus her attention on the young woman at her side. Now that Emily had made appropriate social appearances and was, she had to admit herself, becoming quite beautiful, Calista had decided they should be friends. After receiving a lifetime of animosity from the girl, Emily found this irritating.

"There are those who say that strange things happen on his plantation."

Emily sighed. "What sorts of things? Ghosts? Goblins?"

"Disappearing slaves."

Emily's gaze sharpened. She remained silent, waiting for Calista to continue, and nearly exploded in annoyance when she realized the girl wanted her to beg for details. "Oh, out with it! What do you mean?"

"I mean that he has only a small, skeleton staff of servants, yet he constantly buys new slaves. And then nobody ever sees or hears from them again." Calista plucked a stray thread from the wrist of her delicately embroidered glove and smiled. "I overheard one of our downstairs maids telling the cook that other plantation owners use it as a threat for good behavior. If they don't see to their duties properly, the slaves will be sold to Mr. Stanhope. I told Papa it was an excellent source of inspiration for hard work."

"Calista, for heaven's sake. Are you suggesting that Mr. Stanhope practices some sort of black magic? Murders them in their slave quarters and then buries them in the cotton fields?"

"Well I don't know, Emily Birmingham, but you needn't be so flip about it! And perhaps you should watch yourself. Dancing with a murderer might not be good for one's health! They're only slaves, but one can't be too careful." Calista cast one final glare in Emily's direction and flounced away in a froth of lace.

Emily rolled her eyes and leaned back against the wall, sliding slowly behind the large fronds of a potted palm. Of all the idiocy. Austin Stanhope might be a womanizer, a gambler, and a wealthy slaveholder, but Emily was fairly certain he wasn't a murderer. She was usually an excellent judge of character, and to her knowledge, her instincts had yet to fail her. Besides which, Calista was frightfully transparent. Emily had noticed her attempts to catch Mr. Stanhope's eye, and she had failed. More likely than not she was suffering from a fit of insane jealousy. To lose the attention of a man to the likes of Emily Birmingham would undoubtedly be keeping the girl awake at night.

Emily smiled slightly in spite of herself.

She located her parents through the fronds of the palm. They stood together, chatting with various city and state officials, looking young and vibrant and beautiful. So Jeffrey was finally accepting a diplomatic mission from Davis. Emily shook her head slightly. Her father had avoided committing himself to any one thing for years. What had finally made the difference?

She would know soon enough, she supposed. They were making their way across the room, looking to the left and the right in an obvious attempt to locate her. Emily reluctantly stepped from behind the palm sanctuary and when they reached her, turned wordlessly and left the stately room with them.

* * *

7 June 1862
Shenandoah Valley, Virginia

Dear Mother and Father;

I write to you again after an intolerably long day of marching. Twenty-five miles we marched in the space of one day! Do you know that others are calling us "Jackson's foot cavalry"? I feel less valued than a horse, that much I can tell you.

The situation under "Stonewall" Jackson is unbearable. He is a religious zealot, convinced we are God's living army, which we may well be, but even still he treats us as though we were cattle! I tell you, I fear my health will fail if I am not soon transferred from under Jackson's command. I have tried to manage things myself, as I mentioned in a former letter, but I find that my contacts here are limited and people seem unusually unwilling to help me.

Father, I must insist that you speak to your influential friends on my behalf. I know they will listen to you. It is my fondest desire to serve directly under General Lee. I would then still be here in Virginia, but I would be serving under a man much more tolerable.

There are things I suppose you would be proud to know; we have stolen tons of goods from the Yanks, so many from under the nose of Union commander Nathaniel Banks that the fellows now refer to him as "Commissary Banks"! We are successful on that score, truly. According to General Lee, one of the Confederacy's best assets is that inept Union general, McClellan. We march around him with our fifty thousand, and he sits in fear with his one hundred fifty thousand! It is a proud time for Southerners, indeed. We may hold our heads high knowing the Yankee idiots cower in fear at our superiority.

On that note, I'll close. Please, Father, do your best to see me relocated.

Your son,
Richard

Richard Birmingham folded the letter and sealed it, sinking wearily back on to his haversack. He would have to post the thing in the morning and hope he had the strength to spend another day marching. To admit his weaknesses to his parents had been galling, but desperate times were calling for desperate measures. He had tried every trick he knew—some clean, most dirty—and had yet been unable to see himself transferred.

What Richard had felt as admiration for the man people called "Stonewall" had quickly turned to fear when worming his way in under Jackson's command. Richard had witnessed Jackson's stand at Manassas the year before and had been so amazed at the man's sense of control, he bribed his way into a transfer. He had lived to regret that move ever since.

Jackson was said to have admired John Brown's stoic composure at his hanging, which did little to dispel Richard's disquiet. John Brown had been a raving lunatic, and there were few in either the North or South who would argue it. What was worse, however, was the harsh disciplinary measures Jackson invoked upon his own troops. The slightest infractions or variance from his orders were harshly punished, even amounting to arrest.

As Richard sat against his pack, he heard four gunshots in rapid succession and felt his pulse quicken. He might have been a recipient of one of those shots himself. Four men in his company had elected to desert earlier in the afternoon, and listening to their brave talk, he had very nearly gone with them. Upon notification of their disappearance, Jackson had immediately dispatched scouts for their retrieval. Just before Richard began his letter home, the four bedraggled men had been forcibly hauled back into camp, and then, as his own ears had just attested, had been summarily shot.

Jackson was focused and deadly, and he didn't seem to care if he lost his own men in the process of fighting the enemy. They were traits Richard would have admired had he not found himself on the other end of the command. He had tried and failed to gain Jackson's trust; even his attempts to appear a devout Christian had not turned the commander's opinions to his favor. He kept largely to his own counsel and would not be bought by flattery.

Richard looked again at the letter he still held in his hand and hoped it would find its way to his home in South Carolina. He had begun his foray into the Confederate army with such high hopes and aspirations, and now he found himself completely spent. His only hope lay in the hands of his influential parents.

* * *

12 June 1862
Charleston, South Carolina

"Memphis has fallen," Sarah said as she met Jeffrey at the front entrance. He was on his way to a luncheon appointment, a letter held loosely in his hand.

He glanced at the newspaper she clutched and nodded. "I read it earlier."

"Jeffrey," she said, and moved imperceptibly closer to him. "I, I wonder . . ." Her voice was hushed, and it was with some effort that she kept it from trembling.

His brows knit in concern as he watched her. "Sarah? What is it?"

She took a step closer so that she was inches from his finely tailored sleeve. How easy it would be to lean on that arm. It was true she had dominated her own husband through the years in her refusal to let him stand at her side as she ran Bentley, but as much as she had continually told herself he was a weak man, she knew he possessed strength.

Sarah lifted her fingers and watched with a sense of detachment as they hovered over his arm. With a small sigh of resignation, she let her hand drop and turned her head to one side. She caught her reflection in the gilded mirror that stood over a polished, mahogany side table. The flowers in the large vase that sat on the table were beautiful and vibrant, and the woman who stared back at her from the mirror was equally as beautiful. She was quickly becoming a shell, however, and she knew it would be useless to deny the fact that she was terrified.

"Sarah." Jeffrey's voice resonated in her ear, and she caught his reflection next to hers in the glass. Such a handsome man he was—so nice to look upon, and the years hadn't changed that fact. If anything, he was more appealing to behold than ever. He touched her hand—held her fingers within his own and tugged on them lightly. "What is it?" he repeated.

"Memphis has fallen," she said, her voice barely a whisper.

He released her fingers and gathered her close. She felt stiff and awkward, and it wasn't until he rubbed a gentle hand across her back that she relaxed and leaned against him, allowing him to comfort her for the first time in all their married years. "We are safe here," he murmured into her hair, and she closed her eyes. If only she wasn't so very afraid.

"I am going to England to garner more support, and we'll be safer than ever," he continued. "Do not worry overmuch."

Sarah pulled back, suddenly embarrassed. "I shan't. I am fine."

He smiled slightly, almost sadly, and said, "I know you are. You will always be fine, Sarah Matthews."

She didn't dare ask him what he meant, so she chose instead to ask him about the letter he still held in his hand.

His expression shifted slightly. "It's nothing, really, just a note from Richard."

"Oh? What does he say?"

Jeffrey shrugged, waving the letter a bit. "Just that he's well, if not a bit tired."

Sarah narrowed her eyes. "What are you not saying?"

He sighed and handed her the letter. She read it and, more importantly, read Richard's fear in it. When she finished, she looked up at her husband. "Can you have him transferred?"

He nodded. "I'll do my best—I'll send a letter to Lee tomorrow before I leave for England."

Sarah gestured to the letter. "He sounds very . . . humbled."

Jeffrey nodded again. "He does. Perhaps his time away has been to his benefit."

"I suppose. He hasn't always been—that is to say, Richard has not always behaved with proper—"

"I know."

Sarah flushed deeply and averted her gaze. "Jeffrey," she said, her voice dropping, "I wonder if you're aware that we have a grandchild?" She glanced back in his direction and studied his face.

He suddenly looked very tired. "I gathered as much," he said. "Sarah, I blame myself. I never took the boys in hand the way my own father did with me, and Richard needed some guidance."

"I didn't allow you to." Her tone sounded brusque and very much like her usual self—even to her own ears. "There was nothing you could have done. We raised one son who set his mind to his own beliefs, absurd though they are, and he sacrificed his way of life for those beliefs. Our other son . . . he . . . he lacks honor," she finished stiffly.

Jeffrey made no reply, as clearly none was necessary. The pause was long and uncomfortable. Sarah shook her head slightly and cleared her throat. "Are you nervous, then? About your voyage to England?"

Jeffrey pulled on his riding gloves and shifted away slightly, signaling his desire to be on his way. He shook his head in response to her comment and said, "I am looking forward to the trip, actually. We need European support, and the sooner the better. I'm anxious to be off."

"And with regard to Emily—I'm taking her with me to Savannah next week. I assume Stanhope has spoken with you about his intentions?"

"He has. I've told him you and I are in full support of his intentions for Emily's hand."

"So we are in agreement, then. Good. She needs to be away from here. She reminds me of . . ."

Jeffrey nodded his agreement. "I know." He finally turned to leave, turning back as though in afterthought. "We may lose Richard," he said, looking into her eyes as though searching for her reaction.

"Yes." Heaven help her, Sarah could think of nothing further to say. Surely she must be a candidate for hell—she couldn't summon a mother's grief. Only when she thought of Richard as an infant, a small child—innocent and pure—could she feel a sense of sadness. *It won't take his death to make me feel sorrow on his behalf,* she thought to herself as she watched Jeffrey descend the front steps and mount his horse. *I have long since missed the life Richard might have led.*

* * *

The morning dawned bright and early, and Jeffrey was off. Sarah stood at her windows on the second floor and watched as Jeffrey's carriage pulled out, making its way down the tree-lined drive that led to Bentley's front door. He wasn't riding in the carriage with his trunks, however. He was seated tall and straight in the saddle atop his chestnut gelding. He turned once and looked directly at her in the window, as if he knew she was looking. Raising a hand to her in farewell, he finally turned back and continued his journey to the harbor.

He would more likely than not stay at the Charleston town home until nightfall and then attempt to get past the blockaders under cover of night. "Godspeed," she whispered, and let the curtains fall back into place over the large window. When he came home again, perhaps she would make an effort to treat him differently—to find company in his companionship. She took a deep breath and let it out again, placing a hand to her forehead for a moment in contemplation.

Shaking her head slightly, she straightened her shoulders. It was best to be about the day's business. There was always much to do.

* * *

13 June 1862
Utah Territory

It was with a certain amount of bewilderment that Earl and several of his fellow militiamen met with Deputy Marshal Robert Burton just south of Kington Fort. They had been summoned home to join with a posse to deal with an uprising in the Morrisite community north of Salt Lake, and the air seemed charged with tension.

"Most of you are familiar with Joseph Morris," Burton told the men. "He's an apostate Mormon who is claiming to be a prophet and receiving revelation for his flock."

Earl nodded. He had heard of the commune—they had moved their headquarters to Kington Fort and were attempting to live the United Order. For many of the group, it had failed miserably. They were also antipolygamy, and for many reasons had left the Saints and moved north. Morris had also, unfortunately, prophesied a specific date on which Christ would arrive. When the Savior hadn't materialized, many of Morris's followers became disillusioned.

Burton continued speaking. "The Morrisites have arrested three of their own apostates who have been trying to recover their property. Chief Justice Kinney issued a writ demanding that Morris release the three arrested men. He also authorized the arrest of Morris and some of his assistants."

Earl took a deep breath and let it out again. How ironic to become a member of the militia and encounter no trouble abroad, only to return to his own backyard for the mayhem. "Morris and his followers have refused to adhere to Chief Justice Kinney's orders, and so we are here to charge them with contempt of court."

"All of the followers?" someone near Earl asked.

"No." Burton consulted a piece of paper he had folded within his pocket. "Joseph Morris, Peter Klemgard, Richard Cook, John Parson, and John Banks. Now," he continued, "I've sent a message to Morris demanding his surrender, and we're waiting for his reply."

One of Burton's men approached him and whispered in his ear. Burton pursed his lips for a moment and then spoke to the assembled men. "Morris has gathered his followers in the open bowery and is awaiting revelation."

Earl cocked a brow but remained silent. Who was he to criticize another's odd beliefs, especially since the origins of the Church had contained much revelation and many visitations from beyond the veil? Many people thought the Mormons were nothing short of insane because of their claims of heavenly visits. As he looked toward the bowery, however, he shuddered. In Earl's opinion, Morris was waiting for a sign from the wrong source.

He heard Burton impatiently order two artillery shots to be fired in warning. Earl watched as the first went overhead, but as he watched the second shot, the blood began to roar in his ears. There was a general groan of dismay as the second shot hit the encampment. As the smoke cleared, two women and a young teenage girl lay on the ground. The women were prostrate and still; the girl moved a bit.

Earl and the rest ducked and took cover as the fire was returned. The Morrisite population didn't have artillery or impressive weapons, but they fired their guns, apparently having decided to fight to the bitter end.

* * *

Earl yawned and responded as he was shoved in the leg by someone's boot. Was it already his turn to continue bombarding the small encampment? "We're goin' in."

Earl opened one eye and squinted at Shaffer, his friend from the militia. "We're doing what?"

"We're gonna storm the fort and demand the men charged come forward." Shaffer paused for a moment and added, "Lucas and Bilford are dead."

Earl's eyes shot to the far side of their makeshift headquarters where two bodies lay covered with sheets. "Just now? How long was I asleep?"

"An hour."

Earl stood, stunned. Burton approached him then, looking weary and frustrated. "I'm taking nineteen men with me to charge the fort. I need you to stay here with the others and protect our backs."

Earl nodded quietly and tried to organize his thoughts. He had assumed, in the last three days of fighting, that the Morrisites would eventually run out of ammunition and that would be that. He never envisioned some of his own dying.

He readied his weapon as Burton and his men approached the fort. Words were exchanged, and the next movements occurred almost too quickly for Earl to follow. There was a scuffle, gunfire, and smoke obscuring the scene. "What happened?" he shouted to the other men who stood with him. *"What happened?"*

As he began to run for the fort, Shaffer, who breathlessly spat explanations, stopped him on the return. "Morris . . . said he wanted to make a speech . . . then he said he'd never surrender and turned and ran . . ." Shaffer reached for his canteen and took a swig of water, heedless of the amount that ran down his face. "Burton shot him and two women who got in the way, trying to obscure his efforts . . . John Banks is also dead . . ."

Earl's head was swimming. What bizarre turn had the whole thing taken? He turned in stunned shock as a woman came screaming out of the compound, pointing back inside. "He shot Joseph Morris in cold blood! Wouldn't even let him speak! And then he shot two of my sisters who objected to his actions!" The woman sank to the ground on her knees and sobbed.

Shaffer's eyes narrowed. "That's not true! Morris said he would never surrender, and he ran!"

Earl looked from one person to the next as they began streaming out of the compound in confused chaos. The remaining militiamen behind him ran to the fort to help Burton regain control, and Earl eventually followed at a slower pace, wondering for the life of him if he'd ever know what had just transpired.

* * *

Dear Ben,

I find myself, once again, protecting the overland mail route and telegraph wires away from home. I don't know if you've heard of the trouble with the Morrisites—probably in the big scheme of the war it's but a small bump, but in Salt Lake, it was big happenings. I was there, and even I'm not sure about the outcome of the whole mess. I remain as confused as ever.

We took roughly ninety Morrisite men to Salt Lake City for trial for murdering two posse members and for their refusal to meet due process of law. I have yet to hear of the outcome, as the trial has been set for March of next year, which is the next session of court. If you were to ask me who was at fault in the scuffle, I naturally seem to side with my fellow militiamen, but I suppose I will always doubt because I wasn't close enough to witness firsthand exactly what was said.

The thought of skirmishing about with Indians now seems relatively tame in comparison to what I've seen the last few days. I deeply regret the loss of the two posse members, and I also deeply regret that those women in the compound died. Things on the mail route remain steady, however, and because the lines are running again, I know you will eventually receive this letter, unless something untoward happens on that end.

I hope you are well and whole. When I briefly saw my mother, she made me promise I would send you her love in my next letter. We miss you terribly, and anxiously await your return home. My mother told me she regularly opens your cabin for airing and cleaning. You know how thorough she can be.

Sincerely,
Earl

CHAPTER 13

"At night I lived over the horrors of the field hospital and the amputating table. If I but closed my eyes I saw such horrible sights that I would spring from my bed. . . . Those groans were in my ears! I saw again the quivering limbs, the spouting arteries, and the pinched and ghastly faces of the sufferers."

—Belle Reynolds, housewife from Illinois and battlefield nurse

* * *

23 June 1862
Alexandria, Virginia

Anne watched the photographer, Alan Shaffer, with interest as he explained the mechanics of the small room perched atop the wagon. "Most people call this wagon the 'What Is It?' wagon. It is odd looking, I must admit. Here, the plates are prepared for photographing. We use what is called a 'wet-collodion' process. First, the plate is covered with collodion from one edge to the other. Then, the plate is immersed in silver nitrate for roughly four minutes. We then place the plate in a specialized holder that allows us to get it to the camera without being exposed to the light. Meanwhile, the subject of the photograph is already seated before the camera, which has been focused and is ready to go."

Anne glanced at Alan's camera, which was seated upon a large tripod. It was roughly the size of a big picnic basket. "So, the plate is inserted into the camera, and then the image is exposed by uncapping the lens?"

Alan nodded. “After the exposure is complete, we then carry the plate back into the darkened tent, and must develop the picture before it dries. If the plate is dry, the image is ruined.”

Anne nodded. “So how, exactly, is the picture developed?”

“The plate is bathed in a liquid solution that fixes the image into place for printing on albumen paper.”

Anne ran her fingers along the wooden box that was seated upon its tripod perch. “This is fascinating,” she said as she looked at the camera. “I’ve never taken the opportunity to learn about it. How long have you been a photographer?”

Alan glanced with obvious pride at the camera. “I’ve been employed by Matthew Brady for nearly eight years now. I’ve enjoyed every minute. He has teams of two all over the Union army—his goal is to create a photographic history of this conflict.”

Anne smiled. “He’s no longer content to photograph merely the rich and famous?”

Alan chuckled. “Apparently not.”

“So where is the other half of your team?”

“He went home to Kentucky—he’s suffered from dysentery now for weeks, something fierce. I’m still waiting for word from Brady as to when I’ll receive a replacement.”

“In the meantime, would you mind terribly if I observe your work every now and again?”

“It’d be my pleasure. Feel free to observe anytime you’d like.”

“I’d enjoy that very much, thank you.” Anne felt her heart race at the prospect of learning something new. What a joy it would be to actually own such amazing equipment! She only wished there was a way to transmit the images over the telegraph wires with her articles. Wouldn’t Jacob be thrilled to receive pictures with the written copy? “Will you show me your development area?” she asked.

“Right this way.” Alan lifted one side of the dark fabric that formed a tent over the plate-developing equipment, and she watched in fascination as he showed her the chemicals used to treat the plates, demonstrating the process as he talked. “Of course, this must be done with the use of an amber light so as not to ruin the image.”

“Amazing,” Anne murmured. She caught Alan looking at her with an expression of amusement.

"You look just like I felt when I first experienced this process," he said. "For the person with an eye for detail and a sense of capturing history, this is a very enjoyable pursuit."

"I'm sure it is. I appreciate your time, very much."

"You know," Alan said, rubbing his finger along his chin. "I've heard rumors about Confederate troop movements in these parts. I may travel with my equipment should any battles occur within this general vicinity. Perhaps you'd like to join me? We could form a team, of sorts—thereby we should be able to travel a bit as journalists."

"I would love to! If I can get permission as well, that is."

"Leave it to me, young man." He smiled. "Yes indeed, you remind me of myself."

Anne turned back in the direction of her own tent, which was situated across a sea of similar tents that lined the field in neat rows. It was a city unto itself. She passed a group of men who had stripped to their trousers and were playing at pugilism as a means of distraction. She smiled at the revelers who had placed money on one fighter or another and wondered who would find himself the victor.

* * *

26 June 1862
Near Oak Grove, Virginia

Richard sat just beyond the walls of General Stonewall Jackson's tent, straining to overhear the man's conversation with his officers.

"Sir," a man was saying, "we have a message here from General Hill. He'll attack McClellan's soldiers around Oak Grove without us. In my best estimation, this is not the time to bivouac. We should be on the move if we are to attack with General Hill."

"If Hill attacks alone," a gruff voice answered in return, "it will be without Lee's orders. We stay here."

Richard faded quickly into the shadows as the men within the tent slowly made their way outside. He was far enough away to avoid detection, but close enough to hear comments made in muted tones.

"Oak Grove was a bloody mess, I hear tell. They used canister shot—made a mess of our boys something fierce. If we don't move now, tomorrow will be certain death for Hill's men."

"You heard the general. Hill shouldn't attack without Lee's orders."

"But Lee intends for us to be there as well! We are to attack together, and—"

"Enough. We don't question the general. If he says we stay, we stay until he decides to move."

As the voices faded, Richard sank back against the trunk of a tree and closed his eyes. If only Jackson would move forward and join with the other regiments, he might just have a chance to force some kind of transfer! Richard shook his head, feeling the bite of the bark at the slight movement. His biggest mistake had been leaving the Palmetto Guard in the first place.

Had it been a whole year already? Yes, almost to the day. It had been Richard's first taste of Yankee blood, and he had reveled in it. Now, however, he was interested only in his own welfare. Marching under Jackson was intolerable. The general consistently denied requests for furlough, worked them like dogs, and treated them like a humorless Sunday school preacher. He quoted scripture and handed out Bible tracts as if tomorrow signaled the end of time. Richard figured he could have put up with all of the religious nonsense if only the man were even marginally reasonable. He was a fanatic, however, driven and ruthless.

Richard thought back to his days with the Palmetto Guard and cursed his own stupidity. Those had been times when he had been the one to wield influence. He had spread lies and half-truths about some who had decided to take a disliking to him, and much to his delight, the internal strife had been to his advantage. He had thrown just enough doubt and question upon the characters of his enemies to tarnish their names and their futures.

He should have stayed where he had ruled. Instead, his admiration of Jackson's power had placed him in a position much to his own disliking. As he stared into the dark, night sky, he wondered if his letter had reached his father, and if so, how long it would be before he heard a response.

* * *

17 June 1862
Gaines Mill, Virginia

"Who is it in reference to?" General Robert E. Lee's staff officer looked at the telegram in annoyance. A collection of the staff officers convened in a large tent a few miles away from severe carnage as they scrambled to communicate.

"It refers to a letter written to General Lee by Jeffrey Birmingham of Charleston. His son is requesting a transfer." A young corporal who had just skirted the battle site stood before the officer, pale with shock.

"Now? You bring this to me now?"

"General Lee is aware of the request, and asked that someone here take care of the details, sir."

"Fine." The officer dismissed the issue with a wave of his hand. "Sergeant Mosby should be near my tent. Have him see to this."

The young boy saluted and backed away, barely registering the conversation that floated around him.

". . . Who is Jackson that he feels he can just show up to battle when the mood moves him? If he had been on time, Porter wouldn't have been reinforced!"

". . . Yes, but we did beat those blue-bellies back into a good retreat! Have you seen the battleground?"

". . . never seen such carnage in all my days . . ."

* * *

2 July 1862
Oak Grove, Virginia

"A good seven days' worth of battles," Anne said to Alan Shaffer as they made their way across the terrain on the photographer's wagon, pulled by two horses. She retrieved a folded map of the area from her pocket and showed her traveling companion. Tracing a line with her finger, she said, "Word is they started here at Oak Grove.

McClellan beat back Lee, and the Union troops took positions around Oak Grove. The next day, Confederate General Hill attacked on his own, without reinforcements, and was beaten back, but for some insane reason, McClellan ordered the troops to withdraw to one of the new supply bases on the James River."

Alan shook his head. "Farther away from Richmond. So much for his glorious campaign to take the Confederate capital."

Anne nodded. "Then Lee pursued the Union into Gaines Mill, but supposedly old Jackson was late with his arrival and our men had time to reinforce and regroup. It only held for a short time, though. We retreated to the James River. On the thirtieth, Lee again pushed our men back from Savage's Station, but a bad thunderstorm halted further defeat and, they say, saved the day for the Union."

Alan glanced at Anne. "How is it that you know all this, young Johnson?"

"I've been intercepting messages over the telegraph lines with my tools." Anne smiled and withdrew a small, metal box from the pocket of her overcoat.

Alan shook his head. "You are a resourceful lad."

"Thank you."

"Continue."

Anne inclined her head with a grin. "At your service. Following the retreat from Savage's Station, McClellan attempted to protect supply trains that were on the James River near Frayser's Farm. Lee pushed us back, but it was costlier this time for the rebels. After this, McClellan ordered a retreat to Malvern Hill, which is a high ridge along the banks of the James River." Anne gestured along the map with a finger that was smudged with dirt. She frowned and absently wiped at the dirt with her other hand, still holding the map and gesturing as she talked.

"Malvern Hill was an advantageous position because McClellan's men couldn't be flanked. Our men stood their cannons side by side and blew the rebels back down the hill each time they advanced. This would have been yesterday," Anne said, reaching for her small notebook. "Yes," she nodded, checking her notes. "Yesterday. And word has it that McClellan's advisors wanted him to pursue Lee, but he refused."

"Crazy little man! He had 'em on the run! Can't imagine Lincoln will keep him much longer. He doesn't fight! And all that talk of taking Richmond is nothing but so much dust now. We're farther away a week later than we were when we started."

Anne nodded and folded her map. "I do believe we're seeing the end of McClellan's vaunted 'Peninsular Campaign.'"

"Did you happen to intercept any casualty numbers?"

Anne took a deep breath. "Well, they may be largely inconclusive at this point, but when I checked this morning, there were roughly sixteen thousand Union dead or wounded and twenty thousand rebels dead or wounded."

Alan looked at her, his jaw slightly slack. He couldn't seem to find the words to express his thoughts, and his gaze again found its way to the road ahead, where the horses plodded along carefully. "You do know, young Aaron," he finally said, "that we may see some unpleasantness in the next day or two."

Anne nodded. They had been on the road since early that morning, having secured permission from their commanding officers to travel to the battle sites for photographic and journalistic purposes. The Ohio 7th had set up camp in Alexandria, with no immediate plans for movement.

"I'll be fine," she said.

Alan glanced at her again. "Good," he said with a nod. "I'll admit I'm not much looking forward to this myself."

* * *

"We could have had those bloody Yanks finished! Do you realize that because of your ineptitude, whereas we could have won this war and sent the boys in blue crying home to their mamas, we instead find ourselves with massive losses and little to show for it?"

Richard listened in fascination as one of General Lee's top aides soundly berated the senior staff officers. He sat in the back of a room in an abandoned church house near one of the sites where the Confederate troops were caring for their wounded and attempting to regroup. His transfer out of Jackson's regiment was complete, and he was intensely relieved. The happiest moment he could remember in ages had come only two days before when, upon his arrival to his new regiment under Lee's command, Sergeant Mosby had told him that he needed a new assistant. Richard pledged his undying devotion, and Mosby had since allowed him to be privy to meetings with staff officers close to the general.

"I say we accomplished our objective," one man close to the back of the room muttered to his companion. "McClellan isn't knocking at Richmond's door any longer."

Any reply was lost to Richard's ears as the meeting broke and men shuffled out the door. Mosby turned to Richard and motioned for him to follow.

"I don't understand all the fuss," Richard said to Mosby in an undertone. "Seems to me that fellow was right. We pushed McClellan back miles."

Mosby glanced at Richard in amusement. "We lost more men than we could afford to lose," he said, and Richard flushed. "Besides," Mosby added, "the point made here tonight was directed at staff officers and their field counterparts. Lee develops elaborate battle plans that would work quite well if communications between the staff and field people were more effective. We should have beaten McClellan's men soundly instead of merely driving them back."

Richard nodded, absorbing the information and filing it away for later use. He was beginning to feel like his old self again, and it filled him with a sense of unshakable confidence. Now that he was amongst people who were willing to treat him like the son of wealth that he was, there was hope.

Never again would he believe his father was good for little, if not nothing. Jeffrey had friends in high places, and Richard was finding that to be as valuable as the family money itself.

* * *

3 July 1862
Savage's Station, Virginia

"Boyd, are you sure you don't want to send something to your other sister as well?" Anne folded the paper on which she had written a letter and smiled at the soldier who lay on the cot. His pale face was marred with scratches and bruises, and his left leg was missing from the knee down.

"I don't think so," he said. "I'm not sure what I'd say to her that I haven't said in that letter. They get together often, the two of 'em, so I'm sure Betsy will share hers with Catherine."

"Well, I think you've been very brave. It must have been hard to stay here in the field hospital while the rest of the army retreated."

His smile was weak. "It's not as though I had a choice. I couldn't very well get up and run."

"You will soon enough, I'm sure."

"You seem awfully young, soldier. Why aren't you home with your ma and pa?"

Anne cleared her throat. For a moment, she had forgotten she was supposed to be a boy. She had very nearly reached out and touched the soldier's forehead, much as her own mother would have had she been there. "I wanted to get me some rebs," she said. It was her tried and true response. She offered it whenever others asked her why such a young boy would enlist.

Boyd shook his head, his voice dropping to a whisper. "Ya shoulda stayed home. I'll tell ya, I ain't never seen such awful bloodshed my whole life. I ain't even sure this is all worth it! Lincoln thinks this country should stay together? I say let 'em leave! They don't want to be part of the United States—I don't see what good forcing 'em to's gonna do."

The boy's lip trembled, and he bit it between his teeth, turning his head away. Anne fought the sting in her own eyes, and barely managed to keep her composure. The task grew even more difficult with young Boyd's next pronouncement.

"There's no way Emma'll want me now."

"Sure she will!"

Boyd turned his face back to Anne. "What woman wants half a man?"

"You're suddenly half a man now because you're missing part of one leg?" Even to her own ears, Anne could hear her resemblance to her no-nonsense mother. "I'll tell you what kind of woman wants a man like you. A good woman, that's who. So if your Emma is a good woman, she'll welcome you home with open arms, proud of your service to your country. You can go home with your head held high."

Boyd nodded, but Anne wasn't sure he believed a word she said. She had half a mind to get Emma's address and write her a stern letter. She looked around her for a moment at the sea of wounded men. Twenty-five hundred soldiers had been left behind in a field hospital with the Union army retreat from Savage's Station. She and Alan had come upon the scene the day before and had stayed to help in any way they could.

They probably all had "Emmas" at home waiting for them, and Anne wondered how these men would be received. The scale of gore she had witnessed in the last twenty-four hours was incomprehensible. Alan had photographed dead bodies lying in ditches and along roadsides. She had pulled her notebook and pen from her pocket more times than she could count only to hold them listlessly while she looked at the carnage, which seemed to spread in all directions.

She left Boyd with a comment that she would return to check on him later and wandered in the waning light of the day until she found Alan. He was just outside the tent where he developed the photographs, looking as exhausted as she felt. "Have you seen enough?" he asked her as he ran a hand through his dusty, disheveled hair. At her nod, he said, "So have I. Perhaps we should return to Alexandria tomorrow."

She nodded again. "Can I be so bold as to borrow your camera for a moment?" she asked.

"Certainly. Is there any way the subject can be brought over here, though?"

"I don't think he should be moved at the moment."

"I'll help you carry the equipment, then."

"Thank you. There's a soldier I'd like to get a photograph of. Just as a memory." She shrugged, not even sure why she felt compelled to take a picture of Boyd.

Alan nodded and, after giving the camera a cursory examination, helped her carry it and its tripod to Boyd's side.

"Do you mind?" Anne asked Boyd, indicating with the camera.

"What on earth for?"

Alan leaned to whisper in her ear. "You get the camera situated. I have a few plates prepared already—I'll go get one."

She nodded and then turned back to Boyd. "You have a friendly face. I'd like to remember it."

"Soldier, you are one odd duck."

"If you only knew how odd." She gave him a genuine smile that faltered a bit as he suddenly focused in on her face as though making a discovery. His eyes narrowed a bit, but then he shook his head as if to disabuse himself of an impossible notion. She could read his thoughts in his expression, and she quickly prepped the camera on its tripod, viewing him through the lens and preparing to take what she hoped would be a good shot of his face.

It was to Anne's advantage that he was weary; he had no trouble holding himself still while the image was exposed onto the plate. When she finished, she thanked him and offered her hand. "Take care of yourself, Boyd," she said, pitching her voice a notch lower than usual and hoping it wasn't noticeable.

"You as well," he responded, his brows drawn in confusion. "Thank you for your help with the letter. You'll post it tomorrow?"

"I will. Good luck to you." Her eyes misted again as she walked away from the young man, hoping with all her might that he would have a good life upon his return home. It was the most any of them could hope for, really; Anne knew the moaning and crying of the wounded would haunt her nights for a long time to come.

CHAPTER 14

"I can't spare this man. He fights."
—Abraham Lincoln in response to public criticism of General Grant

* * *

17 July 1862
Charleston, South Carolina

Ben felt almost guilty for sneaking back again to watch Mary. Almost. It was the fourth time in eight days that he had taken a few moments from his precious free time in camp to hide in Bentley's small forest. Mary was becoming a regular visitor to the tree house; he could count on her arrival there like clockwork. He wondered what she thought as she sat there, stealing some quiet minutes for herself. He knew what a precious commodity those moments were. Unless things had changed in the years since he'd been away, she undoubtedly wasn't afforded many.

She was so beautiful it stole his breath. Her hair was always pulled back into its simple bun, and she never wore anything other than her plain brown dress and worn pinafore, but her skin was flawless—smooth and a shade darker than his own. In reality, his skin was much the same tone as hers with the amount of time he'd been in the sun lately.

How ironic.

Ben felt the familiar temper flare, and clenched his teeth to keep from cursing aloud. The same old injustice he'd long felt on those grounds was still there. It seeped into his bones from the very earth on which he stood. He wanted to scoop Mary into his arms and take her far away, where she could live a life of her own choosing. If the country were still united, in fact, he'd now have a legal right to do so. Congress had just passed the Second Confiscation Act, which freed the slaves of all rebels. Of course, the Confederacy was not wont to follow the rules of the United States. So, if Ben valued Mary's life, he'd best leave her where she sat.

He sighed aloud, and, much to his horror, watched as Mary turned her head toward him in alarm.

She rose quickly and moved toward him, and as he rose to run, he tripped over a protruding log and fell headlong onto the ground. His blue uniform alerted his senses as he scrambled to right himself—had he been wearing gray, he might not be cause for alarm. As it was, all his efforts were in vain; he tripped again and this time, Mary caught up with him.

He slowly turned his head up to face her, and managed a weak smile at her expression. She stood rooted to the spot and watched him with eyes as large as saucers. She opened and closed her mouth several times, but all that came out was an inconsequential squeak.

Ben stood, dusting his pants and arms as he did so, wishing for all the world he didn't feel so vulnerable. He reached to tip his hat to her only to find it had fallen from his head—probably the first time he had tripped. He dropped his hands to his sides with a small shrug and whispered, "Hello, Mary."

* * *

Mary felt her knees buckle, and she dropped to the ground, never once taking her eyes off Ben. Fate was a cruel, cruel thing, for it had endowed Ben with even more handsomeness and appeal than he had possessed as a young man. And here he was, in the flesh, and all she could do was fall to the ground in a near faint.

To his credit, he moved quickly as she sank, holding her arms and kneeling on the ground next to her while she tried to catch her breath. It was absolutely impossible that Ben was here. He was supposed to be thousands of miles away in the West. Yet here he was, wearing Union blue . . .

Union blue—suddenly it didn't seem so impossible. In fact, if the Ben she knew were to ever don a uniform, it would undoubtedly be Union blue. She barely registered the words he was saying.

". . . enlisted with a Massachusetts cavalry regiment . . . I'm stationed on Hilton Head but have been camping the past two weeks near Folly Beach . . . just wanted to see . . ."

"Oh, Ben," she moaned. "You've finally come home."

Ben gathered her limp form into his arms, and they sat on the ground together, neither saying a word for several long moments. When Ben finally drew back, he looked at her face with something like regret. "Well," he murmured, "I'm not exactly home."

Mary closed her eyes. "No. I suppose not." When she opened them, she very nearly expected to find him gone. Yet there he was, sitting beside her, still holding her hand like a dream come true. But her dreams could never come true, and the reality of it stung so much her eyes filled with hot tears.

"Mary," he said, and wiped away a tear that fell down her cheek, "don't cry. You'll break my heart if you cry. I left you a young girl, and now you're a beautiful young woman and you're breaking my heart."

"You . . . you have no idea," she said as the tears began to fall in earnest. She quickly looked around them to be sure they were alone. "It's been so hard for us these years. You wouldn't even recognize Emily. Oh Ben, she's so confused. And she hurts all the time . . . she's just like you, you see, and she doesn't get on well with your folks, and . . ."

"Shhh," he said, wiping away another tear and cradling her face in his palm. It hurt her so much for him to touch her so, knowing he did it out of a sense of brotherly kindness.

"I will take care of things somehow, Mary. I don't know how yet, but you must trust me. I couldn't before, but so many things have changed now—the future is bright with possibility."

She couldn't help but laugh. "Ben, men are dying by the thousands, and if the Confederacy succeeds—" she caught herself on a sob, "then my life will continue year upon year the same, and Emily will never be happy, and Ruth will die an old woman here, and Rose—"

Ben shook his head and shushed her again, pulling her close for another brief embrace. He rubbed his hand softly along her back and whispered in her ear, "I will take care of you."

She almost believed him. But she knew it could never be—that he would have to leave, and if she were ever to have any kind of life that didn't involve unpaid servitude to another, it would be up to her to find it. When he released her, she tried to smile. "Emily will never believe you're here."

"I don't know that she would want to see me," he said.

"Yes, she certainly would! She has missed you so—you have no idea." Mary anticipated telling Emily that her brother was close enough to touch, but then felt the sting of disappointment. "She's in Savannah."

"Savannah? Why?"

"Because your parents fancy her married to Austin Stanhope. He has a plantation there, and he's extremely interested in courting Emily."

Ben nodded, unable to hide his disappointment. She could see it in his face. He shrugged and said, "Perhaps we'll be here long enough for me to see her when she returns. Is Clara gone as well, then?"

"Yes. Rose went with them, too."

"Why didn't you?"

"Mama Ruth needs my help. She's not been feeling well lately."

"I'd like to see her, too," Ben said. "But my time today is spent. I'll visit again in three days, exactly this hour. Is there any way you can meet me here? Possibly Ruth, as well?"

She would meet him again or die trying. "Yes, absolutely. And Emily should be home within the month. I hope she'll return in time."

"I do, too." Ben stood and offered his hand to Mary. She marveled at his good heart. He had always treated her well. With Ben, she had never felt like a slave. He embraced her one last time and placed a soft kiss upon the back of her hand. "Three days," he whispered, and then he was gone.

* * *

Ben lay in his bedroll that night, his heart pounding each time he remembered his encounter earlier in the day. Luke had been ecstatic that Ben had been able to talk to one of his loved ones; he had maintained all along that Ben should try to see his family and friends regardless of the bad feelings his parents still harbored.

Ben couldn't believe that after five, no *six*, long years now, he had actually been able to talk face-to-face with someone from Bentley. And a beautiful someone she had become, too, he thought as his heart flipped again. Mary had grown into womanhood in a most becoming way, and Ben wished with all his heart that she had beautiful clothes to dress up in and parties to attend.

Somehow he'd finish what he'd started all those years ago! He'd get them all away from Bentley and into lives of their own if it killed him. Mary, Ruth, Rose, Joshua . . . Joshua! He'd been so besotted with the grown-up version of the little girl he'd left behind that he hadn't even thought to ask her about Joshua! Surely he was still at Bentley or Ben would have heard otherwise. Wouldn't he? It had been ages since he and Emily had corresponded, and for all he knew, Joshua had been sold or traded.

His heart ached at the thought of his friend. He and Joshua had been closer than friends. He regarded Joshua with more love and compassion than he did his own brother, Richard. It was sad, really. He didn't even think to ask after Richard's welfare.

It was Joshua he wanted to see, and if Ben wasn't certain he'd be arrested for desertion, he'd mount his horse that very moment and ride for Bentley. *Ah, well,* he thought as he drifted off to sleep, *I'll try to see him next time . . .*

* * *

19 July 1862
Savannah, Georgia

Emily tried not to be impressed as she sat on a swinging chair beneath the shade of a giant weeping willow. The air was surprisingly cool in the shade, especially in the midst of a hot Savannah summer. Thankfully, the breeze off the Atlantic traversed the city and swept across Austin Stanhope's beautiful plantation lands of Willow Lane. The property was even more beautiful than Bentley, and although Emily hated her home, she had never once denied the beauty of it.

She closed her eyes as the breeze drifted across her face and took a deep sigh. She knew well that Stanhope was interested in seeking her hand in marriage—he had said as much to her mother the night before. Sarah was enthused—even young Clara's eyes had sparkled when Austin made a special effort to learn some signs so that he might communicate with her.

It seemed the only person opposed to a marriage between Emily and Austin was Emily herself. He was a very nice man, handsome and attentive, if a bit arrogant, and had generously opened his home to her family, but Emily felt a pang of pain that was becoming altogether too familiar when she envisioned herself in the arms of anyone but Joshua. How scandalized her parents would be if they knew—horrified, even.

She reluctantly opened her eyes and drew her lower lip between her teeth. Things were not going at all according to her plans. She was supposed to be spying for the Union—gathering valuable information from the Confederacy elite with whom her father associated and passing it along to the Yankees. So far, all she had managed to do was bring herself to the brink of betrothal.

She spied a slave woman who carried a basket of baked goods from the cookhouse and was making her way across the lawn to the mansion. Emily drew her brows together in confusion as she tried to recall the nonsense Calista had spewed forth the night she had seen Emily dancing two waltzes with Stanhope. Something about disappearing slaves? It had all seemed utter idiocy at the time, but now, sitting in the shade of the man's own trees, Emily had to wonder if Stanhope was involved in something strange.

Disappearing slaves . . . disappearing slaves . . . could it be? Was there a possibility, no matter how remote, that Willow Lane acted as a station for the Underground Railroad? It seemed too outlandish to even be real. What plantation owner in his right mind helped slaves escape?

As though her very thoughts made the man himself materialize, Stanhope approached from the house, and Emily observed his even stride as he approached the swing, where she still moved slightly with the breeze. She made no attempt to hide her curiosity as he walked to her and asked if he might take a seat next to the swing. Emily inclined her head without comment and continued to study his face, as if she might find the answers hidden there.

"Miss Emily," he said as he made himself comfortable on the beautiful, wrought-iron bench, "I trust you're enjoying your stay?"

"I am. Thank you for your hospitality."

"Now what a perfectly prosaic thing to say."

Emily stared. "I beg your pardon?"

"I expected something a little more unusual."

"What on earth should one say? 'My stay, Mr. Stanhope, has been one of complete and utter charm and excitement!' Is that what you expected?"

He smiled, unruffled by her tone. "I've come to hope that your lack of convention will keep me entertained. I'm rarely disappointed."

She sniffed. "I've behaved with the utmost decorum on this visit."

"Indeed you have. I suppose I was hoping for something a bit reckless."

"Really?" Emily arched a brow. "Then perhaps you've come to the wrong person."

"Oh, no. I think I've come to exactly the *right* person. Emily," he said, then leaned forward, propping his elbows on his knees. He steepled his fingers together and examined them, for once seeming to lose a bit of his unshakable calm. "I spoke to your father last time I was in Charleston about you and his hopes for your future."

Emily watched him but made no move to reply at his pause. The wind blew a curl across her cheek, and she pulled it away with one finger. He looked at her, his gaze roving over her face as if trying to read her thoughts. She was determined that he not see them.

He cleared his throat and again looked down at his hands. "He indicated to me that he would not be averse to a possible union between you and me."

Emily looked to her right, across the vast lawn and plantation buildings, and took a deep breath. He had said the words, had finally come to the point she knew he had been trying to make for weeks, and now she would be forced to respond in some way. He was a kind man, and for some reason she couldn't begin to fathom, she didn't want to hurt him.

"I will not be the mistress of a plantation, Mr. Stanhope."

"Please, won't you call me by my given name? I've given you leave to do so now for days."

"Fine. Austin, I refuse to own other people. I refuse to be married to a man who owns other people. You've said on more than one occasion that you admire my lack of convention, and in fact, you encourage it. I'm sure I've now shocked you beyond all comprehension." She still looked out over the land, finding she didn't want to see the look of distaste that surely would cover his features. "Well, now you can see that we are as mismatched as two people ever were. A 'union,' as you call it, between the two of us would be impossible. I doubt I shall ever marry. I don't believe there's a man alive who would find my way of thinking appealing."

"On the contrary."

Emily started in surprise when Austin moved from his perch on the chair to sit next to her in the large swing. It moved as he sat, and the sudden swoosh took her breath. He planted his feet on the ground and slowed the movement of the swing, bringing it back to its former gentle motion.

He made no move to take her hand, but his shoulder was nestled against hers, and his thigh brushed up against her skirts. She looked down at the contrast between his black, tailored pants and the frothy spill of her pale pink dress. When he spoke again, his voice was hushed. "Why do you think I initially made my trip to Charleston all those weeks ago, Emily?"

She stared at him, discomfited by his close proximity and thrilled at the same time. "I'm sure I have no idea."

"I went to find you." He looked at her, gauging her reaction.

"I'm confused," she admitted, wishing he would back up just a little bit.

She breathed an inaudible sigh of relief when he turned his attention from her face and looked out toward the vast, green lawn and profusion of flowering plants instead. "Word gets around, from plantation to plantation. I'm sure you're aware of this."

"Yes."

"I've been hearing for nearly a year now about Jeffrey Birmingham's unconventional family. About how his wife is the one who takes business matters in hand and is the actual owner of Bentley. About how his oldest son left home after a failed attempt to free some of the family's slaves. And most of all, about how his redheaded spitfire of a daughter is sure to never land herself a husband because of her unconventional, bluestocking approach to life and her uncommon habit of spending entirely too much time in the company of the family slaves. In fact, there have been whispers, horrified of course, that the redhead may be altogether too much like the oldest son."

Emily's heart thudded in her chest. She had known that there were never secrets amongst high society—but such details about her own life, reaching the shores of Savannah, Georgia? She felt herself clenching her teeth together in an angry defense. He must have sensed it because he held up a hand to forestall a retort.

"It is those things that prodded me to search you out."

She shook her head in confusion. "But why?"

"Because of what I do."

Ah ha! Triumph! He *was* an Underground Railroad stationmaster! "And you hide slaves," she said.

"No."

She glanced at him in surprise. "No?"

His voice dropped to a whisper, and he took her hand, lacing her fingers within his own. She should have been upset at the assumption, but oddly enough wasn't. "I buy them and send them north."

"You send them north? To be slaves in the Union?" Her voice rose against her own will.

"Emily, you surprise me. No, not to be slaves. I give them their papers. I free them."

"Wh . . . why? Why would you do that? This plantation has been in your family for years—it's not as though you're a Bostonian abolitionist masquerading as a Southerner!"

"You're not a Northerner, either, Miz Birmingham," he drawled. "And yet you're an abolitionist if ever there was one. And so am I."

Emily looked away from his face, sitting in stunned silence, her fingers still interlaced with his. It was impossible. It was unthinkable. He bought slaves only to set them free? But Willow Lane was a fully functioning plantation. How on earth did he fund his efforts, and who worked the fields?

When she asked him about it, he smiled. "Every Negro person you see here is a freed man or woman. They know of my efforts, and at risk to their own safety, they stay here and work the plantation with me. I pay them for their work, and they have the understanding that once the war is over, if the Union should prove victorious, they can leave and go wherever they wish with no ill will on my part."

"And if the Confederacy wins?"

He winced. "They can still stay, if they choose, but if they'd rather, I'll happily send them north. It just won't be . . . well, I feel it won't be pleasant for the Negro population if the Confederacy wins this war. I believe the backlash will be tremendous."

Emily's mind swirled with thoughts to which she could barely put a voice. "Why come looking for me, though?"

"I'd like to marry," he said. "I'd like to have children. Obviously I need a woman who won't be averse to my 'occupation.' On her deathbed, my mother swore she'd rally the children she wanted as her grandchildren and send them down to me, and so I'd better be quick about finding myself a good woman."

Emily's eyes widened fractionally in dubious disbelief. "And you chose me?"

He laughed then, and gave her fingers a bit of a squeeze. "I chose you. When I heard the rumors, I knew I had to see you for myself. And once I did . . ." His voice dropped to a whisper and Emily felt his eyes on her face. She flushed. "Once I did, I knew I was lost."

Emily turned to him in confusion. She already loved one man. How on earth could her heart be flipping and tripping over yet another? "I don't know what to do," she admitted softly.

"Marry me."

"I don't know you, and I . . . I . . ."

He cupped her face in his hand and touched his lips softly to hers. It was the briefest of contact, much like the breeze that had been blowing across her skin all afternoon. He drew back and she opened her eyes—she hadn't even realized she'd closed them. "Marry me, and together we can do much good. We're of a like mind, Emily, and we can make a difference for people."

Emily's mind flashed to Mary, Ruth, Rose, and Joshua. *Oh, Joshua.* Her eyes filled with hot tears, and she gritted her teeth in anger as they fell from her eyes. To kiss another man seemed the ultimate betrayal. She was betraying her heart. And yet, if she married Austin, and could convince Sarah to let Mary and the rest come with her to live at Willow Lane, she could finally, *finally* see them to freedom. It had been her aim all along. Her dreams were within her grasp, and yet she hadn't ever realized that she would have to sacrifice her heart to achieve them.

What were her other options, though? It wasn't as if she could marry Joshua as it was, and now she finally had a chance to offer him his freedom. Was there even any choice?

Her tears fell in earnest as she nodded and whispered, "I'll marry you, Stanhope. I think it only fair to tell you, though, that for many years my heart has belonged to another. Another that I can never have."

He gave her a pained smile. "I'm besotted enough with you, Emily, that I'm afraid I have no pride. I'll take you any way you'll have me, and I hope that eventually you'll find room in your heart for me as well."

She made an effort to smile through her tears but succeeded only in the loosest of terms. "I'm making room already," she admitted on a quiet sob. "I think that's what makes me feel so wretched."

He wiped away a tear with his fingertip and she closed her eyes. He kissed her eyelids one by one and then placed another gentle kiss on her lips. "I can't say I regret that, but I do promise to try to make you happy. Let me make you happy, Emily."

She caught her breath again and looked down onto the fabric of his fine, snowy-white shirtfront. She nodded miserably, knowing that if she allowed it, he undoubtedly *would* make her happy, and she wasn't sure how she would live with the guilt.

"There are some slaves," she said, sniffing, "that I would give my life to see living free. If I can persuade my mother to agree, will you . . ."

He nodded. "In a heartbeat. I'll buy them from her, if she'll let me, and then they can live and work here or go up north—whichever they choose. Will you be at peace, then?"

"I'll be a step closer, I believe. Thank you." She suddenly felt very awkward.

"I have only one request of you now."

"Oh?"

"I insist you stop calling me 'Stanhope.' Please, *please* call me 'Austin.'"

She laughed in spite of herself. Very gently, he placed an arm about her and guided her head to rest against his shoulder. They sat, slowly swinging in the chair as the breeze grew cooler still with the setting of the sun.

CHAPTER 15

"Please proceed with all dispatch to Bermuda in pursuit of the rebel steamer, Nashville, *which vessel on Saturday last ran the blockade from Charleston."*

—U.S. naval communication in reference to one of the first Confederate raiders

* * *

24 July 1862
New Orleans, Louisiana

Daniel was beginning to feel much like a common criminal. Once a week, sometimes twice, he was allowed shore leave from the *Kennebec,* and each time, he somehow found his way to the street where Marie Brissot lived. He was becoming familiar with her comings and goings. He knew the sound of her step upon the street and the elusive scent of her perfume as he sometimes followed her at a discreet distance when she went into town.

He told himself that he was just curious about her, but in truth, he feared for her safety. Ever since the Union had taken control of New Orleans, the citizens had adjusted to the shock with mayhem, hostility, and looting of their own. It didn't help matters at all that the man the citizens called "The Beast," Benjamin Butler, was making the transition so, well, beastly for the citizens.

In May, shortly after Farragut had steamed his way into history, Major General Benjamin Butler had issued an order stating that because the women of New Orleans had treated the invading soldiers with insult and contempt (one woman going so far as to dump the contents of a chamber pot on the head of Flag Officer Farragut), that if they were to further insult or degrade them, they would then be "regarded and held liable to be treated as a woman of the town plying her avocation."

Daniel had read Order Number 28 with disbelief. It was true that the reception of the New Orleans citizenry had been less than cordial, but it could hardly be faulted. Did Butler assume the Confederacy would welcome the invaders from the North with open arms? Daniel was inclined to agree with the folks of Louisiana when it came to the major general.

He drew his thoughts to the present and melted back into the shadows of the full trees and shrubbery across the street as the front door to Marie's home opened and she stepped out onto the porch. She held a basket over one arm, and because she was leaving from the front entrance, Daniel observed, she was obviously traveling into the city on foot.

He frowned. She often did that, and it worried him. What was she thinking, walking? It wouldn't be a problem except that she often left in late afternoon, as it was now, and she then returned to the house when it was dark. He didn't mind so much when she took her horse and carriage—at least then she was afforded a measure of safety, but he couldn't for the life of him figure why she ever chose to go on foot.

He followed her at a discreet pace and wondered when he would finally summon the courage to introduce himself to her. He had long since abandoned the notion that she considered herself above him in station. That notion had been an instantaneous and defensive reaction to her request that they not meet; he had automatically assumed it meant that she didn't think he was good enough to be acquainted with her in the flesh. As he had given the matter consideration, however, while following her all over New Orleans the past weeks, he realized that such a superior attitude on her part flew completely in the face of the personality he'd come to know through her letters. He knew her to be kind and intelligent, compassionate and humorous from his correspondence with her, and observing her interactions with New Orleans's less fortunate citizens confirmed what he had believed of her from the start. It couldn't possibly be him she was uncomfortable with.

That left only *her*, and he was confused as to why. Why wouldn't she want him to meet her? As far as he was concerned, she was darn near perfection! It didn't make sense, and as he saw how hard she worked all day in that little school of hers, and then making numerous trips to the market throughout the week buying more food and supplies than she'd ever consume herself, he had to wonder what it was she was hiding.

* * *

It was back. That certain sense that she wasn't quite alone, and Marie wondered at it for the third time that week. She felt as though she had a shadow that had been dodging her for weeks, and her nerves were frayed with the worry. Sometimes it was a quiet footstep behind her, and when she turned there was nobody there. Or often it was just a familiar scent—not unpleasant, necessarily; in fact, it reminded her of the soap her father used to use.

She wished it were her father. The thought of him dead still spread an ache through her chest that left her feeling breathless and in pain. It had taken her poor mother a month, apparently, to convince herself she needed to tell Marie that Jean-Pierre had died, never having recovered from his unconscious state. Marie had cried so many tears she was convinced she was completely dry, only to begin again and find solace leaning on Pauline's gentle shoulder.

The Fromeres had been her salvation. Without their company, she feared she might go mad. Her school, also, went a long way toward helping her forget about the void her father had left in her life, and she was grateful for the distraction. Now, if she could just shake the feeling that more often than not, someone or something was dodging her footsteps, she might sleep more soundly at night.

She made her way toward the small shops she frequented when needing to stock up on the fruits and vegetables she didn't have in ready supply. Pauline was such a good woman—she always made sure the pantry was full of fresh bread and butter, that there was a warm meal waiting for Marie when she returned home from school in the late afternoon, and she even went so far as to pack a small lunch for Marie to take to school with her each day.

In return, Marie shared her home and provisions, and taught the Fromeres everything she knew. They absorbed knowledge like sponges, and she was constantly amazed at their progress. The time would present itself, she knew, when she would somehow be able to get them to safety in the North. It was just a matter of time. That she had been able to keep the family a secret thus far was a divine miracle.

Marie turned and acknowledged a greeting from a casual acquaintance, and as she did so, she caught a glimpse of a man she knew she'd seen before. He was dressed in the uniform of the Union navy, and he was blonde and broad shouldered; the reason she recognized him was because of a jagged scar he bore just above his right cheekbone. She had wondered if he had suffered a childhood accident, or if it was from a wound more recent.

She smiled as she passed him, making her way back down the street after finalizing her purchases, and very nearly stopped short; it was his scent that had her alarmed. She caught the barest whiff of it—her father's soap—and felt a hint of alarm. Had this man been following her?

Marie quickly moved through the crowd of people and walked toward her neighborhood. The fact that night had not yet fallen was of little comfort; the city had been virtual mayhem for weeks now, day or night. If the man she saw was bent on mischief, she wasn't altogether certain she'd be able to summon help. He was a Yankee, after all—and after The Beast's General Order Number 28, all a Union soldier had to do was suggest a woman was harassing him, and she then was left in the position of trying to defend her good name.

Marie nearly laughed in desperation. She didn't have a good name anyway, although it was history and no fault of her own. Time was dulling the gossip, a feat she never thought possible, but there were those whose memories were long and unforgiving. She felt a presence behind her, and for the first time since her father had been attacked, she felt genuine, paralyzing fear.

She quickened her pace even more, and by the time she was within the boundaries of her own neighborhood, she was nearly running. She darted behind a bush thinking to throw him off; she didn't dare lead him right to her front door! If she were smart, she would lead him on a circuitous maze through the streets so that she might prevent him from seeing where she lived.

What was she thinking? He probably already knew where she lived! Heaven only knew what he was about. She crouched down low and hoped with all her might that the strange man, whoever he was, would give up the chase and leave her alone.

Her hands tightened around the basket as she heard running footsteps. The sound grew louder until he was very nearly upon her, and then he ran past. He must have seen her out of the corner of his eye, however, because he happened to glance back at her and then come to a dead stop.

"Are you," he began, breathing heavily and approaching her, "are you all right? Is there something wrong—is someone chasing you?"

Was he mad? "*You,* sir, you were chasing me! And I'm beginning to think this isn't the first time. I've heard you before!" Despite her attempts to be brave, Marie's voice shook.

He put out a hand in supplication. "Oh, no, you misunderstand. I . . . please accept my apologies." The sailor ran a hand through his hair and took a deep breath. "Miss Brissot—Marie—I am Daniel O'Shea. It's been some time since we corresponded last, and I don't know if you quite remember me . . ."

Marie closed her mouth. It had fallen open sometime during his speech. Daniel O'Shea? Oh, dear heaven. She had wanted to meet him so badly, and then knew he would find himself disappointed in the end . . . why on earth had he sought her out? She had told him expressly that she didn't want to meet him.

"So I see you've completely disregarded my wishes." She shifted her basket from one hand to the other. If only he weren't so tall, she might have a better time of chastising him. It hardly seemed effective to have to deliver a good set-down while looking up. "I seem to recall writing to you that this wasn't a good idea."

"You did." He flushed a bit and shoved his hands into his pockets. "I saw you one day in the city, though, and recognized you from your daguerreotype. I—the streets are not safe these days, and I suppose I've taken it upon myself to see that you come and go unmolested."

"And were you ever going to introduce yourself to me?"

"No. You said you didn't want to meet me."

Oh dear. It wasn't that she hadn't wanted to meet him, but rather that she didn't want him to meet *her.* Rubbish. It hardly made sense to her! Well, best to disabuse him of any notions at the start. She drew herself up to her full height. "Mr. O'Shea, the reason I didn't think we should meet had nothing to do with you. I'm not a woman of good standing in this community, frankly, and I didn't think you would appreciate it. I apologize for not mentioning it in our written correspondence. Truthfully, I doubted we would ever meet in person."

With that, she turned to leave and finish the short walk to her home. Her legs trembled, and hot shame flushed her face. She vowed to keep any threatening tears from falling until she was safe in her bed that night.

"Wait!"

Drat. Did the man not have any sense? She had just given him the perfect excuse to leave her alone!

"Miss Brissot—please wait."

She reluctantly stopped and turned as he jogged to her. She swung the basket from hand to hand until she realized she was fidgeting, and then mentally commanded herself to stop. She gripped the basket handle and waited for him to speak. Ordinarily she would have attempted to put a person at ease, and he obviously was in need of such kindness; however, he had chosen to put them both in this awkward position, and she left him to fend for himself.

"I'm not concerned with your 'reputation.' I very much enjoyed our correspondence and have missed it greatly. Your letters helped me—" He looked away, a muscle working in his jaw. "You helped me when I was feeling very confused. I've been—unhappy . . . and our exchange was very . . . you've had a very calming influence on me that I have appreciated."

Still, she watched him but said nothing.

"I'm very sorry for disregarding your wishes. I have no desire whatsoever to make you unhappy. I've missed you, I suppose."

He trailed off and was silent, and she tried to still the heavy beating of her heart. How very genuine he seemed, and she regretted that she was not a woman of impeachable character that he could take home to his mother. "I've missed you as well, Mr. O'Shea, although I confess it's strange to say so when we've never even met."

"You know," he said, "you tell me your reputation suffers, and yet I can hardly believe it. Surely people are mistaken in their judgments."

Marie shook her head, averting her gaze. His expression was too earnest, too probing. "They're not mistaken. I've earned my reputation. Years ago, but still—things don't necessarily change much over time. If you don't mind, I'd rather not discuss it any further."

"Fine. Consider it dismissed. Now," he said with the hint of a smile, "the hour grows late, and I wonder if you might allow me to accompany you home rather than follow a discreet distance behind."

Marie looked at his handsome face and crisp uniform. That uniform could well mean trouble for not only her, but also the Fromeres, should someone choose to interfere in her life. "I hope you won't take offense at this," she told him, "but my neighbors will likely not look kindly on my association with the enemy. They despise my family as it is, and . . ."

"Say no more. I hadn't even thought of that." He glanced down at his clothing with a wry grin. "Perhaps if I were wearing rebel gray, things might be different."

"Perhaps."

"I've been meaning to ask you," he said suddenly, "how is your father? Has he recovered?"

She felt her heart thump as it always did when she thought of her father. "No. He passed away several weeks ago."

"Oh, Marie," he said softly, "I'm so sorry."

She shrugged. "It's probably just as well. Who knows if he would ever have been able to live a full life again, as wounded as he was. He would have hated being an invalid."

"I'm sorry for your loss. And your mother's. Will she come home now?"

"No. I told her to stay with her family in Boston. This place is in such turmoil right now—I hardly think it healthy for her."

"What about you, then? Surely you can go to Boston now, too."

Marie shook her head. "I have responsibilities here that I will not leave. When the time is right, perhaps, but not now. And your parents? How are they?"

"The last I heard, everything was fine."

"Are they taking care of your home for you, then?"

Daniel nodded. "It's not much to care for—only the house itself. I don't have any animals that need tending."

Marie smiled. There was so much more she would have liked to be able to say, but standing on the street corner less than a block away from her house with a man in enemy uniform wasn't wise. "I hope you find everything just as you left it when you return home." She suddenly felt very sheepish. "I apologize for speaking rudely earlier. I wasn't sure of your reaction, and . . ."

"Say no more. Again, I apologize as well, and I wish things could be different. Is there no place at all where we could talk sometime?"

Marie chewed on her lip. "I suppose you could come to my schoolhouse. It's two miles north and quite secluded. The area itself is inhabited by people who generally don't run in these circles," she said, indicating the neighborhood with her finger, "and they've been kind to me."

"I would very much like to sit down with you," he said. "I've come an awfully long way to meet you."

She laughed, and he smiled with her. "Surely you didn't enlist just to meet me," she said. "One might question your sanity."

"Believe me, my sanity has been in question more than once."

There was a slight pause as they simply looked at each other, and then Marie finally broke the silence. "I must be going home," she said.

"I'll stay right here," he promised, "but I'll watch until you reach your front door."

"Very well. It isn't necessary, though. I appreciate your thoughtfulness, but you needn't go to the trouble."

"I do. For my own peace of mind."

* * *

It was laughable. Daniel doubted very much he would ever enjoy peace of mind again. Now that he had met her, actually conversed with her, he was convinced he'd think about her for the rest of his life. She had been everything he'd hoped she'd be, right down to her tone of voice. For the first time in ages, he was thinking of someone other than himself, and he found that he rather liked it.

He had obtained detailed directions from her regarding her schoolhouse and was looking forward to the following week when he'd have time to visit her there. Perhaps nothing significant would ever come of their association, but for the time being, she was like a breath of fresh air.

Daniel whistled all the way back to the harbor.

CHAPTER 16

"We are coming, Father Abraam, three hundred thousand more.
From Mississippi's winding stream and from New England's shore."
—Words from a poem popular in 1862

* * *

3 August 1862
Boston, Massachusetts

Camille Birmingham placed an arm around Abigail's waist and pulled her close. "It's bound to get easier, Abby," she said. "Your mother is proud of you, I'm sure."

Abigail nodded through eyes that looked very moist. "I'm trying. I just don't think I'm as strong as I *thought* I was. I'm not my mother."

"You don't need to be. She was enough."

Abigail laughed. "She was, wasn't she? She was wonderful. I keep thinking that I'll see her mingling here with someone. I still can't quite believe she's gone."

Camille squeezed Abigail's waist again and placed an affectionate kiss on her cheek. "My mother says you'll see her again. Dolly's in heaven waiting for you."

"I hope so."

Camille looked around the room at the Society's members, feeling for them a genuine affection that caught her by surprise. Had she known a year ago that she'd change her social circle and become an entrenched member of the Abolition Society, she would have fainted outright. And yet here she was, enjoying the woman she was becoming and enjoying even more the people with whom she associated.

Her mother, Elizabeth, winked at her from across the room, and Camille felt a warm glow. She was making her mother proud, and it pleased her. It was funny, in a way—Camille had never really cared for her mother's good opinion until after she came home from Washington last year with the Sylvesters. Suddenly, everything had changed. Her whole world had changed, and she knew she could never change it back to the way it had been before. What was even more surprising was that she didn't want to.

"Here comes your friend," Abigail said quietly, and Camille looked in the direction the girl nodded.

"He's not my friend," Camille muttered, and scowled at Jacob Taylor, who was walking toward them with a smile. "He won't leave me be! I've told him I don't want to write for his column. Just because Anne was content to pursue manly occupations doesn't mean I am."

Abigail rolled her eyes a bit, and Camille bristled. "What does that mean?"

"It means that writing isn't necessarily a pursuit reserved only for men, Cammy. You should know that by now. Haven't you been listening at the suffragette meetings?"

"Yes, I have. But I'll be hanged if I'm going to put on men's pants and run around town pretending to be a boy."

"As I recall, he's not asked that of you. He doesn't want you to put on a disguise at all."

"Not now, but he will! You just watch. I think he's sneaky."

Abigail snorted and moved subtly to her right. Before Camille knew what she was doing, her friend had disappeared into the crowd. "Abby!" she whispered, but to no avail.

Jacob Taylor was upon her. "Have you been deserted?" he asked.

"You needn't smirk. She just went to get some punch from the refreshment table," Camille said. "In fact, I'll join her."

"Miss Birmingham, I do believe you are trying to avoid speaking with me."

"Now why on earth would I do a thing like that?"

"Because you know I want you to work for me."

"Work." She sniffed. "What an utterly ridiculous concept."

He laughed. "Now, I know better. You might have been of such an opinion at one time, but I happen to know for a fact that you are waiting hand and foot on two grieving women." He sobered a bit. "And they need it. How is your aunt? We haven't seen her out much lately."

Camille clenched her teeth. She hated it when Jacob Taylor was nice to her. It made her think he might be a reasonable man after all. "She's coping. My aunt Jenny was never one to be down for long. I suspect she'll be herself soon."

Taylor nodded. "I hope so. Do tell her hello from us at the Society."

"I will, thank you. And now, if you'll excuse me . . ."

"I don't mind at all. In fact, I was feeling a bit thirsty myself. I'll walk with you to the refreshment table."

Camille glanced at him in annoyance. Had he no social graces at all? She had just dismissed him! "It's fine, really. I can make it myself."

"Oh, I don't mind a bit." He took her elbow and began to stroll toward the table. Camille clamped down on an outraged gasp that he would be so forward and glared up at him.

"Why, sir, will you not leave me be?"

His expression was one of feigned innocence. "My dear Miss Birmingham, whatever do you mean? I simply desire your good company. Is that such a bad thing?"

"It wouldn't be if I weren't convinced you have ulterior motives."

"Now that sounds simply accusatory. Do you think my purposes are threatening?"

"Annoying."

"Well, that's a matter of opinion."

They reached the table, and Camille took a small glass of punch and sipped it, looking around for Abigail. When her friend materialized, Camille would give her an earful.

"Truly, Mr. Taylor," Camille huffed out when he seemed inclined to stand by her side for the rest of the evening, "why is it that you keep pestering me about writing a column for your paper?"

"Because, Miss Birmingham, in all seriousness, I find you very intelligent and quick-witted. I also know that you hold a somewhat jaded view of society—high society, in particular. I would very much like to introduce a light, short gossip column, if you will, with some of your observations."

"I see a potential problem, Mr. Taylor. I no longer associate with many of those to whom you refer."

"Could you? Your mother still does."

"Precisely! My mother still does. Why not badger her for your column?"

Taylor smiled. "I don't want your mother, Miss Birmingham."

"Bother," Camille muttered, and firmly set her empty glass on the table. "If you leave me be for, shall we say, at least two weeks to think it over, then will you dismiss the matter altogether if I decide once and for all to say 'no'?"

He inclined his head. "Your wish is my command."

"Ha! If that were true, you'd have left me alone long before now."

"Perhaps I'm missing your sister. You remind me of Anne."

Camille frowned. "I miss her, too. I never thought I'd say it, but I wish she'd come home."

"You didn't object to her leaving originally?"

"I suppose, but now sometimes with things as they are, I worry for her safety." Camille glanced at Jacob Taylor and saw a quick change of expression, almost a wince, but then it was gone so fast she wondered if she had imagined it.

"Chicago is safe, I'm sure. I'm certain she's fine," he said, and placed his empty glass on the table next to Camille's. She observed his movements with an objective eye; Abigail certainly found him attractive, and Camille had to admit he was handsome in a new-money kind of way. There was a part of her soul that would always love clothing and socializing, and she had to admire his presentation. He currently wore buff riding trousers, a crisp white shirt, and a dark blue coat and cravat. His sense of style was impeccable, and he always looked very well turned out, even if he wasn't from old money.

Camille had to smile at herself. The Birminghams weren't "old money" either, and there had been a time when she would have gone to great pains to hide that fact. It was of little consequence now; the country was torn in half, war was exploding on numerous fronts, and her brother was an enlisted man. Her smile faded a bit.

"What is it?" Jacob asked her.

"I worry about my brother, as well. He's in much more immediate danger than is Anne."

There was a pause—so long of a pause that Camille looked directly into his face. "Yes," he finally said. "Your brother is in a dangerous position."

Camille nodded slowly, looking at him with a curiosity brewing at the back of her mind that she couldn't quite define. Something about the way he spoke or the words he was using wasn't quite right—almost as though he and she were speaking of two different things entirely.

"But not any more dangerous than Anne's?"

"I didn't say that."

Camille shook her head slightly. "I don't know what you're saying or not saying. Mr. Taylor, I'm beginning to believe you might just be a bit daft."

"Well, now, that's a kind observation."

"Justifiable, though—you must admit."

"If I'm truly daft, as you say, then I doubt I'd know whether or not your statement really is justifiable."

"You're making my head spin. I'm going to find my mother and Abigail, and you're going to stay here. Remember, you promised me two weeks of unmolested contemplation."

He sketched a dramatic bow and smiled. Mercy, the man did have white teeth. Lots of them—rather brought to mind the image of a hungry wolf. "As you wish, my lady," he said.

She shook her head one more time and made her way across the room to where she saw Elizabeth in conversation with some women. Something tickled the back of her mind, something she still couldn't put a finger on. Something Taylor had said, or not said . . . oh, curse it. Who knew what the man meant. She had been granted a two-week reprieve from his probing eyes—she'd best make good use of it.

* * *

Jenny Stein Brissot placed a fresh bouquet of flowers on Jean-Pierre's grave and pulled a small weed from the earth by his head-stone. Her face was dry; she had no more tears left. She had grieved for a long time now, and was beginning to feel selfish surrounded by loving family while Marie was left to suffer through her pain all alone.

It really was time that Jenny returned to New Orleans. She wanted no part of it now, though, other than to collect Marie. The problem was that, according to Marie, the city was in utter turmoil, and getting there might prove to be a difficult issue. There was another problem, and that was Marie herself. Jenny knew she would never be able to convince her strong-willed daughter to leave when she still felt so committed to her students. It was probably easier, too, for Marie to have her work. She was able to immerse herself in it and not dwell on the reality of Jean-Pierre's death.

She would write again to Marie and see how things stood with her. If she wished to stay in New Orleans, Jenny knew that nothing she said or did would convince her daughter to join her in Boston. It might actually be the kinder thing to do, to leave her daughter be. Jenny herself had found distraction in trying to comfort Abigail. The decision to take up temporary residence with the pretty young woman had been utterly spontaneous.

Upon further reflection, Jenny realized that she was trying to escape the memory of Jean-Pierre's demise. He had never been to the Van Dyke household, so therefore Jenny could surround herself with things that had nothing to do with his death. She much preferred the memories of her husband as he truly had been in life. He was young and vibrant and gentle. He had been everything she could have hoped for in a husband, and she would never find another like him.

It suited her to find solace with Camille and Abigail. And in some way, comforting Abigail, who was roughly the same age as Marie, helped Jenny feel just a touch closer to her daughter. It was a blessing to be staying at the Van Dyke residence, and she was grateful to Abigail for allowing it. She, Abigail, and Camille had made a comfortable rhythm for themselves, and Jenny determined to stay for a bit longer, if Marie wished it.

"I can't believe you've left me, my Jean-Pierre," Jenny murmured in French. "I shall never fill the void." Much to her surprise, Jenny found that she truly did have a few tears left. They filled her eyes and rolled down her cheeks. The late afternoon sun filtered through the leaves on the cemetery trees and created shadows on her husband's tombstone. She felt a hatred in her heart for the faceless, nameless cowards who had put her husband in his grave. Beneath their anonymity, however, she knew who they were. She also felt a stab of fear that Marie was still among them.

Confusion and despair rolled around in her heart as she made her way toward the cemetery gates. War was a cruel thing, she decided. It took more lives than just those meeting on the battlefield.

CHAPTER 17

"In the face of this wide earth, Mr. President, there is not one disinterested, determined, intelligent champion of the Union cause who does not feel that all attempts to put down the rebellion and at the same time uphold its inciting cause are preposterous and futile—that the rebellion, if crushed out to-morrow, would be renewed within a year if Slavery were left in full vigor . . ."

—Horace Greeley, editor of the New York Tribune, in a public letter to Abraham Lincoln. The letter later became known as "The Prayer of Twenty Millions."

* * *

29 August 1862
Charleston, South Carolina

Charlotte Birmingham Ellis looked at her husband over her needlework. "I fail to see how it concerns me, William."

"It doesn't necessarily, but I thought it might be nice for us to actually appear as a married couple every now and again."

"Why?"

William let his breath out in a frustrated sigh and reached for his cigar, which sat in the ashtray, lazy circles of smoke rising from its end. "Charlotte, do you intend to stay married to me for an extended period of time?"

The question surprised her. "Of course I do. People don't divorce. Respectable people don't divorce."

"Then can we not at least maintain the pretenses?"

"I thought we were doing at least that, William. I didn't realize you weren't satisfied with our charade." She heard the cynicism in her own voice but was well past feeling sorry for it. Her husband had married her for her family's money, and she had been the only one in all of Charleston who hadn't known that. She glanced again at his face before turning her attention again to her handwork. He was still so handsome, and the stab of pain she felt whenever she looked at him was as strong as it had been when they had first married, years ago.

"It's the charade part I'm dissatisfied with, Charlotte. This is about us, not your parents, your sisters, or your brothers. I'm speaking of you and me." He rose and replaced his cigar, coming to stand before her. When she didn't indicate for him to join her on the settee, he did so of his own accord.

She stiffened unconsciously. Her defenses went up whenever he was around; she was constantly afraid of being played for the fool. It had happened once—who was to say it wouldn't again? "What game are you playing at, William?"

"I'm not playing, Charlotte. I'm tired of the cutting remarks, tired of being your lapdog—a lapdog you despise. I would like a sense of normalcy as it concerns us."

"The way we've been living *is* normalcy for us. There never was anything else."

"Yes, there was." His voice was husky, and it made her shiver. The fact that she would react to him against her will after all this time made her angry.

"No, there wasn't! I may have felt something, William, but you never did. For you to even pretend is cruel. There! You can be satisfied with yourself that you have managed to hurt me as much as I've hurt you." She gathered her material and thread and moved to stand.

He put a restraining hand on her arm and said, "Charlotte, please, I beg of you. Stay and listen to what I have to say."

Something in his voice gave her pause. There was a note of sincerity, of desperation that she had never heard in it before. She sank back down into the cushions and folded her hands over her needlework, allowing him the space he wished to speak his mind.

"I didn't marry you despising you, Charlotte. My feelings may not have been as strongly engaged as were yours, but I wasn't as colhearted as you would like to believe. The arrangement I had with your father is not so much unlike a dowry. I had debts and obligations, and he paid those for me. Your parents saw your affection for me, and I believe they wanted you to be happy."

"My parents wanted me to be someone else's responsibility." Her voice was soft and vulnerable, and she hated it.

"Then they were fools," he murmured. "Charlotte, you're a beautiful woman with a quick mind. I've come to admire your strength and your character."

"William, I don't understand. You know very well I turn a blind eye to your indiscretions. I do not interfere in your pursuits, regardless of what they entail. Why on earth do you plague me like this now?"

"Charlotte, I would dearly love a son. You are my wife, and I believe you might enjoy a child of your own, yes?"

It was true, and she resented that he knew it. "I would have to consider the notion for a while."

"I understand. And I would certainly hate to give the impression that I'm rushing you, but I must tell you that I've considered enlisting."

"What?" She sat unmoving, trying to sort through his words and wishing they'd make some kind of sense.

"The war effort is not going to be resolved soon; I believe we all know this. Citizens are facing conscription, and I would rather enlist on my own terms than be called against my will."

"William, you know very well we can buy your way out of it."

"Leave me at least a shred of self-respect, Charlotte. I may not have behaved like a man in the past, but I intend to do so now."

"So it is your objective to go off to battle and leave me home with child? You may well die—what would be the purpose?"

"First of all, I don't believe for a moment you or the child would suffer if I were dead. You have enough support here for five women. Secondly, my purpose is that somehow I will have left a part of myself in the world. I do not wish to be of so little account that when I'm gone, there will be absolutely nothing left. I haven't supported you or added anything of consequence to this family, and I have no parents or siblings left either. You, Charlotte—you are my only chance for solace."

Sometime during his speech she had stopped breathing. Charlotte now sucked in her breath and let it out again on a shuddering sigh. It wasn't fair that he should ask for the one thing she swore she would never give. Her intimacies, her heart, were hers alone, and she had guarded them selfishly as a married woman. The walls around her were thick and solid, and she didn't want the one man who had helped put them there to ask her to tear them down for him.

She rose as tears threatened. "I'll think on it, William. Please leave me in peace for now."

* * *

Emily marched into the drawing room to find William, her brother-in-law, seated on the settee and staring into the empty hearth. She stopped short. "William? Are you ill?"

He shook himself as though from a daze and looked at her, his eyes coming into focus. "No, no. I'm well." He rose and, without another word, left the room.

Emily looked after him for a moment before shaking her head in dismissal and remembering her purpose for entering the room in the first place. Yes, there it was—the newspaper.

She didn't have to look far to see that what had been rumored was indeed true; it was splashed across the front page: "Rebels Beat the Yanks a Second Time at Bull Run/Manassas!" Emily sighed and sank onto the vacated settee, reading the article with growing discouragement. What was wrong with that darned Union army? They constantly outnumbered the rebels, yet they consistently lost! And so much for Lincoln's new general, Pope. He wasn't any better than McClellan had been apparently.

Speaking of McClellan, there he was again, mentioned farther down in the article. "Lincoln decided to give you another chance, eh Little Mac?" Emily murmured as her eyes scanned the lines of print. "Let's hope you can prove yourself this time around."

"Who are you talking to?" Someone had entered the room without Emily realizing it. She smiled when she saw who it was.

"Mary, you've caught me talking to myself. Lincoln has replaced General Pope with McClellan again."

"Hmm." Mary walked to a side table, where she placed a newly crocheted doily. She smoothed it into place and stood back a bit to survey her work.

"You're cynical, Mary. Don't ever accuse me of it again." Emily strolled to her friend's side and put an arm about her shoulders.

"I've learned from the queen cynic," Mary said, and reached her hand up to grasp Emily's. "Have you spoken with your mother?"

"Yes. She told me she'd consider it." Emily was grateful the house was so blessedly empty. Sarah was in town for the week, and Charlotte was set to join her later that afternoon. William spent his time who knew where, and Jeffrey was on his way to England. With Ben gone and Richard away fighting his Yanks, the only two actual Birminghams in the house would be Emily and Clara. Emily knew Mary would never have dared be so comfortable with her physical gesture of friendship if the house had been full of the family.

"I don't think she'll let me come with you," Mary admitted, leaning her head upon Emily's shoulder.

Emily, in turn, rested her head upon Mary's. "Austin promised to pay her a substantial amount of money for the four of you. I think she'll consider it."

"She *might* let me go, and possibly Joshua, but Mama Ruth? Never. And I've been thinking—how wise is it to have Rose and Clara separated?"

"Mary. Would you really want to deny Rose a life of her own just to keep the girls together?"

"I don't know." Mary shrugged, and Emily felt her misery. It had been all well and good for Emily to breathe fire all these years regarding the freedom of those she loved most, but she hadn't taken into consideration how drastic changes might affect them.

"Maybe my mother will let Clara come and live with us. Then the girls could be together for . . ." She stopped as Mary squeezed her hand. Mary was right—it wouldn't do at all to make reference to Austin's activities. The walls often had ears. "Well, you know," she finished on a whisper.

"I seriously doubt your mother would let Clara go, too. Then she'd have nobody left but William and Charlotte."

"She'd have Bentley."

Mary didn't respond. She didn't need to. The two women stood in silence for a moment, gently swaying together as they looked at the doily on the side table. "Have you spoken with Joshua yet?" Mary whispered finally.

Emily closed her eyes. She had been avoiding Joshua ever since her return from Savannah as an engaged woman. She had immediately sought out Mary and told her the news and of her possible pending freedom, and then had requested that Mary share the information with Joshua because Emily had much to do. It had been a lie, and they both knew it.

"I haven't had time to," she said, opening her eyes.

Mary pulled back and looked at Emily. She took both of Emily's hands in hers and said, "What is it that I haven't been told?"

Emily shrugged. "I don't know what you mean."

"Yes, you do. You should've come home ecstatic, running straight to the stables to talk with Joshua after you told me. Instead you asked me to give him the news, and you've been avoiding him like a plague. All you've ever wanted is our freedom. You even decided to try to spy for the cause, and now you look as though you've been whipped. You told me you're developing positive feelings for Mr. Stanhope, so I'm having a hard time understanding why you're so unhappy."

Emily felt her eyes fill, and she looked at Mary through blurred vision. She averted her gaze to the window instead and said, "I'm leaving my home—things will change."

Mary snorted softly. "You hate this home."

"Not everything about this home."

Mary released her hands and moved to the door, closing it softly. She drew Emily to the divan and sat next to her on it, wiping away a tear that had fallen from Emily's eyes. "What is it about this home you love so much?"

Emily finally looked at Mary, knowing her anguish was clearly written upon her face. "Joshua."

Mary's expression was puzzled, uncomprehending for a moment, and then her eyes widened. She closed them then, and drew Emily into a tight embrace. "Oh, dear friend. All this time we've had even more in common than we knew."

Emily released the shuddering sobs she'd been keeping locked inside since returning from Savannah. "What do you mean?" she managed as she drew back and searched for the lacy handkerchief she'd stashed in her sleeve.

"You love my brother, and I love yours."

"Richard? *Richard?*"

"No, not Richard!"

Emily's mouth dropped open. "Ben!" She thought she shouted his name, but was surprised to hear it come out as a whisper. "Oh, Mary. Oh . . . Mary." Emily drew her friend back in for a quick squeeze and began to laugh. Mary joined her, and soon the two of them were laughing so hard they were breathless.

Emily fell back against the divan and shook her head. "Aren't we a pair?" she murmured, and looked at Mary, who was wiping her own eyes. "Do you realize how impossible we are? We are both pining away for loves we'll *never* have. Ever!"

"Do you think I don't know that?" Mary's lips twitched, but her eyes were sad. "I've lived with that knowledge since I was a girl. I thought it would fade with time, but now it's worse."

"At least the object of your affection is miles away. I envy you that."

Mary turned pensive, looking at Emily and chewing her lip. "I've been meaning to show you something since your return, but the opportunity hasn't arisen. Until today—in fact, that's why I came looking for you. Can you spare a few moments tonight around ten o'clock?"

"My goodness, Mary—something clandestine?"

"Of sorts. And I'm also wondering, since I have much to do at the house here today, if you can ask the same of Joshua—have him meet us at the old tree house."

"Mary, that's unfair. I don't want to talk to Joshua."

"Yes, you do. Please? For me?"

"Very well. But let it be said that I think you're a cruel woman."

"Fine. And now I must be getting upstairs. I have a dozen projects to finish."

Emily walked with Mary to the front staircase and watched as Mary ascended, her form graceful and lithe as always. Emily then turned and exited the front door, making her way around the enormous porch to the back of the house, where she stepped out upon the massive lawn and headed for the stables.

She didn't even know what she'd say when she saw him. Probably he didn't even care, so why should she? She was still mulling things over with a frustrated frown when she entered the stables and found Joshua near the back, tending to a wounded mare.

He had wrapped the horse's foreleg and was checking his work. He must have heard her soft approach, for he looked up at her and held her gaze, saying nothing for a long time.

Finally, he patted the horse gently and arose, standing before Emily, crossing his arms over his chest and leaning against the side of the stall. "We've been friends for a long time, Emily," he murmured. "Why didn't you come and tell me your news yourself?"

Her breath caught, and she cursed herself soundly, vowing not to shed another tear. She had never been one to cry overmuch, and it was becoming irksome. "I didn't want to have to tell you myself."

"It's very unlike you to be a coward."

She flinched at his honesty. "Why does it matter who the messenger was? You're going to be a free man, if I can convince my mother to let you come with me. I would think you'd be dancing in the streets."

"I should celebrate the fact that you're sacrificing your life to give me mine?" His tone was sharp, and it stung.

"I'm not sacrificing my life, Joshua." Her tone rose to match his, and she belatedly reminded herself to keep her voice down. She glanced from one side to the other.

"We're alone," he assured her. "Jackson is overseeing the fieldwork today, and everyone else has run errands into town."

She nodded and looked at the mare he had been tending to when she entered. For the first time in her life, she couldn't think of something to say to him.

"If I were certain you'd be happy, I might be a bit more enthusiastic about my own turn of events," he told her quietly.

In spite of her pain, she couldn't help but smile. His voice, his speech, his choice of words—they spoke of his education and intellect, and she knew he and Mary both would do well for themselves up north, given half a chance. "Joshua, I've loved you all my life," she said evenly, still looking at the mare, "and I can think of nothing I'd rather do than help bring about your freedom."

He was silent for so long that Emily finally looked at his face. It was blank, and except for the telltale movement of a muscle in his jaw, she wouldn't have guessed they were discussing anything more harmless than the weather. "Are you sure this man will be good to you?" he asked, his tone flat.

"I believe he will," she said, picking at a bit of lace on her dress. "He's a good man."

"There isn't a man good enough for you, Emily Birmingham." Again, his face was still impressively impassive.

"Well, there is one, but he won't have me." If her tone was sharper than she intended, it was because she felt as though her heart were being torn from her chest. "I would have run away with you, Joshua. I would have taken whatever you would have given me." The dratted tears came back, making their familiar journey down her face.

Instead of the softening reaction she had hoped for, his face hardened. "Do you believe I think so little of you that I would compromise your virtue or your good name? That I would offer you a life fraught with danger or homelessness?"

"No, I—"

"I don't know you as well as I thought I did, apparently."

"Joshua! How can you say that to me after . . . after the last time I was in here with you? You told me I must leave because, because—"

"Emily," he interjected, "I think you may have placed too much importance on our embrace. We're friends, and we've always been friends. That much alone is nothing short of a miracle, given the stations of our birth."

She stared at him through her tears. What was he trying to say?

"I care for you deeply, as one would a younger sister. I wanted to be sure your fiancé is all that you could ask for. Now that I know, I am at peace. As you're nearly a married woman, you probably ought not come in here alone anymore. I believe I mentioned that the last time we spoke."

Emily finally nodded, dumbly, as though she had no sense. As she turned to go, she stopped for a moment. "I nearly forgot," she mumbled. "Mary has a surprise for us—we are to meet her at the tree house at ten o'clock tonight."

"Did she say what it concerns?"

"No."

With that, she left the stables and made her way slowly to the mansion, her eyes on the ground until she reached the door.

* * *

Joshua sank down onto the floor of the stable and buried his face in his hands. His shoulders heaved in great, gulping breaths, and he fought the impulse to take every tool he could find and hurl it against the wall. He wanted to run out of the stables and scream the injustice to the skies, cursing heaven and hell and everything in between. For the first time in his life, he wished he were a field hand so that the constant physical labor might take his mind off of his aching heart.

He would never forget Emily's stricken expression, the haunted look in her eyes, the pain so clearly etched in her features. He was responsible for that pain, and it was nearly his undoing. It had been necessary, though. Emily was about to give herself in marriage to another man—appropriately a white man—and it was infinitely for her own good that she not nurture lingering feelings for one of the family slaves.

It was quite likely that her affection for him stemmed from the fact that he reminded her of Ben, the brother she had adored and then missed more than anything in the world. She was young yet—it was true, she was approaching eighteen years of age and was marriageable without a doubt, but she seemed so innocent and vulnerable. Perhaps age and time with her husband would replace childhood infatuations and impossible dreams.

He, now—he was another issue altogether. Joshua was a man of roughly twenty-five or twenty-six years of age. He had known a hard life and impossible conditions. His spirit yearned for freedom, for what *could* be, but he was no stranger to reality. He loved Emily Birmingham with all of his heart and soul, and would until the day he died. *He* wanted to be the one she married—the one legally and morally allowed to claim her every affection. He wanted to be the one who held her until they both grew old with age. He wanted to die in her arms only to embrace her moments later on the other side of life.

"Oh, dear God in Heaven," he moaned softly into his hands.

"How am I to watch her with another man?" Even as he prayed, he wondered why God didn't strike him dead. He was soon to face freedom—an elusive dream he had never dared to hope for—and still he complained. "Forgive me, please forgive me," he whispered.

Finally, he pulled his emotions together and rubbed his head and aching neck. What was it Emily had said when she left? Something about the tree house and ten o'clock. He hoped to have completely regained his composure by then.

* * *

Emily made her way to the tree house in the dark without stumbling or groping about. She knew well the path that took her into the small forest on the edge of the property. As a very young child, she had followed Ben and Joshua while they roamed the plantation, always returning to the tree house as their favorite spot. Thoughts of Joshua brought a fresh wave of pain that she tried very hard to ignore.

Now, with the light of the moon filtering through the trees, she waited alone for Mary and her surprise. What on earth could warrant a meeting out here, of all places, under the cover of night? It wasn't long before she heard a light shuffle and glimpsed two figures coming toward her.

At Joshua's familiar shadow, she bit her lip. She would *not*, under any circumstances, cry anymore. He had made his feelings, or lack thereof, more than clear. He didn't feel for her as she did for him. He had made her feel silly and shameful, and she regretted ever opening herself to him. Twice now, she had told him she loved him, and all he felt in return were brotherly affections. Never again would she divulge her feelings to him, but it wouldn't change the fact that she would love him forever. No matter whom she married, no matter where he went, she would always remember him and ache for what could never be. She steeled her resolve to be the strong person she always had been as he and Mary approached. He would not see her weak side again.

"Well, Mary," she whispered as the two reached her, "here we are. *Why* are we here?"

Mary looked into the darkness for a moment and said, "Shhh."

Emily glanced at Joshua's dubious expression but remained silent. Before long, there was a nearly imperceptible rustle in the leaves. The noise came from the direction directly opposite the plantation. Emily squinted her eyes in the dark, trying to see what was coming. She looked at Mary in question; Mary's eyes were trained on the darkness. Presently, she smiled, and Emily looked back over her shoulder.

A shadow emerged from the trees, a person she didn't recognize. She felt a thread of fear when he stepped closer to them and the blue cast of his uniform became obvious. She glanced at Joshua, sensing his palpable tension. It wasn't until the shadow moved continuously forward, coming to stand just before her, that a flicker of recognition flashed across her mind.

He removed his hat and ran a hand through his black hair. The green eyes, so very like her own, glowed back at her in the dark. It couldn't possibly be. She looked at Mary, whose eyes had filled with tears. Mary smiled at her, tenderness clearly evident in her luminous brown eyes.

"Ben?" Emily felt the blood drain from her head, her vision blurring. She tried to suck in a breath, and wished she had changed out of her blasted corset before leaving the house. Stumbling sideways, she felt Joshua's arms around her waist, and she clutched at his shirtfront.

Ben moved forward and took her from Joshua's arms, holding her so closely she felt her ribs would break. The tears came then, great gulping sobs, and he shushed her even as he laughed softly in her ear.

"Mary did the same thing," he said in a voice that cracked with emotion.

Emily felt one of his arms leave her side, and she glanced up as Ben embraced Joshua. As for Joshua—he appeared too stunned to speak. The three of them stood, locked in a tight embrace, for what seemed an eternity.

Emily was eventually released, and she promptly sank to the ground, heedless of the damage to her clothing. Ben and Joshua crouched down next to her, searching her face for signs of illness.

"I'm fine," she whispered. "I just need to sit."

Mary moved to sit next to Emily on the ground, placing a supporting arm around her waist. Ben glanced at Joshua with a grin and sat as well. Joshua shrugged and joined them on the ground, shaking his head at Ben as he settled into place.

"What on earth are you about, my friend," he asked Ben, his voice husky with emotion. He clapped Ben hard on the shoulder and shook him, and Ben wiped at his eyes with a laugh.

"I enlisted in the cause," Ben answered. "I left Utah for Boston and joined up with a Massachusetts cavalry. You remember Luke, my cousin? He joined with me."

"And where is he?"

Ben motioned with a thumb over his shoulder. "Back at camp, about five miles out. We're leaving soon to go back to Hilton Head. Who knows how much longer we'll be there—I had to see y'all."

He smiled and clasped Emily's offered hand. "Dear heaven, Ben, I've missed you," she said.

"And I you." Ben kissed her knuckles and leaned forward to wipe a tear that streaked down her face. "Mercy, little sister, you're a woman now. I would never have recognized you."

"And you're even more grown up than you were. You look wonderful," Emily said, wondering what Mary thought of Ben's maturity. She reflected back on their conversation earlier in the day. She had said Mary was lucky that Ben was so far away. How wrong she'd been, and Mary hadn't even corrected her.

"Mary!" she said, glancing at her friend who still sat close. "You didn't say a word!"

"The last time he visited, you were in Savannah," she said. "Joshua, you were gone away on errands, and now you can't see Ruth," she finished, looking at Ben. "She's in town with your mother."

"For how long?"

"Another week, at least."

Ben nodded, looking as if he were trying to swallow his disappointment. "At least I got to see the three of you, though," he said, squeezing Emily's hand and thumping Joshua on the back.

"You may have the opportunity to see Emily again, once you're back at Hilton Head," Mary murmured with a glance at her friend.

"Why is that?"

Emily cleared her throat. "I'm getting married. My fiancé's home is in Savannah."

"*Married?* Emily, already?"

Emily avoided Joshua's eyes, although she could feel his gaze on her face. "I'm of marriageable age, Ben. You've been gone for a long time."

"I have," he agreed softly. "A lifetime, it seems." He looked over at Mary and then at Joshua. "My friend," he said to the other man, "I cannot tell you how much I regret having failed you."

Joshua shook his head, his eyes bright in the darkness. "You did all you could, Benjamin. It was more than I could ever have hoped for. You'd have done me no good dead, and if you'd stayed, it would have happened." His voice broke, and he stopped. He shook his head, swallowed, and clasped Ben again on the shoulder. "I've envied you, but I've missed you more."

"When this is all over, things will be different. We will all spend time together—we'll stay close."

Emily glanced at Joshua and Mary, wondering how much she should divulge to Ben. In the end, she chose to keep Austin's secret just that. If Ben knew, he might inadvertently let it slip somehow, somewhere in conversation . . . it just wasn't worth the risk.

Joshua and Mary kept quiet, as well. Apparently they were content to follow her lead, and they kept their thoughts about their pending freedom to themselves. Emily looked at her beloved brother and felt her heart constrict. Perhaps she was doing him a disservice; after all, he had tried a slave escape himself years ago. He certainly knew how to keep secrets. *I owe it to Austin,* she thought. She had felt guilty for sharing the information with Mary and Joshua—she must not spread it further.

"I hope you can somehow find time to see me in Savannah," she said to Ben. She told him of Willow Lane's whereabouts.

"When is the wedding to be?"

"One month."

"That seems awfully soon. Is Mother not planning the celebration of the ages, then?" Ben's mouth quirked at the corner.

"The war, apparently, has put a damper on most parties these days," Emily said.

"Doesn't it though." Ben tried to see beyond the dark trees. "Has anything changed around Bentley?"

"Not much," Joshua answered for the three. "Things probably run much the same as when you were here. Of course, Richard is now next in line to inherit, but I don't think he wants it. Doesn't seem to show much interest in it, anyway." Joshua paused. "Did you know that Richard is serving somewhere in Virginia?"

Ben nodded. "Uncle James told me. How is Richard? What is he like?" Ben looked at Emily when the other two were silent. "You hinted at something in your letters . . ."

Emily shrugged and deliberately avoided looking at Mary. If Mary wanted Ben to know what had happened, she would tell him herself. "He's just not a very nice person, Ben. He's, well, he's mean. Always was, though, even when you were here. It's nothing new."

Ben frowned. "I know. I suppose I had hoped things would be different . . ." He shrugged. "How are Clara and Rose? I know I wouldn't recognize them at all."

Emily smiled. "They're sweet. They've learned so much—I've been teaching them—and Rose is as proficient in signing communication as is Clara. They speak together so quickly I can barely follow sometimes. Clara's also become an excellent lip-reader. I'm proud of her."

Ben was able to relate but a small portion of where he'd been spending his time and the people he'd left behind in Utah before he reached for his pocket watch, as though just remembering the time. "I need to go before I'm missed," he said. "I wish I could stay." He drew Emily close and placed a kiss on her cheek. "You're a beautiful woman, Emily, and I'm so proud of what you've become."

"Oh, not more tears," she muttered as her eyes filled. "I've cried enough now to last me a lifetime." Why was she so worried that she'd started a habit she'd be unable to finish? Something whispered that her tears had only just begun.

As they stood, Ben and Joshua embraced one last time, and Ben said, "This is not the end. We will see each other again, and we will build a life for you."

Joshua nodded and managed a smile. "It's very good to see you again, Benjamin."

Mary stepped forward then, and Emily noticed a change in Ben. Whether it was the quick intake of breath or a slight alteration of his features she couldn't be sure, but there was something different in his regard for Mary. She watched as Ben folded her in his arms and placed his lips next to her ear. "I will see you again, as well," he murmured, and Emily felt her eyes widen slightly in comprehension.

She turned her head to hide a sad smile. Ah, poor Ben. He was just as cursed as the rest of them. He would have undoubtedly noticed Mary's uncommon beauty—it was commented on by slave and white man alike—and not only was she beautiful, she was incredibly bright. If Mary and Ben had spent more than a few moments together in the past weeks, he would know it by now.

"Well," Emily murmured, "we're all in this together."

"What?" Joshua whispered, as Ben and Mary were still talking quietly.

"Nothing." She looked up at Joshua, who was watching her closely. "I was thinking aloud."

He nodded and continued to look at her. She tried to memorize the handsome angles of his face, the broad set to his shoulders, the shape of his eyes. Her memories would soon be all she had of him, and they would have to be enough.

So much was changing, and so swiftly. And to make the chaos complete, Ben had returned as though from the dead. She shook her head as she glanced at Mary and Ben, who were reluctantly separating, and then again at Joshua. "What a mess," she muttered.

Joshua raised a brow but said nothing. It was just as well.

There was nothing more to say.

CHAPTER 18

"The truth is, when bullets are whacking against tree trunks and solid shots are cracking skulls like egg-shells, the consuming passion in the breast of the average man is to get out of the way. Between the physical fear of going forward and the moral fear of turning back, there is a predicament of exceptional awkwardness from which a hidden hole in the ground would be a wonderfully welcome outlet."

—David L. Thompson, Union soldier, after the battle of Antietam

* * *

16 September 1862
Keedysburg, Maryland

Ivar sat outside the tent, stretching his aching muscles and sewing a mismatched button onto the other of his two good shirts. He was becoming quite proficient; his mother would be suitably impressed.

He thought of his family as he worked on the button. He wondered what little Inger was doing at that very moment. She was nearing her fourth birthday—something he could scarcely believe. How much she must be speaking now! And if his mother had her way about things, and she usually did, Inger was probably well on her way to reading and writing as well.

He smiled. When he got home to Ohio after his term of enlistment was over, he would hold Inger on his lap and listen to her chatter. He would kiss her blonde curls and hold her close, and only when she squirmed to be free would he let her go. He would hug his mother and kiss her cheek; he would tell her how much he loved and appreciated all she had done for him. Merely sewing buttons had made him appreciate her. And sewing buttons had been the tip of the iceberg that was her life's work.

Ivar chuckled to himself as he thought of hugging and embracing his father. Per would undoubtedly think him mad, but Ivar liked to believe the embrace would be returned. He knew his father was proud of the efforts he was making on behalf of their adopted country, but Ivar wondered on a daily basis how his father fared. His mother had mentioned in a few letters that some of the neighbors were helping with the small farm, which was a comfort to Ivar. Per's leg problems had worsened since Ivar's enlistment, according to Amanda, and Ivar worried over it.

The regiment had seen much by way of marching and skirmishes over the past month, and although the men currently lounged and relaxed, there was a level of unmistakable tension in the air. General Lee's men had taken up position on the other side of Antietam Creek, and the Union soldiers in the area knew they would soon see action again.

Ivar was tired. They were all tired. The weather was unspeakably hot, the men were weary of the constant marching, and each time they faced the enemy, whether in a battle setting or minor skirmish, the heart-pounding anxiety of uncertainty was taking its toll.

They each found their own kind of diversions. Jed and Mark sat next to Ivar at a small table they had erected, playing a game of cards. Mark cursed soundly under his breath as Jed beat him for the third time. "You wait until you're healthy again," Mark told his gloating friend. "I'll wrestle you to the ground until you cry 'uncle.'"

Ivar smiled to himself and noted Jed's color, which was returning. His pneumonia had held on stubbornly through the summer, but was abating. He was slowly regaining his strength after having spent some time in an infirmary. They were still together, the three of them, and he fervently hoped they'd go home together, too.

"Where's our young friend today?" Mark asked Ivar over his shoulder.

"He's taking pictures with Alan."

"You know, at first I thought it was a complete waste of time," Jed commented as he dealt another hand of cards, "but now I'm thinking the boy knew what he was doing when he made friends with that photographer."

"Why?" Mark asked.

"Because it's so bloody boring to sit, day after day, doing nothing but wishing we were home. At least Aaron has found another hobby."

Ivar nodded his agreement. Young "Aaron" had indeed found herself another hobby, and she had thrown herself into it with all her might. She seemed to enjoy picture taking the same way she did writing. He wondered if it wasn't so much a diversion for times of boredom as it was for times of horror. They had all seen more gore in their year of enlistment than they cared to admit, and hiding behind a box, distracted by getting the process just right, sounded mighty tempting, even to him.

"Perhaps he'll show us how it works sometime," Ivar said to his friends as he tied a knot in his thread and bit it off with his teeth. He examined the button and held it up for inspection. "What do you think?"

Mark cocked his head to one side. "You should be the camp seamstress, Gundersen. Looks like young Johnson isn't the only one finding new talents." He and Jed then laughed as though they were quite funny, and Ivar shook his head.

"I've seen your button repair, both of you. We'll see whose lasts the longest."

"We'll just come to you for help, then."

"I'll refuse." Ivar stood, his lips quirking at the corners, and went into the tent to place his shirt in his haversack. His mother would be proud—even in these most primitive of conditions, he took the time to care for his clothes, wash whenever he could, and fold things neatly into place. In truth, it was these simple things that kept his sanity from abandoning him. The little routines of daily life helped him feel a sense of normalcy, as though there were at least a few things under his control in a world where the boredom of camp life was punctuated by brief moments of terror.

He turned at the sound of someone entering the tent and answered Anne's quick, "Hello, there." She bent over her haversack, pulling things from it and throwing them on her bedroll. "What are you looking for?" he finally asked when he could control his amused curiosity no longer.

"An article I wrote for Jacob. I had it here yesterday . . ." She continued rummaging and eventually pulled a crumpled piece of paper from the bottom of her bag. She stuffed the displaced items back into the sack and stood, taking a deep breath. "I wrote this piece and then tore it from my notebook because I didn't like it." She smoothed the paper against her leg with slim fingers that had become adept at firing a gun and wielding a bowie knife. "I'm glad I didn't destroy it, though, because Alan has some pictures that will complement it perfectly. I'll send them via the mail pouch to Jacob in the morning."

She glanced at Ivar with a smile and then turned and left the tent as quickly as she'd come. He looked at her messy bedding for a moment before shrugging and turning his attention to his own matters. He was glad that she'd found a way to deal with their reality. Some men didn't do that so well, and trouble often brewed because of it. The woman was lucky; she was small enough of a "boy" to have been picked on mercilessly had she not been so personable in communicating with the other soldiers. They all liked her, and she had been able to avoid trouble because of it.

In truth, he had to admit he'd never in his life seen someone who was so adept at reading people and responding appropriately. She was almost like a chameleon. She changed colors depending on with whom she spoke. With the educated among the group, she was scholarly. With the farm boys, she was conversant in a more rural exchange. When speaking with those who favored sports, she knew all of the rules and game strategies. She had even learned enough of military strategy and tactics to fully comprehend conversations she sometimes "accidentally" overheard coming from the vicinity of the officer's tents. Ivar knew of several who lacked the capacity to understand the simplest of maneuvers.

In addition to all her good traits, Ivar supposed the thing that surprised him the most about Anne was that he genuinely *liked* her. Perhaps it was because she was so unique—perhaps it was because she pretended to be a man and somehow he even thought of her as such. Whatever the reason, she was pleasant to be around, and given their current set of circumstances, that was a nice bonus.

* * *

Anne awoke in the dark of night to voices just outside the tent. "We need to be mobile in fifteen minutes." Ivar lifted the tent flap and stepped inside.

"Did you hear?" he asked her.

Anne nodded and stretched, rubbing her eyes and wondering for the millionth time why she wasn't home in Boston, sound asleep in her bed. She pulled on her socks and boots, grumbling something unintelligible to Mark and Jed, who were also stirring and asking why everyone was awake.

"What time is it?" she asked Ivar while collecting her weapons and canteen.

"Nearly eleven," he said as he gathered his own things.

The four tent mates joined the others in their company who had likewise been roused. They all moved forward as commanded, falling into their ranks and approaching the creek that ran its course through the countryside. Fording the waters of Antietam Creek, they eventually took up their positions at three in the morning, where they slept until the first light of dawn.

* * *

"I overheard something interesting," Anne whispered to Ivar as they sat quietly on the ground after awakening.

"I'm sure you did," he answered.

"Our illustrious Commander McClellan has known for days now of Lee's northern invasion plans. When some of our troops took over a vacated Confederate camp, they found a copy of the plans wrapped around some cigars."

"Hmm." Ivar nodded and considered what she was saying. Anne felt a surge of impatience as she watched his face. He wasn't considering things quickly enough for her liking.

"Don't you see?" she hissed. "McClellan has known all this time, *we* even knew that Lee was across the creek, and yet we wait all night to attack? Why?"

Ivar shrugged. "They say he's cautious."

"He's too cautious! And his record shows the folly! Every time he defeats Confederate forces, has them on the run, he never pursues them. Why is that?"

"Are you suggesting he's soft on the Confederacy?"

"No! I'm suggesting he's relying on faulty information! Time and time again, he discovers after the fact that the Confederate numbers are *thousands* less than his scouts have informed him they are. You watch," she said, crunching into an apple she'd found in a nearby orchard. "Our numbers here are nearly into the ninety thousands. From what I heard last night, Lee's numbers are only in the fifties. If we take the day in this battle, send Lee on the run, and then don't pursue him . . ."

"Then that will tell us what about McClellan?"

"That he's . . ." Anne tapped her temple with her finger. "He's not using his whole brain to think matters through!"

Ivar smirked, and Anne fought the urge to smack him with the butt of her rifle. "You haven't liked McClellan since that friend of yours in Washington wrote you that letter last year," he told her on a yawn.

He was referring to a letter she'd received from Isabelle Webb over a year ago, and she had to grudgingly admit that Belle had colored her opinion of McClellan, perhaps *slightly*, but that still didn't mean the man was a good general. He might have been good for morale, especially after that buffoon Pope, and he certainly knew how to train troops. He just didn't know how to pursue his advantage after battle. He never felt he had one.

Anne sniffed. "Well, that's true, but you watch, my friend. You just watch."

Conversation around them eventually ceased, and Anne wished it would continue. There were thousands, *thousands* of men waiting to slaughter each other, and she was terrified. To her left were Ivar, Mark, and Jed. To her right was Alan, who was doing his best to maneuver his camera conveniently; truth be told, though, he would probably have to wait until the aftermath to photograph anything. The action was simply too quick for live shots. She knew he was prepared, however, to capture history as best as he could.

* * *

The ensuing battle broke itself into three fronts. It began in the vicinity of yet another church—Dunker, it was called—and Anne felt the irony with a shake of her head. She made mental note of as many details as possible for later scribbling into her notebook. However, by 10:30 that morning, her eyes were glazed over and her senses dulled. She constantly reminded herself to stay alert, and ran along blindly behind Ivar when the order came to form a column, four deep, to attack Confederate soldiers who had taken position in a sunken road that was a friendly division between two farmers' fields.

The morning had started near the church, in a cornfield wherein green stocks were now flattened to the ground and red with the blood of thousands upon thousands of dead and wounded. The battle had moved back and forth upon the bedraggled cornfield fifteen times. When the orders came to make way to the sunken road, Anne had been altogether too happy to move on.

The Union commander leading the charge was a sight to behold. He rode ahead of the troops to be a vision of encouragement, and behind them, a regimental band urged them onto victory. Anne's focus shifted slightly, and events slowed to a surreal pace as she watched the commander atop his horse, the merry music stirring from behind. It was so out of place! The band should have been playing in a great social hall, and all of the soldiers, Union and Confederate, *Americans all*, should have been seated side by side in congregational delight.

They moved closer and closer to the sunken road, which actually formed a perfect trench for the Confederate soldiers. So close that Anne heard the Confederate order to commence firing, she watched with clenched teeth as the commander atop his horse was shot and killed instantly. The men around her wavered, faltered a bit, but regrouped and came back at the road, charging five times.

The noise from the guns and artillery was deafening, and Anne winced as two people directly in front of her fell to their faces, one thrashing in pain and the other still in immediate death. She found herself grateful for the hours of drilling and training, for her body took over where her mind seemed wont to shut down altogether.

Line after line of Union blue fell, and Anne stepped back, reloaded, and charged forward again with Ivar, Mark, and Jed. It was with some desperation that she watched so many Union troops fall, and began to wonder not *if* she would join them in death, but *when.* She thought frantically of her mother and father. They thought she was safe in Chicago, working for Pinkerton. She thought of Camille and Robert and little Jimmy. She thought of Luke and wanted to weep. Her throat clogged tightly and her eyes began to burn, and she mentally screamed to herself that she didn't have time to fall apart.

She heard a groan to her right and cried out in horrified shock as both Mark and Jed fell to the ground as if felled by the same bullet. "No!" she heard herself scream amidst the cacophony of noise and destruction. "Oh, no, no, no!" She fell to her knees beside the two men, whose bodies were twisted in grotesque, unnatural angles. Heedless of the stampeding of feet and trampling of other Union soldiers, she shook the two men, dropping her rifle to the ground.

"Oh, please," she sobbed. "Please get up!"

She heard, as though from a great distance, a familiar voice yelling to her. "Johnson! Aaron Johnson, come here!" It was Ivar, but she didn't move. She didn't care about anything except for awakening Mark and Jed. They didn't move—they both stared unblinkingly in different directions, not flinching, not moaning, but horribly, horribly still.

A rough hand under her arm lifted her while a voice in her ear snarled, "Anne, pick up your weapon. Now." Ivar hauled her forcibly to her feet and tore her away from the two men who lay prostrate and lifeless on the ground. "Look!" he said as he pointed to a unit of Union soldiers who had found an advantageous spot on slightly higher ground.

He began running toward them from the side, dragging Anne with him. She stumbled and struggled to keep up with his long-legged stride, yelling at him repeatedly to release her arm, but he held fast. By the time they reached the unit, which was now identifiable by their regimental flag as a group from New York, Ivar was practically dragging her along the ground.

He pulled her again to her feet and looked her directly in the eye. "Are you with me?" he barked.

She nodded.

"You stay by my side, and you fire your weapon. Do you understand me?"

"Yes," she said, feeling tears burning a path down her filthy cheeks. Ivar's eyes were a haunting, burning blue amidst the dirt and grime on his own face. He had long ago lost his cap, and his blonde hair was disheveled and dirty as well. As she tore the cap from her cartridge and loaded her weapon with hands that shook so much she feared she'd drop it, she noticed the blood spattered liberally in dark, gruesome patches all over his uniform.

She glanced down at her own clothing and noted the blood, other peoples' blood, smeared across her midsection and arms. Fighting a wave of nausea, she finished loading her gun, raised it to her shoulder, and fired. The sound echoed in her head, and she knew she'd hear it in her dreams for the rest of her life . . .

* * *

The next morning dawned bright and warm, and Anne stumbled along next to Ivar as they passed what was being hailed as "Burnside's Bridge," the third and final front of the previous day's battles. It was a draw, really, but because the Union had effectively halted Lee's advance northward, it was already being hailed a Union victory.

Once the troops from New York had found the more advantageous spot on which to return fire on the rebels in the sunken lane, the Confederates had been beaten where they stood. The lane, having already been renamed "Bloody Lane," was piled so deeply with bodies that it was impossible to walk across.

"You were right," Ivar muttered as they worked their way down the dusty road that was littered with bodies and blood. "McClellan isn't pursuing. Seems like a likely course of action, and yet we stay here."

Anne nodded but said nothing. She took little pride in winning their argument of the day before. Had it only been one day? It seemed like a lifetime.

Ivar took a good look at her face and, taking her by the arm, this time with a gentleness that surprised her, steered her off the dusty path and into a small copse of trees. Her gun hung limp in her hand, and her canteen had long since vanished. She was thirsty, hungry but had no stomach for food, and was exhausted to the very marrow of her bones. She looked at Ivar and wondered where he found the strength to even speak.

"Are you ill, Anne?"

She was too tired to even chastise him for using her given name when others might overhear. She shook her head, but knew she'd probably be ill forever.

He studied her for long moments, his perceptive blue eyes seeing too much. She knew what was coming before he even said it. "I'm going to tell them who you are."

It was enough to shake her from her daze. "No. I'll be fine." She rubbed her forehead and massaged her eyes. They were gritty from dust and gunfire smoke. "Please," she said as she dropped her hand. She gripped her weapon more firmly and steeled her resolve. "I want to stay."

"Why." His question sounded more like a flat accusation than anything.

"Because I want to finish what Mark and Jed can't." She felt her eyes tearing up again at the thought of their fallen friends, and angrily brushed the moisture aside. The tears definitely wouldn't help her convince Ivar that she was coping well, and besides, they hurt her eyes.

Ivar shot her a look of impatience and shifted his rifle from one hand to the other. "I told myself when I realized you were a woman that I wouldn't interfere," he hissed, "that what you were doing was your own business. Now, however, I'm starting to believe that my place will be in hell after this life if I don't find a way to make you go back home."

"You're not responsible for me. This is my own doing, and I'm a woman, not a child." Anne thought of her mother and straightened her spine. "I'm not a minor, nor some irresponsible chit who hasn't thought things through. I knew what I was getting myself into when I enlisted, and I intend to see this through to its fruition."

"I don't understand you. Not a bit."

"You don't need to. But I find myself a little frustrated that you can't comprehend I could be here for the same reasons you are."

"I'm here because I saw my friends enlisting—friends who had more responsibility at home than I did, and yet they were doing the right thing by heeding the call of their country. *You* enlisted because you wanted to see something interesting to write about. You were bored."

"How dare you! How dare you minimize my intentions!"

"Tell me I'm wrong!"

Anne stood before him, fuming and shaking in exhaustion and fury. "You have no right to suggest you know me! To suggest that you know where I came from or why I'm doing this!"

He moved his face close to hers and dropped his voice to an angry whisper. "Tell me I'm wrong, Anne!"

She clenched her teeth together so hard she was sure they'd all crack. She hated him, then—hated him because he was right.

"I don't have to tell you anything," she spat out, and spun on her heel. "And I'm not going home," she said over her shoulder. "If you tell anyone about me, I'll find another way to get back in. I'm staying until I'm dead or this war is over."

She could feel his gaze boring into her back as she walked, and when he caught up to her in a few angry strides, she could almost feel the fury that radiated from his body. In that moment, she knew he might be angry with her, but he wouldn't tell. Her secret was hers to keep, for the meantime, anyway, and she breathed a sigh of relief. She didn't want to go home yet. Nobody would understand the things she had seen or done—she wanted to stay for a while with the people who could relate to her.

* * *

Ivar mentally turned a blind eye as the Ohio 7th took on the duties of recovering the dead and wounded from the battlefields. His first task, with Anne stubbornly at his side, was to retrieve the bodies of his friends. His heart groaned in pain at the sight of their intertwined limbs and lifeless faces. So close in life, they had joined each other in death, and surprisingly, it made sense.

He thought of their wives and children at home who would have to receive the news of their death, and his hands trembled as he moved them, one by one, onto crude stretchers. How close he had come to joining them! It could have been Per and Amanda receiving news of *his* death—left to raise his child without him.

Ivar noted with a certain amount of sadness the state of the Confederate dead. He had heard rumors about the shoddy state of the rebel armies, but to see it firsthand was sobering. Many of them were dressed in what could be called clothing in only the loosest of terms. The shirts and pants were torn rags, and there were more soldiers with bare feet than he could count. Their soles were cracked and bleeding, some obviously having marched so far without shoes or boots that their feet had toughened on their own.

Anne stayed with him the entire day, and showed almost no emotion at all until they came across a familiar face, lying still and lifeless on the ground next to an amazingly intact camera. "Oh, Alan," she groaned. She sank next to him in the mangled cornfield and wiped a hand across his bloodied face. She picked up one of his hands and held it to her cheek, finally placing a kiss on his knuckles and letting his hand fall back to his side. Ivar glanced around to see who might have noticed; if Anne wanted to maintain her charade as a man, she probably ought not indulge in such feminine displays of affection. However, he had to admit, he had seen much emotion, raw pain, and tears over the course of the last twenty-four hours. Perhaps nobody would think her odd at all.

"Can we take him now?" Anne asked, looking up at him, and his heart constricted at the sadness in her eyes.

He nodded and motioned for some of the men in their company to come forward with a stretcher. Anne took the camera and held it as she would an infant while they placed the photographer's body on the board. She walked beside him silently, and for the rest of the day kept the camera with her.

It wasn't until the dark of night, when he returned back to their camp and fell upon his bedroll, that he truly felt the loss of his good friends. He looked over at their vacant bedding and felt the hot sting of tears burn in his eyes. He closed them tightly and willed them to stop, but heedless of his wishes, they seeped from his eyelids and trailed a path onto his blankets. He heard Anne's quiet sniffing next to him and knew she was affected by their absence as well.

He hadn't imagined it would hurt so much to lose them, and in such an awful way. The pain cut deeply—it was even worse than when his wife had left him and their young daughter; he had imagined he would never hurt in a worse way than he did then. Hoarse sobs rose from his chest and into his throat, and he choked with the effort it took to keep them inside.

Theirs was not the only tent from which such noise emitted. There were soft cries of despair and moans from wounded men all over the camp. The task of removing all of the dead and wounded from the fields of battle had taken all day and well into the night, and still the task remained unfinished. The sorrow abounding throughout not only their regiment, but also numerous others in the groups that comprised the Army of the Potomac, was heavy and painful.

Anne seemed to know what he needed most; she didn't try to speak to him or comfort him in any way. She left him to his space and, when his sobbing quieted and the tears slowed their flow, she remained silent and allowed him to fall into a fitful sleep.

CHAPTER 19

"Gentlemen, I have, as you are aware, thought a great deal about the relation of this war to slavery. . . . My mind has been much occupied with this subject and I have thought all along that the time for acting on it might probably come. I think the time has come now. I wish it was a better time. . . . I have got you together to hear what I have written down. I do not wish your advice about the main matter, for that I have determined for myself."

—Abraham Lincoln to his cabinet in reference to his preliminary Emancipation Proclamation

* * *

23 September 1862
Boston, Massachusetts

Dearest Luke,

I miss your company now more than ever. My mother's death has left me feeling much like a ship adrift at sea, and I find myself scrambling to keep from thinking of her. She would be angry with me, however, for carrying on so, and I must find other ways to distract myself.

I'll begin my distraction efforts by telling you what has happened lately here and in general. Your sister Camille is staying with me, as is your Aunt Jenny. I'm sure you must know this from correspondence from both your mother and Camille, but I must tell you personally how much of a strength they are to me. I have selfishly taken advantage of their generous offers of companionship and have not one regret for it! I believe our time together has also been a strength to your aunt. The loss of your uncle has been difficult for her to bear.

I don't know if you will have heard this news by the time you receive this letter, but the preliminary text of an Emancipation Proclamation has been published today! I can scarcely believe the direction in which matters are now progressing, but am thrilled, of course. This early draft is not nearly as conclusive as most of the Society would like; the proclamation frees only those slaves who reside in the rebel states. The slave-holding border states that Lincoln so fears losing have not been included in this draft.

I can't help but feel, however, that this is a much-needed step in the proper direction. Surely total emancipation of all slaves will be quick to follow, and then we shall see the dreams of so many, for so long, realized.

Congress has also haggled over the issue of allowing free blacks to enlist and fight for the Union. It became officially supported in July, but we still hear murmurs amongst all levels of society against it. Frederick Douglass has been most vocal in support of such a thing. How fitting for a black man to be able to fight for his own freedom!

Lincoln has been extremely cautious, it is said, in his delicate balancing act of trying to maintain the border states while at the same time appeasing the ever-growing contingency here in the North that pressures him to officially declare the aim of the war as total emancipation of all slaves. The voices here grow louder and stronger, and while I shout along with the rest, I don't envy Lincoln his task. I believe his heart is true and with us—he has denounced slavery as an evil for many, many years.

I find myself thinking of you constantly, Luke, and hope you are well. We receive news telegraphed from the battlefront—the details are unthinkable. Matthew Brady has an exhibit in his New York studio with photographs of the aftermath of Antietam. I hear they are horrific. We are slaying each other in peoples' backyards! I can hardly believe I live in a time when such a thing is reality for this country. It seems that more and more, every family I speak with has a relative, if not a direct son or father, who has died or been wounded. How much longer can this continue?

But enough of my worries—it's hardly fitting that I write to you and fret when surely you would benefit more from words of encouragement. Please know that I love you, Luke. I have never said the words to you aloud, and I look forward to the day when I can whisper them in your ear. Please take good care for your safety and know that I will patiently await your return.

My love always,
Abigail

Luke folded the letter and creased its edges thoughtfully. She had said she loved him! He smiled a bit with a feeling of relief. He had loved her for a very long time, and couldn't wait to tell her, either. Perhaps it wouldn't be hasty of him, then, to formally ask her to marry him. In a perfect world, he would have wished to do so in person; however, who knew how long it would be until he returned home? He had two years left in his enlistment, and if the war didn't end before then, it would be at least that long until he could be with her again.

It was true, he could feel her worry in the lines she penned, but he would rather have received a whole letter from her full of naught but complaints and fear than nothing at all.

The drills for the day were finished, and the men were left to tick away the hours as best they could. The weather was warm, and the soldiers were in their shirtsleeves, the cuffs rolled up to reveal arms that had tanned brown in the sun. Luke glanced at Ben, who sat across their empty fire pit with his head bent over one of two letters, his expression unreadable.

Seated on a blanket that had seen better times, Luke leaned back against a fallen tree log and stretched his legs outward, yawning. "Trouble?" he asked Ben, who glanced up from his letter as though startled that he wasn't alone.

"No, not trouble, exactly." He rubbed his forehead and closed his eyes. Gesturing with the piece of paper, he said, "This is from Emily. The wedding is in one week, out on the lawns at Willow Lane."

"Is the whole family in Savannah, then?"

"Everyone but my father and Richard."

"I'm surprised they wouldn't wait for your father, at least."

Ben shrugged. "Who knows when he'll return?"

Luke looked at his cousin's face and debated whether or not to pose his next question. "Did you know," he began, and stopped.

Ben waited, and when Luke didn't finish his question, he said, "Did I know what?"

"Did you know beforehand that your father was leaving for England?"

"No. By the time I heard, he was already gone. Why? Did you suppose I knew and did nothing to alert the blockaders?"

"Well, I did wonder. He is your father, after all."

Ben shook his head. "He may be, but my political loyalties have nothing to do with family. I'd have told in a heartbeat if I had known."

"It would have been hard for me to do, were it my own father."

Ben's smile didn't reach his eyes. "And there's the difference between the two men, isn't it? Your father is a man of strong character."

"So is yours. You just don't happen to agree with him."

Ben snorted and looked off into the trees. A twitching muscle in his jaw betrayed his agitation. "If my father had a strong character, he would have done something definitive long ago."

"What should he have done? Leave your mother?"

"Luke, he should never have married my mother."

Luke was silent for a moment, and then finally dared voice that which bothered him the most when thinking of Ben's life. "What are you going to do when this is all over?"

Ben looked back at his cousin. "What do you mean?"

"Your life. What do you plan to do with it?"

"I'll go back to Utah."

"Were you happy there?"

"Happier than I was here. I felt welcome."

Luke studied him for a moment longer in silence. "Do you have someone special you'd like to share your time with?"

Ben flushed a bit and looked down at his hands. "I've . . . yes. But I don't know that it will ever become a reality."

"Might I suggest something?"

"You're going to, even if I say no." Ben smiled slightly and softened the statement.

"When this war is finished, regardless of the outcome, you're going to become a bitter old man if you don't release much of your anger."

"You sound like someone's mother."

"It's true. You hate your family; you despise your parents so much it's eating what little optimism you have left."

Ben sighed. "I don't hate my family. But just imagine for a moment, Luke, if you had been raised in my place. James and Elizabeth are people of strong moral fiber. Mother and Father care little for anything that doesn't revolve around Bentley and the money it generates." Ben stood and paced to their tent and back again. "They *worship* that plantation, Luke. It's a god for them. They support a war that is being waged to give them the right to continue worshiping that ground and the system that makes it possible! Now, you can't tell me you would be able to brush those things aside."

He did have a point, Luke had to concede. Furthermore, now that he had tossed out his grandiose suggestion that Ben abandon his anger and move forward, he had no idea how he should suggest his cousin accomplish that. He finally shrugged. "I wish I had answers for you, Ben, but all I know is that if you live the rest of your life embittered, you will have allowed the system to beat you."

Ben sank back down onto the ground and leaned against another large log they had placed around the fire pit. He looked at Luke and finally shook his head. "You're right. But I have no idea how to change. Anger is a comfortable companion."

Luke motioned to a letter Ben had been reading earlier. "Is that from your friends in Utah?" he asked, although he knew it was an obvious change of subject.

Ben nodded and retrieved the letter with a smile playing about his lips. "Earl Dobranski's latest update," he said. "I miss that boy." He looked at Luke with a shake of his head and a small laugh. "Earl got himself a pair of boxing gloves not long before I left to go to Boston, and I could swear, I thought my life was over. He's built like a lumberjack, and we used to fight with each other for sport. His mother had to tend to my scrapes and bruises afterward, and I think she scared me even more than Earl did."

"What news does he have from the West?"

"They have a huge twenty-fourth of July celebration every year to commemorate the anniversary of the first Mormon pioneers into the Salt Lake Valley. All the government and Church dignitaries attend—people make large feasts, there are parades, it's quite a big to-do. They've done it all again this year, and apparently they've welcomed in a new governor. Harding," Ben said, consulting the letter. "They like him very much. He's made some very favorable comments about them and seems to be trying to understand the religion and the culture. He's avidly antisecessionist and pro-Union."

Luke nodded. "Sounds like he may do right by them."

"I hope so. There've been some problems in the past."

"So you really feel like one of them?"

"I do. I felt as though I belonged from the moment I joined them. I was frustrated with what I'd left behind, but they welcomed me like family."

"Why don't you let me take a look at that Mormon Bible of yours—I'll tell you what I think."

Ben stared at him, his mouth slack, and Luke had to laugh. "Did you think I'm not the least bit curious?"

"I didn't want to offend you with it, or push it onto you . . ." Ben stammered.

"You can't very well push something on someone when you don't even offer it."

Ben rose and entered their tent, returning in a moment with a small, black book. "I hope you enjoy it," he said. "I know I have."

Luke took the book from his cousin with a mental shrug. He had asked to see the book more out of kindness toward Ben than anything. It couldn't hurt to read it, though.

* * *

23 September 1862
Charleston, South Carolina

Ruth talked constantly as she helped Mary pack her things. She knew she was babbling, but she couldn't seem to stem the flow of chatter that spewed forth; a little bit of nothing and everything.

"You must take care of yourself once you're in Boston," she said. "Just because there are many abolitionist folk doesn't mean every white person's friendly."

"Yes, Mama Ruth." Mary smiled at her.

"I've already said that, haven't I?"

"Yes. But I don't mind."

"I want you to remember everything I've taught you, and don't you go doubting yourself, not even for a moment, do you hear? You have talents, my girl, and you are smart. You don't let anyone tell you otherwise."

"I won't." Mary paused. "Mama Ruth, I'm afraid I'll miss you dreadfully. I almost don't want to leave."

Ruth approached her granddaughter and gathered her close. "Don't talk like that. This is what I would wish for you, above anything else in life. I'll be along in due time." She pulled back and looked at Mary's eyes. "All right?"

Mary nodded. "You'll be well here?"

"I will. I don't want you to give me a second thought."

Mary laughed without humor. "As if I'll go a day without thinking of you. You're the only mother I've ever had. I don't want to leave you behind."

Ruth shook her shoulders lightly. "No more of that. D'you hear?"

Mary nodded.

There was a quick knock at the door, and Joshua poked his head in. "Have you said your farewells?"

"We have. Do you have a hug for your Aunt Ruth?"

"As if I could leave without one." Joshua smiled and embraced the older woman, and she rubbed her hands gently across his broad back, remembering when he had been an infant.

"You take good care of yourself, young man. Mind your manners, but hold your head high."

"I will. You'll be all right here?"

"Yes. My, how you two children do fuss! Enough nonsense. I'll be along when I can."

A short hour later they climbed into a carriage with Emily, and then they were gone. Ruth indulged herself by returning to her quarters for a moment and crying for all she was worth before drying her tears and returning to her duties.

* * *

30 September 1862
Savannah, Georgia

If he had only taken the opportunity to let his mother know he was there, she might, *might* have let him give the bride away. Ben shook his head from his lowly squatting position in a large clump of bushes that were liberally outfitted with stickers and briars. There was no chance at all that Sarah would have allowed him to even see Emily, let alone attend her through the wedding ceremony.

It was evening at least, and the hot sun had dimmed its fervor somewhat, so that the small gathering of people situated on Willow Lane's beautiful lawns were afforded a measure of comfort. Emily's letter had said the ceremony would be followed by a formal dinner, and that the newly married couple was to spend their honeymoon period right there at the plantation. Apparently, wartime didn't make for the best festive travel. Ben smiled a bit at Emily's caustic humor and again glanced at her, standing next to the groom.

She wore a gown of beautifully simple white, her red hair elaborately plaited and covered by a gauzy, white veil. Her hair was in such stark contrast to the white of the material that she had taken Ben's breath away when she first appeared. She was a vision, and he was grateful to at least be able to see her.

Emily smiled at the small cheer that went up when the vows were finished and the bride and groom exchanged a chaste kiss. Every now and again, in the hustle and bustle that followed—the round of hugs and kisses, the congratulatory wishes—he saw her look about discretely as though trying to find someone. Ben knew she was looking for him, and he wished he could call out to her that he was there.

He stayed in his prickly bushes until well after dark, thankful he had been able to obtain a day of furlough. His presence in the regiment wouldn't be missed. When he was certain the revelers had all gone home or were bedded down for the night, he finally emerged, scratched and sore, from his hiding place.

He stood quietly, looking at the large house for a moment in confused speculation. Why on earth would Emily marry a plantation owner—an owner who obviously employed, purchased, and traded slaves? It flew in the face of everything she had said to him in her letters over the last six years. It didn't make any sense. His only thought was that perhaps she was hoping to free Mary and Joshua.

He had seen the two slave siblings earlier as they helped prepare for the wedding. He had to wonder what they were thinking of the whole affair, and wished desperately to be able to speak to either one of them. Well, truthfully, he considered as he felt his face flush, he would rather have spoken to Mary.

"Ben!" a voice whispered from the trees.

Startled, he nearly ran, but then trusted his better instincts and went in the direction of the voice. Deep into a small grove he followed the sound of retreating footsteps until, at last, he saw Mary.

He couldn't help but smile. "I merely think of you and you appear!" he whispered to her as they embraced.

She chuckled quietly and pulled back. "I knew you were here," she said. "I just had to wait until you showed yourself."

"Is anyone else here?"

Mary shook her head. "Only me. Everyone else is down for the night, I believe. The wedding is finished; the guests that live here in town have gone home."

"You're tired," he said, noting the fine lines of fatigue under her eyes.

"Just a bit." She smiled. "Emily will want to see you again. Will you be at Hilton Head for a long time?"

"I don't know. There's talk of splitting the brigades and sending some up north to join up with the Army of the Potomac. I suppose we'll see."

"I'll get a message to her if there's a time you can come back."

Ben thought for a moment. "I suppose I should wait at least a week. I can't get furlough again, so it'd have to be when I can manage some free time . . ."

"One week, then?"

He nodded. "One week, it is. Right here, if she can manage it. If the city were in Union hands, I might just march right up to the front door, but as it stands, I suspect I should continue hiding."

Mary smiled. "That's probably very sound thinking." She fidgeted with her hands for a moment and then added, "Ben, I'm glad I saw you again, because I want you to know how much I appreciate everything you did for me as a child. If it weren't for you, I wouldn't even know how to read or write, and, well, I'm grateful."

"Mary, it was my pleasure. You were such a sweet girl, and so ready to learn. I'm glad you've been able to retain everything." He paused. "It's amazing, really, the difference a few years makes. When I left, you were so young. Now you're practically a grown woman."

She nodded but said nothing.

"Do you, that is, have you . . . a beau?"

"Ben, you know how things are here. Even if I did, any relationship or marriage would be little more than a sham."

"Of course." He felt his face go hot. "How insensitive of me—please forgive me. I just wondered . . ."

"If I fancy anyone?" He could see her smile and her even, white teeth in the dark.

"Yes, I did wonder," he mumbled, wondering when he had lost his social graces.

"No," she said with a smile that looked fleetingly wistful. "My heart remains unattached."

He nodded, feeling strangely relieved. "I wish I could say I'm sorry to hear that."

Her eyes widened. "Why?" she whispered.

He shrugged, feeling strangely, sheepishly, like a schoolboy. "I should be getting back to camp," he muttered.

She nodded, her shoulders sagging a notch. "I hope to see you again," she said.

"Meet me next week with Emily."

"Oh, no. I should let her have her time alone with you."

"Please, I'd like to see you, too."

"You would?"

He nodded. "And is there any way Joshua could come, too? Will you ask him?"

"Oh. Oh, yes. I'll ask him."

They both stood, saying nothing but neither moving to leave. "Well, Mary, you take care of yourself," Ben finally said.

"I will. You do the same."

"You go now, and I'll watch to see that you make it to your quarters unharmed."

Mary laughed. "Oh, Ben. Always chivalrous. Even to a slave." She shook her head, gave him a quick hug, and turned and ran before he could respond.

As he watched her run toward the slave housing, he wondered what her future would hold. *Come to think of it,* he mused as he walked slowly away from his sister's new home, *I wonder what it will hold for all of us . . .*

* * *

Emily sat in the parlor of her new home two weeks after her wedding, still feeling no more like a plantation mistress than she had before. The home ran smoothly without her influence, although the staff had graciously asked her opinion on matters in which the woman of the house would have ordinarily had a hand.

Her husband was attentive and gentle, and she had no complaint with him. Her world should have been idyllic and peaceful, even with the country at war, but she felt useless. She did have one last remaining goal, and that was to see Joshua and Mary to safety in Boston.

With that purpose in mind, she rose and made her way to her husband's study. It adjoined the library, which was full, floor to ceiling, with more books than a body could count. She entered through the large room and walked to the French doors that separated the library from Austin's den. Seeing they were open and that he was seated behind his desk, alone, she entered.

Hearing her, Austin rose from his paperwork and smiled, his face lighting up with obvious pleasure. Emily couldn't stop the flush that crept up her neck and spread across her face. "Austin, I wonder if we could address something."

"By all means," he said, making his way around the desk. Placing a hand on the small of her back, he led her back into the library, to a divan that faced a large wall of windows overlooking the gardens at the back of the house.

Once seated comfortably, she tried for a moment to collect her thoughts. Since her marriage, she had felt very much unlike her old self. She was now a married woman and wasn't sure exactly how to comport herself. She was hardly a society lady burning with a desire to entertain or go to tea, and yet she wasn't really a child anymore, either.

Austin was an enigma. He was handsome, charming, and even-tempered, and she couldn't for the life of her understand why he loved her. He was never demanding, he made time in his schedule for her, they discussed politics together, and much to Emily's delight, they were of a like mind concerning anything important. He still felt very much a stranger, though, and she found herself on uncertain ground.

"I'm thinking of Mary and Joshua," she began. "I'm wondering when we can send them to Boston."

Austin nodded. "I had planned to accompany three people north in about two weeks. Usually, however, I try to secure some sort of employment for the person before we leave. I don't happen to have anything ready for Mary and Joshua yet."

Emily looked out the window for a moment, tapping one finger to her lips. "If I can arrange employment for them, will you be able to take them with you this next time?"

He nodded. "I will. Speaking of that trip, I've been meaning to ask if you'd like to come along. The front will be even more convincing if we are traveling as husband and wife. All of this time I've been going under the guise of business travel—it would be a welcome change to have a different, yet still viable, reason."

Go with Joshua and Mary to Boston? Her heart pounded. She'd be witness to their faces as they took their first breaths on free soil. "I would love to," she said. "Thank you, Austin. And thank you for paying my mother such an exorbitant sum of money, as well."

"It was my pleasure," he said as he took her hand in his own. "I only wish we'd been able to convince your mother that Ruth and Rose should come along as well."

Emily shook her head. "I knew she never would agree to it. I'm afraid the only way Ruth will ever taste freedom is if the Union wins this war."

"*When* the Union wins this war."

"Yes."

Austin frowned. "Are you not well, Emily? You seem subdued."

"I'm perfectly healthy."

"Are you happy?"

"I . . . yes. I'm just feeling a bit unsure of myself, I suppose. It's not a feeling to which I'm accustomed."

Austin nodded. "I should have expected it, and I apologize that you feel uncomfortable. Is there anything I can do to help?"

Truly, could a woman ask for a better husband? "No," she said. "I'll adjust eventually. Thank you, though." She smiled and leaned forward as he kissed her cheek. "Will you be going into town later today?" she asked as they rose to leave.

"Yes, in a few hours. Would you like to come?"

"I would. I'll have some letters to post."

* * *

It was too much, just as Joshua had known it would be. Stanhope was a good white man who was worth his word, and that meant something. Because he truthfully had no need for other servants when he purchased Joshua and Mary from Mrs. Birmingham, he asked Joshua what kind of work he might like to do, to which Joshua replied, "I'd like to try my hand at furniture making."

Stanhope had promptly shown him to the wood shop, wherein Joshua found more tools and kinds of wood than ever a person could imagine. "This shop was used by a carpenter who made his way north a few years ago, and it hasn't been used since. You're welcome to it." The friendly smile and genuine manner had been beyond unexpected, and Joshua had felt a measure of warmth in it.

But to watch Emily as a married woman, knowing that she now "belonged" to Stanhope, was more than he could bear. She appeared content, if somewhat subdued, and he was glad for that. Knowing, however, that she had married one man while loving another, and that it had been for *his* sake, broke his heart. The sooner he was away from her, the better.

CHAPTER 20

"New Orleans gone—and with it the Confederacy. Are we not cut in two? The Mississippi ruins us if it is lost. . . . I have nothing to chronicle but disasters. . . . The reality is hideous."
—Mary Chestnut, famed Civil War diarist

* * *

27 September 1862
New Orleans, Louisiana

The day had been long and tedious, and Daniel wondered for the millionth time how he had managed to once again find himself shuffling papers behind a desk. He was at sea, for heaven's sake! Well, truthfully, they were in port, but the point remained the same—he was stationed aboard a ship; he had hardly expected to be spending his time doing office work.

Nundry was quickly becoming a thorn in his side. The man envied Daniel's position—a position for which Daniel certainly hadn't lobbied—and Nundry constantly looked over the sailor's shoulder for potential flaws or mistakes.

It was a welcome relief to find two minutes alone, away from Nundry and the majority of his shipmates. The small pub where Daniel sat was one he frequented when he could. It was generally quiet, on a side street where few people seemed to venture, and the customer base consisted of mainly Union soldiers and sailors.

He sat over a mug of local ale and contemplated his current situation. He wasn't altogether certain he was achieving his objectives, but then, he couldn't be sure what those objectives had ever been. He had enlisted to get away from home, and that much he had certainly done. Would things be different, though, when he returned? What was it he hoped to accomplish with his life anyway?

Daniel checked his pocket watch and had to glance twice at the face. It was nearly time for him to meet Marie, and he didn't want to be late. Tossing a few coins on the table as he rose, he had nearly made it to the door when he was halted by a loud voice.

"I knew it was you! This fella's the best brawler in all of New York City, boys!"

Daniel groaned inwardly. When the man stood and barred the entrance, he said, "I need to be going."

"Aren't you O'Shea?"

"Yes, but I don't fight anymore."

"Aw, come on! Butros here says he can lick anybody!"

"I'm sure he probably can." Daniel tried to shove past the arm, but it wouldn't budge. A man easily a head taller than Daniel and twice as thick through the chest and arms rose from the corner table and sauntered over to the door. Daniel raised a hand, hoping the man would listen to an appeal of logic. One whiff of alcohol on the man's breath quickly disabused him of the hope, however.

"I don't fight anymore," Daniel said to the man's glassy eyes.

"I do."

With that, Daniel found himself flat on his back, seeing stars. He shook his head and tried to focus as the man called Butros hauled him to his feet. The cheering erupted around them, and Daniel noticed that money began to leave pockets and wallets, much as it had in the days when he had been paid to fight at home.

He fuzzily dodged another punch and shook his head again, hoping his vision would clear before the man could land another good hit. Thankfully, the large man had consumed so much ale that his movements were a bit slow. Daniel maneuvered his way toward the door, his hands raised in defense.

"I just want to leave," he said to the thug.

"Yer yella."

"I'm leaving."

"Yer yella!"

Daniel danced to one side in an effort to avoid the fist that came toward his midsection, but he didn't move fast enough. The huge fist caught him square in the ribs, and he felt something crack. With a groan, he slid up against an empty chair, his tumble sending the occupants of the table scurrying in all directions.

Cradling his side, he prepared himself this time as the large man came at him. The teeth that grinned at him were yellow and half rotted. Focusing on those teeth as the man advanced, Daniel waited until the very last moment and then, with all the strength and skill he possessed, planted his fist in the man's mouth.

Butros's eyes widened in shock and then rolled a bit as he fell back, his hand flying to his mouth. Blood spurted out from between his fingers and rolled down his hand. Seizing the opportunity, Daniel made for the door just as the pub proprietor came screaming from the back rooms. Limping out into the night, he quickly lost himself amongst the trees and thick undergrowth along the street, and skirted as many main thoroughfares as he could. The noise behind him gradually faded into the distance, and he allowed himself to relax a bit as he continued on his way to Marie's home, clutching his left side with a right hand that was most assuredly broken.

* * *

Marie impatiently checked the time and looked down the street yet again. Perhaps Daniel was unable to get away today. It wasn't as though he didn't have other things to do. She regretted the fact that they could meet only under the cover of darkness, and wished things might be different—that they could somehow have met in a different time, under different circumstances.

The Fromeres were down for the night, tucked away safe and snug in her upstairs bedrooms. Every time night fell and all was quiet, Marie breathed a sigh of relief that they had made it through another day without detection. They couldn't stay thusly forever. Marie had maintained the large garden plot to the back of the home and was grateful for it, but often when she went out to purchase what she couldn't grow or produce on her own, she wondered how long it would be before someone grew suspicious at the amounts she carried home.

The ideal situation would be to somehow get the family to Boston; the question remained *how.* It was true, Lincoln had freed the slaves in rebel territories, but then the Fromeres were already free, and they had encountered trouble from all sides! People refused to allow them the space they needed to live their own lives, and young troublemakers in town who had framed young Noah for a beating he didn't commit were the reason she was harboring the family in the first place.

She looked around her at some of the vacant homes up and down the street. Many people had fled just before the invasion, choosing to vacate to their homes in the country or stay with relatives elsewhere rather than face the "Northern horde," as many called it. More still had managed to leave the city after the Union army took control, and Marie began to feel as though she were living on a ghost street.

It was just as well, though. She was much less worried about someone seeing Daniel or thinking anything odd of the fact that he was in the neighborhood. To be safe, they kept their time spent together at night, but her anxiety was much less than it had been when he had first arrived.

He was sincere and charming in a rough, uncultured sort of way, and it had been a delight to see his personality up close as opposed to thousands of miles away in letters. She smiled a bit as she anticipated his arrival, but the smile slowly faded as she spied the shadow of a man limping toward her house as though he could barely walk.

With a small cry, she realized that the shadow was Daniel. Heedless of who might see, she ran out the front door and to his side, insisting that he lean on her as they stumbled up the steps and into the house. His eye was swollen nearly shut, and a trickle of blood had dried on the corner of his mouth. What alarmed her the most, however, was his sharp intake of breath as she eased him into one of her sturdy kitchen chairs.

"What happened to you?" she asked as she rushed to the kitchen pump and wet a dishrag. She wrung it dry and applied it to his eye, then moved to put a kettle on the stove.

"My past came back to haunt me," he mumbled, and clutched at his left side as though it was all he could do to remain upright.

"I think you should lie down," Marie said, and rose to help him out of his chair.

"No, no. I'd rather sit for a bit."

"Who did this to you?"

"One of my own." Daniel shook his head. "I used to fight professionally, you might say, and someone recognized me from home." He waved a hand wearily and told her what had happened at the pub. "I'm sorry, Marie," he said. "I'm not fit company for you. I never really have been."

"Of course you are," she said, and took a seat opposite him, seeking to lift his mood. "I told you—people around here think I'm a harlot. They would expect me to have a friend who fought."

He shook his head, trying to smile. The effort cracked open the sore at his mouth, and he winced. The kettle whistled, and Marie stood, happy to have something to do. With hands that shook, she poured Daniel a cup of mild tea and brought it to him at the table.

"Can you drink this?"

He shrugged and then winced again at the movement. Tentatively moving his left hand forward, he wrapped his fingers around the cup, making it look comically small. He took a sip and closed his eyes, then carefully placed the cup back onto the saucer.

"My mother would like you very much, Marie Brissot."

"Really? And why is that?"

"You make a good cup of tea."

Marie smiled and tried not to allow herself to become emotional over the state of her friend's battered body. "Your side," she said. "What do you suppose is wrong? Would you like me to fetch a doctor? Do you have one aboard ship?"

His face blanched slightly. "Please, if you have any regard for me at all, do not find a doctor for me. It's just my ribs. They may be cracked, I think."

"Oh, Daniel. How are you going to do your work? How will you sleep comfortably in that hammock?"

"I'll manage. These days all I'm required to do is paperwork, and the hammock is surprisingly comfortable." She could hear the effort he made to keep his tone light, and she tried with all her might to match it.

"Well, then, you're living like a king, aren't you."

He smiled and opened his mouth to say something when he looked slightly over her shoulder and froze. Alarmed, she whirled around to see young Noah peering around the doorway. The sixteen-year-old fled the room, and Marie leapt from her chair to stop his frightened flight.

"Noah," she called when he reached the stairs. "It's fine. Don't worry—he's a friend of mine."

Noah retraced his steps and stood before her, looking extremely sheepish. "I'm sorry, Miss Marie. I done heard your voice and you sounded scared. I come down here to check on you."

"Thank you. I'm fine, though. Please go back to bed and get your rest."

The young man returned to the second floor, and Marie stood at the stairs for a moment, wondering how she would explain his appearance to Daniel. She made her way slowly back into the kitchen and resumed her seat.

"You have slaves?" He sounded surprised.

"No, no. I am helping a family of free blacks who are in a bit of trouble." She chewed on her lip for a moment. "Nobody knows they're here, though, and if you wouldn't mind . . ."

"I won't say a word." He pretended to lock his mouth and toss a key over his shoulder.

"Thank you. I appreciate it very much." She fidgeted with a stray thread on her skirt until she realized she was making a mess with the material, and commanded her restless hands to be still.

"It's very fitting, you harboring a family in need," he murmured, adjusting the cloth he still held on his eye. "I'm not surprised in the least."

"You don't disapprove?"

"Of course not. You remind me of my mother."

"That's the second time you've mentioned her tonight. Do you miss her?"

Daniel nodded, although it seemed reluctant. "I miss my parents very much. My father is a very enthusiastic immigrant, you might say, and although he often made me feel insane with his rosy attitude, I find myself missing his company."

"Your father sounds like a wonderful man."

"He is." Daniel cleared his throat a bit. "I wish I could have met yours."

Marie nodded, feeling her throat swell. Drat—would she never be able to think of Jean-Pierre without crying? She quickly cast about for another safer topic of conversation.

"So, will there be trouble aboard for you because of this tonight?" she asked, gesturing toward his battered frame.

"Most likely not," he answered. "There was nobody from my ship that I recognized, and I left before it became a matter of monetary damage to the pub."

"I'm glad."

"You're not . . ." He paused and looked at her as though trying to solve a riddle. "You're not appalled by the fact that I'm basically nothing short of a street brawler?"

"You're much more than a street brawler, Daniel O'Shea. And as for your fights, I'm assuming you probably had good reasons."

Daniel shrugged and winced again. "I don't know that they were good reasons," he said, shifting slightly in his chair, "but I fought because I was angry."

"Angry at your opponents?"

"Angry at all of America. And angry at my brother for leaving me." He looked so embarrassed that Marie felt a tug of sympathy on her heart.

"I can understand that," she said. "I'm angry at my father for leaving me. Perhaps I should fight someone—will it help?"

He chuckled and sucked in his breath. "You must believe me when I say it doesn't solve a thing," he said after the pain had obviously subsided a bit. "I wouldn't recommend it."

"Well, then, I shall have to think of something else."

"How are your students?"

Marie felt a stab of sadness. "They're not coming to school so much anymore," she said. "Their mothers are feeling the pain of being without husbands and are hurting for help on their farms. Even the young ones are required to work from sunup to sundown. I haven't gone to the schoolhouse for the last two days. There's nobody there to teach."

"I'm sorry." Marie glanced at him in appreciation. The amazing thing was, he really *did* seem sorry for her sake. What an amazing thing, to find such a good friend. She hadn't felt so relaxed since Gustav had been home—and Daniel was even better companionship than Gustav. Daniel didn't seem to want her to be anybody other than who she was.

At the thought of Gustav, she said to Daniel, "I was just informed the other day that one of my good friends is missing—nobody has seen him since Shiloh."

"I'm very sorry," he said. "I wish I had better comfort for you."

She shrugged. "There's really not much to say, is there. This war gets uglier by the day. He was a good friend—a simple man who just wanted to fish the bayous for the rest of his life. He didn't require much."

Daniel nodded, but left her to her thoughts. He took another sip of his tea and sighed a bit. "Well," he said after a moment of comfortable silence had passed, "it seems tonight was the night for sharing secrets. You learned that I'm a fighter, and I learned you're hiding people in trouble. And yet here we are, still friends." He grinned crookedly and cursed under his breath at the trickle of blood he released again.

Marie chuckled and rose to dampen another cloth. She placed it against his mouth and removed her fingers when he lifted his hand to hold it himself. He now held one cloth to his eye and one to his bleeding lip, and her laugh increased in volume.

"Yes, here we are, still friends. We seem to be suitable company after all, you and I."

"Hear, hear," he said, and nodded toward his teacup. "If I had another hand, I'd raise my drink in a toast."

"If you had another hand, I don't think you'd have been allowed to enlist." He laughed a bit and then groaned, and Marie couldn't help but continue to smile. The conversation was silly, her mood was light despite her concern over his health, and she felt as though a burden had been lifted now that somebody else knew of her efforts on behalf of the Fromeres. It was less frightening, somehow, as though she were no longer alone.

"I'm glad you followed me home," she murmured, and smiled at his battered face.

"As am I, Miss Brissot."

"You look exhausted. I'll take you back down to the docks in my carriage."

He laughed and groaned again, and shot her a look of pure incredulity. "Do you honestly think I'd be party to you driving to the docks at this time of night? It's bad enough down there in the daylight."

"Well, you certainly can't walk. Take one of my horses and leave it in the livery. I'll fetch it tomorrow. Can you ride, do you suppose?"

"I believe I can manage." He held his breath and stood, slowly straightening. "Thank you for the tea and for the use of your tea cloths," he said, and moved the material from his eye and mouth.

"Keep them," she said, her mouth twitching at the corners.

"Well, many thanks," he said, sketching half of an elaborate bow.

"My pleasure. Your eye is probably going to turn several pretty shades of green and yellow before long."

"It won't be anything that hasn't happened before."

She felt her mood sober a bit as she accompanied him outside to the small stable. "You will take care? I should hate to see you break something even more vital than ribs."

"I will."

Marie saddled the horse, gently brushing away his hands as he moved to attempt the task on his own. With a certain amount of difficulty, he managed to hoist himself into the saddle.

"Thank you," he said, looking at her for a long moment with the one eye that still remained open.

"You're welcome. Call on me again soon, and take care."

* * *

Marie sat in the parlor long after Daniel had gone and looked across the room at a portrait of her parents. She found it amazing that she could finally look at it without becoming teary eyed. The pain hadn't gone away, but at least the outward manifestation of it was wearing off.

"Miss Marie?" The voice at the door startled her, and her eyes darted across the room to see who was there.

"Oh, Noah." She laid a hand on her chest. "What are you doing up so late?"

"Sorry, miss. Didn't mean to scare you."

"No, no. Come in and sit down."

Noah was the youngest of the Fromere children, and was becoming a handsome young man. He settled into the chair opposite hers and looked at her as though making an assessment. Of all the Fromeres, Noah had always been the most frank, as well as the one least intimidated by her. His older brothers were quiet and reserved. They rarely sought her out for conversation, and she was grateful Noah had taken it upon himself to strike up a friendship with her.

"Did you hear of the new regiment formed today?" he asked after a period of speculative silence.

"I did. Isn't it actually the same regiment that was formed last year under the Confederacy?"

Noah nodded. "They offered their services to Butler, and he mustered them all in today. The first officially recognized black unit in the Union army."

Marie heard the unmistakable note of pride in his voice. While understandable, something in it made her wary. She kept that thought to herself, however, and said, "It's marvelous, truly."

"It is! We can finally fight for our own freedom—do you know how that feels?"

"I can just imagine, Noah." She smiled at the young man, feeling a sense of companionship in his joy. Somehow, he was like family.

"I need to be a part of it, Miss Marie." His eyes shone. "I want to join them."

Marie sighed. It was what she had been dreading. "Oh, Noah. I know you want to be part of it, but it's dangerous for you. Someone who recognizes you—that Bussey boy, for instance—might realize you're still here in town and see you punished for beating the mayor's son."

He scowled. "You know I didn't do it."

"I do. But that's the whole reason your family's in this house. We must keep you all safe until we can get you to Boston."

"If my family can be safely transported somehow, then I'll enlist."

"That still doesn't eliminate the potential damage to *you.*"

He laughed. "I'm goin' off to fight! I'll probably die anyhow!"

"That is not funny. Don't even say such a thing."

"Well, it's true. What're the odds of me comin' back in one piece?"

"I'd say they're fair enough if you're careful and blessed with a bit of luck."

He shook his head. "I'd have to be blessed with a lot of luck, you mean."

"Then help me understand. If you truly feel you're enlisting to die, how can you do it with a cheerful heart?"

"Because I'll have the *right* to do it!" Noah sat forward in his chair. "Beggin' your pardon, miss, but you never had your rights questioned before. You don't walk down the street and worry that someone'll snatch you up and demand to see your papers or threaten to sell you to someone else."

"I know." She tried to smile gently, but felt a sudden surge of protectiveness, as though she wanted to put her arms around him and make everything in his life good. "In truth, I've felt the sting of some of it," she said. "Not in terms of my skin color, but my gender. *I* can't enlist."

He inclined his head slightly in acknowledgement.

"But it's nothing compared with the trials you face in your life, and I wish I could make things perfect for you."

"Aw, Miss Marie. You already have."

Her eyes burned with tears that collected and then trailed down her cheeks. "It's nothing," she said, feeling sheepish and casting her glance about for something to look at other than his sweet face.

"It's not nothin'. You saved us from folk who were ready to string us all up."

She sniffed and tried to control her emotions. She must be tired. She was always emotional when she was tired. "Well, then, I'm glad our paths crossed."

"Me too, miss."

"Noah, please think long and hard before you decide to enlist."

"I will. I don't want to do anything that will put my family in danger."

"I don't want you to face danger, either."

He smiled. "That's just life, ma'am. We all face danger of some kind or other eventually."

They sat in companionable silence for a moment until Marie glanced at the boy and said, “Noah, why did you come looking for me tonight?”

He grinned. “I figured if I could turn you in favor of me enlistin’, then my mama won’t object too awful much.”

Marie shook her head and dried the last vestiges of her tears with a reluctant smile. “You’re incorrigible, Noah. You’ve figured out how to play us as your pawns.”

He relaxed back into his chair with one eyebrow cocked. “And me a stupid colored boy. Who da’ thought?”

CHAPTER 21

"He is an admirable engineer, but he seems to have a special talent for a stationary engine."
—Abraham Lincoln, speaking of General McClellan

* * *

15 October 1862
London, England

Dear Sarah,

By the time you receive this letter, I may well be home. My ship will leave London in approximately one week, but the mail packet embarks tomorrow, and I wanted to apprise you of recent happenings here.

I fear we were unable to convince the government to officially recognize the Confederacy now that Lincoln has his Emancipation Proclamation in the works. The day it was announced in London, we witnessed dancing in the streets. Our hopes of official recognition from the queen, here, or from any European power, are now a thing of the past. There is no way, anymore, to assume that we may count on those quarters for support.

I have heard by now of the battle at Perrysville, Kentucky, on the 8th, and Braxton Bragg's failure to invade the North. How discouraging it is to fail a second Northern invasion; I hope that the armies quickly regroup and find themselves able to at least protect the ground we still hold.

I have been thinking, Sarah, of many things I plan to discuss at length with you when I return home. The first of these is a confession; I have been investing modest amounts of money through the years in my brother James's iron stock. I'm sure you are aware of his fantastic good fortune since the business's humble beginnings, and the money I invested, admittedly without your knowledge or consent, has grown and expanded in ways I certainly never expected in the beginning. I had hopes, of course, and trusted in my brother's good sense and ability to work, but have been caught pleasantly surprised at the return on my investments. Should anything perchance befall me at some point, I wanted you to be aware of it.

The second issue I wish to discuss with you is of a personal nature. I admire you greatly, and often find myself in awe of your strength. Things have not been warm between us for some time, and I hope to remedy this. I have remained true to you, Sarah, and our vows. I have led a lonely existence in our fine home, and I find that as we grow on in years, I do not wish to be alone any longer. If you have ever felt a shred of compassion for me, I sincerely hope that you will allow me the opportunity to properly court you. Regardless of the war, regardless of Bentley's prosperity or failure, I am still here and will stay by your side. It is my fondest hope that you may find pleasure in my presence.

Until we meet again.

My love,

Jeffrey

* * *

20 October 1862
Utah Territory

Earl Dobranski stood on the steps of his home east of State Street as the United States military troops passed by. The troops were under the command of a Colonel Connor, a man who had made no bones about his disdain of the Mormons. He had called them murderous, traitorous, and whores, descriptions that didn't settle well at all amongst the Saints.

Clearly, the troops were ready for battle. They were nervous, looking about themselves as they marched past the homes and people who had come out in droves to observe their passage. It was little wonder the troops were antsy, Earl thought to himself, if Connor had filled their heads with stories of the Mormons' treachery.

The crowds gathered on the street and on doorsteps did nothing to distract the men—they didn't cheer or yell disparaging things—they merely watched. The troops, roughly six hundred strong, made their way east of the city to a new encampment that overlooked the entire valley. Word was that Connor wanted to keep an eye on things.

It was ironic, really, that he should detest the Mormons so. He was strongly pro-Union and very staunchly committed to the government of the United States. The Latter-day Saints were as well, except for instances where they knew the government had done them wrong. The night before at the dinner table, his mother had said, "They just don't understand where we've come from and what we had to live through. The government didn't care one whit for our lives or our safety, and allowed us to be driven from our homes and murdered."

Now, as the troops marched up the street, he could only hope that there would be no friction—that the men who were to coexist with the Mormons would at least try to understand some of their history, some of their bitterness, some of their pain.

* * *

Over a week later, Earl sat in a meeting with his family as President Young addressed the congregation with regard to the troops sitting east of them on the benches. He seemed to have lessened a degree in his wariness of the men, as it had become clear that they meant no harm but felt it necessary to "watch" the Mormons, most likely to try to catch them in something unlawful or treasonous.

The prophet admonished them, as he had before, that the men were to keep their families away from the fort to the east, that if they chose to conduct business with the troops as far as selling of goods or services, they should respond kindly but maintain their self-respect. Earl leaned slightly to the right as his brother Enos, who was nearly eighteen years of age, whispered in his ear, "The prophet was told the troops want the members of the Church to offer some kind of oath of allegiance before we are allowed to sell them anything. As if their presence here isn't enough of an insult! And you know what the prophet said?"

Earl shook his head.

"He said if a soldier asks for a bushel of potatoes, then the Mormon should say, 'Do you want me to take the oath of allegiance? If you do, go to hell for your potatoes.'"

Earl snorted and was swiftly elbowed in the ribs by his mother. He attempted to swallow his laughter and nearly choked for his efforts. Much to his relief, he hadn't interrupted the proceedings, and sat through the rest of the meeting chuckling to himself.

As the Dobranski family left the meetinghouse and began their walk home, Earl looked up to the side of the mountain to the east and wondered, for the millionth time, how it could be that only a few months back in the summer he had been in the service of his government, and now, he was being spied on by them. He shook his head. Connor certainly hadn't made any friends in the valley with his inflammatory attitude and remarks to a San Francisco newspaper earlier in the year.

The situation was complex, and the little settlement in the desert had grown and would continue to grow as more people flocked to the hills. He worried a bit over the situation with the United States government and wondered if the relationship between them and the small band of people in the far reaches of the West would ever come to some kind of amicable agreement that would result in statehood for Utah.

The government maintained that polygamy was as much a treasonous system to the Union as was slavery. Earl wasn't a philosopher by any means, and seldom did he think of himself as a deep thinker, but he had long found slavery distasteful, and he knew it was because of the influence of his friend Ben. It was troubling, though, to think that a nation viewed something his people felt was a religious directive as treasonous. Polygamy was not a condition that had always existed in the Church, however, and perhaps the day would come when it would no longer be a necessity. It was an issue in which he exercised all the faith he could summon, and left it in the hands of the Lord. When the time was right, things would fall nicely into place. He had to believe it.

"So you missing bein' a soldier, Earl?" his youngest brother, Elisha, asked him as they neared their home.

"Naw. It was fine for a while, but I'm glad to be sleeping in my warm home. Those poor fellas are up there in their adobe huts. Is that where you'd like to be?" He ruffled the boy's hair and pulled his neck close in the crook of his arm. The boy squealed as Earl knuckled the top of his head.

"Maybe I'll be a soldier like Ben someday!"

"Heaven help those poor people if the war is still goin' on by the time you're allowed to enlist," Ellen murmured from behind the boys, where she strolled arm in arm with their father.

"'Poor people?'" the young one asked. "Sister Rushley says it serves 'em right!"

"War doesn't serve anybody right," Ellen answered. "It destroys people."

"Does it make Jesus cry?" Ellen regarded the young boy for a moment with a pained smile. "I think it does, Elisha."

* * *

16 November 1862
Charleston, South Carolina

Sarah's stride was firm and sure as she walked back to the mansion from the cookhouse. She was grateful that her outward appearance was steady, because inwardly she was in turmoil.

Bentley was losing money. With the blockade so effectively halting shipments, the goods sat on the docks and collected the proverbial dust. The Confederate states had been entirely too confident in European dependence on Southern exports. England had not only stockpiled goods, especially cotton, over the past two years, but was quickly learning to rely on herself and her own interests in Egypt and India. What had begun as a smug assumption on the part of the ruling Southern class was quickly turning to panic, and even the wealthiest plantations were beginning to show the strain.

How could it have come to this? Where was the glory of the Confederacy? Bentley had never lost a penny, *ever.* Sarah had run the plantation in the same sure, responsible tradition as her father before her had, and now she felt as though her entire life was slipping from her grasp. She didn't relish the thought of having to tell Charlotte that they would not be buying new dresses for Christmas this year—but that was the least of her worries.

She thought of the letter she had tucked in the top drawer of her vanity table in her bedroom. If Jeffrey didn't return home soon, she wondered how she might be able to go about the business of cashing some of the stock he mentioned. When she had first read the letter, she had been shocked. Even more, though, she was impressed at his foresight and initiative. She wouldn't have believed he had it in him in those early years to do anything at all behind her back. The Jeffrey she had married all those years ago lacked a certain strength that the Jeffrey of today possessed.

Thinking of him and the letter made her frown slightly. He should have returned home by now, although she knew better than to think there might not be trouble with the blockade, or upon the open seas, for that matter. She flushed slightly as she thought of the other matter he had mentioned. She was lonely too, although she was loath to admit it. She wouldn't discuss it at much length with him, but she was willing to forge a more affectionate relationship. The things he had said struck a chord with her. She was aging, her family was growing up and going away from home, and for the first time in her life she was beginning to doubt the ability of Bentley to sustain her.

She entered the parlor and was busy marking sagging figures in her finance book when a soft knock on the door alerted her attention. "Yes?"

"They's a gentleman to see you, missus. Shall I show him in the parlor?"

"Who is it?"

"He say he from Richmond and must speak with you."

Sarah rose, a frown wrinkling her brow. "I'll take him to the parlor myself," she said, dismissing the young slave. The girl nodded her head and backed away, melting into the shadows of the main hall. Odd, Sarah thought as she made her way to the front door, she had always made it a point to be personally acquainted with the house staff, and knew every name. It was a sign of her own strain that she didn't know the girl at all, other than by a fleeting recognition.

The gentleman standing next to the door, examining the high ceilings and impeccable woodwork, was wearing an impressive dress uniform of Confederate gray. Sarah might have appreciated the fact that he admired her home, but any sense of pride she would have felt faded away in the face of her growing agitation at his presence.

"May I help you?" she asked as she approached.

The man looked startled, but composed himself quickly. "Are you Mrs. Birmingham?" he asked, doffing his hat and holding it with two hands.

"I am."

"I am Lieutenant Colonel Stafford, from the Confederate War Department, ma'am. I wonder if we might have a seat for a moment and talk?"

Sarah's heart thudded once, hard, in her chest, and then began a staccato beat that irritated her. Surely he was here to pass along information to Jeffrey.

"If you need to get messages to my husband, I'm expecting him any day now," she said to him, folding her hands together and willing them to stay still.

The man flushed slightly. "I would dearly love a cup of tea, Mrs. Birmingham. Is there not a place where we could take a seat?"

"Of course," she murmured after a short pause. "How crude of me to forget my manners." She turned and led him to the parlor, which was situated to the left of the entry hall. Pulling on the bell cord, she gave instructions to the servant who materialized to see to her wishes, and then sat down on a richly upholstered chair.

Her visitor sat across from her, offering her a smile that was decidedly strained.

"Why don't you tell me what it is you're here to say," she said. It must be about Richard. Had he been wounded? Taken prisoner?

"Mrs. Birmingham, I cannot tell you how very much I regret that I must be the bearer of bad tidings, but I'm afraid it's in regard to your husband."

"Jeffrey?" She frowned. What on earth could be wrong with Jeffrey?

"Yes." He paused and ran a finger under his collar. "We've only recently obtained evidence that his ship has been lost at sea in the North Atlantic."

She narrowed her eyes at the man. What was he saying?

"I'm . . . I'm very sorry. I bring you the most heartfelt condolences from President Davis and his cabinet."

"What?"

By this time, the tea had been brought into the room, the bearer having set the tea tray at her elbow for pouring. Stafford rose and went about the business of pouring the hot liquid into a cup, and placed it on a saucer, handing it to her. She might have laughed under different circumstances. Gentlemen did not pour out. She took the saucer without thinking and held it in both hands.

"What are you saying to me, sir?"

"Mrs. Birmingham." The man knelt down on one knee before her and looked into her eyes. "It is very likely that your husband, Jeffrey, has died."

"That's impossible. Jeffrey is an excellent swimmer."

"I'm sure he was, ma'am. But nobody has seen or heard from the ship in days. He should have been here by now."

Try as she might, Sarah could not make sense of the fog that had enveloped her brain. *Impossible, impossible, impossible . . .*

In the activity that followed, Sarah would only remember vague images. Stafford calling for help from the staff, someone summoning Ruth . . . Ruth taking Sarah to her rooms on the second floor and urging her to lay down upon the blue-and-white quilt Mary had made only six months before . . . It was the middle of the day—surely it wasn't time to go to bed. And she was fully dressed, and wearing her clothing atop the bed, which had been made hours before . . . she didn't want to rumple the quilt . . .

Bentley was failing her. Jeffrey was failing her. Her father had failed her. Ben was gone, Emily was gone . . . Richard was a scoundrel with no integrity . . . Charlotte was an embittered version of her mother . . . The darkness finally overtook her muddled senses, and it was a blessed relief. *Sleep . . . I want only to sleep . . .*

* * *

2 December 1862
Savannah, Georgia

With a sense of profound shock, Emily read the letter as she sat with Austin in the breakfast room. "My mother is incoherent, and has been for two weeks!"

Austin took a sip from his glass and wiped his mouth on a fine linen napkin. "Is there something we should do?"

Emily shrugged, looking up from the paper with eyes that were wide. "I have no idea! My mother's never been incoherent in her life." She gestured with the letter. "Ruth says she barely eats, she refuses to leave her room, and although she's awake, she just stares and refuses to speak to anyone. It must be severe," she added, as though thinking aloud, "for Ruth to risk writing to me."

"She must be deeply mourning your father. When my father died, my mother was shortly on his heels. She didn't function well without him."

Emily shook her head. "I don't think you understand. My parents aren't, *weren't,* like that. There never seemed to be any love lost between my father and mother, even on a good day." She stopped for a moment and waited for the fresh thrust of pain to pass. She had received word in November of her father's disappearance, and she had been surprisingly sad over his loss. It was odd that she should feel anything at all when she had convinced herself through the years that she hated her parents. What a disappointment to realize she'd not been entirely in the right.

Jeffrey's memorial service had been one of grandeur, and had shown Bentley off at its finest. The people who came to pay their respects to Sarah were enormous in number, and Emily had stood next to her mother, accepting their words of thoughtfulness and kindness while Sarah had barely managed to shake their hands. Emily had assumed that her severe level of shock would wear off, that in time she would again be able to function.

Emily folded the letter slowly and placed it on the table. Austin paused in the act of buttering his roll and said quietly, "Would you like to go to her?"

"I don't know what I would say. My mother doesn't like me much."

"I think she respects you."

Emily smiled. One of the things she was coming to love about Austin was the fact that he didn't patronize her. He could very well have demurred and said, "Of course your mother likes you—she loves you!" and they would both have known it was probably a lie. He dealt with her honestly, always, and yet his manner was kind.

"Well," she said on a sigh, "she may respect me, but I doubt I would do her much good. She needs Richard. He always knew how to charm her."

Austin raised an eyebrow. "From your descriptions, I would never have expected him to be charming."

"Oh, he's not," she said, stabbing at a piece of ham with her fork. "Not in general, anyway. But when he wants something, he can manipulate people to his advantage. Mother always seemed to be particularly vulnerable to his attentions. And if she wasn't, she at least turned a blind eye to his indiscretions. He's a handsome devil," she muttered. "I suppose she made allowances for him based on his face."

"I do believe the pig has already been slaughtered," Austin said with a mild tone, and tore a piece of his roll. Emily looked down at her ham to find that she had employed her fork and knife with a certain amount of enthusiasm.

"It never hurts to be certain," she said and, piercing a piece of the meat, she placed it in her mouth and chewed with a scowl.

Austin gave her a wry smile and continued eating his roll. "I do believe I shall turn the conversation away from Richard and on to more pleasant topics. So, my wife, do you believe this war will end before we are utterly ruined here in the South, or will we soon find ourselves restored to the Union?"

"Your idea of pleasant," she said, and took a sip of water, "is a bit morbid. But to answer your question, I do believe we shall be utterly ruined."

He nodded. "As do I."

"It's funny," Emily said as she toyed with a poached egg, "when I was at Bentley, I didn't care one whit about saving the plantation. Now that I'm here, I admit I would be sad to see this home and lands destroyed. I suppose it's because I know that the workers are here of their own free will, they are handsomely paid, and they are not slaves."

"Yes, it would be sad to see the home destroyed," he agreed, his tone mild. "Not to mention the fact that we would find ourselves in the streets."

"Hmm." Emily chewed her food thoughtfully and winked at Austin. "Might be a bit of an adventure, though."

He inclined his head and raised his glass. "To adventure."
She raised hers as well. "To adventure."

CHAPTER 22

"A chicken could not live on that field when we open on it."
—Confederate artillery officer at Fredericksburg

* * *

13 December 1862
Fredericksburg, Virginia

Richard walked to and fro with Mosby as his new friend and mentor delivered messages between high-ranking staff officers and the officers in the field. Their position on the heights above the town of Fredericksburg, Virginia, was an optimal one, and one which General Lee had taken ample time to establish. They were behind a twelve-hundred-foot-long stone retaining wall at the far side of a wide-open field that was roughly six hundred yards across, and were dug in for the duration. Any Union charge would be completely and utterly repulsed. He almost felt sorry for the poor bluecoats.

Burnside was now the man in charge of the Union Army of the Potomac, and word was that not only was he an inexperienced and incompetent commander, he willingly admitted it. He replaced McClellan only at Lincoln's insistence, and Richard believed the new Union general might be the South's biggest asset.

"McClellan would never attack us in this position," Mosby had told him earlier in the day, "but all the Union activity on the other side of the river tells us that Burnside probably will."

Richard looked down over the town and to the river, where the Union troops were waiting for their pontoon bridges so that they might cross and attack. He shook his head. They were doomed to fail; there were Confederate sharpshooters placed strategically throughout the town. He seriously doubted the boys in blue would even make it across the river. Pity. He tried to hide a smile.

"Rather than divide his army in three, Burnside should have kept it as one unit and moved on to Richmond," one of the staff officers was saying to Mosby.

Another interjected, "His stupidity is our gain. I suggest you don't go run and tell the blue-bellied general where he's made his mistakes."

There was general laughter all around, and Richard listened with interest. He was learning much just by paying close attention. Sometimes, as he settled in for the night, he even made notes about opinions, comments, and certain people's strengths and weaknesses. Certain he would find a use for the knowledge one day, he took full advantage of his new friends.

* * *

Richard stood shoulder to shoulder beside other Confederate soldiers as they took down successive Union advances. He marveled at the density of the Union general, who kept sending his boys to charge across the open field only to be slaughtered. Not one blue-dressed soldier made it within even fifty feet of the Confederate defensive position behind the stone wall.

The field was littered with blue. There were more dead and dying bodies than the eye could count. Richard had to give them credit—they had certainly followed their orders without shirking their responsibilities. The Union soldiers had lobbed artillery round after round into the city of Fredericksburg to eliminate the threats coming from the Confederate sharpshooters. Once their passage across the pontoon bridges was secured, they had plowed their way through the town to confront the Confederate forces dug in at Marye's Heights.

Richard was tapped on the shoulder and momentarily relieved of his position. He moved to the rear of the four-deep line and took a deep breath, stretching his tired muscles. He worked his way back toward the groups of commanding officers, hoping to catch sight of Mosby. When he did, it was with a certain amount of shock.

"Who is that?" Richard asked, and pointed to a young blonde child about three years of age who sat happily atop the lap of one of the officers.

Mosby shook his head. "Denman was behind a house, taking final shots at the Yanks before we withdrew from the city, and he saw this girl chasing after an artillery shell as though it were a plaything."

Richard's mouth dropped open. "So he ran to fetch her?"

Mosby nodded. "Scooped her up and ran for us up here at the Heights. She's been keeping us company ever since."

"Where is the girl's mother?"

"Nobody knows. She doesn't seem overly concerned."

Richard looked at the child. It was true—she seemed entirely blasé about her present circumstances or lack of a mother. He shook his head slightly. Denman was a fool. To leave his cover and grab some silly child who had no better sense than to stay with her family? Of course it would be viewed as heroic, and Denman would receive all sorts of accolades and congratulatory sentiments.

He shrugged and turned his attention elsewhere. From his vantage point well behind the lines, he could see that wave after wave of blue kept advancing, and all were shot down as though they were fish in a barrel. It wasn't long before fires were set to kill the wounded still on the field who could not escape. "I hope Lincoln keeps Burnside as commander of that army forever," he murmured to Mosby, who silently agreed with a shake of his head.

* * *

15 December 1862
Washington, D.C.

Dearest Aaron,

My, how some things change, and yet how they remain the same. I write to give you Washington's perspective of matters thus far. Lincoln is, of course, more than frustrated with his lack of effective military leadership. He recently said, "If there is a worse place than hell, I am in it." Lincoln advised Burnside not to attack at Fredericksburg, and the man did anyway. It seems there is no happy medium; McClellan had to be forced into battle, and Burnside must be held back.

Have you heard the casualty totals? The Union lost 6,000 men in Fredericksburg, and more than 6,700 were wounded. The Confederates report 5,000 losses. Today a truce has been established to recover the dead of both sides. I don't envy the soldiers their task. I understand that toward the end of the battle, Burnside was in tears and was determined to lead the next charge himself. His officers held him back, naturally, but he was beside himself with grief and has taken full responsibility for the deaths.

It is my understanding that the Army of the Potomac will settle into winter quarters for a while, and may God help them regroup and heal.

I hope all is well with you, and that this letter finds you healthy and strong. I look forward to the day we shall again meet and embrace.

Yours affectionately, dear friend,
Isabelle

* * *

28 December 1862
Dumfries, Virginia

Anne read Isabelle's letter with a tired smile. Yes, amazingly enough, she was healthy and strong, and had survived yet another battle, this one brought to them at Dumfries courtesy of one Jeb Stuart, Confederate cavalry general. The regiment had been hit hard, yet had held and shoved Stuart's men back, but with heavy casualties. Throughout the whole of it, Anne had found herself blessedly numb.

She glanced over at Ivar, who was writing a letter home, with spectacles perched on his face and looking for all the world like a scholarly farmer. Which he was, really. He wasn't a soldier, yet he was adapting well. Anne counted it a blessing that she'd been placed with him in the Ohio 7th. He was a constant source of strength for her, and she was grateful.

They currently sat in their tent, each writing letters or reading by the light of a small lantern. Anne and Ivar had been assigned two new recruits upon the deaths of Mark and Jed. It was just as well—nobody else knew Anne was a woman, but she and Ivar both did, and it might have been uncomfortable had they bunked together alone.

The two new tent mates, Thomas and Justin, were young men from a small Ohio town near Ivar's. They had come aboard full of zeal and ready to fight. After the encounter with Stuart's men, though, they had mellowed considerably but tried not to let it show. It had been an interesting transition to observe, and Anne imagined that she had been much the same herself.

"What's on the agenda for tomorrow?" Thomas asked.

"Most likely picket duty or roadwork," Ivar answered, his head still bent over his letter.

Thomas flopped back down onto his bedroll with an emphatic sigh. "I could've stayed home and done roadwork," he muttered.

"Would you rather fight?" Ivar asked him, still not looking up.

"Well, maybe I would! That's what we came here for, isn't it?"

Anne glanced over at the boy. "Yes, it's what we came here for. Can you honestly say, though, that you enjoyed it?"

"No, but it's better than sitting around."

"The winter will pass quickly enough, and then you'll probably see all the fighting your little ol' heart can handle." She folded Belle's letter and placed it in her haversack. "I, for one, would like for it to be over."

"I would too," the boy mumbled, and Anne pitied him. "I just think that as long as we're here, we might as well do the job."

Justin groaned slightly and turned over on his bedroll. "Shut up, Thomas. I'm trying to sleep. We've marched enough in the last two months to kill a horse."

Anne's lips twitched. "We have horses in the regiment. They're still alive and well."

"You shut up too, Johnson. Just because you like to move around doesn't mean the rest of us do." The boy braced himself up on his elbows. "Do you know, I've done some figgerin'. We march an average of ten miles a day. Some days more, some less."

"Yes. It's rather a necessity when we need to get from one place to another." Anne wrapped herself in her blanket and wished they could build a fire right there inside the tent. Nights had been cold lately.

"It's boring!"

"We got to see the president himself in October. That was exciting." Anne yawned and closed her burning eyes. Mercy, she was tired.

Justin gave up and laid his head back down. "I wasn't even here then," the boy muttered, and closed his eyes as well. "What are the chances that'll happen again?"

Ivar extinguished the light from the lantern and settled himself in for the night. As was his habit, he bundled himself tightly and scooted his bedroll closer to Anne's. He seemed to do it unconsciously, and it often made her smile. She wondered what he'd say if she asked him about it.

"It's late," Ivar said. "Everybody go to sleep."

And that was that.

CHAPTER 23

"Resolved: That the emancipation proclamation of the President of the United States is as unwarrantable in military as in civil law; a gigantic usurpation, at once converting the war, professedly commenced by the administration for the vindication of the authority of the constitution, into the crusade for the sudden, unconditional and violent liberation of 3,000,000 Negro slaves . . . and which we denounce as an uneffaceable disgrace to the American people."

—"The Emancipation Proclamation Denounced," state of Indiana

* * *

4 January 1863
Savannah, Georgia

Emily was smiling as she entered the study. "My aunt responded," she said. "She answered me over two months ago, but it's taken this long to reach me."

Austin stood from behind his desk and stretched. "What does she say?"

"She has positions for Mary *and* Joshua!"

He smiled and walked around the desk, wrapping Emily in a warm embrace. "I'm thrilled," he said in her ear. "I look forward to meeting this Aunt Liz of yours. Now," he said, taking a step back but holding her hands, "will you be ready to leave in two days?"

"I'd be ready to leave in an hour," she said. "I want you to know I'm grateful that you postponed this particular trip until I got word from Boston. I've also thanked Aristotle and Jonah for their patience. And now, I'm going to find Mary and Joshua."

She smiled again and kissed her husband, beside herself in excitement. When she went to dash off, he tugged her hands and, catching her off balance, pulled her forward for a more prolonged kiss. He finally released her and she felt herself flushing. Honestly! She'd been a married woman for months now—why on earth was she still so self-conscious of his attentions?

Austin winked at her and released her hands, and with a grin, she fled the room to find her friends.

* * *

"We're going to Boston, we're going to Boston!" Mary stood stunned in Emily's tight, tearful embrace. "Can you believe it? Mary, you're going to be free!" Emily stood back and took Mary's shoulders in her hands. "Say something to me!"

Mary looked at Emily and tried to put her thoughts to words. "I can't believe it," she finally whispered. "I absolutely cannot believe it's going to happen."

She sank onto a sofa behind her, suddenly feeling light-headed. She had been in the parlor, working on a piece of fine linen embroidery, when Emily had come dashing in as though the hounds of hell were chasing her.

"My Aunt Elizabeth in Boston said she just lost a good seamstress and has been looking for another!" Emily said, sinking next to her on the sofa. "And not only that, she said that Uncle James has contacts who are in need of all manner of workers, and that he'd have something lined up for Joshua by the time we get there!"

"Oh, Emily," Mary whispered. "I don't know what to say!"

Emily crushed her in another hug, and Mary felt Emily's hot tears fall on her neck. "Mary, I can't stand it, I just can't! I'm so happy I could die."

Mary's eyes filled with tears, and they fell suddenly in a torrent of emotion that she wasn't sure she could contain. Her whole body shook as great sobs escaped her small frame, and she was grateful for Emily's support.

When she finally calmed a bit and pulled back from Emily, who was attempting to mop her face with a sodden handkerchief, she finally felt the first hint of misgiving. "Emily, I'm scared," she whispered. "Maybe I should just stay here with you—it's not as though I'm your slave, really. You're paying me, after all!"

"Mary, are you *insane?* This is what we've wanted for you our whole lives!"

"I just wish Mama Ruth were going . . ."

"Mary." Emily ran her fingers along Mary's arms and down to her hands, which she held firmly within her own. "Sweet friend, I'm scared, too. I can't imagine being without you, and I'm still scared of being a married woman. But you can do this! You *must* do this! People have been risking life and limb on the Underground Railroad for decades now—your 'escape' will be relatively uneventful. Think of how envious all those people who have gone before you would be."

"I'm not trying to be ungrateful, Emily." Mary's face felt hot.

"I know you're not, and I'm not trying to make you feel bad. I just think that . . . oh Mary, you're so very intelligent and capable. I cannot wait to see what kind of woman you become when out from under the shadow of the South. Away from me, from everybody, having to rely on your own brain and instincts, and yet you'll be with people who are very kind and supportive."

Mary caught her lip between her teeth and chewed on it, cursing at the fresh tears that started up again. "I know," she said. "And I'll go, gladly. I'm just very, very afraid."

Emily gave Mary's hands a little squeeze. "You know, if the Union goes on to win the war, Lincoln's Emancipation Proclamation will stand, and you can come back here, if you'd like. You can go anywhere you want to!"

Mary tried to smile, but it felt forced. She could only imagine what it looked like. "People aren't going to change their opinions overnight. I very seriously doubt I could come back here or anywhere in the South. Probably ought to be careful where I go in the North, as well."

"That may be true, but in theory and by law, you'll be free. What other people choose to do with that is their own business. God will bless you, Mary." Emily's voice cracked, and her tears ran afresh. "He will bless you, because you are His child. I will pray to Him every night to keep you safe."

Mary nodded. "I believe you then, Emily. I'll believe you because I must." She took a breath that became a shuddering sigh. "When will we leave?"

"In two days."

"I . . . when was the last time we saw Ben?"

Emily frowned a bit. "A week ago?"

Mary nodded. "So he won't visit again for probably another week. Will you please tell him . . . tell him . . ."

"I'll tell him you're at Aunt Liz's. He will write to you up there, and you can finally answer. You can sit at a desk and write without worrying that someone will find and whip you."

"Very well. I . . . very well."

Emily kissed Mary's cheek and stood. "I'm off to tell Joshua."

"Would you rather I did it?"

"No. I'll be fine."

* * *

Joshua was in the workroom, planing a long board. What a delight it was to create something with wood—he had never known he would do so well with carpentry. He awoke every day to a sense of purpose, a sense of happiness that he would be doing something he enjoyed.

When Emily appeared in the doorway, her presence startled him, and he sucked in his breath. When he saw her tearstained face, his senses went on alert. "What is it? Are you hurt?"

She shook her head and entered the room with a brave smile, her eyes bright and shiny with tears that threatened. When she shared her good news, he stood rooted to the spot, stunned.

"I didn't think Stanhope had secured employment for us yet," he finally stammered.

"He didn't. I did."

"Oh, Emily." His arms folded around her as she rushed at him for a hug. She wrapped her arms around his neck and laughed.

"Can you believe it, Joshua? You're about to be a free man!"

He closed his eyes in disbelief and gave her a huge squeeze. It was only when he heard her struggling for breath that he quickly released her to the ground. "I'm sorry!"

She laughed, took a deep breath, and waved away his apology. "I'll survive," she managed, and then laughed again. "Joshua, I'm so happy. It's everything I've ever wanted for you."

His smile remained in place, but he felt it dim a bit. He could think of only one thing he wanted as much as he wanted freedom, and she stood before him, married to another man. It wasn't to be—it had never been, and he could only be grateful that through her, he would obtain his life. His own life.

"Emily," he managed, his voice sounding rough, "I can't thank you enough. I know why you married Stanhope, and I . . ."

Emily shook her head. "We will not speak of it." She forced a smile and said, "The future, only. Yours will be bright, and I insist that you write and tell me how you're getting on."

"It's the least I can do. Again, thank you."

"It's my pleasure," she whispered, then turned and left.

* * *

10 January 1863
Boston, Massachusetts

"The battle at Murfreesboro, Tennessee, finally concluded on the third," Robert commented to his father as they read the newspaper after dinner. "Braxton Bragg retreated. They're calling it a 'costly draw.'"

James nodded, his expression grim. "I heard," he said. "Combined casualties of twenty-five thousand."

"I confess I'm a bit disappointed in Grant," Robert said as he moved on to another article. "His General Order Number 11 is not at all in keeping with the Society's way of thinking."

"Well, I don't suppose Grant has ever even pretended to be an abolitionist. What does the order entail?"

Robert sighed and folded the paper. "Apparently some Union citizens have been taking advantage of Union blockades on cotton and other goods, and have been exchanging items needed in the South for cotton. Grant assumes these citizens are all Jews, and issued the order to expel all Jews from his area of operations. Lincoln ordered Grant to repeal the order, of course. He says it 'proscribed a whole class, some of whom are fighting in our ranks.'"

James nodded. "You're right. Not at all in line with the Society. His opinions reflect the larger part of the Northern and Southern states anymore, though." James's lips twitched a bit. "I wonder what Grant would think of your great-grandfather."

"My great-grandfather, the Jew?" Robert grinned. "He could say all he wanted to, but I'd bet my inheritance that he doesn't hesitate to use weapons provided by your iron company, even with your tainted Jewish blood." He winked at James.

James laughed at Robert's outright sarcasm and set his newspaper aside, changing topics as he did so. "You'll be finished with your schooling soon. Have you given any thought to what you'd like to pursue afterward?"

"I've been thinking of enlisting."

"You'll be barely seventeen."

"True, but they won't turn me away. They need men too badly."

James nodded slowly. "I always assumed it would come to this with you. That's why I've taken the liberty of speaking to some friends—you can virtually choose your regiment and locale."

Robert frowned. He didn't necessarily want special favors—if he chose to, he could stay away from the enlistment office altogether. "I don't have a preference as to locale *or* regiment," he admitted. "I would like to be a quartermaster, however."

James smiled slightly. "I thought as much. And I think that with your quick brain, you'd be an excellent quartermaster. When you are closer to enlisting, would you like me to ask around and see what can be turned up?"

Robert nodded. "I hate to use unfair advantages, but yes, I'd like that." He was silent for a moment. "I don't understand why you're being supportive about this. I assumed you'd try to keep me out of the military."

"I thought about trying to keep you away from it," James admitted, "but I knew you'd find your own way around me, sooner or later. I'd rather have you doing something you'd be good at than wasting away at something you'd hate."

"I appreciate that."

James leaned back in his chair and stretched, crossing his legs at his ankles. "A father's work is never done," he said with a sigh. "I'm going to check in on Anne next month when I do business in Chicago. All this time and the girl hasn't visited her mother so much as once!"

Robert tried to hide a smile, but failed. James used his wife as an excuse. In truth, he was probably missing his daughter more than anyone.

"What?" James asked, looking askance at his son.

"Nothing." He paused, and then added, "I miss her too."

James nodded soberly and gazed out of the window at the fading winter day. "This is a hard time for a young woman to be away from her family. I hope to convince her to come back to Boston for a while."

Robert snorted. "I wish you luck. Anne has a mind of her own."

"I know that. I need to think of something enticing."

At that, Robert laughed out loud and stretched his legs, unconsciously taking the very pose his father held. "And what might that be, I wonder? A potential husband? Money? She doesn't need either one."

James smiled a bit. "She is rather fond of Susan B. Anthony, isn't she?"

"She is. But she's also fond of Elizabeth Stanton, and *she's* a married woman and mother of several children. Perhaps there's hope for Anne yet."

"Perhaps. But she's in Chicago, doing what she undoubtedly sees as exciting investigative work. I can't imagine she'll want to come home." James sighed again. "I'm probably fighting a lost cause. I just wish she'd come home if only for a short time. Then I could convince Camille to come back for just a bit . . ."

"And then Luke would magically come home, and we'd all be here together just as we were in the old days," Robert finished for his father, and felt a stab of sympathy. The family was growing, and growing apart. The fact that they were all fond of each other didn't change the fact that they were far, far away from one another. It *would* be wonderful, if only for a moment, to see everyone together again in the same house.

James smiled, looking a bit sheepish, and glanced at his son. "Robert, we sound like a pair of old women."

"Indeed, we do. What would Mother say?"

James laughed. "She'd tell us to pull ourselves together."

"Then I suppose we must." Robert rose from his chair and stretched a bit. "I have exams to study for," he said and, giving his father a mock salute, left the room.

* * *

27 January 1863
Boston, Massachusetts

Camille stood on the docks with assorted family and friends while the Union ship was secured and the gangplank lowered for the passengers. "Now tell me again how Stanhope managed this?"

"Yes, I'm not entirely clear on that point myself," Abigail murmured as she watched the ship.

Robert stepped closer to the women and said, "Apparently before the war he was able to hide two of his freed 'slaves' in travel trunks while two actual slaves accompanied him in full view. He always told anyone who asked that he was going on business and needed his servants. Then, once here, he delivered the slaves to their predetermined locations and occupations, and then returned home with the two employees he had been hiding."

"Ah," Camille said. "So to all others, it appeared he was going and then returning with two slaves."

"Exactly."

"And how is it different now?" Abigail asked.

"Well, he's unable to come and go as he pleases on Confederate ships, obviously, with the blockade. So he travels on Union ships, with captains who are aware of his plans and sympathetic, and meanwhile he tells his Confederate neighbors that he travels north to buy sensitive information to aid the Confederate cause."

Camille shook her head. "Seems awfully risky to me."

"It is," Robert agreed. "But I can't think of a more worthy cause."

Abigail smiled at Robert. "Well, well. Another young Birmingham to add to the growing list of abolition supporters."

Camille stared as Robert flushed and mumbled something incoherent in response. How had she not seen it? Robert was sweet on

Abigail! Oh, how awkward for him. She would hate to be in love with her sister's beau. She would have to ask him about it later. Or perhaps she would be kind and leave him in peace. But when had she ever been kind? She grinned, and her devilment must have shown in her eyes because Robert snapped at her.

"What are you smirking at?"

"Nothing." Camille caught movement out of the corner of her eye. "Oh, look—they're disembarking!"

The passengers left the ship singly and in pairs, and it wasn't long before Camille spied a young woman with a bonnet that tried but failed to cover a head of thick, red curls. "It's Emily," she said with a smile. "I'd know that hair anywhere."

"That must be Stanhope she's holding onto," Robert said in reference to the tall man whose arm Emily held as they walked down the gangplank.

Camille caught her breath at the next sight. There, preparing to descend, was a young black couple. The man was tall and handsome, with a straight back and broad shoulders. He took a deep breath with his eyes closed, and finally opened them, looking around with an air of accomplishment. The young woman on his arm was a petite young thing, with beautifully sculpted, high cheekbones and a regal bearing. She, too, took a deep breath and looked about in wonder.

"Oh," Camille said, and put a hand to her chest. Tears clogged her throat, and she wondered at the sudden burst of emotion.

She felt an arm about her waist and looked to her side to see Abigail, who also was overcome. A tear trickled down her cheek, and she whispered to Camille, "Isn't it the most incredible thing to watch a person take his first breath of free air?" She studied the couple a moment longer before adding, "I guarantee you, those two had at least one white parent. I'll bet my life savings it was an overseer or the master of the house."

Camille raised an eyebrow. "I would think my Uncle Jeffrey would have conducted himself with more decorum and respect, especially since my aunt is such a battle-ax, but then I suppose one never knows."

"It was the family overseer who sired them both," Robert murmured under his breath to the two women. "I overheard Mother telling Aunt Jenny. She knew about it when they were born—the young woman's grandmother was Aunt Sarah's personal servant, and she told Mother."

"I wonder what Aunt Sarah thought."

"Probably nothing. It happens all the time."

Abigail pursed her lips and wiped at her eye with her finger. "That is just deplorable," she said. "No respect whatsoever for the sanctity of marriage or the virtue of the slave woman."

"The slave has no value as a real person to them," Camille muttered, and wiped at her own eyes. "A woman's virtue is probably the furthest thing from the mind of a lusty male."

Robert blushed slightly and moved away from the women. Camille heard Abigail's gentle chuckle and felt her fingers squeeze her waist. "You're embarrassing your poor brother," she whispered.

"I think he's already embarrassed," Camille whispered back, "and it has nothing to do with me!"

"What do you mean?"

Camille was saved from having to elaborate by the arrival of their guests. She moved forward to embrace Emily, surprised at the growth of the young woman and her beauty. Emily had been such a gangly, awkward young girl. She had blossomed into a rose, and Camille told her as much.

Emily laughed. "As have you, cousin. Why, I never would have recognized you on the street!"

"My dear," Elizabeth said as she embraced her husband's niece, "you sound just like your mother!"

Emily grimaced. "I suppose the proper response would be one of gratitude."

Elizabeth laughed and covered the awkward moment. "Not necessary, if you don't feel it."

The laughter and handshakes continued all around the small group as Emily introduced first her husband, and then their two companions, Mary Birmingham and her brother, Joshua Birmingham.

The siblings graciously accepted the effusive welcome and continued to look around as though seeing the world for the first time. Abigail stepped forward and placed a hand upon Mary's arm. "I must tell you," she said, "that my mother was an abolitionist my entire life, and only recently passed away. If she were here, she would love you as her own and welcome you with open arms. I gladly do so in her place, and to tell you both that we will all do everything we can to help you and to ensure that your adjustment to Boston is a comfortable one."

"Thank you so very much," Mary said in a soft, Southern tone, her voice trembling slightly. "I'll admit to being a bit nervous."

"It's perfectly understandable," Abigail said, and patted Mary's hand. "But truly, you are safe and amongst friends."

Camille scanned the small crowd and wished she had a camera so that she might capture the moment permanently. It was a scene she never wanted to forget; she had the privilege of witnessing the beginning of complete freedom for two human souls, and the thick feeling in her throat was still present. It worsened when she glanced at Emily, who was openly weeping. She didn't make a sound, but the tears coursed down her face and she leaned heavily on her husband's arm.

With a smile and a laugh, Mary looked at Emily, her own tears falling; Mary walked to Emily and embraced her, and the two women stood for a long moment, clinging to one another. Camille glanced over at her mother, who was also in tears, and she rolled her eyes when her own started to fall. "Oh, this is ridiculous," she muttered, and swiped at her eyes, receiving several laughs that seemed to lessen the intensity of the moment.

It was only as they were leaving that she noticed Joshua, who had stood stoically until that moment, was dropping a few tears of his own.

* * *

Later, in the quiet of her own room when the entire house was asleep, Camille sat at her vanity and scribbled her impressions on a piece of wrinkled paper. She wrote so quickly her hand began to ache, and even still it was as though she couldn't pour her thoughts out fast enough.

The smell of the air, the color of the sky, the expressions on the faces of the two young Birminghams as they looked around their environment knowing for the first time that they had the freedom to go where they wished and say what they pleased. Camille hoped with all her heart that Boston would be kind; in truth, there were many who were not freethinkers, but there was an overwhelming contingency of abolition supporters who would welcome them into the fold and help care for them.

She glanced down in surprise some moments later to see that she had filled the whole page with hasty scrawls and still had more to say. “Hmm,” she said aloud. “I wrote something down.” What it meant, she didn’t care to speculate.

CHAPTER 24

"The day was cold and raw, yet a large number of our citizens were present. . . . Up to that time scarcely any of the citizens had set foot within the encampment, but now there was quite a score of carriages from the city, many equestrians and a large concourse of people on foot."
—Eyewitness to the burial of federal dead after Bear River

* * *

4 February 1863
Utah Territory

Earl stood alongside his family as three volleys were fired in tribute to the soldiers who had recently died in a skirmish with Indians who had entrenched themselves in the Bear River Valley.

Following the ceremony, he turned and made his way back down toward the city with his family, who had all made the walk on foot. With them was a friend of Eli Dobranski, Joseph Henacker, who lived in Logan, Utah.

"I can't say I've held Connor in high esteem lately," Henacker was saying to Eli in reference to the commander of the federal troops, "but his attack on the Indians was a godsend. They have plundered the Cache Valley area, wreaking havoc and killing people indiscriminately for quite some time now. I know what the good prophet has said about being kind to the Indians, but it has been frightful for us up north."

"Is it true the Indian chiefs charged the troops while carrying scalps of white women?" Elisha jumped up and down as they walked down the street.

"Elisha Dobranski! Mind your tongue." Ellen shot a look to the boy that should have had him quaking in his boots. It had certainly worked on all the rest of her sons through the years. Death, warfare with Indians, and scalpings were too exciting for a boy of seven, however, and he was willing to risk his mother's wrath to uncover the grisly details.

"I don't know about that, young Dobranski," Henacker answered the lad with lips that twitched, "but I understand the whole affair was quite dramatic."

Elisha's face fell, but he must have realized he wasn't going to get any more details out of the man because he fell silent, scooping handfuls of snow as he walked, balling them up, and throwing them into the street.

"After the battle with the Indians," Henacker continued, "the soldiers made their way into the city, and those who were too frozen or injured to move were rescued and treated with all we had to offer." He sniffed slightly. "Connor, of course, says that the Mormons have done nothing to help at all, but it simply isn't true. I was right proud of the outpouring of Christian support."

Earl glanced at his mother, who remained quiet. She was of Indian heritage, and when she'd heard the news of the battle, her reaction had been mixed. On the one hand, she knew of the troubles the settlers had experienced because of the Indians, but on the other, she couldn't condone what she viewed as an outright massacre.

Elisha abandoned his snowball throwing and again danced alongside the visitor as they continued their walk down the street. "Is it true that Porter Rockwell helped bring the soldiers back home?"

"That is true, my friend. Are you a fan of Porter Rockwell?"

"Yes. I want to be strong like him someday."

"A worthy goal. A worthy goal indeed." Henacker glanced at the rest of the Dobranski boys, who all filed dutifully down the street, one looking much like the other in bulk and strength, the only difference being their heights that matched their respective descending ages.

"I'm thinking your brothers here are every bit as strong as our friend Porter Rockwell, though. I'd say that bodes well for you, young Elisha."

The boy scrunched up his nose in thought. "I s'pose so."

"And you, Earl—have you made a decision regarding your future yet? You'd make an excellent missionary, you know."

Earl nodded, feeling a bit uncomfortable. "I've considered it," he admitted, wishing people would stop asking about his life. It was his business, after all. "I'm thinking I might be a down-and-backer for a while, though."

Ellen glanced at him in surprise. "You are? You hadn't mentioned it to us."

"I've only just been thinking about it, that's all."

By this time they had reached the family home, and Brother Henacker was invited to stay for luncheon. Following the meal, the family dispersed to see to their various activities, but Eli halted Earl at the front door.

"Do you have a minute to spare, son?"

Earl nodded. "Of course."

Eli led him to the small front parlor and took a seat. Earl sat opposite him and wondered what his father was about. His air was solemn, as though he was thinking on a matter, and very seriously.

Earl took a moment to study Eli. The hair that had once been dark like his own was now turning to gray and white, but the flesh seemed as firm and solid as it had when Earl had been just a young boy. He had enjoyed such a warm relationship with his father then—they had wrestled and worked side by side. Eli had been his idol and his mentor. Then had come the time when Eli had agreed to serve a mission for the Church, and it had taken him away from the family for years. By the time he returned home, Earl was a young man, and he had finished growing up without his father. The relationship should have been a comfortable one, but of late it had been strained.

"Son," Eli began, "things have been distant between us since my return, and I feel as though you resent the time I was gone."

"No, of course not."

Eli only looked at him, saying nothing, and Earl had to amend his statement. "Perhaps a bit, sir," he admitted, feeling shame.

"I understand. I missed you horribly, and when I returned, I could hardly believe that the young boy I left behind was the man I saw before me. I don't suppose I felt I knew you anymore, and therefore you wouldn't want my interference."

Earl crossed one ankle upon the other knee and tried to make himself comfortable in the chair. He shrugged a bit, but could think of nothing to say.

"I suppose I want you to know that I'm proud of you, and I'm proud of the way you helped your mother while I was gone. You've become a fine man, and I'm glad to be your father."

Earl glanced up in surprise. It certainly wasn't what he'd expected to hear from the man who'd become such a stranger to him. "Thank you, sir."

"Do you believe my time away was well spent?"

"Of course." This time, he spoke the truth. Ben had told him on more than one occasion how grateful he was for the man who had brought the gospel into his life. He loved Eli Dobranski for that, and had made sure that Earl knew it.

"Do you have a testimony of Christ?"

"I do."

"I hope you'll consider sharing it someday, in whatever capacity you might find yourself."

"I will consider it."

"Well, then, that's all I will ask of you." Eli stood, and Earl joined him. Earl extended his hand, but his father surprised him by clasping him forward for a quick hug followed by several successive slaps on the back that he was sure would leave handprints.

"I love you, son."

Earl felt a sting behind his eyelids. "I love you, too," he whispered.

* * *

6 February 1863
Charleston, South Carolina

Ruth missed the young people something fierce. Mary and Joshua had left Bentley in August, and to Ruth it had been an eternity. She hadn't realized how much she loved their companionship until they were gone.

Her heart was gloriously glad for them, however. She had received a letter, delivered by an anonymous servant, from Emily a couple of weeks back that said, "We are about to head north to Boston to complete my husband's business transactions." It could only mean that the time had come for Mary and Joshua to leave the South, and

Ruth wondered every day, every *hour*, how they were doing, and wished to see them again.

Ruth turned at the sound of footsteps in the main hall. Charlotte approached with a piece of paper in her hand, and judging by the bright expression on her face, it must have been a letter from William. The slight alteration in her step due to her broadening midsection was discernable, even from far away. William had enlisted nearly seven months before, and interestingly enough, Charlotte was nearly seven months into her pregnancy.

There was a softness to the woman now that had been absent before. William had obviously encouraged intimacy before he left, and Charlotte had become much of the same person she had been as a young child. She was likable again, and Ruth was amazed at the change. A little love went a long way to making a body happy, that much was evident. Ruth allowed herself to think of her own dear, late husband for just a moment while Charlotte continued her journey toward her.

"William is well," Charlotte said, slightly out of breath. "He says he is bitterly cold, and several of the men in his regiment have frozen to death, but he is strong and has hope that he'll stay healthy."

"I'm glad to hear that, Charlotte," Ruth said to the young woman, noting the worry in her eyes. "And only a handful more weeks until the weather warms in the North. I'm sure he'll be right as rain."

"Yes." Charlotte nodded. She wandered away from Ruth and down the hall to the parlor, where Ruth knew she would sit and reread the letter through the day. Ruth shook her head a bit and moved to the grand staircase in the front entrance. She climbed the stairs slowly, considering life's extreme strangeness.

She never, in a million years, would have anticipated that Sarah would utterly collapse over *anything*, let alone the death of her husband. Ruth remembered times when Jeffrey showed an inclination to favor *her*, a slave, since he received virtually no attention from his wife. Ruth had declined, of course, and thankfully Jeffrey had treated her as a gentleman would.

And now, here was Sarah, barely eating enough to sustain life and communicating very, very little. She didn't seem to care about anything, and Ruth knew that it wasn't just because Jeffrey was gone. Bentley was in dire straits, and Sarah knew it. The Emancipation Proclamation had been signed, and it was murmured that surely it was only a matter of time before total emancipation of all slaves became a ratified amendment to the Constitution.

So everything that Sarah held dear was crumbling. Everything she believed was turning out to be a sham, and it would soon, more likely than not, become a thing of the past. Ruth knew that Sarah knew it, but Ruth was amazed that it had brought Sarah to her knees.

Ruth had thought of trying to leave on more than one occasion. Just because things were changing, however, didn't mean she could merely pack a bag and depart. Slave bounty hunters were still a dime a dozen, and the South in general didn't think kindly of Lincoln's proclamation. No, Ruth was not yet a free woman, and even if she had been, she wasn't sure she would have bolted for the front door immediately.

Something about Bentley was drawing her ever closer, daring her to try to save it. It was probably because Ruth was now fully in charge that it held a heady sort of challenge for her, and she was intrigued by trying to see how far they could all stretch the plantation's resources.

But do I want to stay here forever? The thought echoed in her head as she made her way down the second floor hallway to Sarah's suite of rooms. No. Bentley was the only home she could truly remember, but it had also been her prison. She had harbored dreams as a young child—dreams of a home of her own. It didn't have to be a big affair; something small and tidy would have done nicely for her, with a beautiful row of delicate flowers in front near the door and a nice little garden out back.

Her husband, her children, and grandchildren all gathered round—it would have been her heaven on earth. But her husband had been dead for many years, as had her only daughter. Her two grandchildren were all that was left of her daughter, and Mary was far away in Boston. Rose still slept in Clara's room on a small cot next to Clara's bed. The cot was a luxury.

There was another, though, and every now and again, Ruth thought of her great-grandson, who lived two miles down the road at the Charlesworth's plantation. The child would be roughly a year-and-a-half old by now, and Ruth wondered how he was getting on.

Mary's little boy he was, forced upon her by Richard before the war had started, back when life had been consistent and all the children but Ben still at home. She wondered if Mary ever thought of the child, if she hated or loved him.

It was a bond Ruth shared with Sarah, although the white woman would never admit it. They shared blood in that small boy who lived down the road. As she opened the door to Sarah's sitting room, she marveled again at the change life had handed her. Sarah was but a shell of her former self, and Ruth was stronger than ever.

* * *

6 February 1863
Savannah, Georgia

"This will be the last time I can visit you," Ben said to Emily and Austin. "I can't thank you enough for allowing me to see my sister these many weeks," he added to Austin. "I'm very grateful."

Austin waved a hand in dismissal. "Think nothing of it. I was glad when she insisted we meet." He smiled at Emily, and Ben was gratified to see her return the affection. She seemed happy, and he was glad for it.

Her expression dimmed, however, with her next comment. "Oh, but you haven't seen Ruth yet! All those times you were at Bentley she was never home, or she was ill, and we never even told her you were here. I had hopes that sometime before leaving, you might make it up her way . . ."

Ben shook his head, feeling heavy. Ruth was indeed the one final person he truly wanted to see. He had also hoped to see Clara and Rose, but they had been small children when he had left home and likely wouldn't know him from Adam. Ruth, however, was the woman he had always wished had been his mother. What he wouldn't give for a chance to see her—he wasn't sure he'd get another one.

"I don't know how I'd manage it. I don't have any more furlough for a long while, and I'm fairly certain we'll be leaving Hilton Head directly without stopping in Charleston."

"Well, pooh." Emily frowned and tapped her finger to her lips. "Where is it you'll be going?"

"Virginia, most likely. We're to be attached to the Army of the Potomac."

"You'll be with Fighting Joe Hooker, eh?" Austin leaned back in his chair and tapped his cigar over an ashtray at his elbow.

Ben nodded. "Let's hope he proves more effective than Burnside."

"Lincoln is said to be very impressed with the manly way in which Burnside accepted total responsibility for the deaths at Fredericksburg," Emily commented. She removed her slippers and curled her feet under her skirts minus the hoops, looking very much like a contented cat.

"I'm sure he is," Ben said, "but manly is one thing. Winning battles is another. And have you heard of the disastrous 'Mud March'?"

Austin nodded. "It's horrible bad luck that man has had. I think his intentions were good—he was trying to cross the river again—who'd have known a two-day storm would turn the road to sludge?"

"I do pity him," Emily added. "One hundred fifty dead animals, stuck in all that muck. And the rebels on the other side jeering at them, offering help crossing the river and then holding up signs that said, 'Burnside stuck in the mud.'"

Ben smiled at his sister. "One would never know you for a Southerner, Emily, if not for your accent. I'd think you were a blue belly tried and true to listen to you talk."

She opened her mouth to respond only to be cut off by a pounding on the front door. She wrinkled her brows in a frown and looked at Austin. He shrugged in response. Ben rose from his seat. "I wonder if I shouldn't be going—I've stayed quite awhile tonight."

Emily nodded and gave him a quick hug. They heard footsteps in the hallway, and after shaking Austin's hand, Ben made a dash for the French doors that led to the back patio. He was barely through them when he heard the doors leading from the hallway bang open.

"Stanhope! Is it true?"

"John, whatever are you doing, bursting into my home like this?" Ben heard Austin's angry voice in response to the man who had forcibly entered the parlor. He poked his head to one side and tried to see into the room, but the white lace curtains on the glass doors partially obstructed his view.

"Mandalay told me you've been smuggling slaves up north. Tell me it's not true!"

"Of course it's not true, and how dare you come in here and frighten my wife with your demeanor and your rumors?"

"He has proof, Stanhope. Mandalay's son was aboard ship with you and your wife last month. I'll wager you had no idea."

"Of course I had no idea, and why should I?"

"He watched very closely, and thought it interesting that you took two servants with you, left them all happy-like with some white folk in Boston, but still managed to come home with two more. And why would you leave two slaves in New England?"

Ben heard Austin heave a sigh. "I sold them to my wife's aunt."

"Ha! Slave owning is illegal in Massachusetts, Stanhope. I don't think you can expect me to believe that!"

"Believe it or don't—my wife's uncle is the twin brother to her father. Do you think two men who are twin brothers don't share the same lifestyles?"

"Not if one lives in Boston, they don't! You'll be hearing from Mandalay." The man turned to go, and then turned back for one final parting shot. "I thought we were friends, Austin."

"John," Austin's voice was weary, "we are friends. You mustn't go around believing every rumor you hear. Mandalay has never liked me, and he's obviously just stirring up trouble."

There was silence then, and Ben moved his face closer to the glass. Peering through a gap in the curtains, he could see that the man had left. Austin had his arms around Emily, who laid her head on his chest. They swayed slowly back and forth, neither saying anything.

Ben quietly left the scene, his thoughts in turmoil as he made his way back to camp.

* * *

6 February 1863
Boston, Massachusetts

For the first time in her life, Mary's bed was her own. It was true that Emily had supplied her with her own bed at Willow Lane, but that had been only a temporary situation. She was now living in a new home, with her room and board paid, and she was *earning a salary!*

The irony that she was still under a Birmingham roof was not lost on her, but oh the difference between the two. In this home, she was valued as a person. She didn't fool herself into thinking that all of New England, or even Boston for that matter, loved and accepted the black population as equals, but the people with whom she shared a roof did, and for the moment it was all that mattered.

Her bedroom was on the third floor of the stately colonial home. There were three small bedrooms on that floor, and hers was the smallest. It also meant that it was hers alone. It was whitewashed and contained a small table that had been adorned with a vase of small, fresh wildflowers on her arrival, and a bed with a fluffy pillow, plain white linen sheets, and a red-and-white log-cabin quilt. The floorboards were covered by a round, red braided rug that kept her feet warm in the mornings when she arose. There was a small armoire in the corner with drawers for her personal items, which were few.

Her work during the day consisted of some light mending of the family's clothing—especially those pieces that were fine and worth repairing—and then decorative work to adorn the house. She loved it. Every minute of it. And the best part was the fact that she was being *paid* to do what she had been doing for years without money.

The first night in her new home, Mary crawled beneath the crisp, white sheets in her snug attic bedroom and lit the small lantern on the table next to her bed. She then opened her copy of *Pride and Prejudice* that Emily had given her years ago and cried. She cried because she couldn't believe her good fortune. She was blessed and lucky, and she knew it. She cried because she was in a beautiful bedroom with an actual bed that was hers alone, with clean bedding, and she was reading a book without fear someone would find her and whip her.

She glanced over to the table at her pen and paper, and the tears continued to flow. She could write to Ben without fear of reparation, and she could continue to nurse her dreams of a life with him even though they would never come to pass. She cried because she was so blessed, and she cried because Mama Ruth and Rose were still back at Bentley, Mama Ruth sleeping in an old bed that sagged (although that bed was a luxury by slave standards!) and old bedding that was threadbare from so much washing, without any kind of pillow, in a shack that provided no heat. She cried that Rose slept on a cot in a room full of things, none of which belonged to her.

Too overcome to actually read her book, she placed it aside on the table and turned down the lamp. In the still dark of night she fell asleep, the words of the Lord's Prayer on her lips.

The shock of her good fortune finally settled in, and she slowly realized it was not all about to be snatched from under her nose. She worked very hard each day to please Mrs. Birmingham, and thankfully, thus far she had. The lady of the house seemed very pleased with her work, and Mary took great pride in it.

The other staff were polite to her, if not completely warm. They were all strangers yet, and Mary assumed it would take awhile before they could consider each other friends. For the most part, Mary was the youngest of the lot. There were three maids, two of whom shared one of the larger bedrooms on the third floor, the other who lived in her own house with her own family. Of the two that lived in the residence, one was a white woman named Jane who said very little to anyone, and the other was a black woman, Josephine, who had been free for five years, the whole time of it in the employ of the Birmingham family.

The cook and her assistant resided in the other large bedroom next to Mary's. The cook's name was Madeline, and she hailed originally from the Jamaican islands. Her assistant was her niece, also from Jamaica, who was probably the closest in age to Mary. Her name was Carmelle, and she was in her midtwenties. She was a chatty woman; Mary loved to listen to her island accent. Madeline constantly told her to "quit runnin' her mouth!" and Mary smiled each time. Their banter was a comforting sound, and sometimes Madeline let her sit in the kitchen while she mended Mr. Birmingham's shirts as long as she promised to "touch nothin' and spill nothin'!"

Griffen, the aging family butler, moved along at a sedate pace—ever proper and solemn, occasionally offering a smile when he felt the occasion warranted one. He was kind to Mary, and perhaps that caught her most by surprise. He was an old white man. He smiled and exchanged pleasantries with a young black woman! What an amazing, amazing thing. Old white men had smiled at her before, but never with respect.

She currently sat in the kitchen, this time mending one of Robert's shirts and listening to the two Jamaican women as they argued over what constituted "normalcy" in the North and what didn't.

"Now," Madeline told her as she kneaded dough for dinner rolls, "don' go thinkin' that just because you have your own room and every other Tuesday off that you suddenly high society. Maids and seamstresses ain' no high society women."

Mary smiled. "I'll remember that."

"An' you all talkin' like a white girl. Why you doin' it?"

Mary glanced up in surprise. "This is how I talk."

Madeline stopped kneading the dough and looked at her. "Like a white girl?"

Like a girl who's been educated. Mary bit her tongue. "My master's son taught my brother how to read, and he taught me. My mistress didn't like people to sound ignorant in her presence, so she encouraged it. I've spoken like this ever since I can remember."

"You thinkin' you somethin' special then?"

"No. It's not hard—do you know how to read?"

"What's a cook need with readin', I ask ya?"

"You could learn new recipes."

Madeline tapped her temple. "Girl, everythin' I be needin' to know I got up here."

Mary nodded with a smile at the woman's rhythmic and musical intonations when she spoke. "That's fine, then. But if you'd ever like to learn, just tell me."

Carmelle spoke up then after an uncharacteristically long silence. "I'd like to learn."

Madeline cackled at her. "You a cook's assistant! Whatchu be needin' it for?"

"Well maybe *I* learn new recipes and teach you a thing or two!" Carmelle snapped at her aunt with the corner of a dish towel and sent Madeline into a fit of shrieks.

Mary laughed out loud at the pair, Carmelle joining her, and was finally rewarded with a reluctant smile from Madeline. "All right, smart girl," Madeline said. "You teach us to read. Then we talk all proper and white like you."

Carmelle shook her head. "I don' wanna sound white. Not too many white folk I like."

Mary looked at her in surprise. "There are many white people in the Abolition Society—you go to the meetings, don't you?"

"Ya, those white folk I like. There are many, many who aren't in the Society, though."

Jane entered the kitchen then with a stack of clean, white dish towels. She set them in their proper cupboard and turned to leave.

"Jane I like, but Jane don' have much to say," Carmelle said.

Jane offered half a smile to the room in general and left.

"What's wrong with her?" Mary whispered.

Carmelle shrugged. "She don' ever say. At first we thought she don' like black folk, but she that way with everybody."

"It's sad," Mary murmured. "I wonder why."

Madeline pounded the dough with a strong fist and sent her long braids to flying about her head. "Everybody have a sad story, missy. Don' have time to be feelin' sorry for everybody."

At that, Mary found herself in partial agreement. "Sometimes it's hard for the heart to hold it all," she said, and went back to her sewing.

Madeline paused in her movements and looked silently at Mary for a moment as though surprised, and then she nodded once and turned her attention again back to the dough. "True, white girl. 'Tis true."

* * *

"I'll tell you what," the grizzled old man said to Joshua as they stood inside the man's carpentry workshop. "I'll give you room and board, but that's all. You can be my 'apprentice,' as you call it, and learn what you will, but I make no promises."

"Sir, you won't regret it." Joshua could barely contain his excitement. He had work as an assistant groomsman with the Birminghams, and in truth, it was kind of Mr. Birmingham to have given him the position, especially since he didn't need another hand with the horses. But Joshua wanted to work with wood. He asked some of the other stable hands where he might go to learn more about carpentry, and they had guided him to the old white man who had a shop near the docks.

For three days, he pestered the old man to let him apprentice. For three days, the man had turned him away with a snarl. Finally, finally today, something he said must have worked, because he had his foot in the old man's door.

"I sleep upstairs, above the shop. I got a room back here that I don't use for nothin' but storage, so you can have it."

"Thank you. I will make this worth your time, sir."

The man looked as though he doubted it, but shrugged. "Suit yourself. And I got a name. You can call me Orson."

"Ah, yes. That would explain the 'Orson and Sons,'" Joshua said, motioning upward toward the battered sign on the outside of the shop.

"Except I ain't got no sons."

Joshua looked at the man expectantly, waiting for an explanation, but none was forthcoming. "Well, then," he said. "Orson, my name is Joshua Birmingham."

"You talk awful proper for a nigra."

Joshua felt his face heat, but maintained his calm. "I'm an educated nigra," he said evenly.

"Well, I'm an uneducated Jew. We should get on fine." The man nodded. "You'll be here in the morning?"

Joshua looked at the man for a moment, trying to follow his reasoning. At the man's irritated raise of the brow, Joshua mentally shook himself and said, "Yes, absolutely. I'll be here in the morning."

As he walked the two miles back to the Birmingham mansion, he wondered if he wasn't making a big mistake working closely with the irascible old fellow. What an odd creature he was. It would be altogether too easy to stay in the comfort of James Birmingham's stables, but he wanted more. And if carpentry was good enough for the Nazarene, it was good enough for him.

He whistled as he made his way to the back of the big house, feeling better than he had . . . ever.

CHAPTER 25

"And now, beware of rashness. Beware of rashness, but with energy, and sleepless vigilance, go forward, and give us victories."
—Abraham Lincoln, in a letter to General Joseph Hooker

* * *

27 February 1863
On the banks of the Rappahannock

"So I reckon it's a mite bit colder up here in these parts than it was down on Hilton Head?"

Ben appreciated his and Luke's tent mate's attempt at conversation. "Just a bit," he said, knowing the unintentional shiver in his voice punctuated his words. "Woulda been nice to stay there longer."

"And miss all the fun up here?"

"Mmm. Fun." Luke stamped his feet.

"Aw, you're a Bostonian! This cold should be second nature to you."

"Ben, I believe ol' Johnny here is laughing at us."

Johnny did indeed laugh. "Misery loves company, and if I've gotta be out in it, I reckon I'm glad you do, too."

"So, do people think you're joking when you say your name's Johnny?" Ben asked, blowing into his cupped hands.

"Naw. They just say I'm fighting for the wrong side—sometimes they call me 'Johnny Reb,' but that's about all."

"Well, since we're the new folks in town, you'll have to tell us all about Fighting Joe's policies."

"He's changed things, that's for sure." Johnny threw another stick onto the small fire and kept his eye on the far riverbank. The men in their company were taking their turn at picket duty, and Ben and Luke were doing their best to adjust to the new setting. "For one thing, Hooker's stepped up the cavalry. But then, you would already know that."

Ben nodded. "Seems like that's about all we do know."

"He's also trying to stop desertion, so he's made a new furlough plan. If Billy Yank takes furlough and then doesn't come back the day he's supposed to, he's court-martialed. Then, if he's still gone, furloughs are cancelled for the rest of his regiment."

Luke whistled between his teeth. "Has it worked?"

Johnny nodded. "Fellas don't want to be responsible for their buddies not getting to leave, so everybody seems to be honoring it. Of course, he's also had some deserters executed, and I'm sure that helps motivate folks, too."

"I'm sure it does. I didn't notice so many desertions down where we were," Ben commented.

"Probably because you were so far away from home. Up in these parts, I heard tell the army was averaging two hundred a day."

"Two hundred desertions *a day?*" Luke stared at the young man.

"Yep."

"Well," Ben muttered, "at least the food is better up here."

"Didn't used to be. Hooker did that, too. We had us a whole mess of corrupt commissary fellas who were selling our supplies and good food to civilian folk on either side of the Virginia border. Hooker got rid of 'em and put in orders for fresh bread and vegetables. You have him to thank for your full bellies."

Ben saluted nobody in particular. He opened his mouth to say something when he heard a slight popping sound in the distance. It was followed quickly by a shout from across the river, "Say, Yanks, there are some fools shooting across the river up above, but we won't shoot if you don't!"

Ben, Luke, and Johnny looked at each other, and Ben wondered if his eyes were as wide as those of the other two. They all shrugged, and Luke finally hollered back, "Fine!"

"That must be the oddest thing I've ever seen in my life," Ben said. "As soon as this weather thaws and things are back in business, that reb will try to blow our heads off."

Johnny grinned. "That's nothin'. A while back, one of our Union officers was invited to a dance by some of the rebel officers over there," he said, jerking his thumb over the shoulder at the river. "They took him to the dance, he had himself a rolickin' good time, and they brought him back before daybreak."

"No!"

"It's true. And only just last week, fellas were trading supplies across the river, using little sailboats. I mean to tell ya, this is one crazy war."

Luke shook his head at the river and stamped his feet some more, trying to warm them. He glanced down at Johnny's boots and said, almost sheepishly, "I don't know why I'm feeling sorry for myself—your boots have holes clear through."

Johnny shrugged. "I figure sometime soon we'll go into battle again, and maybe I'll come across a fallen reb who has the same size feet as me. 'Course, their gear is in worse condition than ours is. Don't suppose I have much to hope for."

"If it warms up soon, it won't be so bad." It was lame comfort, and Ben knew it. He hadn't realized how sheltered he and Luke had been on Hilton Head. The most they had done was train and defend the island from minor picket action. All in all, he finally felt like he was contributing, as though by suffering he was somehow more fully supporting the cause.

His one major regret about leaving the South behind had been his inability to visit with Ruth. All that time he had been there, and she hadn't even known. Emily maintained her silence and encouraged the others to do the same so that Ruth wouldn't waste her time hoping to see him. If she did, it would be a pleasant surprise.

Ruth wasn't the only person he missed, though. He hadn't heard from Emily, and he wondered how they fared—whether or not the neighbors had caused any more trouble for Austin and his "business." He also missed Mary something fierce. He thought of her in Boston and wondered how she was doing. He never would have dreamed in a million years that he'd find himself so taken with her. When he left home, she had been but a young girl. As a young woman, she was captivating, alluring, and intelligent. He loved every stolen moment he had managed in her company.

He almost felt guilty for not missing Joshua as much as he did Mary. Joshua was well and good, and he was a dear friend with whom he hoped to have close contact once the war was over, but Mary . . . Mary was amazing . . .

" . . . not even listening—he's somewhere in fairyland."

"What?" Ben looked at Johnny, having no idea what the man had just said.

"I said, it's about time for us to change our shift. Are you ready to head back to the tent?"

"Doesn't really matter if I'm ready or not, does it? I swear on my life, when I get home after this is all finished, I'm never setting foot in another tent. Especially in the dead of winter."

"Don't know why you would," Johnny said as they noted the approaching replacements. "Seems like a stupid thing to do."

Ben rolled his eyes as they began the journey back to the heart of camp. "That's what I mean . . ."

* * *

27 February 1863
Savannah, Georgia

Emily stood to the side of Austin's bed as he packed the barest of belongings into a small haversack.

"This is grossly unfair. It's extortion!" she fumed.

"It's called blackmail, my sweet, and I'm afraid I have no answer to it."

"There ought to be someone to whom we can appeal, somebody who . . ."

He stopped packing for a moment and put his hands on her shoulders, giving her a small smile. "Somebody to whom I can say, 'My neighbor knows I've been freeing slaves, and if I don't enlist and leave the state, he's going to turn me in to the authorities?' Who would listen to that and help us?"

Tears filled her eyes. "I don't know! There must be someone! Something! Someone up north."

"Sweet Emily, I have racked my brain through every possible solution only to find there are none. I'm afraid they've closed every possible avenue, up to and including threats on the lives of my Northern counterparts. I cannot endanger them by turning to them for help."

"But to be forced not only to enlist, but to fight for the Confederacy!" She choked on the words as though she would gag.

"I won't put my heart into it. Will that help?"

She laughed in spite of herself only to lapse back into tears. "No, it won't help. You may well die, and I'll be left to raise our child by myself."

"I won't die, I'm resilient. And . . . what did you say? Emily, are you . . ."

She nodded miserably. "I am. At first I wasn't sure, but now I know I'm nearly two months into it, but I didn't want to say anything in case I lost it, and . . ."

He crushed her into his arms. "Oh, Emily." She felt his cheek resting against her hair, and it saddened her even more.

"Austin, what will I do with you gone?"

He held her at arm's length and gave her what she assumed was supposed to have been a stern look. "Where's the brave young woman I married? The woman who sacrificed her whole life to free her best friends?"

She flushed. "I didn't sacrifice my life," she mumbled.

He laughed. "Yes, you did. I hope that it's been pleasant thus far, though."

"It has." She smacked at his chest. "You know that it has. I've come to . . . to . . ." She cursed inwardly as the tears flowed again. "I love you, Austin, and I didn't think I would. I don't want you to leave."

"I love you too, Emily." Once again, he pulled her close. "I'll be home before you know it. And if I see your brother and cousin, I promise not to shoot them."

"That's very thoughtful of you. But are you sure Mandalay has proof of your activities?" She tried one more time.

"He does." Austin sighed and turned back to his packing. "He showed me—I don't know how, but he cornered some of the men I've sailed with in the last three years and coerced signed statements from them." He shook his head. "I'll serve my time with the army and then I'll come home. Perhaps I can even do a bit of spy work."

Emily snorted. "I thought I'd try that as well, and I ended up getting married."

He considered the matter carefully for her sake, hoping to draw a smile. "Well, as I'm already married, I suppose that option is out of the question. I shall have to think of something else." When she didn't so much as lift a corner of her mouth, he stroked her cheek with the back of his finger. "I will be fine. I will return, and we will get back to the business of living a fairy tale and be proud, happy parents of a little, redheaded baby."

Emily smiled then, but it took extreme effort. If he didn't leave, then he wouldn't die. If he didn't die, then perhaps she *could* have the fairy tale—at least some semblance of one. He wasn't necessarily the prince she would originally have chosen, but she had come to love him.

"There is one thing I don't understand—what does Mandalay have to gain by your enlistment?"

Austin's smile was bitter. "Revenge. Several of the slaves I took to Boston I bought from him. I'm sure he sees it as the ultimate form of betrayal. But on to more pleasant matters. Emily, I need to tell you that this plantation is in dire straits."

"Pardon me?"

"I'm sure you've noticed that the South is suffering."

"Well, yes, I do read the papers."

"We've been relatively isolated here—I've made excuses to keep you with me because I suppose I wanted to shelter you somehow, but Savannah at large is beginning to show strain, and Willow Lane is close on her heels. I had stockpiled food and necessary items in case of emergency—my parents are actually responsible for that habit—but our stores are nearly depleted, and the cotton embargo has ruined us."

"And you're leaving. This is delightful."

"Emily, the only reason I burden you with this is because you need to be aware of what we're facing. Gwenyth is knowledgeable in the day-to-day functions of this plantation, and she knows what to try to buy or sell in town. Work with her and do your best. When I return home, we'll see if we can't salvage somehow. Until the war is over, I fear we must be . . . resourceful."

* * *

The next morning, he was gone, and Emily wandered back and forth in the front hallway wondering what on earth she was to do with herself. How could she have accomplished her life's goal at eighteen? Mary and Joshua were free in Boston, and therefore Emily had no purpose anymore.

That's the stupidest thing a body ever thought, she said to herself as she passed the front door again. Ruth, Clara, and Rose were still in Bentley's clutches, not to mention the staff at Willow Lane. Somehow these good folk had to eventually make their way north—if they wanted to.

"No time like the present," Emily muttered to herself, and went in search of the housekeeper, Gwenyth. She found her in the cookhouse with the cook, planning the week's menus.

"Gwenyth," she said without preamble after entering and closing the door firmly behind her, "what are your intentions?"

Gwenyth blinked. "Ma'am?"

"Do you want to stay here or go to Boston?"

Gwenyth exchanged a glance with Janet, the cook. "Come and have a seat, Mrs. Stanhope."

"Oh, for heaven's sake. Call me Emily." She took a seat with the two women at the butcher-block table that was smooth with years of use.

"When we were hired by Mr. Stanhope, it was with the understanding that we would have the choice to either remain here, freed and in his paid employ, or eventually go north to Boston with the others he was sending."

"And now that we are living on the losing side of a war? What do you wish to do?"

"I can't speak for Janet, but I wish to stay."

"I do too, ma'am."

Emily looked at the two women. "I appreciate that, very much. I still feel much like a stranger here, and I confess, I have no idea how to run a plantation. Austin told me that you are aware of the comings and goings?" she asked Gwenyth.

The woman nodded. "I would be happy to work with you," she said. "I wouldn't want you to think I'm trying to usurp your authority—Mr. Stanhope asked that I continue—"

Emily held up a hand to forestall the woman's explanation. "Continue away, Gwenyth. I am utterly ignorant in all of this, and I desperately need you. Please, teach me all you know and keep me apprised of your wishes. You're not obligated to stay."

The woman's eyes filmed over, and she cleared her throat. "Ah, but I am. Mr. Stanhope bought me my freedom, taught me to read and write, and he pays me to do work that once was forced on me. I owe him my life, as does Janet."

Janet nodded, her eyes also teary.

"Oh drat, now you're making me feel weepy again," Emily muttered, her eyes burning. "He is wonderful though, isn't he?"

Gwenyth laughed. "He is. The society mamas around here were green with envy when he went chasing after you, missus."

"Well, he caught me. And now, I find that I'm . . ." she paused, suddenly feeling very shy. "I'm carrying his child."

"Oh, chile'" Janet said, clapping her hands together. "My mama worked here for the first Mrs. Stanhope and birthed your husband. Now, I gets to see the whole new Stanhope generation."

"Well then, I'm glad you're here. I don't know the first iota about babies, so I'll depend on you for help."

"With pleasure, missus."

"Emily."

"Oh, I couldn't."

"I insist. Emily."

Janet ducked her head. "Emily."

Emily smiled. How wonderful to have friends again! "Splendid. Oh, and have you heard that the Massachusetts governor just received the authority to raise black troops? They're already organizing the first officially recognized black regiment from the North!"

"Isn't it marvelous? They say Frederick Douglass was very supportive of the proceedings. And the commanding officer of that regiment is the son of some wealthy abolitionists. Some good white folk up that way, I hear."

Emily nodded. "Good folk indeed. Some of them are my relatives." She felt a surge of pride and suddenly realized she wasn't the only one in her family besides Ben who cared about racial injustice.

Janet scowled a bit. "The Confederate Congress say black troops and their commanders is criminals, and any black prisoner of war will be sentenced to death or slavery."

"I'm not surprised," Emily muttered. She shook her head and changed the subject. "And now, Gwenyth, how bad is it here? Do we have food for the week?"

"We do, for several more weeks. We're down to the last of our reserves, though."

"Well, I don't require anything elaborate, and with Austin gone, there's just those of us in the house and the few workers still in the fields." She paused. "Do we still have workers in the fields?"

"Yes," Gwenyth answered. "We have a skeleton crew, and although this is . . . well . . . *was* a functioning plantation, it is rather small in comparison to some."

Emily nodded. Willow Lane was roughly one-third the size of Bentley.

"So I think you'll find that there aren't as many mouths to feed as you might suppose. I reckon we'll get on fine for a time yet to come."

"Good. And do you happen to know if Austin had planned any other journeys to Boston in the near future?"

"I don't think so. This last trip up was supposed to have been his last for a while, at least. I reckon he knew his neighbors suspected him of something."

Emily nodded, suddenly feeling very morose. She had grown used to his company, and the warmth in her bed at night. They had separate bedrooms, as was the custom in most wealthy homes, but more often than not Emily awoke in the middle of the night to find her husband's warm form cuddled next to hers after he had spent a long night in his study, going over figures.

She closed her eyes briefly and then shook her head, impatient. Enough already. Moping wouldn't bring him back home. "No more maudlin nonsense!" she said to herself as she approached the house and wrenched open one of the French doors leading to the parlor. "I'm hungry."

CHAPTER 26

"Since poverty has been our crime,
We bow to the decree.
We are the poor who have no wealth
To purchase liberty."
—Anonymous New Yorker's response to the Conscription Act

* * *

3 March 1862
Boston, Massachusetts

". . . don't believe I'm actually standing in a newspaper office," Camille muttered to herself, and looked with distaste at the stacks of papers and books scattered here and there atop Jacob Taylor's desk and around the room. "This is insane. What am I doing?" She had very nearly convinced herself to turn and leave when Jacob finished his conversation in the hallway and entered the room.

"Sorry to keep you waiting, Miss Birmingham." He walked to his desk, kicking aside a stray newspaper that had fallen to the floor, and indicated for her to sit. She eyed the chair, wondering what might imprint itself on the back of her dress if she chose to take him up on the invitation.

"It's clean," he said, eyeing her with unmasked amusement. "People have been sitting in it all day. Whatever might have been on it before has been swept off just for you."

She arched a brow but sat gingerly on the edge of the seat. "You didn't know I was coming."

"Ah, but I had hopes."

Camille shook her head. "Mr. Taylor, you are an enigma. I'm not here to discuss *you*, however, but rather myself."

Jacob sat in a chair next to hers and settled in comfortably, one ankle swung up upon the other knee. He folded his hands in his lap and smiled. "I'm altogether willing to discuss you."

She flushed. The man seemed to take great pleasure in twisting her words. "My writing, rather."

"Your writing? Well, well. I see I must have planted a seed."

She sniffed. "Believe what you will, but I have come to the realization that I do indeed enjoy putting words to paper." Camille shuddered. "I shouldn't wish for it to become common knowledge, however. A woman writer is most . . . most . . ."

"Unsophisticated?"

"Vulgar."

"Vulgar?"

"Oh, you know very well what I mean. In my circles, it just isn't done. It was bad enough when we discovered Anne's silly business, but that she disguised herself was beyond the pale."

"One would think you might be grateful she disguised herself."

"Mr. Taylor, she pretended to be a *boy.* Had nobody but family discovered it, I might be able to rest in peace, but people know."

Jacob laughed. "*People* don't know. The Van Dykes know. Or knew, rather. Now that Dolly's gone, it's just Abigail. You would have told her eventually, anyway."

"Perhaps, but that's not the point."

He waved his hand. "All right, fine. Nobody will know you're writing. Now, what do you have for me there?"

He pointed to a paper that Camille clutched in her hand. "Oh. Yes, well, these are just some silly ramblings from something I experienced the other day, and I thought you might like to take a look at them. If not, it means nothing to me, really. I mean, I can do without writing, heaven knows that, and—"

"The paper, please?"

Camille hesitated and then slapped it in his outstretched hand. She tried not to fidget while he read it, telling herself that the only reason she was studying his face for a reaction was because he was interesting to look upon.

He finally glanced up at her, and she made herself angry by holding her breath.

"Miss Birmingham," he said, "this is very, very good. It's a very tender observation of freedom's first breath, and I'm quite surprised at your insight. Not to mention your skills with the pen."

"Well, I did pay attention to my tutors, you know. I can answer correspondence with the best of them."

He waved the paper a bit. "This is more than a casual answer to an invitation for tea. You're very eloquent with the written word. Do you read much?"

She felt herself flushing. "Well yes, but only because my mother forces me to!"

He laughed long and hard. "Miss Birmingham, you're going on, what, nearly twenty years now?" At her nod, he continued. "Your mother can only force you into doing so much at this point, especially since you're living away from home."

"How do you know I'm living away from home?"

"I pay attention. Now tell me honestly—you've never snuggled up under your covers at night with a good novel?"

"Perhaps once or twice," she muttered.

"And which author, might I ask?"

"Jane Austen," she said, her tone even quieter and largely indiscernible. "A bit of the Brontë sisters . . ."

"Ah ha! And from thence we see the source of your beautiful prose. Miss Birmingham, you're hired."

She flinched. "Oh, do lower your voice."

"I'll pay you per article."

"Please don't tell anyone." She closed her eyes in mortification.

"And I have an assignment for you. In your meanderings about town, see what you can overhear regarding people's opinions of Lincoln's Conscription Act. He signed it today. Have you heard?"

She shook her head.

"It's a mandatory draft of males aged twenty to forty-five, but if a man has three hundred dollars to spare, or a hired substitute, he can be exempted."

"Hmm. I shall have to pose a few questions at our next tea with the neighbors . . ." she said, already thinking of how she wanted to begin.

"And be considering a pseudonym. It worked well enough for your sister."

"Speaking of Anne," she said, suddenly remembering, "have you heard from her of late?"

"No, why do you ask?"

"Because her correspondence over the past several weeks has been surprisingly scarce. My parents are a bit concerned. In fact, my father has business in Chicago soon—I think he intends to stop in on her and see how she fares."

Jacob stared at her for a moment, his expression blank. "And when is he going?"

Camille shrugged. "I don't know. Soon."

He shifted his gaze from her face to his desk, his brows furrowing slightly into a frown.

"Why?" Camille asked.

"No reason, really. But you know Anne—she hates for people to think she can't care for herself."

Camille snorted unintentionally. "I know. She's a bit too independent as far as I'm concerned."

Jacob didn't respond, but continued staring at his desk as though deep in thought.

"Mr. Taylor? I should be going now." Camille stood, and he rose alongside her, managing a smile although it was obvious his thoughts were elsewhere.

"Thank you, Miss Birmingham. I shall look forward to hearing from you soon. Shall we say, no later than a week?"

Camille nodded. "That should be sufficient." As she left the office, Camille had the distinct impression that Jacob Taylor was losing his wits.

* * *

3 March 1862
New Orleans, Louisiana

Cleaning the decks was infinitely preferable to sitting inside a cabin, doing paperwork. Daniel was almost grateful for the barroom brawl that had been the reason for demotion. Nundry, of course, had been beside himself with joy when word made it back to the ship that O'Shea had put down a man twice his size with one good punch. He had been lectured to, "punished" with extra shipboard duty, and told he was no longer allowed to oversee the ship's logs.

He had tried to look contrite, but he was overjoyed. Nundry could have it all. He only wanted to serve his time, stay out of trouble, and decide how to convince one Marie Brissot of New York's virtues. He adored her. He had felt more of an instantaneous connection with her, even through the letters, than he had with his late fiancée, and although he was ashamed to admit it, it was true. Surely Alice wouldn't have wanted him to live a lonely life—he told himself as much, anyway—and he wondered every day if Marie thought of him as much as he did her.

The war continued on its steady course—the fleet of ships at the door of New Orleans patrolled day and night, keeping an ever-vigilant eye open for blockade-runners. Rumor had it that Grant was busily digging canals through the murky, difficult bayous around the Mississippi in order to capture the one final Confederate stronghold on the river—Vicksburg. Daniel doubted the effectiveness of the canal venture; by all accounts he had heard from people familiar with the area, he was attempting the impossible.

Daniel tucked the supplies back in their proper compartments when he finished his duty for the night and glanced at his pocket watch. Tonight would be his first free night in several weeks, and he was anxious to see Marie.

He walked with purpose to the corner lot near her home. It was deserted, as was the home next to it, and by slipping between the bushes and into the backyards, he was able to approach the back of her house undetected by any eyes. When he knocked upon her back door with their signal—three knocks—she didn't answer.

He waited for a moment and then knocked again. This time, the wait seemed interminable, and he swallowed his crushing disappointment. She wasn't home. Well, it was hardly her fault; it wasn't as though she had known he was coming. He turned and left slowly, knowing he could wait on her back steps but not wanting to cause trouble or anxiety for the other occupants of the house.

He wandered back into the heart of the city, noting absently that he had to choose a different tavern than the one he formerly frequented. If the same men who were there the last time were there again, he didn't want a repeat performance. After strolling down several side streets, he wandered into a taproom that was small, dimly lit, and fairly crowded. He found a vacant table in the far corner and sat with his back to the wall, his chair tipped up on two legs. At his signal, a woman who looked to be well into her forties but was probably much younger plopped a glass of ale down on the table. He nodded his thanks and as she left, he eyed the glass with distaste. Nothing was of good quality, it seemed, with the Union having done such an effective job of slowly squeezing the South to death. He heard that the folks and soldiers up near Richmond were faring even worse.

He listened with half an ear to the conversations around him. Most of the people in the room were Union soldiers or sailors. Interspersed with them were the few odd locals who could stomach the presence of Yanks for more than five minutes and a general assortment of women looking to make a coin or two.

The table next to his hosted four men—he assumed them to be locals from their dress and manner of speech—who were hunched over their glasses as though they had been there for a while.

"You gonna enlist again when you heal up?" one of the men asked another.

"Not if I can help it. The only part of the war I miss is some mighty tasty conquests just south of the Mason-Dixon."

"No, the best conquest yet was well before the war, Gregory Buckland. You thawed the ice queen."

There was a chortling sound and a snort coming from the man on the far side of the table, whose image was blocked from Daniel's view by the two men seated with their backs to him. One of them perked up and said, "I ain't heard that one."

"Oh, it was the best. Gregory tells this little Frenchie girl that he loves her and he wants to marry her. None of the rest of us thought he could compromise her, but he did! And she was willing!"

"Well, it wasn't a complete compromise," the man on the other side of the table admitted. "It would have been if the lady of the house hadn't caught us out in her gardens."

"Oh, you don't mean it was during a society party?"

Daniel tipped his chair forward and leaned his elbows on the table, one hand on his mug. He tilted his head to catch a view of the "compromiser." The expression on his face was a smug one. *"Mais, oui,"* he said to his friends' delight.

Daniel narrowed his eyes. He could well understand why a young woman might fall for that handsome face. His eyes were large and amber in color—they seemed to give off a light of their own, even in the dimly lit tavern—and his face was sculpted and lean. The thick, blonde hair was styled to perfection in the current fashion, and Daniel imagined the man probably spent a fair amount of time before a looking glass as he prepared to leave the house each day.

He was exactly the kind of popinjay that Daniel despised; he was every wealthy, cruel child he had gone to school with as a poor Irish immigrant. He was every man who looked down his snooty nose at Daniel's character but who was more than happy to lay down good money for the furniture he made.

Daniel felt an instant kinship with the poor young woman of whom this man had made such sport. He curled his hands around the handle of his glass mug and prepared to bring the foul brew to his lips when the words at the next table stopped him cold.

"You almost didn't get away with it, though, Buckland. I thought Miz Brissot was gonna tear your head clean off your shoulders. Can't say I really blame her, though. You finished that girl's reputation but good." The man seated next to Gregory leaned forward and said to the other two, "The good women of this town *still* give Marie a wide berth when she walks down the street. The men give her a good look, once up and down, and then maybe up again. Then they pretend they're all innocent-like when the wives smack 'em a good one."

The laughter at the table became a dim echo as Daniel's hand tightened on the mug. His heart pounded in his chest with such force it was a wonder it didn't explode. He rose, and very, very slowly walked to the next table. He put his hand on Buckland's shoulder, and when the man glanced up in surprise, he leaned down close to his ear.

"The only reason I'm not going to tear out your throat with my bare hands is because I have hopes for my future. Look at my face—do you see my face?"

Buckland's nostrils flared, and he moved to stand, but Daniel tightened his grip on the man's shoulder and shoved him back into the seat. "I want you to remember my face," he muttered, "because if I ever hear you talking about Marie Brissot again, you will see this face when you're in your bed at night, and it will be the last thing you *ever* see."

"Who the bloody blazes are you?" Buckland was maintaining his bravado, but he winced slightly under the increasing pressure of Daniel's thumb, which was now deeply entrenched into his collarbone. "You can't threaten me! I'll report this to your commanding officers!"

"Do you think they'll care?"

"Yank," Gregory fumed, "you'd better hope I don't find you alone some night in a dark alley."

"*You'd* better bring a big gun and hope I'm feeling generous." Daniel stood to his full height, straightened his strong, Irish back, showing his thick frame to its advantage, and glanced at the other men at the table who were staring at him, slack jawed. With a final squeeze to Buckland's shoulder, he turned and left the tavern.

What were the odds he'd encounter the source of Marie's ruination in that huge city? Providence was indeed kind.

Hoping for one last chance to see Marie, he jogged the distance back to the neighborhood where she lived and took his secret route to her back door. This time when he knocked, the door opened. There she stood, looking shocked and delighted. "Let's sit out here tonight," she said, and reached for a shawl that hung on a hook next to the door.

She led him to a double swinging chair that was suspended from a large tree branch. The swing overlooked what was once probably a beautiful flower bed, but which had faded from its former glory. "Are you sure?" he said as they sat together on the swing. "It's a bit brisk."

"It feels wonderful. Pauline and I have been baking all day, and the kitchen is frightfully hot." She turned to him with a small pat on his leg, which sent his heart racing, and said, "Where have you been? I was beginning to worry."

He pointed to his face, where the bruises were faded and nearly gone altogether. "I was chastised for fighting."

"Oh, but it wasn't your fault!"

"They didn't seem to care. It's fine, really. No, don't look at me like that—I don't mind a bit. It relieved me of some chores I found rather . . . mundane."

"So what are you doing now?"

"Swabbing the deck."

She laughed. "You are unique. Has anybody given you any more trouble—fighting, I mean?"

"Well, no. I'm afraid I dished out some of my own tonight, though."

A few tendrils of hair escaped her bun and blew in the breeze. She turned her face toward it and closed her eyes. "Now why on earth would you do a thing like that?" she asked, allowing him to control the motion of the swing.

"Because the man was a bit of an idiot." He paused, not wanting to upset her, but figuring she had a right to know. "Does the name Gregory Buckland mean anything to you?"

Her eyes flew open, and she shoved her feet to the ground, halting the swing. She said nothing, merely looked at him with wide eyes.

"He was boasting to his friends about his 'conquest' of you—I overheard him tonight in a bar," he told her gently.

"What did you do?"

"I threatened to kill him."

Marie slowly lifted her feet from the ground and settled back into the swing, shifting slightly and turning her face away from him.

"I'm sorry. I don't know if you still have feelings for him, and I know it's not my place to interfere, but Marie, I just couldn't let him sit there and squawk like some idiot hen."

She shook her head but remained silent. He wished he could see her face. He took a deep breath, feeling strangely hurt that she still obviously cared for the lout. "I apologize," he said, his voice coming out stiff, the sentiment forced. "I'll keep my nose out of your affairs from now on." It wasn't until after he said it that he winced at his choice of words, hoping she didn't think he was making a crude attempt at a double entendre.

Again she shook her head, and as he glanced at her, he saw a tear escape and trail a path down her cheek. It was worse than he imagined.

"I should go," he said quietly, and moved to stand. She placed a restraining hand on his leg, however, and so he sat back down, waiting.

Finally she whispered, "It was why I didn't want to meet you."

"Why? You thought I would threaten to kill your past beaux?"

"No, no." She lifted her hand from his leg and wiped her tears, then rubbed her hands together in an attempt to dry the moisture. She sniffed and laughed softly through her nose at some jest only she comprehended.

"Marie, I don't understand."

She sighed. "I know you don't. I never told you, Daniel, that the good people of this city—at least this little corner of the city—see me as soiled goods. They think little more of me than they would of a passing harlot."

He nodded slightly. He had gathered that much from listening to the men at the bar, and it still made his blood boil.

"I didn't want to trap you into a friendship with a 'fallen woman,' but at the same time I took such pleasure in corresponding with you that I . . . I allowed myself to forget for a moment . . . and then the next thing I knew, you were here." She finally turned to face him, her eyes flashing. "I tried to stop you! I told you I didn't want to meet you, and this is why!"

He narrowed his eyes on her face, trying for the life of him to understand her reasoning. "At some point in this conversation, I'm thinking I must have somehow gotten up and left, yet here I still sit."

She thumped a fist on her leg in frustration. "How can you not understand?"

"Understand *what*?"

"That I didn't want you to associate with a harlot, and I tried to protect you from it! You didn't listen, though—you just went ahead with what you thought was right, and now your reputation will be ruined, too. Of course, things are different for men, but surely your mother would be mortified if she knew—"

He laughed and belatedly remembered to lower his voice.

"I even *told* you when we first met that I am less than desirable company . . ."

He put a hand over her mouth to shush her and finished laughing. Just when he was convinced there was no more mirth to escape, however, he started chuckling again. "Marie," he finally managed to breathe out, "what do you think I am?"

Her eyes above his hand narrowed in confusion.

"I am the son of two penniless Irish immigrants who worked their way into a small farm on the outskirts of New York City. I am nearly thirty years old, I have nothing to my name but a very small house and carpenter shop, and I used to brawl for money. Now, I swab decks. You were worried about what *I* would think? I was worried you wouldn't say 'hello' to me, even if you had known I was the one who's been writing to you all this time."

He removed his hand, and she said, "But—"

"Furthermore, my mother has a heart of gold, and she leaves all judgment to God. She would be thrilled beyond her wildest imaginings to know you are my friend, and she'd probably try to bribe you into joining the family.

"Marie, I can match you to perfection when it comes to bad reputations, but I must say that while mine is entirely deserved, yours is not."

His heart fell as he watched the tears again cloud her violet eyes. She shook her head. "I was willing," she said, and looked down at her hands.

"Because you thought he *loved* you. You thought he wanted to marry you."

"That doesn't make it right."

"It makes it *different.* You are not a harlot. You were not a woman who walked the streets looking to make money. You were a young girl who trusted entirely too much." Just thinking of Buckland made him fume all over again. He should have knocked him out cold when he'd had the chance.

She shook her head again and leaned back in the chair, blowing the air from her mouth with a puff of her cheeks. "I didn't think I still cared," she muttered.

"But do you really? Yes, you can still feel the embarrassment and the shame, but do you care what they think?" He made a motion with his arm to the world at large. "Did you even then? Did you like all of those women who were so quick to condemn?"

"No. It hurt horribly, though. And it reflected badly on my parents. My mother was alarmed at my lack of discretion."

"But she forgave you your lack of discretion."

"How do you know?" Her voice was flat.

"I've met her. And I saw her face when she spoke of you. And I have it on good authority from what I overheard tonight that she very nearly killed Buckland herself."

Marie's lips twitched in a reluctant smile, and she wiped at her face. "Wouldn't that have been a sight?"

"I'd put my money on her."

"Spoken like a true fighter.

He suddenly felt awkward. "Just because I'm not what society calls honorable doesn't mean, that is—I wouldn't have you believe, Marie, that I'm all you're worthy of. You could be the bride of a crown prince."

She bit her lip and shook her head. "*You* are a crown prince."

He closed his eyes for a moment and put his arm around her, pulling her close. She laid her head on his shoulder and as the swing rocked, he figured that he could have stayed in that one moment forever. He wished more than anything that they were back in his little home, with the world, the war, all of it locked outside.

She raised her head and looked up at him. Without thinking, he touched her lips with his own. The kiss was soft—almost featherlike, and when he pulled back, her eyes were closed. "*Now* you're compromised," he said, "because I'm not leaving."

She opened her eyes and smiled. "My father would have liked you," she whispered, and knowing how much she had loved her father, he felt complimented. He suddenly understood why men were willing to sacrifice everything for the love of a good woman.

* * *

Marie awoke the next morning feeling as though something exciting had happened, but she couldn't remember what it was. With a rush of memory, she thought of the time she shared with Daniel out on the swing and of the gentle kiss that had sealed her heart. The old, familiar doubts crowded back in again, though, and before long she was feeling much as she always had when she thought of her future possibilities with a good man.

He was too good to be true. Surely it was all a dream that would end badly—he'd realize he didn't want to saddle himself with a woman nobody respected, or he'd die in battle, or, or, or . . . The possibilities stretched endlessly before her, almost as though her mind dared her to believe she could have a happy ending and then mocked her for it.

She dressed and went downstairs, comforted by Pauline's familiar humming and the smell of fresh muffins. Justis Fromere and the boys were in the backyard, tending the vegetable garden and coaxing every last bit of goodness they could from the earth. The yard was secluded and bordered by thick, high trees and bushes. As long as the Fromeres were quiet, she wasn't worried for their safety.

She sat at the dining room table with a book she planned on using to teach Noah the last of his lessons. He was still insisting he wanted to enlist, and she hoped to teach him as much as possible before he made his dream a reality. Just as she was settling in for the day and trying to ignore her heavy heart, there came a knock at the door.

Startled, she jumped a bit and glanced back into the kitchen at Pauline, whose eyes were large with apprehension. Pauline fled to the backyard to warn Justis and the boys, and Marie opened the front door.

"Cecile?" Gustav Deveraux's mother stood at the door, her face pale.

"Marie," she said in heavily accented English, "now we know why it has been so long in hearing from Gustav. He died at a place they call 'Shiloh.'"

"Oh, Cecile. Come inside."

The woman shook her head. "No, no, I cannot. I must be going—my husband is not faring well—it seems I am about to lose him as well as my son."

"I'm so sorry, Cecile. Thank you for taking the time to tell me."

"Here is this," she said, and handed Marie a folded piece of parchment that was splattered in a dark brown color. "He wrote this for you, probably just before the battle. When he was buried, one of his company emptied his pockets and kept his belongings until he returned home to give them to me personally." The woman's eyes teared and overflowed. "Oh, Marie, I shall miss him so."

Marie grasped the woman in her arms and held her close for a moment, then released her. "Take care," she whispered to Gustav's mother.

"*Tu aussi, ma chérie.*"

Marie closed the door after she left and wandered slowly into the study at the back of the house. She waved through the window at the Fromeres that all was well, and then sank onto a chair. With trembling fingers, she opened the letter.

* * *

"Ma chère Marie,

The dawn hour approaches, and I find myself at the fringe of battle . . ."

By the time Marie finished the letter, the tears flowed liberally from her eyes. It was as though her dear friend, the only one of her peers who hadn't judged her harshly, who had remained steadfast through it all, had reached beyond the grave to soothe her worried heart.

" . . . you must not let the actions of one night, years ago when you were but a child, rob you of the happiness you so richly deserve. You were a trusting innocent, and he was an utter cad. You were in love and thought it was a sentiment returned; he sought to satisfy a juvenile wager. And you must remember, chérie, *you know in your heart of hearts that your innocence remains. Mussed hair and a disheveled appearance do not equate to loss of virtue, regardless of what New Orleans's 'finest' would have you believe."*

How could he possibly have known that she would need to hear these things from him? She read and reread those passages that seemed so perfectly to apply, to address the very concerns that had been running through her mind all morning.

"You are worthy of the best this world has to offer, and I pray with all my heart to that God who dwells above that you will find it. If I return home, I hope it will be me, because, of course, I am among the best ever."

She laughed out loud through her tears and remembered his simple arrogance. Life had been merely a matter of black or white to him. He saw things as he chose to see them, and he never wavered.

"If I should die, however, find that someone who will love you and make you smile. Do not spend your life defined by the dictates of a society

who condemns the most innocent of acts and yet perpetrates far worse behind closed doors. They are not worthy to trod in the dust dislodged from the soles of your boots, dear woman.

I hear now the bugle call, and so I must close. I will fold this missive and keep it in my jacket, close to my heart, addressed to you in hopes that, should I fall, some kind soul will see it through to its destination.

Ever yours,
Gustav"

Sweet, sweet friend. Marie traced a finger softly over the dark smudges on the paper. Not mud, but blood. He had indeed kept the letter close to his heart—the very paper she held in her hands touched him as he breathed his last. She hoped that he suffered little pain, that his sojourn into the next life was effortless.

She would miss him, and miss him horribly. She lay down on her bed in the back of the study and allowed herself to curl up into a ball and sob. She cried for his loss, for the loss of her father, for the loss of so many years when other people had been cruel and she had been hurt.

Marie cried herself to sleep, and when Pauline crept in to check on her an hour later, rather than wake her, she covered her with a soft blanket and kissed her cheek. "You jus' sleep, sweet girl. You jus' sleep," she murmured, and tiptoed from the room, quietly closing the door behind her.

CHAPTER 27

"Near a deserted hut we met four children crouched at the side of the road. . . . Their mother was dead and their father had abandoned them. They wept while asking for something to eat. The soldiers immediately gave them enough provisions to last them several days. . . . But what became of these children? This is the horrible side of war."
—P. Regis de Trobriand, New York officer

* * *

2 April 1863
Richmond, Virginia

Isabelle stood on the streets of the Confederate capital, accompanied by her friend Lucy Lockhart. "This looks very volatile to me," Lucy murmured under her breath to Isabelle. "Not the best of times for you to come here on a social visit."

"No, I suppose not." Pinkerton suspected Miss Lockhart of spy work, and had sent Isabelle south to see what she could discern. Thus far, Lucy had given away nothing. "I was becoming frightfully bored in Washington, though."

Lucy glanced at her with a wry smile but said nothing. Isabelle turned her attention to the women who clamored in the streets, the same women who had marched on Capitol Square, demanding that Governor John Letcher do something to ease the burdens of Richmond's starving populace.

"If so many people hadn't flocked to this city after it was announced as the new capital, some of this might have been avoided," Lucy muttered. "This much growth in population would have been trying under the best of circumstances, let alone during a war!"

Isabelle nodded. She had to agree. She had been horrified earlier in the day to learn that the weekly cost to feed a small, Southern family had risen to sixty-eight dollars and twenty-five cents! Before the war, it would have cost only six! It was no wonder the people starved.

"I question the wisdom of Davis allowing so much more Confederate money to be printed," Isabelle said to her companion. "It's no wonder the Confederate dollar is now worth only eight cents."

Lucy nodded. "I fear we're approaching the end, Miss Greene. We don't have the resources to sustain this conflict much longer. I would never have believed this if I hadn't seen it with my own eyes."

Isabelle wondered if she spoke of the war in general or the increasingly agitated state of the women in the street. Before long, the women began chanting, "Bread, bread!" Suddenly, Isabelle heard the sound of crashing glass, and looked to her right as the window of a store was broken and women rushed inside. The sound of shards of glass quickly echoed up and down the street as shops were summarily broken into and looted.

Women ran from the stores carrying food, clothing, jewelry—anything they could get their hands on. Isabelle looked at Lucy, who glanced back at her with wide eyes. "Never in my wildest dreams," Lucy murmured.

It wasn't long before the governor appeared with members of the state militia, giving them orders to fire on the women if they didn't disperse. Isabelle dropped her jaw as the mayhem continued, and out of the corner of her eye, she spied an approaching carriage. A familiar character emerged and climbed atop a wagon, shouting at the women.

It was Jefferson Davis himself. He chided the women for stealing jewels and other items when they were screaming for bread. "You say you are hungry and have no money—here is all I have." He then emptied his pockets and threw money into the crowd. Pulling a pocket watch from his vest, he then announced that if the rioters did not disperse within five minutes, the militia would open fire.

"I think you should come and spend some time in Washington with me, my friend," Isabelle said to Lucy.

Lucy shook her head at the scene in disbelief. "I'm beginning to wonder, myself . . ." She turned to Isabelle and said, "Not everybody here is still staunch in support of the Confederacy, as if you needed further evidence of that." She swept her arm at the women gathered. "I am also one who began in heated fire that has since dimmed."

She pulled Isabelle away from the crowd and linked their arms. "I know who you are," she said.

Isabelle glanced at her askance, saying nothing.

"I know you are not all you seem, and I suspect someone has sent you to examine me. You should know that while I once willingly gave all of my time and efforts to the cause, I find I have no more will."

To trust, or not to trust? Isabelle relied on her instincts, which rarely failed her. "You remain here then, Lucy. I will bring you all that I can, and you will be my eyes and ears. Will you do that?"

Lucy nodded, her eyes on the ground. "Rose Greenhow would be most disappointed in me."

Isabelle snorted. "Rose Greenhow was a zealot with more daring than sense."

Lucy's lips twitched slightly.

"Come to my hotel room," Isabelle told her. "I have food. I'll leave it with you and return to Washington. You will stay here, then?"

Lucy nodded again. "I'll stay here."

* * *

15 April 1863
Charleston, South Carolina

The sweat stood out on Ruth's brow in beads. Her forearms strained with the effort of aiding the baby's entry into life, and she wondered if they would, in the end, lose not only the child but the mother as well.

"Oh, Ruth!" Charlotte was so weak from twenty-six hours of hard labor that her screams had given way to animal-like groans. "Please, I am begging you, get it out. Please get it out." She sobbed then, and Ruth gritted her teeth, offering another prayer to God. How many had it been now? She had lost count of the number of times she had offered supplication to the heavens, and she wasn't sure anymore where one prayer stopped and the next began.

"Where is my mother?" Charlotte cried. "Where is she?"

Angel bathed Charlotte's face with a wet rag and cradled the white woman's head in her arms. "Easy now, Miz Charlotte," Angel crooned. "Your mama be up here soon as she can."

If ever a soul was doomed to hell for lying, it was Angel. Ruth paused as the baby slipped momentarily from her grasp. If the child would just manifest itself enough for her to firmly grasp the shoulders . . .

Charlotte tensed again, her distended abdomen rock hard with another gripping contraction, wrenching a moan from her lips that Ruth was sure she would hear for the rest of her life. She had delivered more babies than she could count, including Charlotte herself, but this was different—something was wrong.

The child inched its way forward, and seizing both one final opportunity and the tiny shoulders, Ruth took a firm grip, murmuring, "Please, most Holy Father—*please.*" The baby eased forward from the birth canal and into Ruth's arms. The little face was blue, and he didn't utter a sound.

Swiftly holding the child by his feet, she soundly rapped him on his behind and was rewarded moments later with a weak, mewling cry. "That's Mama Ruth's good boy," she said to the infant, and held him close to her blood-spattered dress. She gently ran her hand over his head and small throat, massaging down onto his little chest as the cries grew steadily stronger. She placed her finger into the child's mouth and swept it clean, heartened at the increasing strength in the continued cries.

Cutting the cord, she handed the baby to Angel, who wrapped him in a blanket they had been keeping in a small box near the warm hearth. "Oh, he's jus' beautiful, Miz Charlotte," Angel murmured. "Here, ma'am. You hold your wee one."

Charlotte turned her head to one side and managed to lift her arms. Angel placed the crying infant into them and resumed her protective stance at Charlotte's head. Ruth finished the afterbirth functions and called orders to the other women who stood in the room, exhausted from the long hours with the mistress.

They cleaned Charlotte and the bedding, and washed the newborn baby with warm water. His little cries grew ever stronger and angrier at the pawing and manhandling, and it gave Ruth hope. As she turned her attentions back to Charlotte, however, the hope dimmed.

One by one, the women in the room dispersed to see to their own duties. It was afternoon, but as they prepared to leave, Ruth followed them into the hallway. "Bentley will keep for the day," she said. "Cook will prepare Miz Sarah's food for the evening, and the rest of you go to your quarters and rest. If Mr. Jackson has anything to say to you, send him up here to me."

Ruth reentered Charlotte's room and surveyed the scene with satisfaction. Everything was pristine and in order, the temperature comfortable, the baby nursing. Charlotte had fallen into a fitful slumber, and Ruth went forward to check on her. Finally, the baby seemed to have had his fill, and Angel took the little one, securely wrapped him in his blanket, and walked quietly from the room so that the mother might rest.

Placing a hand on Charlotte's forehead, Ruth frowned at the obvious rise in temperature. The woman was on fire. Ruth was so unbelievably tired. She hadn't slept in over twenty-four hours, and her head was beginning to throb. She located a clean cloth and dipped it in a basin of cool water. Wringing it well, she returned to the bedside and, folding the cloth carefully, placed it upon Charlotte's head.

Rotating her head on shoulders that ached from strain, she left the room and made her way down the hall to Sarah's suite. When she reached the sitting room, Sarah was exactly where Ruth had guessed she would be. She sat at one of the window seats, looking out over the vast plantation.

When Ruth entered, Sarah glanced at her and said, "The fields aren't looking quite right for this time of year. My father is going to be most disappointed—I must ask him about it when he returns from Atlanta."

It was no use telling Sarah that her father was dead. In her mind, she seemed to have reverted back to the time when she had come of age and her father was training her to assume her duties as Bentley's mistress. Every now and again she seemed to remember she'd had a husband, but on those occasions her only comment was, "Jeffrey left me." She'd usually stare off into space for a moment and then she was gone, returning again to the time when her life had been happiest—with her father.

"Sarah," Ruth said.

"Yes? What is it, Ruth?"

"Charlotte has had a baby boy. You're a grandmother." Again.

Sarah slowly looked away from the window to Ruth. "I think you must have been drinking some of father's spirits, Ruth. You're talkin' nonsense!"

Why couldn't Sarah be lucid, just for a moment? Her daughter needed her, and she wasn't there. Ruth shook her head a bit and turned, leaving the room.

"Ruth—tell father I wish to see him as soon as he returns," Sarah called after her.

"Yes, ma'am." Ruth walked down the hall and had reached the landing above the mansion's entrance when she heard voices below.

The footman was closing the front door, an envelope in his gloved hand. "What is it, Edward?" she called down to him.

"A telegram, Miz Ruth."

She walked halfway down the large staircase, her hand extended. He met her on the stairs and handed it to her. "I'm thinkin' you should know, too," he added, "that Jackson just up an' left."

Ruth stopped and stared at the young man. "He what?"

"He done left. Said there's money to be made elsewheres."

Ruth inhaled and held her breath for a moment, finally blowing the air out and feeling her energy go with it. The overseer had left. The world around her was changing moment by moment, and she struggled to keep up. It was no wonder Sarah's good sense had deserted her; nothing was as it used to be.

"Edward, please gather the field hands and the house staff together and have them assemble on the back lawn. I'll be outside in a moment."

"Yes, ma'am."

In an odd way, the system of slavery had a hierarchy of its own, and at Bentley, Ruth was the head Negress. She commanded a measure of respect because of her position at Sarah's side, managing the household and everything in it. Ruth only hoped she held enough sway over Bentley's small army of slaves that they would at least hear her out before leaving as well. Not that she'd blame them. She was tempted to run out of the front door and never look back.

She turned on the stair and began her ascent, opening the telegram as she walked. By the time she reached the top stair, she stopped again and stared at the paper in her hand. William had been wounded. He had been the victim of a small skirmish just outside Memphis. He was recovering in a Confederate infirmary in Tennessee and would return home as soon as he had healed.

Ruth's hand fell limp to her side, and she stared at Charlotte's closed door. She made a decision and crumpled the telegram into a tight ball, then entered the room. Walking to the fireplace, she tossed the telegram into it and watched as it quickly became a small ball of light that burned bright for one moment and then was reduced to blackened scraps.

"Ruth?" Charlotte's voice was little more than a whisper.

She walked to the bedside. "Yes, Charlotte."

"Is my mother coming?"

"She's ill, child."

Charlotte was quiet for a moment. "She doesn't even know I'm here, does she? She doesn't know I've had a baby."

"I'm sorry. She just doesn't seem to . . . remember things . . ."

Charlotte's face was a sickly pale color. "All I ever wanted was to be like her."

Ruth nodded a bit. Charlotte had done a right good job of becoming like her mother, but Ruth didn't think she could voice that opinion without making it sound like an insult, so she said nothing.

"Mother always liked Ben the best of all. Even after he left."

"Charlotte, you should try to get some rest." Ruth lifted the quilt back to check on Charlotte's condition. Her heart rate increased upon seeing the large smear of red blood she found beneath the woman's legs. A small amount of bleeding after giving birth was normal, of course, but if Charlotte kept losing blood at such an alarming rate, she doubted the young woman would make it through the night.

Ruth momentarily considered sending for the aging doctor who lived down the lane—he was one of the few who had been too old to go off and fight. She discarded the notion as quickly as it came, however. All he would do was get out the leeches, and it had never made sense to Ruth. If a patient was losing blood, why try a remedy that would merely exacerbate the problem?

She changed Charlotte's clothing and bedding, the poor woman being so drained of strength that she was able to offer little by way of help. The blood continued to flow, however, and Ruth did her best to staunch it.

Charlotte held up a hand and said, "Ruth, please just hold me for a moment. I'm so very tired."

Ruth hesitated for a moment and let the quilt fall to cover the young mistress. Climbing gingerly atop the bed, she gathered Charlotte close and cradled her head and shoulders in her arms.

"Ruth?"

"Yes?"

"When William comes home, will you tell him I was happy to give him a son?"

"You'll be able to tell him yourself, Charlotte. Your little one needs his mother now, so don't you think you can leave just yet."

"I'm bleeding, Ruth."

"Yes, but I'll stay with you. We'll stop it. You be brave now."

Charlotte closed her eyes for a moment. "Ruth, I've not always been . . . that is, I've treated you with something less than respect on occasion . . ."

"Now, since when does a slave deserve respect?"

Charlotte threw Ruth a look that bespoke exasperation. "Don't pretend for a moment you believe that, Ruth. You're as smart as, probably smarter than, any of the rest of us, and we all know it. You've been the one to hold Bentley together, thank goodness, since my mother has deserted her senses."

Charlotte winced and fluttered her hand toward her abdomen. "It hurts," she whispered.

"I know. Try to be still. It won't hurt forever."

"Anyway, Ruth," she murmured as her eyelids fluttered closed, "I would have you know that I do respect you." Her voice trailed off. "You took care of me when I was small . . . like a mother . . ."

Forgetting that she had instructed Edward to gather the slaves, Ruth lay beside Charlotte for hours into the night, sleeping intermittently only to awaken and hear the sound of Charlotte's thin breathing. She staunched the bleeding as the hours dragged by, and continually applied cold, wet cloths to the girl's forehead, neck, and chest. Ruth glanced at her in pity; Charlotte was becoming engorged and would need the child to eat soon to relieve some of the pressure. The baby was with a wet nurse, but Ruth determined to bring him in to his mother by morning. No sense in Charlotte becoming infected and adding to her discomfort.

A tear welled in Ruth's eye and fell atop the young woman's head as morning finally dawned and Ruth realized Charlotte had made it through the night. The bleeding had finally stopped, and her breathing was deep and even. Her skin felt normal to the touch, and when Angel cracked the door open, Charlotte looked at the young woman and said, "Can I see my baby? I think I should feed him."

Ruth looked toward the ceiling and mentally offered a small prayer of thanks. She turned her attention to Charlotte when the new mother spoke to her. "Ruth, you've saved my life," she murmured. Her face was pale, but her eyes were bright. "Please, you won't leave Bentley?"

"No, Charlotte. I won't leave."

* * *

"No rest for the weary," Ruth muttered to herself as she climbed the hill to the mansion, freshly bathed, dressed, and still tired. She viewed the assembled group—her people—and felt a sense of duty. Not to Bentley, but to them.

She surveyed the crowd of dark faces, all of whom looked on her with a certain amount of curiosity. "Mrs. Birmingham is not well—most of you know this."

There was a general nodding of heads. "Charlotte has just given birth and has expressed to me that she has no desire at this time to take over the duties of running this plantation."

There was a general murmur in the crowd. "With Mr. Birmingham gone, that leaves Ben to inherit, and of course, he isn't here. Who's to say how the war will end, but Mr. Lincoln has declared us free—a feat we will see accomplished only if the Confederacy fails. I do not know what to suggest that will benefit all of us, except to say that if you stay and continue to help with maintaining what is left of this plantation, I will find a way for all of us to be compensated."

"How you gonna do that, Miz Ruth?"

"You leave that to me. It may not be much, but it will be something. It is my understanding that the Union general Grant has begun a siege on Vicksburg, Mississippi, after a failed attack. When Vicksburg falls, I suspect we won't have much longer to wait before seeing an end to the war. At that point, we'll all be free to choose where we'd like to go."

She paused for a moment as her words sank in. She then added, "My friends, my family, nobody wants to see you lead free lives more than do I. At this point, however, it may be in your best interest to stay here at Bentley—not because you're being forced to, but because you choose to. You'll be safer, for one thing, and you'll be able to work without the whip of an overseer hanging over your backs. As I'm sure you know, Jackson is gone, and I have no intention of informing Miz Sarah of that fact."

A cheer went up, and as the noise settled back down, she said, "If we work to keep the plantation afloat as much as possible, then we will not only be able to continue feeding ourselves and our families, but depending on who inherits, we may see some just financial rewards. I have no guarantees, though."

She cast an eye over the children, who sat in rags. "I have access to material," she said, making a snap decision, "and will provide it for any needing new clothing, beginning with the children. We must use care, however, because once it is gone, there is no more. The cities are swept bare—plantations and homes everywhere are making do with what they already have.

"Please inform me of your decision—whether to stay or leave—and I will keep a record of the work you do. When Ben returns, I will show him."

"Ben's comin' back?" There was a ripple through the crowd.

"Emily sent a letter saying that he enlisted some time ago with the Union army. I have hopes we may see him sometime."

* * *

1 May 1863
Boston, Massachusetts

"You do good work," Orson muttered to Joshua. "Ye've got a good eye for the wood."

"Thank you," Joshua murmured, concentrating on the work and feeling absurdly pleased. Wringing compliments out of the old man was like trying to squeeze water from a rock. Anytime Orson offered feedback, whether positive or negative, Joshua paid close attention.

Orson left him to his project—he was working on a chair leg—and moved to the front of the shop, where he had work of his own to complete. Joshua lifted his head when Orson said, "Here comes that colored man again."

Joshua didn't have to ask which colored man. He knew. With a sigh, he straightened his back and shoulders, making his way to the front door. "I'll speak to him outside," he told Orson, and left the shop.

The "colored man" was a recruiter for the Bureau of Colored Troops. He had approached Joshua on four separate occasions, begging him to consider enlisting with one of Massachusett's newly forming black regiments. The problem was that Joshua was enjoying his new life. He worked sunup to sundown with Orson, learning more each day about furniture, about wood and the tools used to create marvels from practically nothing. He didn't want to leave—he imagined himself happy living and working forever with the cranky old man.

Never in his life had he been more content. He had attended Society meetings with Mary and the Birminghams, had met many other freed blacks (even Frederick Douglass himself!), and had found a kinship with these good people. Boston was far removed from the war, although it was the only thing most folk talked about, and he didn't want to go back into a situation sure to churn up his insides and his feelings.

He constantly ignored a voice at the back of his head that told him he owed it to his fellow people still in bondage to fight the fight that would make them free. He ignored the voice that said he should find himself a good woman and begin a family. The only woman he wanted lived thousands of miles away, and had red hair and white skin.

Joshua smiled tightly as the man approached and extended his hand. "Mr. Birmingham," he said to Joshua. "Mighty nice to see you again."

"Likewise. I just stepped out for some fresh air."

"It just so happens I was on my way to pay you a visit."

"Is that so? Well, how fortuitous of me to take a break now, then."

"Indeed. I wonder—have you given much more thought to the things we've discussed?"

"Mr. Dobson, I remain unchanged since the last time we talked. I have no wish to enlist."

"Are you aware of the Massachusetts 54th? The commander is Robert Gould Shaw, who is very sympathetic to the cause and is a wonderful commander. It is my understanding that such is the case with all of the commanders who will lead colored troops. Should your reservations be over the leaders, I can assure you they are compassionate and enlightened men.

"Joshua," Mr. Dobson paused, "please, please do give it some more thought. We need as many good men as we can get. By merely being allowed to fight for our own freedom, we send a message to folk everywhere, black and white."

But I don't want to lose my life now that I've only just found it, Joshua thought as he studied the man. *I left the South, and I don't want to go back.* "Do you understand what you're asking me to leave?" Joshua finally murmured to Dobson.

"I do." The older man laid a gentle hand on Joshua's shoulder. "Believe me, son, I do. But do you understand how important this is? It's bigger than just you or me."

Joshua nodded. Finally, after an extended pause, he said, "I will consider it. Come and see me again in a week, and I will give you my answer. And then, I trust that it will be settled one way or the other, for good."

Dobson nodded. "Fair enough. A week, then."

CHAPTER 28

"[The army] has strong limbs to march and meet the foe, stout arms to strike heavy blows, brave hearts to dare—but the brains! Have we no brains to use the arms and limbs and eager hearts?"
—William Thompson Lusk, Union soldier, in a letter to his mother following Fredericksburg

* * *

2 May 1863
Chancellorsville, Virginia

"So you've got a new bride at home then," a companion said quietly to Austin Stanhope as they quietly skirted the Union encampment.

"Yes, and I already miss her." Austin marched along with the rest of the troops following Stonewall Jackson, the man who intended to strike Fighting Joe Hooker's weak right flank at Chancellorsville. Nearly a week before, Hooker had moved his Army of the Potomac back toward Fredericksburg, this time dividing it into three separate entities. Approximately one third of the forces were to make a diversionary strike against the rebel troops still entrenched in their stronghold in Fredericksburg, but instead of a full frontal attack, this time the men were to cross the Rappahannock above Fredericksburg and attack the weaker left flank and rear.

Roughly ten thousand of Hooker's troops were sent to disrupt Lee's lines of communication with Richmond, and the remainder of the army was situated near Chancellorsville as a backup to the other two movements. Austin had to shake his head in admiration for General Lee. Not only had the Confederate commander anticipated Hooker's attacks, he then made plans to foil them that would undoubtedly catch the arrogant Union commander by surprise.

As he moved into position with the rest of his regiment, Austin looked on the Union encampment with a tremendous surge of pity; they sat playing cards, cooking dinner, and making jokes with one another. It was roughly two hours before dusk, and the attack would come as a supreme surprise.

He was right; the Union soldiers were shocked. Those who weren't immediately shot dead scrambled for their weapons or ran into the trees. As the rebel troops followed, many stopped to fumble about in the pockets of the dead men before pursuing the enemy, and Austin looked upon the whole scene of death and mayhem with a sick stomach.

They pursued the fleeing Yanks nearly as far as the temporary Union headquarters, set up for Hooker in a plantation home called Chancellor House, before Union reinforcements arrived to offer a fair fight. This was the first time Austin had seen anything of the sort, and he wished more than ever to be home in the warm arms of his wife.

* * *

Richard Birmingham sat next to Mosby as Stonewall Jackson and his immediate advisors searched the darkened woods for a possible night assault. He reviewed the events of the past few days with a feeling of smug satisfaction that he was firmly entrenching himself in the upper echelons of the Confederate command. Only the night before, he had observed Generals Lee and Jackson, seated upon barrels, discussing the intended operations of the coming days.

The woods became ever darker, and the air about him was charged with an agitation that was nearly palpable. Nights were unpredictable, and the Yanks could well pop out of anywhere and begin an attack. Mosby, to his left, tapped incessantly on the barrel of his gun until Richard was ready to bash him in the head with his fist. "Stop doing that," he hissed.

Mosby looked at him with one eyebrow cocked, said nothing, and continued tapping on the barrel of his gun. Just as Richard was preparing to wallop his friend a good one, they heard a cry from the left flank. "Union cavalry!"

The pop of the guns rang out through the night, and the figures upon horseback reared and headed toward Richard's position on the right. "Fire, fire!" The command was shouted out, and Richard wasted no time in firing his weapon alongside Mosby. It was only after they and those around them had fired several rounds that Mosby's weapon went slack and he began murmuring, "Oh, no, no, no . . ."

"What?" Richard asked. "What is it?"

"That's Jackson."

"No, it isn't."

"Yes it is! Look!"

Richard took a closer look at the man at the front who had obviously been hit, and the sight made him feel faint. They had just shot their own commander.

The walk back through the ranks with Jackson on a stretcher was a treacherous one. Four men bore the stretcher, one at each corner, shoulder height, and Richard cursed the fates that demanded he was close enough to be asked to help. It wouldn't have been so bad had the Yanks not decided to open fire upon the road they traveled through the trees in an effort to get the wounded general to an ambulance wagon. He had been hit three times—once in the left wrist, once in the right hand, and once in the arm between the shoulder and elbow.

Richard glanced at the man upon the stretcher whom he so disliked. Personal biases aside, however, Jackson was a brilliant general. Richard shuddered as shots flew through the air, whizzing around their heads and smacking into trees that lined the path on either side.

The stretcher teetered and was very nearly dropped as one of the men carrying it was hit and dropped to the ground. The fallen man was quickly replaced, and the stretcher steadied before its occupant had time to fall. Richard gritted his teeth. He would have to write home again—this was absolutely intolerable. His father was dead, more the pity, but his mother still wielded influence. Surely as the widow of a man devoted to the Confederate cause, she would be able to insist, and with good results, that her son be allowed to stay at the back from now on, near the generals and decision-makers who were usually kept safe and protected so that they might persevere and continue to lead their troops. Richard was every bit as bright as any of them—it was high time he be made a staff officer.

Once he was, he mused as they stumbled along, the burden feeling extremely heavy, he might just be able to find those who had seen to his dismissal at West Point a few years back. He had been looking for them since his enlistment, hoping to exact his revenge. He planned to enjoy every last minute of it.

A searing pain tore through Richard's chest and neck as he pondered on his future plans, and he fell to the ground. The stretcher was not rescued a second time, and the general was dumped to the ground as well with a thud and a groan of pain. The others who had been walking alongside scurried for the trees, save one of the stretcher bearers who threw himself atop the general as he attempted to rise. After a moment of quiet, the man helped the general to stand and, with Stonewall leaning heavily upon his helper, they staggered off into the trees.

Richard raised a hand in supplication, his throat and chest feeling as though his vital organs had all been exposed. He was on fire; his breathing was suddenly cut short and he felt his mouth fill with a metallic-tasting liquid that could only have been his own blood. As he stretched forth his hand on the ground, his eyesight growing dim, the last person he saw was Mosby, crouched next to the general as they attempted to place him again on the stretcher. Jackson was speaking to General Pender, and then they raised him again to continue their journey, leaving Richard behind without a backward glance.

As his lifeblood flowed out of his body and onto the dirt, he marveled that he should end this way, alone and friendless. He could swear he saw his grandfather in the distance—that was good. His mother's father was there, and he was a man of some influence. He had owned Bentley, after all, had raised it from the small plantation *his* father had begun, and created a powerhouse of wealth. Yes, his grandfather would help him be placed in a better position, one that would keep him out of harm's way. Perhaps at Richmond, or somewhere well behind the lines . . .

* * *

3 May 1863
Chancellorsville, Virginia

Austin lay on the ground in a large thicket of trees that most of the soldiers had come to call "The Wilderness," and groaned in pain. His left leg had been shattered below the knee, and he struggled to find his way to safety behind the Union lines. The problem was, he wasn't sure where they were. All around him lay dead and dying soldiers, both Union and Confederate. With thoughts of Emily uppermost in his mind, he crawled along the ground, wincing in pain, his breathing shallow.

It's so hot, his mind told him, and he couldn't make sense as to why. Shells continued to explode both within and around the perimeter of The Wilderness, and it wasn't long before the acrid smell of burning wood filled his nostrils. As he looked about himself in horror, he realized that the trees, shrubs, and dry leaves that liberally littered the ground he lay upon were ablaze from the shells. Thick smoke soon engulfed him, and he struggled to breathe.

Placing a hand across his nose and mouth, he inched his way along the ground, dragging his bloody, mangled leg behind him. He almost wished it had blown clear off—at least then he wouldn't have such a hard time of it. To his right, through the smoke, he saw soldiers wearing both gray and blue as they dragged men who struggled along, much as was he, to safety.

The fire inside his bursting lungs became secondary to the searing pain and heat that shot through his feet and then his legs. He struggled forward, inch by inch, on his elbows until he felt two hands grasp him beneath his arms and pull him forward out of the trees. A heavy weight then pressed upon his legs and beat him until he felt he would die from the pain.

He struggled to draw breaths, feeling as though the whole of his lungs must be blackened and burned. Dry, rasping coughs shot forth from his throat, and he felt as though he were drowning. A man in a blue uniform knelt close to his ear and said, "Hold strong there, Johnny, hold strong." The soldier turned him slightly to his side and poured a trickle of water from his canteen into Austin's mouth. The liquid seared in pain as it made its way down his burned throat, and after he had swallowed, he struggled for breath in lungs that were completely saturated with thick, black smoke.

Please, please not yet, he thought as the pain below his waist and in his chest became too much to bear. He tried to cry out and relieve some of his misery, but his throat had been scorched by the poisonous, billowing clouds. *Emily, my Emily,* he thought as he lay upon the ground, the burning in his legs more than he could stand.

"Stay with me, Johnny," his rescuer murmured close to his ear. The next thing he knew, he was being lifted onto a board and carried across the landscape, his head knocking painfully against the wood of the stretcher with each jump and dodge of the stretcher bearers. The noise was infernal—a sick combination of shot from artillery and the roaring crackle of a fire to which he had very nearly succumbed.

If he lived, he owed it to the brave man in blue who had rescued him. As he turned his head to one side, he saw blurred images of blue and gray as they worked together to haul wounded men, some on fire, from the inferno that the forest had become. He would have to find his rescuer and thank him.

* * *

Anne gasped as Ivar dragged her from the burning forest, his arm around her waist, hers around his neck. He finally grew impatient with her feeble attempts to keep pace with him as he ran, and he lifted her up against his side. She was painfully jarred with each step he took, but she wasn't about to complain. Far better to be bounced about during a rescue than burned alive.

He dodged and took refuge behind trees and shrubs as he ran, and it was all she could do to hang on. He ran around a mass of blue uniforms toward the rear of the muddled and frantic engagement, and when they neared a small grouping of trees well behind their own temporary lines, she begged him to stop. "Here," she said, pointing to the trees. "I have to talk to you before we see anybody else."

Ivar carried her into the trees, and she glanced around, feeling intensely relieved that for the moment, at least, they were alone. He set her gingerly on the ground, an action which was almost comical given the contrast between that and the method he'd employed to get her to that spot. "Are you hit anywhere but your leg?" he asked her, breathing heavily.

"No," she managed, taking gulping breaths. "Ivar—I want you to remove the bullet."

"*What?*"

"Please. The doctors—I've seen how they operate. They'll give me a stick, tell me to bite down on it, and then dig into my leg with their filthy butcher knives. At least I know your penknife is clean. Besides," she added, perilously close to tears, "I trust you."

"Anne," he groaned, and sank beside her, gingerly touching her torn thigh with his fingertips, "I can't cut into your leg."

"Yes you can. Please, Ivar, you must." The tears came then, no matter how much she'd tried to keep them at bay. "I'm horribly, horribly frightened. I've been so stupid—to think of how many lives I've endangered by enlisting. You could have been killed trying to save me, and—"

"Stop," he said, putting a finger to her lips. "You've been more brave in the months I've known you than many a man I've seen. No more talk like that—you haven't endangered anyone." He glanced over his shoulder as the sounds of the battle raged on. "I really think we should find a medical tent and hope it holds its ground long enough to have you looked after," he said. "Who knows how long we'll be here before we're overrun."

"Then just hurry, please?" She gripped his hand. "Please, I am begging you. I don't want someone else digging around in my leg. Besides, what if they have to tear off my pant leg—someone might notice, or suspect . . ." Anne felt her face redden.

Without another word, Ivar reached into his pocket for his small knife. Along with it he retrieved some matches, which he quickly set to burning the blade.

"What are you doing?"

"Something my father did once on my arm. I had fallen on a large stick that protruded from a fence post on the farm." He talked quickly as he continued to burn the knife. "He removed a chunk of wood that was lodged underneath my skin, but before he did it, he burned his knife and said it would help the wound close." Ivar shrugged. "I had a fever for a few days, but after that everything was fine."

"I trust you," she whispered, and he glanced up at her face for a moment, his expression unreadable. Finally he decided he was ready, and tore a bigger hole in the leg of her pants, exposing the wound that housed a lead ball in the top of her thigh.

"Come here," he said, and helped her scoot along the ground until her back was up against a tree trunk. "Now, grab my shirt, clench your teeth, scream if you must, but don't try to push my hand away. All right?"

She nodded and clutched a handful of his shirt with her left hand. She bent her right knee to her chest and wrapped her right arm around it, braced and ready. "Do your worst," she said, and closed her eyes.

The scream that ripped from her throat was anything but masculine, yet she was too consumed with pain to register that fact. Ivar leaned with his weight on her leg, holding it steady as he probed for the bullet. "Stay with me," he muttered through clenched teeth as she drew a breath and felt light-headed. She coughed and choked, doing her best to hold her body still as the knife dug deeper into her flesh.

"I see it," Ivar breathed, and with a final twist of the knife, he brought the ball to the surface. He closed his fist around it and reached into his pocket, drawing forth a white handkerchief that he pressed against the wound. It was quickly saturated a dark red, so he removed his shirt, leaving him clothed in only his trousers and undershirt. He wrapped the material tightly around her leg, tying it off in a knot.

He put a hand to her face and she opened her eyes, tears still streaming down her cheeks. The concerned look on his face drew her away from her own pain for a moment. If she didn't say something soon, he'd regret having done what she insisted he do. "How is it that you manage to keep your underclothing so white during a war?"

He glanced down at his undershirt and then looked at her with a weak laugh. "My mama didn't raise a sloppy boy," he said. "Are you all right?"

She nodded. "Thank you."

He glanced down at her leg with a dubious expression. "I think I waited too long after burning the knife," he said. "It didn't seal quite like my wound did, but hopefully you'll heal quickly."

"I'm sure I will."

He glanced up and stood for a moment, moving to the edge of the trees. "Anne," he said, his voice terse. "We must go. Now."

"What is it?" she asked as she shifted and tried to stand.

He lifted her right arm around his neck and again pulled her close against him, cursing fluidly as she groaned in pain. "I'm sorry," he said, "but we've lost ground. Do you see?"

To her dismay, she could. The sea of blue that had been so close before had retreated, leaving makeshift medical tents, wounded, and dead in their wake. Approaching was a large mass of gray. "If we stay close to the line of trees and foliage, we might slip through."

"Or you might not," a voice said behind them.

They turned to see a Confederate officer and a group of roughly fifteen or twenty soldiers standing just behind them.

"Your weapons, please." The man in gray was neither nasty nor pleasant. He seemed weary and looked as though he'd very much like to go home.

Ivar very slowly handed the man his gun.

"Where's your weapon, soldier?" the man asked Anne.

She closed her eyes briefly and pointed to the tree where she'd been sitting with Ivar. One of the men in the group retrieved it, and Anne took a deep, shuddering breath, the pain in her leg so intense she felt as if it were in flames.

"Congratulations, you two Yanks," the officer said. "You are now officially prisoners of war."

This is all my fault; it's all my fault. The phrase ran through Anne's head as Ivar asked if he could help her walk. The man nodded his curt assent, and so they limped along, accompanied by the rebels as they led them to a position guarded carefully by an entire company of men. The blue-clad soldiers who sat on the ground in their midst ranged in condition from near dead to spry, alert, and angry.

If only she hadn't made Ivar stop, they would have been safe. He was a prisoner of war now, and she was entirely responsible. *I will never forgive myself, never . . .*

* * *

11 May 1863
Union Encampment, Rappahannock River

"Total Union losses, seventeen thousand. Total Confederate losses, thirteen thousand." Johnny sat back against a tree, his legs crossed, his left arm in a sling. He held a newspaper with his right hand. "Did you know that sometimes the generals get their news from the papers more quickly than their intelligence officers can supply it to them?"

Ben shook his head and added another log to their small fire. Rabbit for dinner was a treat they all intended to enjoy. "I can't say I'm entirely surprised." He glanced up at his friends and reflected on the mess they had witnessed firsthand at Fredericksburg, and then at Chancellorsville. "Well, frankly men, I'm amazed we're all still here to tell the tale."

Luke nodded, also leaning against a tree trunk, and closed his eyes. "Only a dislocated shoulder among the three of us. Given the odds, I'd say that's not too bad."

Johnny picked up the paper again and scanned the articles. "Stonewall Jackson, dead at the hands of his own men. Who'd've believed that?"

"I thought it was the pneumonia that got him in the end," Luke said.

"It was. Pneumonia that set in because of the gunshot wounds. They amputated his arm below the shoulder, but it wasn't enough to keep him from getting ill."

"I hate to say it," Ben admitted, "but with him gone, we may actually stand a chance."

The other two men nodded in agreement. Johnny chuckled then, but without much humor. "Lincoln reportedly said, 'My God! My God! What will the country say?' when Hooker told him we'd retreated back here to our original ground. Would you like to know what the country's saying?"

Ben and Luke eyed him expectantly.

"'Abraham Lincoln, give us a man!' they're saying. I wonder how long it will be before Lincoln relieves Ol' Fighting Joe of his command."

"*I* wonder how long it'll be before Lee decides to push northward," Luke murmured, his eyes still closed.

"You think they'll try another attack on Union soil?" Johnny asked, still reading the paper.

"What does he have to lose?"

"His entire army."

"He could do that in the South. Might as well push his advantage in loss of Northern morale and try for the whole pot. They might at least be able to negotiate a truce, then."

"Lincoln won't negotiate a truce," Ben said as he moved the rabbit meat around in the cooking pot.

"He may have to if we're beaten badly enough."

There was no response then, and Ben scrambled around for some kind of logical argument. Unfortunately, Luke was right. And if the Union made peace, that meant recognizing the Confederacy as a separate country—which also meant that European support might follow.

If the Confederacy remained, so too would slavery. He clenched his teeth together and shook his head. If it came to that, he would probably suffer a fit of apoplexy. Well, one thing was for certain—he would free Ruth and Rose or die trying.

CHAPTER 29

"We are utterly cut off from the world, surrounded by a circle of fire. . . . The fiery shower of shells goes on day and night. . . . People do nothing but eat what they can eat, sleep when they can, and dodge the shells. . . . I think all the dogs and cats must be killed or starved. We don't see any more pitiful animals prowling around."
—Diary of a young woman in Vicksburg during Grant's siege

* * *

30 May 1863
Vicksburg, Mississippi

"Lucy Lockhart, if that even is your real name, I will grind you into the mud when I find you." Isabelle Webb dashed from one mud home to the next, beginning her day with a search, as she had done for well over a week.

Pinkerton had obtained information suggesting that Lucy was still operating as a Confederate spy, and not only that, but she had made her way to Vicksburg from Richmond to share intelligence with Confederate officials there. Pinkerton ordered Isabelle to find her, but unfortunately, Isabelle had become trapped in the city before she could locate the woman.

Union forces bombarded the city day and night, lobbing in artillery shells with a never-ending consistency that was beginning to make her head pound. Grant had attempted an attack on the city that had failed, and now it was clear to the city dwellers that he intended to starve them out.

"How on earth did I get myself into this?" she wondered aloud as she banged on the door of yet another cave that had been dug into the side of the hill. The resourceful residents of Vicksburg had made themselves temporary homes and furnished them in all the finery from their actual homes, which were now being pummeled into oblivion.

As the door was cautiously opened, Isabelle said, "Hello, I'm looking for . . . you!" She spied Lucy standing back in the cave, and she shoved the door aside. "You told me you were going to stay put in Richmond! You also said you were no longer a Confederate sympathizer!"

Lucy sniffed and stepped back a bit as the cave owner advanced on Isabelle. "Now see here," the woman said, "who do you think you are?"

Isabelle held up a finger at the woman and said, "Not now." She turned to Lucy again, feeling her nostrils flare. "I gave you my food!"

"It was good, too."

"You lied to me—you're a liar!"

Lucy advanced a step. "No more so than you! When we first met, you pretended to be someone you're not, and it's no different than what I do, so you can climb down from your lofty perch, 'Miss Emma Greene.' You're no saint, either."

Isabelle held back a sharp retort. Drat it all, she did have a point. Her nerves felt frayed and tattered, she had eaten more rats and dogs than she'd ever care to admit, and she was intensely worried that she would never escape the godforsaken city.

Exhausted and filthy, she sank to the earthen ground next to the entrance and put her head in her hands. "If I die here, Lucy, I will haunt you forever."

Much to her surprise, Lucy sat next to her on the ground. "Since we seem to be such similar creatures, I daresay we'll be good company for each other, then. Have you had decent food today?"

Isabelle shook her head. "I haven't had decent food since I left Washington. The people I've been staying with here have been kind enough to share their emaciated farm animals and rodents with me, though."

Lucy threw back her head and laughed. "Well, it so happens that we have bread, at least, and some vegetables. This is my sister Lindy."

Lindy was still eyeing Isabelle as though she thought her a guaranteed candidate for bedlam. "How do you do," she muttered.

"Very well, thank you. I apologize for barging into your home uninvited."

"Heaven forbid this remain my home forever," Lindy said, and went to the table, where she uncovered a fresh loaf of bread.

"How on earth have you been baking bread?"

"With an oven we dug into the hillside."

Isabelle sighed and dropped her hands to her sides. "Do you have a husband? Children?"

Lindy nodded her head to one corner, where an infant slept in a small bed. "That's my daughter. My husband died at Second Manassas."

"I'm sorry to hear that," Isabelle murmured.

"No, you're not."

"Yes, actually, I am. I hate to see people's losses. This whole insane conflict was completely avoidable."

"How? If we had simply rolled over and allowed the North to dictate our way of life?"

Well, something like that, Isabelle thought, but didn't say it aloud. "This country was founded as one, and we need to remain as one."

"With equal rights for all, I suppose?"

"With equal rights for all."

"The Constitution makes provisions for census counting in terms of a man's slaves. Now, to me that means slavery is sanctioned by the Constitution." Lindy attacked the bread with a fierceness that had Isabelle's eyes widening.

"With all due respect, especially given that you're wielding a dangerous weapon," Isabelle said, "the very nature of the Declaration of Independence states that all men are created equal, and that we 'hold these truths to be self-evident.' In my mind, that nullifies anything else concerning slaves and census."

Lindy sniffed. "Here. Eat your bread and don't talk to me anymore."

Isabelle rose and took the bread from the woman. "Many thanks," she said as she took a bite and felt herself float to a metaphorical heaven. "I'll be polite if you'll keep feeding me."

* * *

30 May 1863
Savannah, Georgia

Emily sat on the floor in the front hall, reading the telegram with disbelieving eyes. Wounded? Already? Part of her felt completely detached as she glanced up at the grandfather clock in confusion. He had been gone only *two months* when he had been at Chancellorsville, according to the date on the telegram.

Impossible. Simply, simply impossible. She had known there were risks, had dreaded him going even, but to already be hurt? Why couldn't he have come home after losing an arm or something, as had other men in the city? They had returned to their families without any drama! A missing arm wasn't something that would bother her—he could lose a leg—even both legs! But lying sick with fever following an amputation? Smoke poisoning in his lungs because of a fire? Too sick to move yet, might die? What had been amputated, his head? The telegram didn't even say.

She ran her hand across her abdomen in an absently protective gesture, wondering their child, only six months in the womb, would feel sorrow for the loss of a father it might never know. "Austin," she said aloud, "if we have been robbed, I will curse heaven forever." Her voice echoed oddly throughout the hall. It was only then, hearing the reality with her own ears as if somehow uttering her thoughts aloud meant he might really die, that she felt the first stirrings of grief that rose from her chest and into her throat as though it would kill her.

Still sitting on the floor, she crossed her legs as she had done as a child and braced her elbows on her knees. She leaned forward then, putting her face in her hands, still holding the telegram, and cried. She didn't know how long she'd been there when Gwenyth came rushing into the entrance hall.

"Emily! Sweet Moses, what is it?"

Gwenyth sank next to her on the floor and took the paper from her limp fingers. With a groan, the woman wrapped her arms around Emily's heaving shoulders and rocked her slowly back and forth, crying with her and yet still murmuring words of comfort.

"He's not dead yet, Emily. He's a strong man, and he'll fight."

* * *

30 May 1863
Charleston, South Carolina

Ruth was dusting Jeffrey's desk when she noticed a corner of paper protruding from one of the drawers. Thinking to put it back in its place, she opened the drawer and closed her fingers around what proved to be an envelope. Obeying the demon on her shoulder that demanded she satisfy her curiosity, she pulled it from the desk, opened it, and withdrew several folded documents that revealed themselves to be stock statements and financial records for James Birmingham's iron company up north.

Ruth raised her eyebrows in surprise. Jeffrey had invested a fair amount of money in the company—money that would easily save Bentley if the funds were accessible. But with the war, not to mention their residence in the leading Southern rebel state, she doubted very much that the Northern banks would turn a kind eye their way. She wondered if Sarah knew of the money. She leaned back in the chair and closed her eyes for a moment. It wouldn't matter if Sarah had known or not. She wasn't aware of anything anymore.

Lately, Sarah had been refusing to eat. She stared out the windows of the home at the plantation and muttered things about her father that Ruth had begun to ignore. In the beginning Ruth had had hopes that Sarah might be able to shake her malady and come to herself, if only to help Ruth decide what should be done with Bentley. With each passing day, though, her condition seemed to worsen.

In an odd way, Ruth found herself disappointed. Sarah had always been a strong woman. What a disillusionment to realize that strength would exist only as long as things were favorable for her. When Ruth thought of the hell Sarah had put her husband and children through, all for the sake of the plantation, it made her angry. Now that life's winds had turned in a different direction, Sarah floundered.

Reminding herself that she was a good Christian woman, she rose from the desk with a sigh and walked to the front door, where Edward was in the act of receiving yet another telegram. She stopped in her tracks. Telegrams these days meant no good. Someone else had died, and given that Richard was the only one left at war, it must be him.

Her suspicions were verified as she read the missive and wondered if she'd ever be able to dredge up even a surge of pity for the boy. He had been nasty as a child, and criminal as an adolescent. She drew a breath and released it, wondering if she should even bother telling Sarah. What was the point? Sarah didn't know who Richard was, and if she did, news of his death would only serve to shake her further.

As she began climbing the stairs to check on the mistress, another thought struck her that nearly again stopped her in her tracks. Ben. The telegram could well have been news of Ben, although the family hadn't had official ties with the boy for years. Emily had finally told Ruth that Ben was fighting for the Union, and one of these days, a knock on the door might herald *his* demise. Then, Ruth knew, she would feel pain.

Ruth paused at Sarah's door and, in the end, passed by. She wandered down the hallway to one of the guest rooms where she had taken up residence. *My, my, but wouldn't the good folk of Charleston pass out cold if they knew that not only had a slave taken up residence in the big house, but that she was running the entire plantation, as well?* Ruth had had enough of pretensions and "knowing her place." She was keeping Bentley afloat, and therefore, she was sleeping in the mansion in a comfortable room with a big fluffy bed and big fluffy pillows. The funny thing was, not a soul argued with her. If any of the staff disagreed with her activities, they kept it to themselves.

In truth, there wasn't much complaining to be done at Bentley because Ruth had worked her fingers to the bone to make things as comfortable as possible for those slaves who decided to stay on. "You are free now—we must have faith that God will deliver us" she told them, and managed to pay them with resources from the house—extra food and material, as well as beds from guest rooms. Perfectly good furniture that had been stored in the attic now graced the slave quarters, which had been repaired and dressed up to be as serviceable and lovely as when they were new. They couldn't all stay in the mansion, but many of them were. Those that weren't made small palaces for themselves out of the shacks they'd lived in all their lives.

She sank down onto her bed and swung her foot, thinking. Richard was gone. That meant Ben, Charlotte, Emily, and Clara were left. Ben would have to be contacted. As the oldest son, he was next in line to inherit, and she knew that Sarah had never actually changed her will. She had told everyone she did—Ben, Richard, even Jeffrey, but Ruth had seen it with her own eyes one day when Sarah was going over some fine details. Ben was still listed at the top. She managed a slight smile. How ironic that Ben was now the rightful owner of that which he had fled.

* * *

2 June 1863
Harrisburg, Pennsylvania

Ben choked on his tea and looked at his cousin, who sat calmly on the other side of the small fire. "You want me to *what?*"

"I want you to baptize me."

"But we haven't even really talked much about the gospel! I haven't told you much of anything!"

"I don't need to know much of anything. I've read your Book of Mormon, and I believe it."

"I thought you had a problem with the 'fourteen-year-old prophet.'"

Luke looked a bit sheepish. "I believe the book. If it took a young man to bring it to light, so be it."

Ben sat back, stunned. He would do it, of course, but he was, well . . . stunned.

"Aren't you happy?"

"I am! I am of course, but Luke—I just can't believe it. Why now, though? I didn't think you cared for organized religion."

Luke closed his eyes. "Ben, I'd like to see my affairs, my life, in order."

A small streak of fear chased down his spine as Ben digested his cousin's words. "Why?" His tone was completely void of all emotion, and he could hear it.

Luke turned his head to Ben and opened his eyes. "I think of the future, and I can't find it."

"What kind of nonsense is that? You've even asked Abigail to marry you!"

"Yes, and I regret tying her to a dead man."

Ben stood and began taking angry strides around the fire. "I want you to stop this right now, Luke. You are not going to die."

Luke chuckled, and Ben glared at him. "We all must die sometime," Luke said. "I have a notion that my time will be in battle."

"You should rid yourself of that notion, then." Ben threw a stick into the fire, and the sparks shot into the night sky. "Cousin, I will not let you die."

Again, Luke laughed. "As much as I trust your strength, Benjamin, I doubt you have the power over life."

Ben came to a stop at his cousin's legs. "When did you start thinking like this?"

Luke sighed a bit and shifted, running a tired hand through his hair. "When we were at Chancellorsville."

Ben sank to the ground in relief. "Thank goodness," he said. "We *all* question our mortality in situations like that."

"You suppose that's all this is?"

"Mercy, yes. I've thought of dying a dozen times—every time I load my gun I wonder who's loading one to fire at me. I try not to dwell on it though."

Luke didn't look convinced. "I'd still like to be baptized, whether I live or die."

"Of course. It will be my pleasure. We can find a secluded spot in the river if you'd like, and whenever you feel ready, we'll do it."

"How about right now?"

"Now?"

"Yes. It's warm out tonight, the camp is quiet, Lee's on the other side of the river, and we're on ours. Nobody's firing anything. No time like the present."

"Well . . . fine, then." Ben scrambled in his mind trying to remember the baptismal prayer. The last time he'd had the privilege of baptizing anyone it had been the young Elisha Dobranski.

"Are you ready?"

"Yes."

* * *

Some time later after all was quiet and nothing moved except the leaves in the wind and the stars that twinkled overhead, Ben crouched low next to the dying embers of the campfire and feverishly wrote a letter.

Dear Joshua,

I blame my cousin Luke for causing me to question my own mortality, but although I don't fear my death, necessarily, I realized that there are things I want to say to you.

Although I enjoyed my time spent in Utah and felt it was a safe haven for me, I never quite moved past the feeling that I had deserted you—that I had horribly failed you. For this reason, my friend, I fight in this war. I am here fighting for you. I do not wish for you to think I am looking for accolades or thanks from you, but I would not have you live your life feeling that I did nothing to honor our friendship or the vows that we made as children—that someday we'd live near one another and be pirates on the high seas or some such. Do you remember all of those dreams? I remember them as if they were yesterday.

I am thrilled beyond words that you are safe in Boston. Word finally reached me of your safe travel and your happiness on your arrival. Would that I might have been there to see it! I shall have to content myself with my own imaginings. I hope that you are able to pursue a life of your choosing—that when next we meet, it will be in times of peace and under good conditions.

Please know, Joshua, of my deepest love and affections for you. You were my best friend as a youth, and I admire the man you've become.

Until we meet again,

Ben

When he had finished his letter to Joshua, he then took a fresh piece of paper and began another one.

Dear Mary,

I find myself feeling a bit sheepish writing to you, but I have some things I must tell you. The past weeks when I met and spent time with you, I was amazed at how you've grown in beauty and intellect. I begrudged the time I couldn't be with you—I would have loved to have spent every moment in your presence, watching you laugh.

I read over these lines and feel I must have become a lovesick poet, and I beg your forgiveness for coming back into your life at a time when you probably would love nothing more than to forget everything associated with Bentley.

I hope you do not find me annoying, but in any case I will keep this letter short. I suppose I just wanted you to know that I care deeply for you, and should something happen to me during the course of this war, I would have you know of my affections.

There is a verse of scripture in one of my Mormon books that states, "The worth of souls is great in the sight of God," and I would wish for you to know of your value in the eyes of your Heavenly Father, despite what the world may tell you.

My love, and may we meet again soon,

Ben

Feeling much better that he had said those things he felt important, Ben was finally able to allow himself the luxury of sleep.

* * *

Luke arose the next morning at the crack of dawn, amazingly enough even before the trumpet had sounded. He left the tent and stretched, feeling strangely . . . happy. Lee's army sat across the Potomac and was moving steadily north—he undoubtedly intended to invade his way toward Washington—and Luke had been feeling lately that his own mortality was in question, yet still he was content.

I could die today, he thought, *and be at peace.* Ben had assumed his decision for baptism had been one sudden in nature, but in truth he had been pondering the issue for a long, long time. It had been weeks since he finished reading the Book of Mormon, and he had found it fascinating—almost eerily so—in the way that many of the battles mentioned in the scripture, fought on this very continent, seemed similar, so familiar.

Finally taking the advice found in the last section of the book itself, he went to the Lord in prayer and asked for His help in discerning truth. Luke had been filled with a measure of peace he'd not felt since he had been at home with his family—before the war, before the chaos, before the destruction and death.

Now that he was baptized, he was ready to face whatever it was the Lord had in store for him. Be it life or death, he did not fear it. He turned his face toward the gentle breeze and closed his eyes, losing himself in the glory of the moment and the light of the morning sun.

CHAPTER 30

"I have no word of encouragement for you. The military situation is far from bright, and the country knows it. The fact is, the people have not yet made up their minds that we are at war. They have not buckled down to the determination to fight this war through. They have got it into their heads that they are going to get out of this fix, somehow, by strategy . . . and no headway will be made while this state of mind lasts . . ."

—Abraham Lincoln in response to a request for encouragement from a group of ladies

* * *

6 June 1863
Boston, Massachusetts

Camille chortled aloud as she read the paper over Robert's shoulder.

"What is it?" Abigail asked as she spooned a piece of grapefruit into her mouth.

"Burnside closed the *Chicago Times* for printing statements disloyal to the Union. Lincoln revoked the order. Poor Burnside must have had his feelings hurt."

Robert laughed with her, and Camille felt suddenly warm—almost as though things were normal again. No war, just family and friends. They currently sat in the Birmingham breakfast room, enjoying the morning repast with the family before going about the day's business.

Camille was happy to note the color in the cheeks of both Abigail and Aunt Jenny. Time was a blessing, if not a downright cure. She took her seat at Robert's right and continued to read the paper with him, agreeing with some articles and fuming at others.

"Oh, look—there's my piece!"

Robert grinned at her. "I thought you were embarrassed about it."

"Well, not with family, anyway."

Robert was a good sport. She didn't bother telling him to read her article; she'd already had him proof it a dozen times before she turned it into Jacob. She was finding herself to be quite a perfectionist when it came to her writing.

"Good morning, everyone," Elizabeth said as she entered the room. "Madeline has outdone herself today, hasn't she?"

The table was spread with all kinds of delights. Camille thought of their starving Southern neighbors and felt a stab of pity. "I wish we could send some of this to Emily," she said.

The group at large nodded and fell silent. Finally Robert said, "Mary seems to be getting on exceptionally well. She goes out and about on errands, she comes with us to Society meetings—I think she's been very brave, what with coming to learn a whole new city and all."

"A whole new life," Abigail added. "Camille and I have quite enjoyed her company. She's reserved, but when she chooses to talk, the most amazing things come out! I know a number of gentlemen in the Society who are quite taken with her."

Camille opened her mouth to add her compliments about the absent Mary when the front door banged open and loud footsteps sounded in the front hall. Before long, her father stormed into the breakfast room looking as though he hadn't slept in days. Indeed, they had expected to see him over a week ago, but he sent a few telegrams saying he'd been delayed. His clothing was rumpled, his hair mussed, and he seemed more agitated than she'd seen him since he'd discovered Anne had been dressing as a boy.

"Anne," he said, and then took a deep breath. Camille nodded. She should have known it would be about Anne.

Elizabeth paused in her movements, setting her plate back down on the sideboard. "What about Anne?"

James's face crumpled, and Camille's heart thumped hard in her chest. She'd never, never seen her father cry. "She hasn't been in Chicago all this time. She enlisted with an Ohio regiment and has been fighting the war."

Elizabeth swayed on her feet, and Camille jumped from her chair, guiding her mother into it. Elizabeth placed her forehead on her hand, her elbow braced on the table. Meanwhile, Robert had risen from his chair and guided James to a vacant one at the end of the table, as he, too, seemed dangerously near collapse.

"I don't understand," Elizabeth said. "We've been receiving mail from her in Chicago."

James shook his head. "She's been sending it through Miss Webb—you remember Isabelle's younger sister?" At Elizabeth's nod, he continued. "Miss Webb forwarded her things on to us, and ours on to her."

Elizabeth's eyes brimmed with moisture. "So where is she?"

A tear escaped James's eye and fell down his cheek, causing Camille's heart to beat even more wildly. She gripped the back of the chair for support and fought the panicky burning in her own eyes.

"I've tracked the movements of the regiment, following the name I suspect she has been using," James said as he drank from a glass of water and cleared his throat. He drew a rumpled handkerchief from his pocket and blew his nose, heedless of his lack of convention to manners. "The last place she was accounted for was Chancellorsville. She and several others from her regiment haven't been seen since."

Elizabeth placed her head down on the table, on her crossed arms. Her shoulders shook with her sobs, and Camille felt her heart break. She was sick with worry about Anne, and very anxious about the effect it would have on her normally unflappable parents.

"There's something else," James added, pointing with a finger that shook. "I've been reading articles penned by that 'Man in the Field, Aaron Johnson.' Interestingly enough, he fights with the Ohio 7th. I thought they sounded oddly familiar—the writing style, the choice of words, the sense of humor—I think Adam Jones became Aaron Johnson, which means Jacob Taylor has known of it this whole time and has said nothing to us."

Camille stood rooted in shock. Could it be true? Would Jacob keep such a secret from a loving family?

Elizabeth eventually raised her head and dried her eyes on a napkin. "Well," she said, sniffing and clearing her throat, "I believe it's time to call in a few favors, James. You speak to your politician friends and tell them that Aaron Johnson is a woman. They'll send her home under a flag of truce—I've heard of this happening already."

"Women enlisting as men?" Abigail asked, her toast dangling from her fingers, where it had been when James first entered the room.

Aunt Jenny nodded, looking pale. "I've read about it as well. Amazingly enough, both armies have behaved with extreme chivalry when finding female enlistees."

"Oh, Anne," Camille muttered. "Why?" The more she thought about it, the angrier she got. Anne ran about willy-nilly with her schemes and never once gave a thought as to how it might affect the people who loved her. Beneath the anger was a stabbing fear. "Honestly," she said as she stormed from the room, "I finally become a woman of intellect, and the other smart sister may not be around to see it!"

"Where are you going?" her mother yelled after her.

"Out for a walk. Don't worry," she bit out, "I'll leave my dress on. I have no desire to wear pants."

Once outside, she called for a carriage to be brought from the carriage house. "I need to see Jacob Taylor" was all she told the driver, and she was off.

The whole ride to the newspaper offices, she fumed. The unmitigated gall of the man! She couldn't wait to give him what for. If she were a man, she'd call him out and demand he meet her at dawn with a brace of pistols and a second!

When the carriage pulled to a stop, she opened the door herself, shocking the befuddled driver, and marched into the building and up the stairs to the third floor. So great was her angry energy that she didn't even notice she was out of breath by the time she reached Jacob's office.

"You!" she said as she slammed the door open.

Jacob glanced up in surprise, as did his two assistants with whom he was meeting. "Would you excuse us for a moment?" he said to the men, who gathered their papers and made a hasty exit.

"Camille, what is it?" He closed the door and moved to take her arm and guide her to a chair.

She snatched her arm back and felt the anger rise hotter than ever. "I trusted you! We all trusted you!"

"Camille, what on earth are you talking about?"

"Anne!"

He stopped then and dropped the hand he'd raised in supplication. His shoulders dropped a notch as well as he sprawled in one of the recently vacated chairs. He motioned to the other one, saying, "Please have a seat, so it won't go about rumored that I sat in a standing lady's presence."

"I don't care what people think!" To her dismay, Camille's eyes filled with hot tears, and it made her all the angrier. "Do you know where my sister is? Do you?"

He looked at her, his expression blank.

"If she's not already dead, she's probably been taken prisoner of war!" The tears continued to fall, and then her angry words became ragged sobs. Her shoulders shook, much as her mother's had. She buried her eyes with one hand, wondering why on earth she couldn't have fallen apart in the carriage. Why in front of this odious man?

She felt his warm arms close around her trembling frame, and for a moment she held herself stiff. "I'm so very, very sorry," he murmured in her ear. "I was wrong. I should have told your family where she was, but she made me promise. And Camille, she is a woman. She is not a child."

Camille relaxed then and leaned against him for support, sobbing until she felt weak. "I don't want her to die," she choked out. "My sister is being shot at. Who knows what they'll do to her in a prison camp. She might already be dead." Her words tumbled over one another, and she barely understood what she was saying herself. Surely Jacob hadn't a clue.

He guided her to a seat and produced a handkerchief bearing his initials. As she was still feeling moderately vexed with him despite his apology, she blew her nose liberally all over the letters. She felt, rather than saw him laugh, but when she looked up at him, his expression was neutral.

"This may come as little comfort, Camille, but most likely she's still alive. They would have sent word to me that Aaron Johnson had been killed in battle. The newspaper address was the one she put on her official papers when she enlisted, and she said I was her next of kin." He paused for a moment. "I take it your father must have gone looking for her in Chicago then."

Camille glanced up at him in surprise. Of course. She closed her eyes. That was why he had acted so strangely when she had mentioned James's business trip. "You might have told me then," she said.

"I couldn't, Camille. I promised."

"There are times when it's acceptable to break a promise."

He shook his head. "Not when the promise is to a friend who is well over legal age."

"She's a woman!"

"Camille." He sat back in his chair, and she could swear she read disappointment in his eyes. "That does not make her less than a man."

She sat for a moment absorbing his words. She knew there were men who attended the Women's Rights meetings as well as Abolition Society meetings—her brother Luke had been one of them. But he had been nothing more than her older brother, and who in her right mind paid attention to her older brother, anyway?

"I know that," she admitted quietly. "But not everybody feels the way you do, Jacob. There are men who would hurt her—horribly."

"In every wire exchange she has sent me, she has told me in a few brief sentences whether or not she was well. The times when she wasn't were the times when she had witnessed battle. Her accounts of her relationship with the men in her regiment were nothing but positive."

"Do you think she's telling you the truth all the time? She could lie—she seems quite adept at it."

"Camille, to my knowledge—and I am a very shrewd man—your sister has never once lied to me. I was hesitant when she first approached me with her scheme. But I can tell you honestly, she would have done it with or without my cooperation. I decided that this way, someone would be informed of her whereabouts, at least occasionally." He paused. "It's been some time since I heard from her. I was preparing myself to do some research about Chancellorsville, truth be told. Now I know," he finished quietly.

"I apologize for screaming at you like a crazed woman," Camille said stiffly. "I was very hurt that someone I've come to admire might be using my sister just to get good press."

"I'm offended, Camille," he said, and the shattered look to his expression showed it. "I have never used Anne. We have had a business relationship that I have always, always allowed her to dictate. I made suggestions, I gave her deadlines, but they were always negotiable."

"Deadlines are negotiable?"

He glanced at her, his face relaxing. He even chuckled a bit, although it seemed reluctant. "Now I've done it," he said. "You'll become the monster your sister is before long."

"No, I won't. I'm much more reasonable than Anne."

"Mmm hmm."

"I am! And if she comes home," she paused, "when she comes home, I'm going to give her a piece of my mind."

"Might I suggest you take the same approach with her that you did with me. I found it very effective."

Camille flushed. "I didn't do that on purpose. It just happened."

"Understandable. Do you suppose I should speak to your parents—tell them my version of events?"

"That's probably advisable. My parents are not happy."

He nodded. "I'll accompany you home, if you don't mind."

"I don't mind. I suggest you brace yourself, however."

* * *

Robert listened as Jacob Taylor explained to James and Elizabeth why he hadn't told them of Anne's enlistment. Although he could see them struggling to appreciate it, they seemed to know he was right. Anne would do what Anne would do. His mother had been saying it for years.

In the end, they thanked him for his candor, which was a marked change from their earlier reception. Robert had stood back in amazement as his father flew into a rage at the man, a rage unlike any he'd ever seen. As they shook hands on parting, Taylor made a cryptic comment about the fact that James was nearly as frightening as his daughter, then turned and left with one backward glance at Camille, who half flushed but then stared daggers at his back.

As for Robert—he felt inexorably ashamed. Retreating to his room after the family dispersed, he mulled some things over in his mind. He had been frightened of enlistment, although he knew it would come to that eventually. His sister had willingly changed her whole identity so that she might have a firsthand view of the fighting.

He felt like much less than a man, and wished a hole would open up in his bedroom floor and swallow him into the pits of Hades. Surely it was where cowards like him belonged.

Well, so much for his reluctance. He sat on his bed and took stock of his future. He had much to prove (much of it to himself), and when his birthday came at the end of July, he would enlist. No prevaricating, no hesitating. He would honorably join his brother Luke and his sister Anne in the annals of Birmingham family history, and do his duty to God and the country.

If he could only quiet the furious beating of his heart, he might be able to do it without fear of collapse.

CHAPTER 31

"Let the black man get upon his person the brass letters 'U.S.,' let him get an eagle on his buttons and a musket on his shoulder and there is no power on earth which can deny that he has earned the right to citizenship in the United States."

—Frederick Douglass

* * *

22 June 1863
Readville, Massachusetts

Joshua carried Ben's letter in his pocket wherever he went. Day or night, he kept it close to his chest, and if he died, the bullet would pass through the letter first before piercing his heart. Upon receiving it, he knew unequivocally that he could not remain in Boston in good conscience.

He regretfully but firmly informed Orson of his decision, who reacted with some surprise. "But you already told that colored fella that you don't wanna fight."

"I didn't think I did. Orson," he had said, pausing slightly and searching for the right words, "I do not want to leave, but I feel it's right. Should I survive, will you allow me to apprentice with you again?"

The old man flushed and shuffled his feet. "I don't want you to go, neither. You hurry yourself back."

With pangs of sadness but resolution in his heart, he had informed the bureau of his decision to enlist. The Massachusetts 54th had already filled their ranks and were entrenched in Joshua's former backyard. The 55th, however, was in need of men.

So thus it was that he found himself training with other black men who had heeded the call of the country—a country in which they'd lived for generations and who had finally decided they were people. Joshua shrugged a bit as he looked around and mused over his philosophical thoughts. At least *some* of the citizens had decided they were people. For now, it was a start.

Joshua shared a tent with three other men. Two were former slaves who had worked on cotton plantations in Georgia, and the other was a free black man, a worker in a textile plant, who had been raised in New York. It was this man with whom Joshua currently sat, enjoying a break in the drills.

"Things are gettin' ugly at home," Davis Moulton said as they sat on a fence and enjoyed a cool drink of water.

"Yes?" Joshua raised a brow, urging him to continue.

He nodded. "The Irish don' think much of the Conscription Acts. They hang up posters that say, 'I fight for Uncle Sam, but not for Uncle Sambo.'"

Joshua shook his head and took a sip of water, wondering if the cool liquid would also soothe his temper. "Makes it mighty hard to be safe at night, I bet," he said.

Davis nodded. "My folks stay indoors all the time. I got a little sister, too—she almost eighteen now. Now, blacks in Boston—they lucky. Their governor's an abolitionist! That's why we got such good officers. They all abolitionists. Can't imagine fighting this fight without them."

Joshua nodded in appreciation. "Makes a world of difference."

"Lincoln just say that all people should be treated fair if they captured, even if they colored." Davis paused. "I hear black prisoners of war have some troubles."

Joshua tried to allay the younger man's fears, but it was difficult when he harbored the same anxieties himself. "We'll stay together. We'll be fine." He nodded once, punctuating his words, and hoped with all he was worth that he spoke the truth. They were undoubtedly headed south after the end of July when their training session was finished. It didn't bode well for those captured alive.

He thought briefly of Emily and wondered how she fared. He had heard she was expecting a child soon, and he carefully chose not to examine his feelings on that issue. He had also heard from the Birminghams via Mary that Stanhope had been injured at Chancellorsville, and for that he did truly feel remorse. Stanhope was a good man who had risked his life and reputation on more than one occasion. He was the reason Joshua stood in New England on free soil, for the moment, anyway. Petty jealousies were difficult to sustain in the face of such profound fact.

Next to the letter in his pocket, Joshua kept a tiny, wooden piece, which he now pulled forth to examine. He had carved it himself; it was a flat rectangular version of the stars and stripes. It was a reminder of all he had gained, and of all he now rose up to defend. Someday when he again met with Ben, he would be able to proudly say, "I fought the fight, too."

* * *

22 June 1863
Boston, Massachusetts

"What's gotcha all riled up, child?" Carmelle asked Mary in her delightfully thick Jamaican accent as they walked from a hat shop in Boston.

"I received a letter from a very special friend," she said, not wanting to share the details.

"Ahhh. It must be a *man* friend to have ya hoppin' about so."

"Yes, it is a man friend. But that's all I'm going to say." Mary knew full well it really was all she could say. If people knew she fancied a white man, her former *master*, for heaven's sake, and that he returned her feelings, she would be laughed out of town. And then, once the laughter passed, anger would follow. Even in Boston, she had seen very few couples of mixed race.

Her heart, though, knew the truth, and it was all she needed. She even considered trying to pass herself off as a white woman. She knew it was possible—her skin was fair, and her eyes more golden than brown. Mama Ruth stayed in the back of her mind, though. She knew without having to ask her that Mama Ruth would be sorely disappointed if she tried to hide who she was. She *was,* in truth, half white. She was also half black. The latter was what had made all the difference in her life, and for better or worse, she would follow her destiny through to its conclusion. The ghosts in her past—Mama Ruth and Rose still in chains, Emily alone and without her, Mary's own child a slave near Bentley—they all stayed neatly tucked away if she concentrated hard enough on other things, on her future.

"Well," Carmelle huffed. "If ya don' wanna tell me, I can hardly make ya now, can I?"

"Not hardly." Mary smiled at her friend and then laughed at her fierce scowl. She linked arms with the woman and said, "We have the whole day off, Carmelle. What shall we do next?"

"The park."

Mary nodded her agreement. "That's exactly what I was thinking, too." They made their way to a park on the outskirts of town, where people strolled and children played and threw bits of stale biscuits to ravenous ducks. Once there, they sat on their favorite bench in the shade of a generous tree and smiled.

* * *

28 June 1863
Charleston, South Carolina

Emily shifted on the window seat for the hundredth time and finally gave up, rising to her feet in an irritated huff. "Ruth," she called, stepping from the front parlor and out into the hall.

"What is it, child?" The muffled voice came from the library.

"Put me to work. I can't sit, I can't sleep, I am in misery." Emily entered the library, wondering if she looked as awkward as she felt. Her midsection was enormous, and she still had at least eight more weeks to go until the baby arrived, by Ruth's calculations.

Ruth had insisted she come home to Bentley to have the child, and with conditions worsening everywhere, Emily decided to leave Willow Lane in Gwenyth's capable hands and stay the last part of her pregnancy with Ruth. She still thought of Austin daily, and usually, by nightfall, she was tired and in tears. She cried herself to sleep, wondering how she could miss a man so when she had only known him for a short time. She had yet to hear from him or the person who had sent her the telegram, and she was left to wonder daily if he was even alive. Gwenyth promised to send word the moment she heard of his welfare.

When Emily arrived at Bentley to find Richard was dead, the whole world took on an eerie feeling of unreality. She couldn't honestly say she missed him. He had been beastly to her, to Mary, and even to Clara, but still, to be alive one moment and dead the next—it was a strange and frightening thing.

Perhaps stranger still, however, was Charlotte. She had changed so completely that Emily didn't recognize her. Even her face had taken on a softer appearance. She was pleasant, she smiled, and she was never, *ever,* without her baby. She carried him from room to room, cooed and sprawled on the floor with him, which left Emily open-mouthed, and the only time Charlotte let the baby from her sight was when she slept at night.

Charlotte had even gone so far as to share a pregnancy story with Emily. Emily had stared at her, saying nothing until Ruth prodded her from behind to respond. Afterward, Emily had demanded of Ruth, "Who is that woman who wanders this house with that infant?"

Ruth had merely smiled. "Sometimes people change, child."

"Yes, they change, but usually just a bit! *That,*" she had said, pointing her finger to where Charlotte had been sitting, "is not my sister!"

Ruth had taken her to a nearby sofa and held her hand. "Emily, William was very, very good to Charlotte just before he left. He showered her with affection, he walked with her in the gardens, and I watched her very physical appearance change. She has become quite beautiful. Much to my surprise, I believe William's affection was genuine. Birthing his child, and now caring for him, has become a pleasure for Charlotte, because she loves William. She was unpleasant before because she felt nobody in her family loved her."

"Nobody in my family loved me, and I wasn't ugly and mean."

"You weren't ugly, no. But *I* loved you, Emily. You let me love you. Charlotte wouldn't let me love her."

Emily had been shamed into silence then, and her cheeks flamed. "I know you loved me, Ruth. You were my salvation. I'm happy for Charlotte, I just don't know what to say to her. She's never been nice to me before."

"Pretend she's a new friend. For all intents and purposes, she is."

Emily drew her thoughts back to the present upon hearing Ruth's voice. "Come with me to your father's office," Ruth said, and slowed her normally brisk pace to accommodate Emily's awkward stroll. When they reached the room, furnished in leather that still shone and mahogany that was faithfully polished each day, Ruth made her way to the desk.

"I need to show you something," she said, and opened a drawer. Fumbling about for a moment, she withdrew an envelope.

Emily looked at it with a slight frown. "What is it?"

"Look." Ruth opened the pages and unfolded them for Emily's perusal.

The girl's eyes widened as she read over the papers, taking them from Ruth's hands without realizing it. "When did he do this?" she asked in regard to Jeffrey's investments.

"Years ago. It would have been when your parents were first married."

Emily shook her head. "Back when he was penniless and desperate for a good life. He probably figured he needed a nest egg for himself in case my mother decided to throw him out on his ear."

"She's not well, Emily," Ruth said in a mild voice. "You should be more Christian."

"Pah. I've seen the work of this area's Christians. A bigger lot of hypocrites I've never heard of anywhere."

"I'm a Christian, Emily."

Emily felt herself flush. She put an arm around Ruth's shoulders and said, "Forgive my pregnant mouth."

Ruth laughed. "You were snippy long before you were pregnant, girl."

"I know." Emily sighed. "One of my worst faults."

"Also one of your most endearing. So," Ruth said, motioning toward the papers, "I thought you should know about this for future reference. I seriously doubt we can access the money now, but perhaps later . . ."

Emily nodded and handed the papers back to Ruth. "Does Ben know he still inherits?" she asked.

Ruth shook her head. "Not unless you've told him."

"I haven't been able to reach him," Emily said. "At least, I don't think the letters have reached him. If they have, and he's answering back, I'm not getting them."

Ruth replaced the letters, and they strolled back into the hallway. "Emily," the older woman said, "I don't think your mother will live much longer."

"I know. I paid her a visit this morning, and I think she looks even worse now than when I got here. It's only been one week. I tried to get her to eat something . . ."

"At least she used to roam the house before. Now she just stays in her bedroom."

"Will you stay here, Ruth, if she dies? Would you like to come home to Willow Lane with me?"

Ruth ran a hand along Emily's hair, which she had left hanging in one long, red braid down her back. "I would love to, girl. But I can't. I have a responsibility to the people here."

Emily would have liked to argue, but she knew Ruth had the right of it. Many of the slaves had stayed at Bentley, and they were the only reason the plantation still functioned with even a modicum of normalcy. And they had stayed because of Ruth. Upon Emily's arrival, Ruth had walked her through the slave quarters and showed her what had been done to make them habitable and enjoyable. The girl had cried tears of delight when she spied the holes in roofs and walls that had been repaired, rugs thrown on floors, bright curtains at the windows, and fresh clothing on the children.

"Did you see the paper this morning?" Emily asked Ruth in a swift change of subject.

"The one that was printed on the back of some wallpaper?"

"Yes! I nearly collapsed in shock. What will happen when the newspaper office runs short on wallpaper scraps?"

"I don't know. Maybe they'll try leaves."

Emily laughed, but it really wasn't so funny. The South was being strangled, and although it was what she said she'd wanted, she freely admitted she didn't like feeling the pinch. "Well, once I got over the shock, I was able to concentrate on the news itself. Did you see that Lincoln has replaced Hooker with George Meade?"

"I didn't have time to read it. What does it say about Meade?"

"Very little. But it looks as though Lee is continuing his move north. He is on one side of the Potomac, and Meade is on the other, shadowing his every step. Oh!" she added, "And we have a new state! Or rather, the Union has a new state. West Virginia was just admitted, and their constitution calls for total emancipation of all slavery."

Ruth smiled. "That is good news indeed."

They had reached the entrance hall just in time to see the wide front door shoved open and two young girls, both nearing twelve in age, rush in.

"Well, there are my girls!" Emily said and signed with her hands for the benefit of her younger sister, Clara, who was deaf. The signing was almost a nonissue anymore; Clara had become so efficient at lipreading and verbal answers that it was easy, at times, to forget she couldn't hear.

"We just got chased by a skunk," Rose said, closing the big door behind them.

"I don't smell anything—did it get you?" Emily asked.

"No. But almost."

"Emily, can we go into town today?" Clara asked.

Emily shook her head. "I'm sorry, sweet pea. It's just not a place I feel safe taking you now."

Clara's face fell, as did Rose's. Ruth laughed to lighten the mood and said to the girls, "Come with me and we'll go see if Nell has anything sweet in the cookhouse. Maybe we can even find a bit of flour and sugar to make some small pastries for desert tonight after dinner."

The girls perked considerably, although the prospect of sweets to a twelve-year-old girl was not as thrilling as it had been in the past. Emily watched them walk away to the back of the house, waving away Ruth's gesture to join them. The girls were growing up in the middle of a war, and Emily's heart turned over. How unfair it was, and yet there was nothing to be done about it.

She turned at a knock at the door, taking the liberty of opening it herself, as Edward was nowhere to be found. On the other side stood a messenger from the telegram company, and her heart fell. It had been her experience that telegrams were not good news, but she had instructed Gwenyth to forward any pertinent mail or messages to her at Bentley.

Thanking the delivery boy and offering him a Confederate dollar, which he waved his hand at in disgust, she closed the door with a shrug. Sighing, she tore open the message and read it.

It was from Mary. She was fine, doing well in Boston, and enjoying her new friends. She missed Emily dreadfully and wanted to see her soon. Lastly, she said with no accompanying details that Joshua had enlisted with a black regiment, and that was the end of the telegram.

Emily walked slowly to the massive staircase and sat upon the bottom step, reading and rereading the message. Joshua had enlisted. It was one of those things she would have to push to the back of her mind or she would never be able to function. He would die, and Austin would die, and everybody she loved would then just keep on dying.

She thoughtfully folded the telegram and stood, pushing herself up with the aid of the railing. Making her way to the back of the house, she left the mansion through the servants' entrance and walked across the lawn to the cookhouse. She managed a smile as she entered and heard the happy sounds of Ruth and the girls making cinnamon pastries. It was a good moment, quiet and unfettered by ugliness, and Emily decided she would live it and forget all else. Walking toward the large table, she placed an arm each around Rose and Clara, and closed her eyes. When she opened them, the girls were grinning at her, for Clara had a dab of flour on her finger that she held aloft for a moment before plunking it down on Emily's nose.

She gave the girls' shoulders a squeeze and smiled.

CHAPTER 32

"Speaking of that legislature, we must remember the good seed are in the army—only the chaff remains at home now."
—Mary Chestnut, in reference to local Confederate politicians

* * *

28 June 1863
New Orleans, Louisiana

Something was wrong—Marie felt it in the air. She had awakened from a sound sleep, but didn't know why. An angry pounding on the front door soon explained it. Grabbing her robe, she thrust her arms into the sleeves as she made her way toward the front of the house, feeling her way in the dark.

When she reached the front door, she grabbed the loaded rifle she kept in the bottom drawer of a hutch. "Who is it?" she called through the door.

"Open up, Marie! We know you've got those darkies in there!"

"What? You're insane! Now get off my property, Mr. Lambert!" Marie recognized the voice of one of her neighbors down the street. She suspected he had been one of the men who'd had everything to do with her father's death. She trembled in both fear and white-hot anger.

"We saw that boy of theirs enlisting today! Now you know darn well that he's the one who beat the mayor's son senseless!"

"He didn't do it! The Bussey boy did it and blamed Noah. Now you leave my property this instant!"

The man beat on the door, rattling it on its hinges.

"Mr. Lambert, I swear by all that's holy I will shoot you in the head if you so much as set foot across my door."

"Now, now, don't go gettin' all testy—we just wanna check your house."

"You are *not* going to check my house! You killed my father, Lambert, and if you think for one moment I've forgotten it, you can think again! Now get off my property—immediately!"

She heard a low murmur of voices, and then Lambert spoke up again. "We'll be back with the authorities and a search warrant! See if we don't, and then we'll see who's high 'n' mighty!"

She listened to the fading footsteps, the weapon still clutched tightly in her hands. They probably wouldn't be able to obtain their warrant in the middle of the night, but they would have one by morning, she was sure.

She glanced at the stairway to see the faces of Justis, Pauline, and the two boys. "Is it true, then?" Pauline asked. "Noah enlisted?"

Marie nodded. "He spoke of it to me earlier. I assumed he was in his bed asleep—he said earlier that he wasn't feeling well."

Pauline sniffed, and Marie edged closer to the stairs. "He stuffed his bed with pillows," she said. "I jus' checked."

"Oh, Pauline, I'm sorry. I should have said something earlier. He wanted to be part of the regiment so badly—he was so proud to think he could be . . ."

"Miz Marie, we're sorry to have brought this trouble upon your house," Justis said, his voice gruff. "Noah didn't think about how he'd be involvin' everyone, I guess."

"Please, don't apologize." Marie set the weapon carefully back in the drawer and stood for a moment, drumming her fingertips against her forehead. "We do need to act quickly, though. I believe it's time for another midnight ride. How quickly can you gather your things?"

"In just a few minutes," Justis answered.

"We're going to try to get you aboard a Union ship headed north. I'll ride to the docks and see if I can't reach my friend . . . wait for me, and hide upstairs in the closets if you hear people come in the house."

They all scurried back upstairs and Marie ran to the study, pulling off her robe. She reached into the bottom of a trunk for a getup she hadn't worn for a long time. The last time she had put on the trousers and men's shirt, she had been rescuing the Fromeres from the Bussey boy and his friends, who were bent on framing Noah for a crime they had committed.

It seemed life always came full circle, she mused as she quickly donned the clothing and pinned her hair, cramming a cap atop the curls and hiding them. She quietly let herself out of the back door, saddled her horse in record time, and was on her way down the street before she'd even had time to really think.

She reached into the deep pocket of the pants, where she'd stashed her gold coins, convinced she'd have enough for an effective bribe or two. Satisfied Lambert and the others were gone, she kicked the horse into a gallop and made her way to the docks, where she knew Daniel's ship sat keeping a vigilant watch in the harbor.

A Union sailor patrolled the area on foot, and she approached him cautiously. "I need to reach a sailor aboard the *Kennebec*," she said, pointing. "It's a matter of some urgency."

The sailor laughed in her face until she reached into her pocket and pulled forth a handful of gold coins. "I'll give you half of these now, and the other half after you bring him to me. Bring his commanding officer as well—bring whomever will come, but hurry."

The sailor's eyes boggled, and she dumped several of the coins into his outstretched hand, depositing the rest back in her pocket. With a whistle, he called for a fellow sailor who stood closer to the water. They conferred for a moment, and after much cajoling on the part of the paid sailor, the other allowed him to climb into a rowboat and begin his journey to Daniel's ship.

The water was dark, and she couldn't see, but she heard shouting over the water. She grew nervous, glancing over her shoulder and patting her horse as though the animal were the one needing reassurance. She wasn't sure her mad scheme would work, but it was the best she could do. What were the odds Daniel would actually be allowed to come ashore and help her? She began doubting herself as time pressed onward, and was nearly ready to give up when the rowboat appeared, this time with three people aboard.

As they approached, she nearly fainted with relief. It was Daniel, and he was accompanied by an older man who looked very much like he'd been awoken from a restful sleep. "Marie," Daniel said, his tired face showing his worry, "what is it?"

She explained as quickly as she could, and when she finished, Daniel glanced aside at his companion. "This is my commanding officer, Marie. Anything we do will have to meet with his approval."

"Sir, these good people are facing certain death if they are not immediately removed from this city. I have been harboring them in my home for months. They are good and have been free blacks for years—the men who are harassing them have no right to do so." She wrung her hands together. "Sir, I have nowhere else to go. Is there not some refuge aboard a Union ship? None that will soon be making its way north?"

The man hesitated for a moment. "We do have a ship in the fleet that will be returning to Boston soon."

"Oh, wonderful." Marie felt weak with relief. "You'll help them, then?"

"Yes, miss. We'll help them. Wait here for a moment, and I'll send some of my men to accompany you back to your home. They can use one of these wagons and bring the family here. Fair enough?"

"More than fair. Thank you so much." Marie felt her eyes burn, and she offered her hand to the older gentleman, who took it and placed a kiss upon her knuckles.

"I can only imagine your loveliness in a dress," he said as he released her hand and shook his head, making his way back to the rowboat. He spoke with some of the sailors standing guard who had gathered in curiosity to watch the exchange. As he climbed into the boat, he called to Daniel, "Wait here, O'Shea. I'll send some men."

Daniel answered affirmatively, and once the officer was again on the water, he turned to Marie. "Are you all right?" he asked her.

"I'm fine." She began to shiver and found it odd because the night wasn't the least bit cold.

"You're not fine," he said as he took her hand and rubbed it between his. "You're frightened to death! Marie," he said, glancing around them, "the way you live is not safe. You cannot possibly continue to stay in that house alone. I don't trust those men who are causing all this trouble—how much longer until they come after you?"

"I've been fine so far. Once the Fromeres are gone, I'm sure they'll grow tired of me again."

Daniel didn't look convinced, and he held her hand tightly until the contingency of reinforcement sailors came ashore. There were roughly ten in number, and they climbed into a waiting wagon and followed Marie, who mounted her horse and rode through the streets to her home.

Once there, she entered from the back and found the Fromeres upstairs, their faces frightened but determined. "Someday, we will repay your kindness," Justis told her. "I don't know how, but we will."

Marie flung her arms around the man and squeezed. Next she embraced Pauline and the boys. "I'll watch for Noah," she told them. "When he's relieved of his duties, I'll send him to you."

Pauline's eyes filled with tears. She nodded her thanks, and they all filed down the stairs to the front of the house where the wagon awaited. Marie wanted to see them board the ship with her own eyes, so she again mounted her horse and rode down the street behind the wagon. Her horse was nervous, and it set Marie's nerves on edge. Daniel watched with vigilant eyes from the back of the wagon, and at his nod at something behind her, she turned in the saddle to see several figures in the shadows. They were gone almost as soon as they'd appeared, and if Daniel hadn't also seen them, she might have thought her eyes deceived her.

The ride to the docks was uneventful, and Marie breathed a sigh of relief when, after a final round of hugs, they were safely ensconced in the rowboat and headed toward a smaller ship out in the harbor. Daniel stayed by her side when the other sailors also made their way toward boats that would take them back to the *Kennebec.* "I asked for permission to see you home again," he said.

She smiled and handed him the reins. After adjusting the stirrups, he climbed into the saddle and reached a hand down to pull her up behind him. Settling her arms around his waist, she leaned her cheek on his back and enjoyed the slow ride back through the quiet streets to her neighborhood. If only she lived farther away! She would have enjoyed a much longer ride.

Feeling so comfortable she very nearly fell asleep, she was startled to feel Daniel's body tense. He cursed under his breath and spurred the horse into a gallop, nearly unseating her. What on earth was wrong? It wasn't until she smelled the smoke that she realized there were flames shooting from the windows of her home.

With a cry, she slipped to the ground when Daniel halted the horse, and she ran toward her house, her mouth open in disbelief. "How could they . . . why . . ." she stammered as Daniel reached her side. She looked up and down the street, but could see nobody. With a stab of alarm, she remembered her other horse at the back of the house in the stable.

She ran toward the outbuilding, Daniel shouting after her to stop. Thankfully, the stable and carriage house were untouched, but if the fire spread from the house . . . She quickly threw another saddle atop the horse and cursed her fumbling hands. Daniel brushed her aside and finished the task, grabbing her arm with one hand and leading the horse with the other.

The animal stamped and panicked at the flames, which had spread with alarming speed throughout the rooms. Marie thought of her life—everything in that house—and felt her throat clog with bitter tears. She would never be free of her tormentors. Her family had never been truly at home with the city's elite, and tonight "the elite" had shown their true colors.

"We need to get help," Daniel shouted to her over the sound of breaking timber and windows. One by one, the neighbors who still inhabited the street made their way out of their homes, rubbing their eyes and staring in shock. It wasn't long before an informal bucket brigade started, and Marie moved to join them.

"Come with me," Daniel said. "I don't want to leave you here."

"But my house!"

"It won't burn any more slowly if you're here—mount this horse and come with me—please!"

She climbed atop the horse, and Daniel mounted the other. They galloped down the street and into the town, Marie leading the way until the sight of smoke in the distance again caught her eye. As she rode toward it, her heart beat faster. The location—it couldn't be—as if her home wasn't enough!

She pulled her horse to a stop and screamed in anguish. As Daniel stopped alongside her, he grabbed her arm. "What is this place?"

"My father's newspaper shop." She sobbed as she watched her father's dreams burn. People came running from all directions and tried to help, but as the time passed and the flames climbed higher, she knew with a certainty that all was lost.

Michael soon appeared in the crowd, speaking in rapid French, his words those of anguish. Marie dismounted and ran to him, throwing her arms around the older man's neck and crying with him as the burning building lit the night sky. Time seemed to stand still as she looked up at the flames that licked the structure and effectively reduced it to crumbling rubble.

She stumbled from Michael, who had turned to hold his crying wife, and wandered through the crowd of frantic people. She couldn't find her horse, didn't see any familiar faces, and couldn't make herself care. Finally, a pair of hands steered her away from the people and down the street.

He forced her to sit and take a sip of water from a canteen. She didn't know where he'd found it, and frankly didn't care. The water was cool and soothing, and it seemed to bring her to her senses.

Daniel looked into her face, carefully assessing her awareness. "Marie, I don't know what to say," he murmured hoarsely.

She shrugged.

"Come with me," he said. "Stay with me."

"Where? Aboard your ship? I don't think I'll be allowed." She leaned back against the building and closed her eyes.

"Marry me."

Her eyes flew open.

"Now. Tonight. My commanding officer can marry us."

"Daniel, I . . ."

"Marie," he said, clasping her face in his hands. "I love you. I think you love me. I've wanted to be with you since your first letter. Please marry me—I'll see if I can get some furlough time, and after that we can get you north to your mother until I'm finished."

Her house was on fire, her family business had been destroyed, and she'd received a proposal of marriage from a man she loved, all in the same night. Somehow, his suggestion didn't feel as nonsensical as it should have.

She nodded. "I'll marry you."

"Can you smile, even a little bit?"

"I can smile for you," she said, making an honest effort, "but not for the men responsible here. Somehow, someday I'll take my revenge."

"Promise you won't do it unless I'm with you." He kissed her quickly and she did smile then, in spite of everything. The Fromeres were safe, and Daniel loved her. He took her hand and helped her to her feet, and after retrieving the horses, the two of them rode back to the docks for the third time.

As she sat in the rowboat, watching the flames rise against the night sky, she bid farewell to her old life. She turned to Daniel then, who smiled at her as though trying to bolster her spirits. "I'll build you a wonderful house," he whispered and pulled her close.

She had no doubt that he would.

CHAPTER 33

"Our people are lashing themselves into a fury against the prisoners. Only the mob in any country would do that. But I am told to be quiet. Decency and propriety will not be forgotten. And the prisoners will be treated as prisoners of war ought to be in a civilized country."
—Mary Chestnut

* * *

30 June 1863
Outside Richmond, Virginia
Confederate Prison Camp

Nearly two months had passed since she and Ivar had been taken prisoner, and Anne figured in that amount of time, they'd probably lost fifteen to twenty pounds each. Ivar stewed and growled at her every day, threatening to tell the officers that patrolled the compound that she was a woman.

Thus far she'd been able to keep her secret, but she wasn't sure how much longer she could hold out. There was one officer in particular—he went by the illustrious name of Bulldog—who continually threw her around. He thought she was a small boy, and took delight in slapping her about the head and harassing her unmercifully. Ivar had already gotten himself thrown into the stockade twice for defending her.

The camp was crowded, and infested with bugs, lice, and rodents. There were roughly twice as many men crammed into a space meant for half that number, and the conditions from the drinking water to the latrines were deplorable.

Anne was suffering. She'd had fevers on and off since arriving at the camp, and the wound in her leg pained her day and night. It seemed to be healing, so Ivar's trick with the matches must have done some good, but it hurt so much that she never really could tell. She'd also developed a raspy cough that kept her and many of the other men up at night.

She sat in a corner of the open field, as was her habit when it became too painful to move around, and glanced up to see Ivar watching her. Poor man; it was all he did. He worried over her like a mother hen, and it should have been the other way around. She constantly apologized to him for being the reason they had been captured, but he wouldn't hear any of it.

The Bulldog relieved his fellow officer of command, and Anne tensed. He sized Ivar up and down, as was his daily routine, and threw some insults Ivar's way before beginning his strut around the yard. Ivar was easily the biggest man of the lot, and Bulldog, who was apparently used to being the big boy, didn't seem to care for it. He taunted Ivar using profane and crude language, and picked on Anne because he knew it made Ivar angry.

She closed her eyes and leaned her head back. She would pretend, just for a moment, that she was at home, sitting under a shade tree and reading a good book. Why hadn't she done more of that when she had the opportunity? She missed Alan's photography equipment, too. She'd only just received word that she would be granted permission to buy it from his employer when they'd moved on Chancellorsville. Who had the camera now? Were the men in the regiment caring for the wagon and all its equipment?

She winced as she felt a boot kick her wounded thigh. She wearily opened her eyes, knowing she'd see Bulldog standing there. Sure enough, there he was, leering at her. "Hey, pretty mama's boy. Why ain't you up and walkin' with the rest?"

"I don't want to," she said. The sun shone hot on her head. She'd long since lost her cap, and her skin was burned from the constant exposure with time spent out in the yard. She felt lethargic in the heat, and knew she needed a drink of water. She was always leery, though, because so many of the men were sick from the river water. She imagined it didn't help that their water source was also an outlet for the latrines.

Much to her surprise, Bulldog didn't have to smack her this time for her face to meet with the dirt. She fell over of her own accord. "What the . . ." she heard Bulldog mutter before shouting, "Medic!"

Ivar was at her side before anyone, and the next thing she knew, she had been placed on a cot in the makeshift infirmary. "Drink this," a doctor ordered, and placed a glass of hard liquor to her lips. It burned a path down into her stomach, and she coughed and sputtered.

She didn't know how he'd managed it, but Ivar was in the room with her. He turned to the doctor and said, "Can I have a moment alone to speak with him?"

The doctor raised a brow and said, "I'll step right outside this door. You try anything funny and you'll probably find a bullet in your skull."

Ivar nodded to the man, who left the room, and then he knelt at Anne's side and discretely covered one of her hands with his own. "I'll not sit by and watch you die, my brave young friend," he said, and she turned her head toward him, trying to moisten her lips with a tongue that felt like sand.

"I don't want to leave you. It's my fault we're here."

"You don't owe me anything, Anne, but I'll never forgive myself if I don't put an end to this madness."

She shook her head. "I want to stay with you."

He laughed, but it sounded more like a groan. "You can't even hold yourself upright! Anne, you will die in a matter of days, and I will not allow it. I'm strong, and I'll survive this place. The Union will probably authorize a prisoner exchange soon."

She looked at him with eyes so dry they couldn't even form tears. She saw moisture in his eyes, though, and it broke her heart. "Don't worry about me," she whispered. "I'll be fine."

He closed his eyes and kissed her forehead. Then he rose and, with a squeeze of the hand, left her side. She heard muted voices in the other room, and then the doctor came back in, looking at her with wide eyes.

"You're a woman?"

She nodded and closed her eyes.

It was done.

* * *

15 June 1863
Boston, Massachusetts

Anne remembered little about her journey home, except that people told her along the way that her parents had had the entire Union on alert for her. Once she reached home, faces faded in and out of her consciousness. People poked and prodded, poured water and broths down her throat, felt her forehead and her pulse, and rubbed salve onto her chapped and broken skin.

When her body had finally recovered enough fluid for her to actually shed tears, she did so. The first night she was coherent and aware of her surroundings, she looked about her former bedroom, turned her face to the wall, and cried. She'd left him behind, and after all he'd done for her! She'd left him there in that awful prison camp, and he was probably not faring much better now than she'd been.

He had no excuse—no reason that would see him sent home under a flag of truce, and that meant it would be up to her. She cursed her body's slow healing—she did him little good lying in her bed hundreds of miles away.

She was sitting up, staring out the window, when there came a tentative knock on the door. It was Camille. Anne smiled a bit and tried not to wince as her lip split open again. She licked it, tasting her blood, and drew her lip into her mouth for a moment to relieve the sting.

Camille pulled up a chair and sat next to the bed. "How are you?" she asked, reaching for Anne's hand. "I think this is the first lucid moment I've seen since your return."

"It probably is," Anne agreed. "I'll live."

"I very nearly didn't recognize you," Camille murmured, and brushed a gentle hand over Anne's short hair. "You're so thin—you're still not eating much." Camille paused and looked down at Anne's reddened, sore hand, softly covering it so that she held it between both of her hands. "Why, Anne, did you do this thing? I'm trying to understand it, but I can't, not for the life of me."

"It was a challenge I couldn't resist." Anne sighed. "I wanted to see it all firsthand—to write about it. The next thing I knew, I was dodging bullets, sleeping in snowstorms, and getting shot in the leg." She shrugged a bit and looked back out the window again. "I hear you and Robert made a trip to Bull Run last year," she said, trying to turn the conversation. She glanced back at Camille, who flushed.

"It was stupid. We've regretted it ever since."

"I'm sorry you had to see it. The Sylvesters should have known better."

Camille snorted. "When have they ever known better?"

Anne looked at her sister in amazement. "Camille, you are not the young woman I left behind."

"Yes, I know. I've become quite the thinking person." She shook her head. "Most trying, I must say."

Anne laughed, which in turn sent her into a coughing spasm that left her weak.

"I'm glad you're home," Camille said when it was quiet again. She fidgeted for a moment and then offered, "I've been writing for Jacob—did you know?"

"I didn't! Camille, that's wonderful!"

Camille blushed. "I've been working hard at my writing, and reading excessively . . ."

"It shows."

"Well, I just wanted to visit for a moment. I'm . . . I was very worried. I'm glad you're safe. Oh," she said as though in afterthought, "we heard from Isabelle's sister this morning. The one with whom you were supposed to stay in Chicago."

Anne had to smile at Camille's hostile tone.

"At any rate, she said that Isabelle's in Vicksburg, Mississippi."

Anne felt her eyes widen. "Vicksburg is under siege."

Camille nodded. "She was supposedly in pursuit of a Confederate spy."

Anne breathed out a sigh. She and Isabelle were quite a pair. They should have known things wouldn't change much after school; they were still getting themselves into just as much trouble as when they were younger women.

"Let me know if you hear anything else, will you?" she asked Camille.

Camille stood and gently embraced her, touching her cheek to Anne's. "I will. And you let me know if you need anything else," she murmured and, placing a kiss on Anne's nose, moved noiselessly to the door. "Jacob came by earlier," she said in a tone that was curiously flat. "Probably to soothe his conscience. I told him you were not to be disturbed."

Anne felt a laugh inside that she didn't have the energy to release this time. "He did it for my sake," she said. "I made him promise not to tell."

Camille muttered something unintelligible, most likely extremely derogatory from the sound of it, and left the room.

"Let me know what you need," had become the mantra of each of her visitors. *What I need . . . what I need . . . I need to get Ivar out of that prison.* It would be her guiding thought, the motivation she needed to move herself forward and to heal. When she was her usual, healthy self again, she would think of a way to see him to safety. She wouldn't be able to enlist again—too many people would prevent that—but there had to be something.

It would help pass the time. She would devise a plan, and when the time was right, she would act on it. It had to work—the alternative was unthinkable.

HISTORICAL NOTES

The reader may note that the quote at the very beginning of the book is what we now consider the fifth verse of "The Battle Hymn of the Republic." There is a slight difference, however, in the version we sing today as opposed to the poem Ms. Howe originally penned. She wrote, "Let us *die* to make men free," and we sing, "Let us *live* to make men free." Interesting, the change. Perhaps it's because in general, the U.S. populace is not called upon to die for freedom, but rather *live* in such a way that we never lose sight of that most fundamental of rights.

Chapter 2—I have Daniel O'Shea aboard the *Kennebec*, which, in the interest of consistency with *Faith of Our Fathers* volume 1, must depart from New York on February 8. In reality, the *Kennebec* departed from Boston, Massachusetts.

Chapter 4—Jimmy Birmingham makes reference to the fact that the *Monitor*, according to his father, looks like a "tin can on a shingle," and according to my sources, this observation was actually made by a Confederate soldier on first viewing the craft.

Chapter 12—"Stonewall" Jackson executes four deserting soldiers through Richard's eyes in this chapter, when in reality, Jackson actually had thirteen of his men executed for desertion, but not until August of that year.

Also in Chapter 12, I detail the Morrisite "war." This was a true occurrence, although I have fabricated the names of the two posse members who lost their lives in that encounter.

Chapter 13—I have Richard reflecting on internal strife he supposedly caused during his time with the Palmetto Guard. The Palmetto Guard was a real regiment, and any "internal strife" with regard to my particular story is of my own making, not documented.

Chapter 18—In this chapter, I detail the battle of Antietam, or as the Confederacy referred to it, Sharpsburg. It may interest the reader to know that as I was doing my research, I placed Anne Birmingham in the Ohio 7th and Luke Birmingham in the 1st Massachusetts Cavalry, not realizing that the 7th and portions of the 1st Massachusetts were both present at Antietam. As it happens, a certain company of the Massachusetts 1st was left behind to patrol and guard the South Carolina coast from Hilton Head Island, and I chose to leave Luke and Ben there for plot purposes with Emily and Mary. Isn't it fascinating, though, that quite coincidentally, two of my fictional siblings could very well have ended up at the same battle? Instances like these—real life instances—happened all during the war.

Chapter 25—The exchanges with the troops across the river and stories told to Ben and Luke by Johnny are all true accounts. Amazing, but truth occasionally *is* stranger than fiction.

Chapter 27—The Richmond Bread Riot is a factual, historical event. The account of Jefferson Davis throwing money to the crowd, however, was an account related to other people by his wife, Varinia. It was never corroborated by anyone else, so it may be more legend than anything. Also, she didn't say whether or not the money he threw from his pockets was worthless Confederate paper money or actual coins.

BIBLIOGRAPHY

Leonard, Elizabeth D. *All the Daring Soldiers: Women of the Civil War Armies*. New York: Penguin Books, 1999.

Long, E. B. *The Saints and the Union—Utah Territory During the Civil War*. Champaign, IL: University of Illinois Press, 1981.

Pflueger, Lynda. *Matthew Brady: Photographer of the Civil War*. Berkeley Heights, NJ: Enslow Publishers, 2001.

Sullivan, George. *Portraits of War—Civil War Photographers and Their Work*. Brookfield, Connecticut: Twenty-First Century Books, 1988.

Vaughan, Donald. *The Everything Civil War Book*. Holbrook, MA: Adams Media Corporation, 2000.

Wheeler, Richard. *Voices of the Civil War*. New York: Penguin, 1976.

Excerpt from

HOUSE OF ISRAEL

THE RETURN

VOL. 1

ROBERT MARCUM

Max watched as Hannah ate the last of her food. She looked so frail, like a porcelain doll that would break if one gripped it too firmly. The last time he had seen her was in New York. They were cousins and both had been present for the marriage of Max's brother Chaim. Hannah and her three lovely sisters had come with their parents from Poland. Chaim had gone to Warsaw for a year to study with a noted rabbi there and had fallen in love with the rabbi's daughter. The marriage had been of one rabbinical family to another, Max's father being one of the prominent rabbis of New York. According to Rabbi Moshe Gruen, Rabbi of Warsaw, it was a marriage made by God himself. New York was where the young couple would live. Hannah and her family had come to witness the event and renew relationships with her only uncle's family.

Hannah shoved the tray aside, nearly off the edge of the bed. Max stood quickly, picked it up, and set it on a nearby table.

"Tell me more, Max. I must hear it all!" she said exuberantly.

They discussed his family and his brother's wife, and two children whom Hannah had never seen. Shortly after Hannah and her family had returned to Poland from the United States, the war had broken out in Europe and they had lost all contact with Hannah's family. Max felt an empty spot in the pit of his stomach. If only they had all stayed in New York! But Hannah's father and the rabbi felt obligated to return. Things had been getting worse in Poland for years—pogroms, special taxes against Jews, then the ghettos. Their consciences simply wouldn't let them walk away to safety while others suffered. The decision had cost both men their lives along with the rest of their families, except for Hannah. She was the only survivor that Max had been able to find. Of twenty people, only she was still alive.

"What is the matter, Max?" Hannah said, seeing the sad look in his eyes.

"I was just thinking . . ." Max said. "It doesn't matter . . ." He tried to put it aside with the wave of his hand.

"No, I want to know. What is it?" she persisted.

He looked at her large eyes, her shrunken body. She had been through so much! "Your father . . . if only he hadn't . . ." His voice trailed off as he sat on the edge of the bed and took her hand.

"If only he hadn't left New York?" she said.

He nodded, his eyes on their clasped hands. Hers were so thin, nothing more than skin stretched over bone.

"Yes, I cursed him more than once for that." She forced a smile. "But my father saved at least a hundred lives before he was killed. He helped them escape to a center that took refugees to Palestine. That is why they shot them like they did." The pain was etched in the lines of her face as the memory came surging back like waves in a stormy sea.

"I'm sorry," Max said. "I don't mean to dredge up such horrible . . ."

She squeezed his hand. "No, it is better to talk of these things. Maybe they will stop haunting me at night if I . . . if we can talk about them." She took a deep breath. "When we returned to our home, it was less easy to ignore the anti-Semitism all around us. Even before Hitler and his army conquered our country . . . well, you know what it was like. Everyone blamed us for something, believed we were trying to ruin the country. Everything that could be done to make our lives miserable was done. It was much worse when we got back, frightfully worse. My father and Rabbi Dallich immediately began getting as many out of Poland as they could. He made contact with the Israeli underground organization in Czechoslovakia and made arrangements. As the first people began quietly leaving their homes on the first leg of a journey we hoped would lead them to Palestine, Hitler came to Poland and our way to freedom was cut off. Father had planned to take us out in only a few more weeks. Instead, they came to our door and imprisoned Father and Mother. My sisters and I were away shopping at the time. When we returned, they were gone. We rushed to the police station, only to see them standing . . ." The tears sprang to her eyes, and her shoulders began shaking with sorrow. "They shot them, Max. I watched them die."

He took her in his arms again and held her close until the sobs subsided and she could get control.

Using a hanky to blow her nose, she continued. "I took my sisters and we fled back to the house. I grabbed everything of value I could and shoved it in a suitcase. My sisters were in shock, unable to help, but I forced them, pushed them, to get some warm clothes together. It was winter and I knew we would need all the warm clothing and bedding we could carry. By the time dark enveloped the city, we were on the outskirts, heading south. My father had told me where to go, how to find those who were helping with the escape. The trouble was, I didn't have the necessary papers. I didn't know how to get them, what to do to get past the patrols I knew would surely be on the roads. So we stayed in the hills. The first night we found a barn to sleep in, but when we awoke the next morning . . ." A sad look filled her eyes, "the farmer had turned us in. The police took us back. They imprisoned us, interrogated us, beat us, trying to get us to tell where others were, where they had gone. Thankfully, my father had not told my sisters. Only I had the secret." Her jaw hardened. "They beat me near to death . . . but I didn't tell them." She pulled up the sleeve covering her left arm. As she ran her hand over the flesh, Max saw the irregularity, a bump in the bone. "He broke my arm with a hammer when I refused to tell and spit blood on his boots!" Her eyes flared with hatred. "If I could have killed him, I would have! Such men should have to go through the same punishments! They should have their arms broken, they . . ." She grabbed a hold of his coat and put her head against his shoulder, sobbing. "They killed Millie because I wouldn't tell. They beat her to death, Max! I know it! It was my fault!" she sobbed. "I . . ."

Max held her again. Would she ever be the same? Could such memories, such horrors, ever leave her? She had been so happy, with a wit as sharp as his father's razor! So much fun! They had ruined her life, butchered her family! Oh how he hoped they would be made to pay!

Long moments passed before she regained control. When she finally lay back against her pillow, he could see that she was exhausted. He must leave.

"I have to get back to Frankfurt," Max said.

She grabbed his hand firmly as if to prevent his leaving. He smiled as comforting a smile as he could muster. "I'll be back, Hannah. I promise."

She tried to smile back. Another promise. So many had been broken, but she had to believe this one. She forced her head to move up and down, used all her will to lessen the hold on his hand, to let him slide free of her iron grip.

He leaned over and kissed her on the forehead. "I promise." He paused. "I am glad you survived, Hannah. So very glad!"

He turned and walked away. She watched until he had left the long hall and disappeared. Slipping off her bed as quickly as her frail condition allowed, she struggled to the window and peered out, hoping to get a last look at him. She saw nothing but darkness. She stayed a moment more, then went back to the bed and snuggled down into the covers after turning off the light on the wall above her. Moments later she fell into a deep sleep—the first she had had in nearly four years.

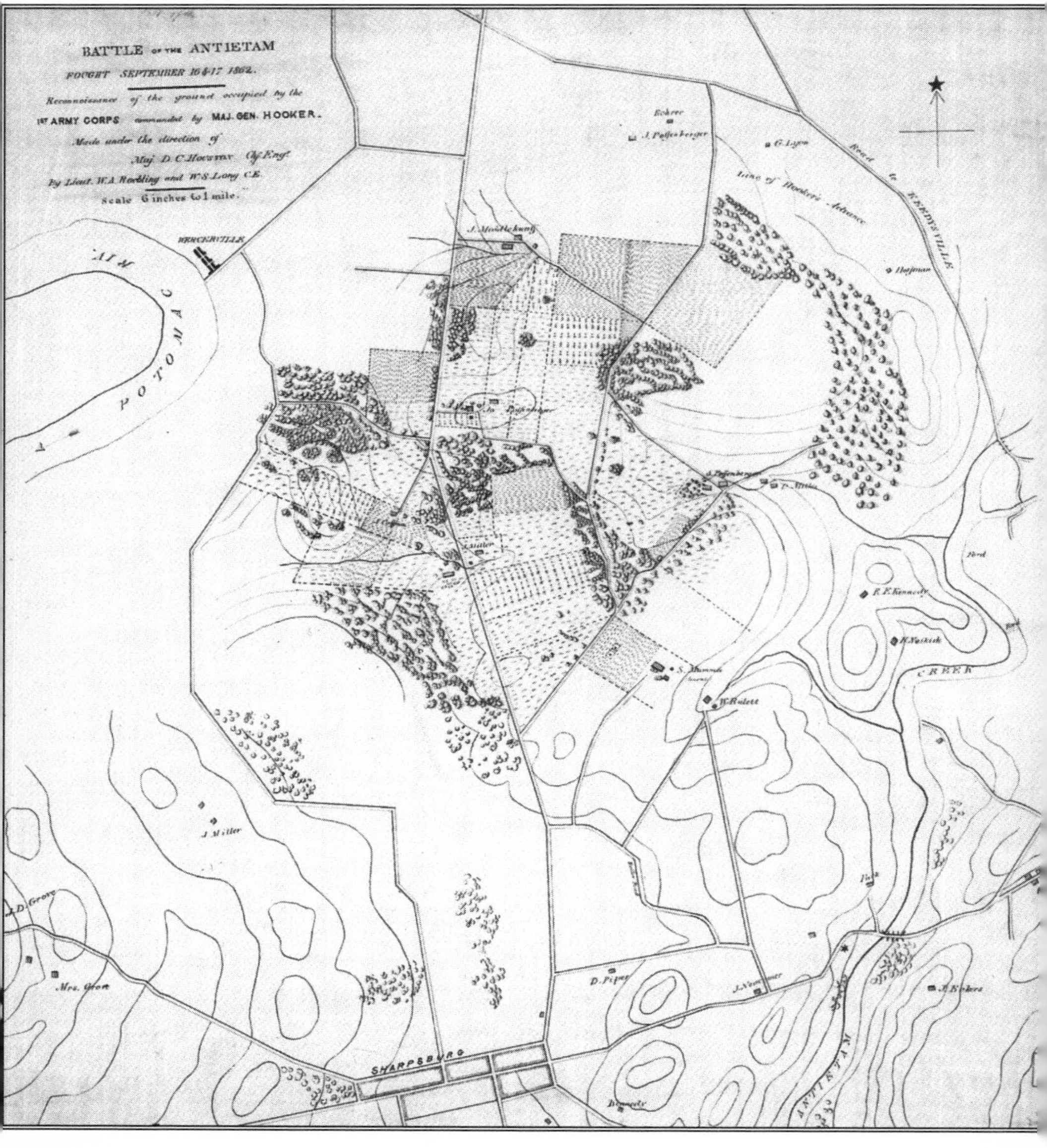

by Washington Roebling & W. S. Lony C.E.; Maj. D. C. Houston (Chf. Engi
Part of the Battle of the Antietam Fought September 16–17, 1862

Geography and Map Division, Library of Congress, Washington, D. C.